Those Three Little Words

USA TODAY BESTSELLING AUTHOR

MEGHAN QUINN

Published by Hot-Lanta Publishing, LLC

Copyright 2022

Cover and Illustrations By: Gerard Soratorio

www.authormeghanquinn.com

For Megan

Prologue

ELI

I'm a fun guy.

Some might say . . . neat.

A solid, trustworthy good time.

If you're looking to have an amusing night out, I'm your man.

No drama.

No worries.

Just good old-fashioned fun.

I learned from a young age that life is short, and you have to fucking enjoy every second of it. So my rule is to say yes.

Say yes to as much shit as you can.

Hornsby, want to go to the pub down the street and get wasted with the locals?

Of course.

Hornsby, do you want to go skinny-dipping in the coach's pool—when he's home?

Absolutely.

Hornsby, do you want to fly to Vegas on our day off and run up the poker tables?

That's a hell yes.

Living in the moment, that's my motto, and up until now, that motto has served me well. It has taken me places I never thought I'd go. It has presented me with opportunities I never thought I would have.

But . . . and that's a big but, a huge one.

This time, my yes has come back to bite me in the ass.

You see, it all happened on my birthday. We had an off day, high from a big win against the Calgary Barnburners. It was Valentine's Day—yes, I'm a Valentine's baby—and we went to the best singles bar in the city that would be crawling with women.

The drinks were flowing.

The conversations were engaging.

And I was by no means calling it a night anytime soon.

That's when she walked into the bar.

In a hot pink dress that clung to every inch of her curvy body, she styled her platinum-blonde hair into long, silky waves, and the lipstick staining her gorgeous lips matched the color of her dress. There was no doubt about it—she was a total smokeshow.

Every guy she came within a ten-foot radius of paused what they were doing to give her a very blatant once-over.

Unmistakably the hottest girl in the bar.

And as she sidled up next to me, unaware of my presence, it felt like the music stopped as she gently placed her clutch on the bar top. Casually, she leaned toward the bartender, her manicured nails drumming along the wood top as she sweetly asked for a gimlet with two lime wedges.

I was entranced.

I was hooked.

I was stolen for the rest of the night.

My mind wanted one thing.

Her.

She had my attention, and no one would steal me away.

2

No one would stop me.

Because in all honesty, I've had my eye on her for a while, ever since I met her two years before.

And that night . . . it was my chance. All excuses, all restrictions, they were tossed to the curb as I laid down the best tool at my disposal to get her to talk to me: it was my birthday.

And fuck, did we have a night. I can still remember the way her dress slid off her body as I held her in my arms. I can still vividly recollect that her lips tasted of lime and danger. And I can still smell her intoxicating perfume floating around me as I drove into her, one pulse after the other until we both came at the same time. *Multiple times.*

It was one of the best nights of my entire life.

But it had to end because we agreed it would be a one-night thing. So that morning, she slipped away undetected, and we both went back to our daily routine. Eat, sleep, and breathe hockey.

Was it the best birthday present I could ask for?

Absolutely.

Did she fulfill my every goddamn fantasy?

More than I could ever have imagined.

And if she came up to me and asked for more, would I oblige?

I would be hard pressed to say no.

Unfortunately, this isn't a fairy-tale story of how my one-night stand turned into a romance for the ages, though.

Nope, that would be far too easy. This story, well . . . it exposes me as the man that I am. The man I feel to my very core. This is the story of how I wear the title "Ultimate Fuckup," because not only did I accidentally get the girl in the hot pink dress pregnant . . .

But I broke bro code.

Because the girl in the hot pink dress is the sister of my teammate . . . and best friend.

Chapter One

PENNY

TikTok Question: If you had a daughter or sister, which one of your teammates would you want her to stay away from?

Silas Taters: Ah, Hornsby for sure.

Halsey Holmes: Hornsby.

Levi Posey: Is that even a question? Hornsby.

Eli Hornsby: Are the guys saying me? Of course they are. *shakes head* Honestly, I'd probably say myself as well. Me or Taters.

Silas Taters: Hornsby said me? That fucker. Too much of a dick bag to say himself.

Pacey Lawes: Who do I want my sister to stay away from? All of them. They're all idiots. They know they're not allowed anywhere near her. But if I had to pick one person in particular? That's easy. It would be Hornsby. There is no way in hell I'd ever allow him to even look at her in that way. Ever. And he knows that.

5

"WHY ARE we going to this bar? You're not even single," I say to my best friend, Blakely, as I pull on the hem of my dress for the twentieth time since we climbed out of the Uber. The dress was cute on the hanger. It was cute on me when I stood still in front of the mirror. But now that I'm walking the streets of Vancouver, nothing about this dress is cute. It keeps riding higher and higher on my thighs. It would be the ultimate success if I skate away from this night without showing off my underwear.

"Yes, but Perry is out of town, and it's fun being your wingwoman."

"I didn't even want to go out tonight," I say. "It feels ridiculous to go out on Valentine's Day as a single person."

"It's not ridiculous." Blakely loops her arm through mine and pulls me in close to her side. A half a foot taller than me, Blakely is a five-foot-ten beauty with chestnut-brown hair, emerald-green eyes, and a smile that only falters when she's been wronged. She's my work wife, best friend, and skin-care expert who's determined never to look a day over twenty-one. "The best time to go out is when you're single because you can hook up with someone just looking to fill a void."

"Ah, yes, because being someone's void filler really screams good time," I say sarcastically.

"Could be a good time if you allowed it to be. Don't you think it's time you start dating? You got the promotion you've worked so hard for, so it's time you relax and have some fun." She is right. I've worked my butt off for the past two years, and there have been many long days and few party-filled nights.

"I don't need a man to have fun."

"Facts," Blakely says. "But getting out of your apartment is necessary. And I didn't want to pull this card on you, but best friends have needs too, you know, and coming out with me tonight is a need."

"Wow, you're going there?"

"Of course, I am. I can't have you grouchy tonight. We need to have fun. Can you do that? Have fun?"

I sigh dramatically. "I think I can manage such a thing."

"Good. Now, when we enter the bar, I want nothing but good spirits from you. And if you just happen to meet a guy, so be it, but that won't be our end goal. Our end goal is to just have fun, maybe do some dancing, and of course people-watch as they navigate this romantic night as singles."

"Sounds like a plan," I say as we reach the bar that Blakely has not stopped talking about.

According to her, on Valentine's Day, the place is decked out in red with balloons, streamers, and singles ready to mingle. Not to mention appetizers are passed around by catering staff, the music is "fire," and it's an exclusive invite list, so not just anyone can join the party.

It sounded like fun when she told me, and now that I'm committed, short dress and all, I might as well enjoy the night. I started as an intern for the Vancouver Agitators and worked my way up to the in-house social media coordinator, specializing in TikTok. And I love my job so hard.

I get to hang out with professional hockey players and make them keep up with TikTok trends, troll fans on our social media accounts, and watch my brother play the sport we're both in love with.

So I might as well celebrate, let loose, and have some fun.

When we reach the door to the bar, a very large and gruff-looking man holding a clipboard greets us. His brow is turned down, and as we draw closer, he slowly takes us in. "Name," he says in a brusque tone.

"Blakely White and guest." She bounces on her heels and smiles at me, clearly excited about our night out.

The bouncer looks through the names on his clipboard, and just when I think he can't find my friend's name, he makes a slashing mark across his paper and then steps aside while releasing a velvet rope.

"No smoking inside. Eat as much as you want. Have fun," he says in such a monotone voice that I wonder how many times he's said that already this evening.

Hand in hand, Blakely and I enter the bar, and I'm immediately struck by the hundreds of balloons pressed against the already low ceiling. Different colors of pink and red, the balloons are the main focus of the decorations, but they don't deter the observing eye from the crepe streamers hanging from one end of the bar to the other and the glitter scattered all over the floor. The balloons alone would be a nightmare but attach the sweaty, dragged-around glitter from the floor, and that doesn't scream good time to me.

But despite the nightmare craft paper clinging to my shoes, the dimly lit atmosphere is filled with peppy music and brimming with boisterous laughter. Not to mention, some suits in here are catching my eye. This might be entertaining after all.

"Over here," Blakely says as she moves us toward the back of the bar, past the drinks and appetizers being passed around, and through a throng of people. "I'm hoping some high-top tables back here are free that we can sit at."

She weaves us through the crowd and around a corner to a much larger room where high-top tables with stools are scattered throughout the space, and the noise is a few octaves lower.

"Ooo, I see a table. Go grab us some drinks, and I'll claim squatter's rights."

The bar is crowded, so I'm not surprised when I receive an elbow to the ribs and a bump to the shoulder on my way to get our drinks.

When I reach the bar, I lean on the slick black top and observe the liquor choices, debating what I should go with just as a female bartender steps up in front of me. "Killer dress," she says.

"Aw, thank you." I glance down at said dress and then back up at her. "It's rolling up my thighs like that's what it was made to do. Could not be more annoying."

She winks at me. "My guess is, that dress will do you some favors. What can I get you, hon?"

Little does she know, I have zero interest in getting involved with anyone tonight. Maybe a little flirting, since there are some options here, but nothing serious.

"Uh, my friend always orders a Malibu Bay Breeze with a cherry, so I'll get that for her, and I'll have a gimlet with two lime wedges."

"Coming right up," the bartender says. She moves around, grabbing clean cups and plucking the correct liquor bottles while eyeing her pours. I'd never be able to bartend, trying to remember the intricacies of every drink ever mentioned while keeping the intoxicated patrons happy. Way too much for me.

"Gimlet, huh? Never would have pegged you as a gin drinker," a husky, deep voice says, coming up to my side.

I know that voice.

I think almost everyone in Vancouver knows that voice.

Turning to my right, I come face to face with Eli Hornsby, the best defenseman in the game of hockey who just happens to play for the team I work for, the Agitators. But more importantly, he's Mr. Prince Charming, the sexiest hockey player in the league, and the . . . horniest. He's easily the most attractive player on the ice, a flirt, and the object of every hockey fan's affection— even the men. He's menacing with a stick in his hand but will captivate you with his charismatic smile—a smile that still contains all of his teeth. And of course, one of my brother's best friends.

"Hornsby, wh-what are you doing here?" I ask, a hitch in my voice, because not a moment goes by when I'm not intimidated by this man and how insanely hot he is.

Also, I'm a little shocked to see him here. A singles bar on Valentine's Day doesn't really seem on brand for him. Then again, he is the biggest player on the team, so he might be out and about on his night off, trolling for someone to hook up with.

Now *that* seems on brand.

"Oh, you know, just celebrating the day I was born." He leans against the bar and takes a sip of the beer in his hand. Casual, in control, and I'm sure aware of how good he looks in his navy three-piece suit.

I don't know anyone, and I mean ANYONE, who wears a suit better than Eli Hornsby.

I've posted a few slow-motion videos of him walking into the arena, highlighting him as the best dressed on the team. His signature cigarette pants paired with no socks and dress shoes is what grabs everyone's attention, not to mention the way he fills out his suit jacket, his biceps tugging on the fabric when he brings his to-go cup of coffee to his lips.

He's a thirst trap I have no problem posting.

But now that said thirst trap is standing in front of me, staring into my eyes, I feel my nerves spike with the urge to either pet his chest or run to the toilet to throw up. Two very opposite reactions, but two very accurate ones.

As casually as possible, I place my hand on the bar and attempt to lean into the wood, mirroring his relaxed position. But where he is the quintessential poster child for how to act appropriately in social settings, I am praying to Cupid himself my dress doesn't curl up like an old-fashioned window blind and slap me in the face while simultaneously flashing my underwear to the hot hockey player.

Oh God . . . what underwear did I put on today? Why can't I remember such an imperative detail?

"Are you, uh . . . okay?" he asks, bending at the knees to look me directly in the eyes.

Oh crap, I haven't said anything.

"Yes, fine. Just great." I snap my fingers aggressively at him. "Oh, that's right. Today is your birthday. I posted a TikTok about it."

"Yes," he says, eyeing me suspiciously. Probably trying to decide if he should be wary of approaching fingers of the snapping variety. "You posted a boomerang video of Posey slapping me in the ass with his hockey stick."

I did. It was really funny. I chuckle to myself, a snort begging to be let out, but someone is looking out for me because I'm able to keep it together. "I thought it was a fitting tribute since the fans seem to enjoy your recent bromance."

Levi Posey, the team's bruiser. Large, bulky guy with the biggest heart of gold. He's an absolute demon on the rink, but outside of the arena, he is as soft and gooey as they come. The most sensitive on the team, who has a penchant for bologna sandwiches and slapping Hornsby on the ass with his stick before the start of every game. It's become a treasured tradition among the fans.

"We share one milkshake, and everyone thinks we're practically engaged." Eli rolls his eyes.

Ahhh, the milkshake. It was the most precious thing I've ever seen. Eli and Levi were at a Children's Hospital event together, and they were given a milkshake with two straws. Locking eyes, they held the drink together, and each took a straw into their mouths. The show they put on was public relations gold. The media team has used it as much as they can. It was even a Top Ten on ESPN.

"It was damning. You are now forever connected at the hip."

"Could be worse." He grins. Ooof, that smile. My hand that's not on the bar rattles by my side from one glint of his pearly whites. "I could have been caught sharing a milkshake with your brother."

"Pacey would never share a milkshake with you," I say, and before I can stop myself, I add, "He would claim you have some sort of infectious disease he doesn't want to contract."

Pacey, my brother, is the star goalie for the Vancouver Agitators. He's the heart of the team and has some of the quickest reflexes in the league. Recently, like . . . a few months ago, he fell in love with a girl named Winnie who just happened to stumble into him during a rainstorm. Long story, but he was bewitched immediately. I don't blame him because she's all kinds of cute and fun. I love hanging out with her, and I'm hoping we're going to hear wedding bells very soon. I've told Pacey many times that he needs to propose. He claims he has plans but is waiting for the right moment. My guess is after the season, when the guys go to Banff, Canada, for some relaxation, Pacey will propose. He's a sentimental guy like that.

But hold on a second. My mind wanders back to what I just said. Uhh . . . did I just tell Hornsby—to his face—that he was diseased? Infectious. Not worthy of milkshake sharing? What on earth was I thinking? I'm pretty sure most of America would want to share a milkshake with him. I mean, I would share one. But here I am, acting like a toddler parroting their parents by repeating what Pacey has said to me.

"I'm not diseased." Eli's face scrunches up. "Your brother likes to make up lies so he has a chance to live up to my beauty," Eli says, making direct eye contact with me and batting his eyelashes foolishly. "But for the record, I don't have any diseases. I just want to clarify that."

I hold up my hands. "Hey, what you do on your own time is your business." But I know a lot of what he does on his own time involves women.

Many long nights.

And always short goodbyes.

The bartender sets my drinks down and then glances back and forth between Eli and me. She smirks and says, "Shall I put your drinks on the hockey star's tab?"

Normally, I'd say no because I don't like to blur the lines with work and my free time, but for some reason, and out of an attempt to match his teasing, I smile at Eli. "Yes, I'd love that." Then I smirk at the bartender. "Thank you."

She winks. "Of course."

Well, now that I have boldly put my drinks on someone else's tab, it's time I take off before I sweat through this dress. I start to walk away when Eli steps in front of me, blocking my retreat.

"Uh, if I'm paying for your drink, the least you can do is talk to me a little longer. Don't you think?"

Uh . . . talk with him longer. That would actually be the last thing I'd want to do. Why, you ask?

Because he intimidates me. Because coming out tonight was supposed to be fun, and even though Hornsby is a great guy, I just don't feel super comfortable around him. This is going to sound really bad, I realize that, but he's just too . . . pretty. I'm not in his league—not that he would ever be interested in me—but I like to keep my interactions with him to a minimum, especially since he's a giant flirt. I don't need my little romantic brain thinking that this overtly attractive alpha male is the least bit interested in seeing me naked. Nope, it's better to let ourselves down easy and not even jump into that realm of thinking.

Therefore, we need to find his friends and scoot him over to their company, not mine. "Did you come here alone?"

"Posey came with me, but he took off within five minutes, claiming he had an upset stomach. Frankly, I think the whole singles bar thing really freaked him out."

Now Posey is someone I could hang out with. Yes, he's handsome, but he's also slightly more down to earth. A sparkling glint doesn't bounce off his teeth every time he smiles like it does with Hornsby.

"Aw, why? He's so loveable. There's potential for him to find a really nice girl."

Hornsby's brow creases. "He finds enough girls. That's the problem. He doesn't like all the attention."

I give him a look of disbelief. "This coming from the biggest player on the team."

His eyebrows shoot upward, nearly kissing his thick hairline. "You think I'm the biggest player?" He points at his chest, feigning shock. Is he kidding? I don't think he's the biggest player. I know he is. Everyone knows it. The team, the management, the fans. It's no secret that Hornsby gets around. I asked Pacey once if Hornsby ever felt bad about going from girl to girl, and Pacey said no because he's always upfront and honest with them. They know what they're getting themselves into with him—one night and that's it.

Call me crazy, but that kind of attitude—one night and that's it—smells distinctively of universal player status.

And I'm ready to tell him that, to stamp him with my label, when his beautiful eyes short-circuit my brain, turning it into a pile of useless, wrinkly mush.

"Uh, ahem . . . I'd like to say . . . well, ooo, is it hot in here?" He shakes his head, smiling. "Yeah, didn't think so, but as I was saying, I well, I heard, you know how everyone talks, that you are, uh, that you . . . well, that you are easily the biggest player on the team." The drinks in my hands feel like they're about to slip out of my grasp and crash to the floor as my palms sweat like they're trudging through the depths of the Amazon.

"Says who?"

Isn't it obvious?

"Everyone." I grimace.

He brings his drink to his lips, studying me the entire time, his uncaring disposition rolling off him carelessly. To have that much confidence, I couldn't even imagine. "You shouldn't listen to other people's opinions."

"Are you saying it's not true?" I roll my teeth over the corner of my lip, and his eyes immediately fixate on the movement.

When his gaze connects with mine again, he says, "I'm saying it's not currently true."

Okay . . . good to know.

I honestly don't know what to do with that or where to go from here. I just want to have a drink with my friend. So, to let him off the hook, I say, "I don't know what you're trying to prove, but you don't need to prove anything with me. I'm not allowed to put players' personal lives, as in hockey players, not the philandering kind of player that you have been described as tonight, on TikTok unless approved, so your extracurricular activities are safe with me."

There, maybe he just wants some reassurance that his horny ways won't be splashed all over an app accompanied by a trending snippet of music.

Although . . . it would make a good post . . . no, I'd never do that.

"Not trying to prove anything." His eyes travel down my body and then all the way back up, his gaze feeling like an infrared light examining me for any inconsistencies. Trust me, he doesn't need a special laser sight to spot them. With a step closer, he says, "Just looking for some company. Are you really going to make me spend my birthday alone?"

Well, isn't that just a kick to my flimsy escape plan?

Blue-green eyes lock with mine as I take in his beautiful face. He's so disgustingly proportionate. From his lips to his nose to the strong, angular curve in his jaw, he's perfect. Actually freaking perfect. Pair that with his towering height, broad, muscular shoulders, his athletic prowess, and his charming disposition and he's a tough one to say no to.

Very tough.

"It's not my fault you chose the wrong person to spend your birthday with," I say, attempting to figure out why on earth he'd want to spend the night in my company.

I'm no one in his world. Sure, I can make a mean quesadilla, and if you were to ask me what season of *New Girl* a certain episode is from, I'd be able to answer you. And not to toot my own horn, but this girl knows how to sew a button, a lost skill among the ages. But other than that, there's nothing special over here, at least nothing of Hornsby's caliber.

"True, but I'm choosing *you* now. Are you really going to turn me down?"

Uhhh . . .

I'm trying to, but failing magnificently.

I'd like to state it's not my fault. Just look at him. I'd love to see any one of you say no to him. Go ahead, give it a shot.

Yeah . . . that's what I thought. Impossible.

Goodbye girls' night.

I had plans, you know, of talking to Blakely about my latest waxing experience—which was a nightmare—and asking her what she thinks of that period underwear you see advertised all over the place. Oh . . . and how I spent two hours the other night watching this beautiful Turkish baker plow her fist into proofed bread dough over and over again.

That is not the kind of conversation that should be had in front of a man like Eli. Nor should he obtain humiliating information like that about me.

Also, I'm not sure he would have a valuable opinion on period underwear.

But it seems Hornsby has other plans, and honestly, I'm not a beast. I can't just leave someone on their birthday . . . alone. So it seems this duo of Blakely and me has become a trio.

"Turn you down?" I glance to the side, spotting Blakely buried in her phone. I swallow hard. "I guess I'm not."

A full-on, mind-melting, panty-splitting smile spreads across his face, and that one look, full of flirtatious promises, makes my legs quiver. Pulse. Possibly spread if I wasn't standing.

I have no intentions of ever hooking up with Hornsby or any one of Pacey's teammates for that matter, but he's chosen me to be his bestie tonight, so that's that.

Without another word, he wraps his arm around my shoulders, and together, we head toward Blakely, who looks up from her phone just in time to catch us walking together.

Uh-oh.

I've seen that grin before.

That grin doesn't look promising for me.

The gears are grinding in her mind . . . her evil, evil mind.

When I set her drink on the table, I can tell I'm not going to like what comes out of her mouth next, and that drink will most likely be consumed by me, not her.

"Eli Hornsby, isn't it your birthday?" she says, the ease in her voice making me envious. She's always had an easy time talking to the players, whereas I nervously sweat in the corner and respond to their questions with weird grunting noises until I warm up. You would think being around hockey players my entire life would have prepared me not to be a nervous wreck, but that is not reality. At least not when it comes to Hornsby.

"It is my birthday." He sets his drink on the small, circular table.

"Well, Happy Birthday," she says. "And I hate to do this because celebrating your birthday seems like a lot of fun . . ."

Uhh, hate to do what?

Why is she standing from her chair?

Why isn't she lifting her drink to take a sip?

Why the hell is she putting her purse strap over her shoulder?

"But Perry called, and he came home early to surprise me.

I'd love to see where this night takes us, but my Valentine is requesting my presence." She pouts her lip, but it falls flat on me.

I don't believe her.

Not even for a second.

"You're just going to leave?" I ask her, panic laced in my voice. I give her a look, the *best friend* look that says, "Please, Jesus, don't leave me alone with him," but because she's the evil wench that she is, she deliberately doesn't translate my plea.

"Yes, but you have Hornsby here to keep you company and possibly be your wingman."

"Wingman?" Hornsby says. "Are you looking to hook up with someone, Penny?"

"What? No!" My cheeks flame with embarrassment. "No, I didn't even want to come out tonight, but Blakely convinced me. I was fine with just hanging out at my place and eating a gallon of ice cream . . . errrr, I mean pint, a pint of ice cream."

Whispers I actually meant what I said. A gallon. A full-on gallon of creamy, delicious milkiness. Possibly even with some sprinkles or chocolate fudge. Definitely cherries.

But of course I'm not going to admit that in front of Mr. Rock-Hard Body.

"She needed to get out. She hasn't even celebrated her promotion yet," Blakely says.

"You haven't?" Hornsby asks. "Well then, it looks like we're going to be ordering another round." He turns his attention to Blakely. "Don't worry, I've got your girl. I'll make sure she has the best evening of her life."

To my horror, Blakely winks. "I'm hoping you do." She then leans into me and gives me a hug while whispering, "Please end up in his bed tonight and tell me all about it after."

"Are you insane?" I say through gritted teeth just as she pulls away.

"I'll miss you too, but we'll catch up at work." She boops my nose with her finger. "Love you." And then she turns to Hornsby. "Take good care of my girl."

"I will," he answers as he lifts his glass toward her. And then, before I know what the hell just happened, I'm left alone with Eli Hornsby, sharing an intimate table in the back of the bar while romantic music plays above us. "Take a seat, stay a while," he says, pushing out a stool for me with his wing-tipped covered foot.

Wow, just wow. I can't believe Blakely did that.

And to my demise, there's not much I can do. I'm not strong enough to set my drink down and walk away without a word. I have to see the man at work, for goodness' sake. My only out was Blakely, and my ex-best friend just left me.

I have no choice.

Succumbing to the trickery, I take a seat and then bring my drink to my lips. Blakely is going to get an earful from me tomorrow. Best friend card positively revoked. She will need to earn that back with lots of presents. Pretty, glittery presents . . . and cash. Yes, I will require cold-hard cash from her to even get back in my good graces. She will need to fan the cash in my face while telling me why I am all sorts of accomplished in button sewing. The price you pay for leaving me.

At least fifty dollars . . . in ones, just to make it annoying.

Maybe ten dollars in quarters.

Five dollars in nickels.

All placed in a jar that is labeled "I'm sorry" with a heart on it. Said jar should be presented to me while she hands me my favorite coffee drink—skinny vanilla latte—a new glittery notebook, and a matching pen. Yup, that will be her penance. Even with that, she'll still be on probation. I'll just *consider* letting her talk to me.

"Hey, are you okay? Are you really that angry?" Eli asks, pulling me from my thoughts of murderous ways to get Blakely back. "Because you seem like you're ready to fist-punch that drink across the room."

I stare at Blakely's drink, considering doing exactly that. A swift punch of it across the room feels satisfactory.

"Irritated," I answer.

"Irritated because you're left with me for the night or irritated because your friend is the one who dragged you out tonight and then ditched you?"

"Both," I say before I can stop myself. "I mean . . . the last one, not both. I don't mind being here with you. You're . . . fine and all."

"Fine and all?" Eli says, looking insulted. "Just fine? You know a lot of people would feel excited to share a drink with me."

"Yes, of course. All of the people. Including me," I say, backtracking. "Very excited." I tap my drink to his. "Cheers to being excited about spending the night together." I take a sip as a smile passes over his lips. "Wait, I didn't mean spending the night together like that, you know, like the way you like to spend the night with women . . . naked. I just meant mutually together in a nonsexual way. Strictly platonic. We don't have sex. That's not something we do. We barely talk, so sex is definitely not something we do."

Jesus, Penny, stop talking.

I take a large gulp of my drink.

But then . . . I keep going.

"Not that it would be bad sex," I continue for God knows what reason. The nerves, and that three-piece suit—and the no socks, his ankles seem so dreamy—the combination is shaking me to my very core. "I'm pretty good at sex—at least that's what I convince myself of. I mean, probably not as good as you because it seems like you get a lot of practice in, if that's what you want to call it. I've had a few partners, one long term, and he was pretty good. We enjoyed sharing a little romp, you know." I elbow him as he just stares at me, his expression full of humor. "Anyway . . ." I blow out a long breath. "You're probably wishing you walked away with Blakely."

"No." He continues to grin. "This is right where I want to be. You are more than entertaining."

"I'm babbling. That's what happens when I'm nervous. I babble. And oh God, I can't believe I just told you that I'm nervous. Not that talking to you about my sex life is better. I just wish that you would stop me from talking so I don't keep going on and on like this." When he doesn't say anything and instead takes a sip from his beer, I say, "Please say something, anything. Put me out of my misery."

He chuckles, a deep throaty sound that vibrates through my bones. "Why would I want to do that when clearly this is the best company I've had in years?"

"Because you're cruel."

"Nah, I just like seeing you squirm, which makes me ask, why the hell are you nervous?"

Yeah, why are you nervous, Penny?

Oh, I don't know, maybe because he's a six-foot-four piece of studliness, and I'm not used to being this close to perfection. Maybe because Blakely wants me to *bed* this man, and now that's all I can think about. Maybe because I wasn't planning on being on my best behavior tonight, but here I am, trying to be professional . . . ehhh, professional would not be the correct term, especially after the sex talk.

"I don't know," I say instead. "Are you nervous?"

"No, why would I be nervous?"

"Uh . . . the pressure of Valentine's Day?" I shrug.

"Never celebrate it, you know, because I'm always celebrating my birthday."

"Right . . . right." I glance at my drink. "You know, I think I'm going to need another one of these."

"Then drink up." He winks, and I swear my uterus flutters.

What on earth is happening to me? Is it because it's Valentine's Day, and the added romance in the air is playing with my head? Because I've had one-on-one's with Eli before. Granted, they've been quick, and I had a task, but still, I didn't stumble around like I am now.

Not to mention, when I'd look him in the eyes while working, he never studied my lips or grinned the way he is now, nor did he ever give me a once-over.

So what's so different about tonight?

Chapter Two

ELI

I remember the moment I first met Penny Lawes. She was an intern, and Pacey was showing her around. We ran into each other in the hallway, right outside the locker room. I made some offhanded comment about Pacey bringing girls around the locker room and asked him if he was starting his own Brentwood Base-ball tradition—they are known for taking the girls back to the locker room. His eyes grew murderous as he said, through a very clenched jaw, that the girl next to him was his sister.

You could imagine my surprise.

I mean . . . Pacey is a good-looking guy if you're into the long, curly-blond-hair look, but his sister . . . Jesus fuck.

Hot.

She's curvy with hips to grip on to and a full fucking rack that I could easily spend an hour exploring. And those goddamn lips, plush and begging to be bruised. Long, platinum-blond hair that I could wrap around my hand and hold on tight while I drive into her. Fucking perfection. Every last inch of her.

Later that day, when I was headed to the weight room to get some legs in after the game, Pacey body-slammed me against the wall and held me there as he told me to stay the fuck away from his sister.

Of course, I played dumb and said I had no idea what he was talking about. Which he replied with, "I saw the way you were looking at her. I swear to God, if you touch her, you're a dead man."

So, I've held on to that little piece of knowledge because although a threat, I know for certain it's most likely a real threat. A threat I didn't want to come face to face with.

Every time I ran into her, walking through the hallways of the stadium or working with her on one of her many TikTok campaigns, I just nodded and smiled outwardly.

But inwardly . . .

Fuck, I ate up her high heels that put the smallest dent on her short stature. I envisioned what those heels would look like wrapped around my waist. I thought about how I'd peel those high heels off and lay her back on my bed, watching as her hair fanned out across the mattress. And those fantasies have collected in my head, filed into a folder labeled untouchable. But they haven't stopped producing, even after knowing I can't do anything about it.

They've just stockpiled.

With every glance from her.

With every moment I hear those heels click-clacking down the hallway.

With every goddamn laugh from her beautiful lips when she's talking to someone else.

My mind has wandered. My imagination has soared, and I've been horny and needy whenever she's been around.

Tonight is no exception.

Except I'm flirting with her tonight—it is my birthday, after all.

Happy birthday to me.

There's nothing wrong with a bit of flirting, right?

"You seem to be drinking that pretty quickly," I point out to her as she sucks on her straw, her cheeks hollowing out, making me dream of what she'd look like if she was sucking on something other than that straw.

"Am I?" she asks after she pulls away from her drink. "Well, I'm thirsty. All that babbling has left me parched."

The fucking babbling. Normally, I wouldn't care for a woman to go on and on about random things, but for some reason, when Penny does it, I'm enamored, and I want nothing more than for her to continue. I want to get lost in those crazy thoughts of hers.

"Do you want something to eat?" I ask her.

"Uh . . ." She glances around. "I think I'm okay. I'm actually not planning on staying long. You know, work tomorrow. I really came out tonight as a favor to Blakely and stayed out because, well, it's your birthday. You know what we should do? We should actually roam the bar and find someone you can go home with. You know, someone who would really know how to celebrate." She waggles her eyebrows at me, and if I wasn't so annoyed with her trying to pass me off on someone else, I'd think it's cute.

"I'm good with you."

"Me?" she asks, pointing at herself. "That's, well, you know, I'm not, uh . . . the thing is—"

"Good with hanging out with you," I say, clearing the air so she doesn't think I'm looking for anything other than her company. She has no idea the number of times I've said *no* to another woman's advances because of an interaction with her on a particular day.

If *she* were to make a move, I'd jump on it so hard. In an instant, we'd be headed to my place with one thing on my mind —getting between her legs.

"Oh, okay." She stares down at her drink. "You don't think I'm boring?"

"Why would I think you were boring? You have been nothing but entertaining since I bumped into you."

"Yes, but I'm not a super great conversationalist."

"Not true," I say before taking a small sip of my beer. "I've seen you with the guys. You're always laughing with them, joking around, teasing."

"Yes, well . . . that's different."

"How so?" I ask while leaning in closer to her. From my position, I catch a whiff of her heady, exotic perfume, and it hits me in my goddamn chest.

She glances away, and I can tell whatever she's going to say won't be the truth. And I want the truth from her. It's rare when I talk to her like this, so I don't want anything to hold her back.

I lift my hand, and with two fingers, I rotate her head so she's looking at me. "Tell me the truth. Why is interacting with me different?"

She visibly gulps as her eyes search mine, bouncing back and forth until she says, "Because you're, uh . . . because well . . ." She swallows again. "You're attractive."

Bingo.

Just the thing I wanted to hear.

Never hurts a man's ego to hear the woman he's been lusting after for two years thinks he's attractive. Nope, I'm going to keep that little nugget of info very close to my dick.

"Well, not that the other guys aren't attractive, because they are, but you're just different, and I don't know why I admitted that. I've only had two drinks. It's not like I'm drunk or anything, so my lips shouldn't be that loose. Honestly, how about we forget I even said that?"

"No fucking way." I let my hand slide back down, only to settle close to hers on the table. "I'm tucking that snippet of knowledge away forever."

She sighs heavily. "Why do you have to rub it in like that? Clearly, it's embarrassing for me to talk about—"

"Rub it in? I'm not rubbing it in. I'm basking in the glory of Penny Lawes thinking I'm attractive."

"Why on earth would you do that?" she asks with a pinch of her brow.

"Uhh . . . because you're a fucking goddess and being recognized by you feels really fucking amazing," I say before I can stop myself.

Her mouth falls open, shock written all over her expression.

"But we don't have to talk about that," I say quickly, not wanting to scare her away. Dropping that hint is important, though. I want her to know that I'd worship her if she let me, but I don't want to make it awkward either. "Tell me something I don't know about you."

She blinks a few times, and then she sits back on her stool while crossing her arms over her chest. Inquisitively, she glances around the busy bar with bustling singles just looking to hook up with someone tonight. Finally, she quietly leans in and whispers, "Is this some sort of prank show that I'm on, and I don't know about it?"

"What?" I ask, confused.

She motions between us. "This . . . this can't possibly be a real thing, so do you have me on a prank show? Oh God, is this for the team? Are there cameras?" She looks around again, lifting out of her chair to get a better look.

I settle my hand on her shoulder and push her back on her seat. Looking her in the eyes, I say, "There is no prank show, Penny. I wouldn't do that to you."

She studies me again, her expression a mixture of humor and confusion. I'm not quite sure if she's about to lay down an onslaught of questions or burst out in laughter.

She chooses the latter.

It starts slow. A chuckle. A small ha . . . until it turns into a full-on guffaw followed by a litany of outlandish laughter so obnoxiously loud that people around us start to glance our way.

The laughter takes over every last inch of her body, shaking her from head to toe to the point of actual tears. Freaking tears. With a napkin, she blots at her eyes, pauses . . . glances at me, and starts laughing all over again.

Annoyed, I take a long, hard gulp of my drink until nothing is left while she continues gripping her stomach and gasping for air. I see a server crossing by us and wave him down for another round for the both of us while Penny attempts to gather herself.

Attempts being the key word.

After another minute, I ask her, "You done?"

She takes a few breaths, lets out a few more chuckles, and then sips her drink through her straw just as the server brings us a new round. He takes our empty glasses and then disappears.

After a few more seconds, she dabs at her eyes one more time and nods. "I'm done." She smirks.

I wait to see if she breaks out in laughter again, but when she keeps it together, I say, "Then would you mind telling me why what I said was so funny to you?"

"Because it's unbelievable," she answers. Straw pinched between her fingers, she sips from her new glass now. "Ask everyone in this bar if what you said is believable, and one hundred percent they would say no."

"I see." I rub the side of my jaw, trying to maintain my composure because now she's really fucking irritated me. I'm a pretty chill guy and can joke with the rest of them. I prefer it, actually, but this conversation has grated on my nerves. It's not only insulting to me, but it's degrading to her. She's so goddamn hot, it's painful being near her and not being able to make a move.

But that very well might change tonight.

I lean in and rest my hand on her bare thigh, sliding it inwardly as I say into her ear, "For your information, from the moment I first met you, I've wanted to fuck you. Don't believe it if you want"—my lips graze her ear—"but it's fucking true. Those lips of yours, I've wanted to own them. Your tits, I've wanted to worship. And your pussy, I've wanted to taste it." Her breath hitches as I allow my thumb to move across her silky skin. "Every time I've run into you, every time I've made eye contact with you, or anytime I've been close enough to smell your perfume, I've thought about all the dirty, naughty, delicious things I could do to you. Dreamed about it. Wondered what it would be like to have you riding my cock, your tits bouncing near my face, your pussy pulsing against my length. So don't for one goddamn moment think what I said was a joke. I'd never joke about fucking you . . . ever."

And with a nip to her earlobe, I pull away and drag my hand off her thigh before grabbing my drink and lifting it to my lips. The whole time, I keep my eyes on her.

Cheeks flushed.

Lips parted in shock.

And her chest is actually heaving just as her eyes slowly lock in on mine.

"I . . . uh . . ." She wets her lips as her face registers shock. I can only imagine what's going through her mind. Hell, I wasn't expecting to lay out my desires for her like that, but she irritated me, and I needed, at that moment, for her to understand the truth. To understand the torture I've endured ever since I met her. Finally, she finds her voice. "I . . . uh, I was told I'm bad at sex."

What the fuck? It's really loud in here tonight, so I must have heard her wrong. Surely, she didn't suggest someone told her she was a lousy lay. But looking at her face, at what looks like utter mortification, maybe I did hear her right. "Penny, did you just say—"

"I know I claimed earlier that I was good, a decent roll in the sheets, but that was a lie to save face. My last boyfriend said I was bad, so . . . you know, just thought that might help your fantasies. No good over here. A no-fly zone for pulse-pounding sex. Sorry."

Bad at sex?

Some dipshit told her she was bad at sex?

Who the fuck says that to a woman?

The only reason a man would say that is because *he's* the one who's actually bad at sex and is placing the blame on someone else so he doesn't have to face reality.

I've wanted to fuck you.

Anger pumping through my veins, I say quietly as I close the space between us, "I don't believe that for one goddamn second." I reach up and push a stray piece of hair behind her ear, lingering at her cheek. "Let me ask you this. Did he ever make you orgasm?"

Visibly uncomfortable, she shifts on her stool. "Well, when I assisted him."

"Assisted him?" I ask, intrigued with exactly how she would do that.

"You know, if I massaged myself while he thrust into me from behind."

The image of her playing with her clit while being fucked runs through my head like a goddamn motion picture on the big screen. I can see it, feel it, but instead of some fuckup behind her, it's me, and the only reason she's playing with her clit is because I demanded that she did, not because she needed it.

I'm *so* turned on. Facing her, I rest my feet on the rungs of her stool and place my hand on her back, closing her between me and the high-top table. "Did you have to do that every time? Massage yourself?"

She doesn't look at me. She averts her eyes to her drink where she plays with the condensation, dragging her perfectly manicured finger over the dewy droplets. "You know, we don't have to talk about this. What about, uh . . . your birthday. Get any good presents?"

"Not yet," I answer. "But I'm hoping I'll get a really good one by the end of the night."

Her eyes shoot to mine, and I hold her gaze, letting her know how fucking serious I am.

She's off limits.

I've been warned.

And I've kept my distance.

But there's something about tonight. Something driving me closer and closer to her, and no matter how many times I try to conjure up Pacey's angry face or threatening words, they're quickly washed away by my desperation.

I. Want. Her.

Need. Her.

Bad.

And I'm not sure anything can stop me from having her tonight.

Chapter Three

PENNY

Booze.

I need more booze.

All of the booze.

Pretend my mouth is the base of a waterfall and just tip all of the liquor right down the gullet because, oh my GOD, Eli Hornsby is causing me to turn all different shades of red.

Not to mention sweat. He is making me sweat down my freaking back.

Yeah, I know, sweating isn't the least bit attractive and no one wants to hear about it. But I'm more than glistening at this point, and it's all because the extremely gorgeous man sitting next to me decided to nip my earlobe.

Have you ever felt a tsunami of arousal take over your body in one giant, consuming wave?

Well, I have, and it was the moment Eli decided to pull my earlobe between his teeth. My freaking earlobe, ladies. I don't think earlobes are the least bit sexy. They're dangling skin bits attached to your head. It's a good thing someone thought to pierce them because they need a little something to make them not so freaky. But yes, here I am, panting and sweating like a freaking hockey player after three periods on the ice from one little nip.

A brief nibble.

It's not like he stuck his tongue in my ear—which by the way, yuck—nor did he suck on my ear or make out with it. His teeth made a brief pass, and before I could register what was happening, he was back in place, sipping his beer.

Yet it was life-altering.

I can still feel it, his teeth on my ear. I can still sense his hand on my inner thigh, his thumb caressing my skin, dragging, teasing . . .

And that provocative voice of his, I can still hear it ringing through my ears, telling me all the dirty things he wants to do to me.

He wants to see my boobs bounce in his face? What on earth?

My . . . *gulp* pussy pulse against his length. I never in my life have heard such a sinister sentence.

That's why I need the booze. Because I'm a bundle of nerves about to either curl into a ball of anxiety or legit pull my boob from my dress and lay it on the table as an appetizer for the voraciously hungry man sitting next to me.

Boob for the taking. Preferably to be used as a sucking device.

DO YOU SEE WHAT I'M TALKING ABOUT?

I've completely lost it.

"Did you get this dress for tonight?" His hand that's resting on the back of my chair slowly drags over the hot pink fabric. When his finger toys with the zipper on the back, my intake of breath nearly startles me right off my stool.

"No," I squeak. "I had it but have never worn it. I always thought it was too slutty for work even paired with a blazer, but thought it would be cute for a date. It was an impulse purchase. It was on sale, and I like the color, and I thought it would show off my short legs, which it does because it likes to ride up my thighs while I walk. It didn't do that in the mirror, but I wasn't walking either. I was just standing there checking myself out. So a very misleading dress if you ask me. But to answer your question, bringing this full circle, this scrap of fabric on my body was not purchased for tonight."

He brushes my hair off my shoulder, his fingers dragging along my skin, burning me, branding me.

Is this his way of seduction?

Is that what's happening?

I mean, he did say he wanted me to be his present tonight, so is that what's happening? If so, it's working.

My body is thrumming, urging me to ask for more.

"Well, I'm glad you saved it for tonight. It looks fucking hot on you."

I chuckle because honestly, I don't know how else to react. This scenario right now just feels so unreal. It's Valentine's Day, and I'm single and sitting next to Eli Hornsby while he flirts with me.

Never in my wildest thoughts would I have ever imagined this scenario to play out.

"Why are you laughing?" he asks, closing the space between us, causing my body to heat another degree.

"Because"—I clear my throat—"this all seems so ridiculous. I mean, what are we doing?"

"Flirting," he says. "Spending some time together. Some innocent time together."

"This is innocent?" I ask.

"Yes, if it wasn't innocent, trust me, you would know."

I wave my hand in front of my face. Thank God it's dark in here because I could only imagine the color of my beet-red cheeks at this moment.

"Well, I don't know what to say to that other than . . . I feel like it's time I leave." I down the rest of my drink, and as the liquid flows down my throat, I think about how I should have left half an hour ago, but for some odd reason, I stuck around.

Not sure why.

I set my empty glass on the table and stand from my stool only for Hornsby to stand as well, blocking me from my retreat.

"You seem to be in the way," I say, looking up at him.

"Because I don't want you to leave."

"Well, that's kind of you to want me to stay, but you see, I fear that if I stick around, I'll do something really stupid like beg you to nibble on my ear again."

A grin falls over his lips. "That's not stupid. That's actually a really good idea."

I shake my head. "No, it's a terrible idea. Really bad." I reach up and pat his chest, his rock-hard muscles doing nothing to tamper my libido. "I should, wow, you are really muscular."

He chuckles and then takes my hand in his and sits me back on my stool. "Stay. I promise I won't flirt anymore. Just don't leave me on my birthday. I've had enough birthdays alone growing up. Give me this one with some company."

He's spent birthdays alone? What does he mean by that? That's so sad.

I realize at this moment that I don't really know much about Hornsby other than the obvious—what's put out in the world for fans. But behind those devilish eyes and sparkling grin, I don't know where he grew up, anything about how he became the hockey star that he is, or pretty much any vital information that made him who he is today.

"Please . . . Penny?"

God, how could I possibly say no to that face?

I can't.

It's why I haven't left yet, and it's why I find myself asking him to order me another drink and some pretzel bites with cheese sauce.

After a quick trip to the bathroom—with a promise that I wouldn't ditch him—I settle back on my stool, pleased to see food and new drinks on the table.

"Told you I'd return," I say while picking up a pretzel.

"I'd like to think it was because you wanted to spend more time with me, but my guess is it's because of the pretzel bites."

While chewing, I say, "Yes, well, I am a sucker for carbs."

He chuckles and picks up a pretzel as well and then smears it in cheese sauce before sticking it in his mouth. For reasons I can't quite pinpoint, I watch as he eats, noticing the fine muscles in his jaw work as he chews or the way his throat contracts when he swallows. It's extremely hot and makes me think I should do a collage of the boys swallowing and chewing for TikTok. A good old-fashioned thirst trap. Then again, it might be a little too sexual, and I'm not ready to lose my job, not when I just earned it.

"So, tell me this, Penny, if Blakely was sitting here instead, what would you be talking about?"

I wash my pretzel down with a giant sip of my fourth gimlet of the night and smile when I set my glass down, starting to feel the effects of the alcohol.

"Well, you for sure. We would probably be watching your every move and then gossiping about it with each other. Possibly trying to figure out who you were hitting on, why, and what you were saying. Possibly betting on who you would take home."

"Is that so? Who's to say I wouldn't have stuck around with you two?"

"Once we started talking about my bad waxing experience, trust me, you would have left."

"Waxing, huh?" He gives me a slow once-over. "You bare down there, Penny?"

Because said alcohol has started to loosen me up, I answer him by saying, "Normally just a short landing strip, but this last go-around, everything went, and I wasn't ready for it. It wasn't my normal lady, so she lit me up with wax."

He wets his lips as he looks at me as if I'm a rare wagyu beef he's been craving for years. "Do you like it?"

I shrug and pop another pretzel in my mouth. "I mean, it doesn't feel much different. I honestly was nervous that doing it all would strip my clit right off, but it's still intact."

He chuckles. "Well, that's good to hear." His hand falls back on my chair as he faces me, his commanding body taking up all of the space between us. "I've gotten my balls waxed before."

"Really?" I ask. "You know I was about to say that's hard to believe, but just by the way you dress, I'd guess you're a waxer. Do you wax your chest?"

He nods. "Yeah. Chest, balls, and ass."

Well, isn't that . . . information.

"I see." I clear my throat. "You, uh, you still do that?"

He nods again. "Yes, I think it makes me skate faster. I got Taters to go with me once. He shrieked like a feral cat in heat and walked around after like someone stuck a hot iron on his nads, but he got used to it and now goes regularly."

"THAT'S . . . hmm, that's fascinating. I should do a video of you two. Call it the story of bare balls."

He laughs. "Pretty sure the front office would not approve."

"Probably not." I shift my body so I'm facing him now and our knees knock together. He spreads his legs wider, and I slip in closer while crossing one leg over the other. His hand that was holding his drink falls to my thigh, and the heat of his touch mixed with the coldness of his palm does strange things to my muscles, contracting them in all different ways.

"What else would you be talking to Blakely about?" His thumb caresses my skin, and I nearly moan from the touch.

Yup, the alcohol has really loosened me up.

"Uh, probably about my horrible sex life because that's what friends in relationships like to talk about with their single friends. That and setting me up with someone to help out with my horrible sex life."

"When Taters was dating Sarah before they broke up, they always tried to set me up with her friends, claiming I was perfect for every single one of them. I think it was just because they had the need to see me in a relationship."

"Did you ever go out with any of them?"

"One," he admits. "We fucked, and that was it." He shrugs. "Have you ever been in a relationship?"

"Not since high school. It's easier not having to worry about someone else with my hectic schedule. I figured when I retire, I'll have plenty of time to find a girl and start a family if I want."

"Is that what you want?" I ask, curious about this man who usually wears a mask of flirtation rather than truth.

"Possibly." He sips his beer. "Haven't put much thought into it. Kind of focusing on the here and now." He sets his glass down on the table and twists it with his large hand. "What about you, Penny? You looking to start a family? Looking to settle down?"

I cringe and shake my head. "No. I don't think I'm mature enough for that. I've been so focused on my career that I haven't even thought about any of that stuff. Not really interested in any of it to be honest. Just having fun."

"Then you've come to the right place." He lifts his glass and says, "Let's finish these drinks and get out of here."

"Oh . . . going home?" I ask, slightly stunned and possibly— just possibly—upset about him abruptly wanting to part so soon.

He smirks. "No, we are going to go get some dessert. I know of a great place."

"Wait, you want me to go with you?"

He rolls his eyes. "Yes, Jesus. Don't I deserve a birthday cake?"

"I mean, yes, of course." My mind reels. "As long as you actually mean birthday cake and not something else."

"What could you possibly be referring to?" he asks with a sparkling glint in his eyes that's damn near blinding.

"You know exactly what I'm talking about." I down the rest of my drink. The alcohol has kicked in, and I'm feeling extraor-dinarily happy. There are no more nerves, no more anxiety. I feel relaxed but also coherent. Like I can make solid decisions that aren't fogged by intoxication.

It's why when Hornsby stands and offers his hand to me, I don't take it right away.

"Are you not going to celebrate my birthday with me?"

"You tend to use the whole birthday thing to your advantage. You realize that, right?"

"I survived another year on this planet. I'm pretty sure that's cause for celebration." He wiggles his fingers. "Come on."

"Wait one second. Before I agree to this dessert, which is actual food, correct?"

"Correct."

"Okay." I straighten my shoulders. "Then I need to make sure that after dessert, we part ways and say good night."

His jaw clenches, and I can see his irritation in the tic of his cheek and the way he glances away. Will he agree? My guess is dessert was a ploy. I might be buzzed, but I'm not stupid. And as I await his answer, I inwardly smirk because I can see right through him. "Okay," he finally says. "After dessert, we part ways."

"Deal?" I hold my hand out.

He lets out a deep sigh. "Deal." He takes my hand in his and pulls me down off my stool. "Follow me."

Together, we weave through the crowd. A few guys notice him and stop him for a fist bump or a handshake. One guy took a selfie with Hornsby, and the entire time, he held my hand, never letting go. It was a whirlwind of appreciation that I wasn't ready to be exposed to.

I get the need to have a little piece of him, though. These men are absolute gods here in Vancouver. To spot them out in the wild and have access to them is most likely overwhelming and a dream come true to any hockey fan.

When we're finally outside, we're whipped in the face by a chilly wind. February in Vancouver in a dress is not a smart choice, but I wasn't expecting to be outside very long.

Hornsby lets go of my hand, and he quickly removes his suit jacket before draping it over my shoulders. The large jacket drowns me in the tailored fabric that smells just like him. Immediately, my body warms from the thought of him being wrapped around me.

"It's a quick walk," he says before taking my hand again and guiding me down the block.

I tug on the hem of my dress as we move quickly. "I didn't think of winter wear when I put this dress on. Thank you for your jacket."

"You're welcome. And that dress . . . trust me, it's perfect for tonight."

"Says the guy wearing pants."

"My ankles are exposed. I feel the chilliness."

"Oh, heaven forbid your ankles get cold," I joke.

"I know, fans around would be terrified they might turn blue. You know there are Instagram accounts dedicated just to my ankles."

"I know. I've seen them," I say. "The comments are absolutely ridiculous."

"Ridiculous or true? Someone said I could easily win best ankles in Canada and America. I mean, that's a title I'd wear proudly."

"Maybe this week you model off your ankles for a TikTok, give your hungry fans more material to work with."

"Give them the goods like that?" He shakes his head, and in all seriousness, he says, "Penny, you can't just give away the milk for free. You have to make them work for it. A little flash here and a little flash there to keep them begging for more. If you just hand it to them, they'll become disinterested. And do you really think I want my ankles to be known as has-beens?"

A loud laugh erupts out of me from how ridiculous he sounds. "The absolute horror."

"Exactly. So, I say we plan a two-year marketing project of showing bits and pieces of my ankles until the grand reveal of a full-on thirty-minute video showing clips of just my ankles. Talk about the ultimate apex. Think of the relief these fans will feel."

"Like a pent-up, edged-out orgasm."

"Precisely," he says, his voice growing deeper.

I glance up at him, and when our eyes connect, all I can see is a yearning in his. I point my finger at him. "Don't even think about it."

"What?" He holds his one hand up in defense. "I wasn't thinking about anything."

"You are such a liar."

We're silent for a moment, and then he mumbles, "You're the one who said orgasm."

"Yeah, and you were the one who alluded to it."

"I alluded to nothing. That's just your filthy mind at work, Penny."

Chapter Four

ELI

Let's be clear about one thing—any woman I take to bed is a willing, consensual partner.

Do I flirt shamelessly to get them there? Of course.

But do I make them go against their own will?

Never.

That's not how I fucking roll.

I want the woman to want me just as much as I want her.

So the way this evening is going with Penny is excruciating because I sense how this night might end. I've crossed a line with flirting with my best friend, my teammate's sister and for nothing.

She's too shy.

She's too levelheaded.

She might be attracted to me, but she's not going to give in.

Am I disappointed? Absolutely.

But that doesn't mean I'll ditch her and find someone else. I actually like her company. She's funny. Interesting. When she's more comfortable, she jokes around, and I like that. She's just a cool person to hang out with.

Honestly, I'm glad I ran into her. She's made my birthday enjoyable when usually it's just a mindless day of me trying to forget I don't have much family, nor do I have anyone who calls me on my birthday other than my teammates.

"Where is this place?" Penny shivers next to me.

"Just around the corner." Releasing her hand, I wrap my arm around her shoulder, bringing her in close to keep her warm.

It's not just cold out. It's borderline bone-chilling. Hat, gloves, heavy jacket kind of weather. My ankles are cold, so I can't imagine what she must be feeling right now.

I turn the corner, and the little bakery that I've grown very fond of has a neon sign in the window stating they are open. Just in time.

"Right there," I say, pointing ahead. We pick up our speed, and when we reach the shop, I open the door for her. I like to say this bakery is the best-kept secret in Vancouver. It's an absolute hole in the wall, a narrow building with a bakery case running the length of the shop, chipped and scuffed black and white tiled floors, and of course, an old man working the front register who has seen his fair share of flour spilled all over the ground.

He glances up from his register, and the smallest of smiles lights up his face.

"Eli, my boy, I was wondering when you were going to come in again."

Right above the cash register is a framed jersey of mine signed and made out to Robert, the man beaming at me. I gave it to him last year as a seventy-fifth birthday present. It absolutely made his day.

"Hey, Robert," I say. "Been busy and also trying to cut down on the sweets." I pat my stomach. "Playoffs are just around the corner, and I need to be in top form."

"I recall the night you came in for some red velvet cake. The next day, you had one of the best games of the season." He lifts his chin. "I told everyone it was because you ate my cake."

"You know, I do believe that was the reason."

He chuckles. "Look at this guy making an old man feel good about himself." He turns his attention to Penny. "And who might this be? I've never seen you bring a girl in here before. She must be special."

I pull Penny in even closer and give her shoulder a squeeze. "She is special. Her name is Penny. I've known her for a bit now, and she decided to spend my birthday with me."

"It's your birthday?" Robert asks. "Well, hot dog. I have just the thing for you."

He walks to the back of the bakery, disappearing for a few moments.

"I take it you come here a lot from how familiar you are with the owner?" Penny asks.

"I come here probably far too much. He makes these chocolate croissants that are so fucking good that I once wept while eating one."

"You did not," she says while poking me and laughing.

"Close to crying. If I was able to tap into my emotions on a deeper level, there would have been tears for sure."

Just then, Robert comes back to the front holding a cake box. He taps the top of it and slides it across the counter. "French silk pie. It's my last one."

"What?" I ask, excited. "You never have any left."

"Today is your lucky day. Happy Birthday, Eli." Robert lends out his hand, and I take it, giving it a solid shake.

"Thank you so much," I say. "How much do I owe you, Robert?" I take out my wallet, and Robert holds up his hand.

"It's on me. Consider it a birthday present."

"You know I can't do that," I say.

He shakes his hand at me. "With the amount of business you've brought me just by talking about my shop, I do owe you this gift. Now take the pie and don't argue with me."

I'd never argue with Robert, so instead, I take a fifty out of my wallet and stick it in the tip jar. With a wink to an annoyed older man, I grab the pie. "Thank you, Robert."

"Anytime." He glances at Penny. "Be nice to this guy. If he brought you here, you must mean something to him. We think the world of him, and I sure hope you do as well."

Looking slightly uncomfortable, Penny says, "He's really great."

Satisfied, Robert offers us a wave, and I head toward the front door. When I open it for Penny, she says, "Where are we eating this pie?"

"Well, since Robert is closing up, we can eat it out here. He always includes forks so we can dig in." When she shivers, I secretly smile to myself. "Or we can take it up to my place, which is just across the street." I point at the modern-looking apartment building directly in front of us.

Her eyes narrow, and she says, "Well, how convenient."

"For me. Not sure about you. I don't know where you live, but like I said, after dessert, we part ways. So we can scarf this down right here, and then I'll be more than happy to find you a taxi to get you home."

"You want me to eat a pie while freezing right outside your place?"

"I mean . . . if you want to warm up, you are more than welcome to come to my place and do so. I have a fireplace we can sit next to."

"Ohhhhh, I'm sure you do," she says with a giant roll of her eyes before walking away.

"Where are you going?" I ask her.

"To your place. There is no way I'm staying out in the cold any longer. I can barely feel my feet."

Smiling brightly, I jog up next to her, pie in hand, and wrap my arm around her. "That's a great idea. Glad you thought of it. And of course, after dessert, I'll help you get back home."

"Uh-huh, sure," she says with a feigned annoyed tone that only makes me smile even larger.

———

"YOU KNOW, I thought your place was going to be more sterile than this," Penny says while glancing around my apartment.

"Sterile?" I ask as I flip the switch to my fireplace. It roars to life in a second, offering a faint orange hue to the dim-lit room.

"Well, you know, like a bachelor pad. Neon signs, beer posters, no texture to your design at all, bland. But look, you have candles and a throw pillow and curtains. And look at that." She points at a picture on the wall. "That's actual art."

I laugh. "I grew up living in the attic of a barn. I told myself when I got older, I'd have a place that felt like a home, so I spent time making this place just that, a home."

She turns around to face me as I rest a blanket along the floor. "You grew up in a barn?"

"Long story," I say, not wanting to get into any aspects of my childhood. Not many know about my childhood, especially the fans and organization, and that's how I want it to stay. *No pity party for me, especially on my birthday.* I set the pie down on the blanket along with two forks. "What can I get you to drink? I have hot chocolate, and I can add a splash of Baileys to it."

"You have Baileys and hot chocolate?" she asks, stunned.

"Yes, why is that so shocking to you?"

She's still wearing my jacket, casually walking around my apartment. "I just pictured you as, I don't know . . . someone who might lean more toward a dark stout or maybe a whiskey than a hot chocolate and Baileys."

"I'm not the cold man you think I am," I say while making my way to my open-concept kitchen that looks over the entire main living space of the apartment.

"I don't think you're cold," Penny says while following me. She takes a seat on one of the stools at the island. "I just had a different impression of you is all."

"Maybe you should start to get to know your players a little better," I say while I start heating up some milk. "Might help with what you post."

"And how do you envision me getting to know the players better?" I turn to see that she has one eyebrow raised at me.

I chuckle. "Well, with me, I say an evening here would be the best way. But with the other guys, a solid questionnaire will do."

"Uh-huh. And why an evening with you?"

"I'm complex. The other guys are superficial. But with me, you really have to dive deep. The more time spent with me, the better. I'm up for an all-nighter if you are."

She shakes her head with humor. "Wow, you never stop, do you?"

"Stop what?" I ask innocently. "I'm just trying to help you do your job better."

"Well, aren't you a benevolent knight in shining armor?"

"I've been known to be called that before." I wink and then grab two mugs from my cabinet . . . and I wait for a reaction . . .

"What on earth are those?" Penny asks. Just as I expected.

I hold the mugs up. "These are my bosom buddies. Taters got them for me one year as a Secret Santa gift." I flash the mugs of a bare chest, one set of dark nipples, one set of light. Both beautiful. Both doing the job of holding hot liquid. "And before you refuse to drink from a pair of breasts, let it be known that these are the only mugs I have."

"You know, I take back my comment about your sophisticated side. This"—she waves at the mugs—"this is what I expected from you."

"Glad I didn't disappoint," I say. She shivers and pulls my jacket closer together. "Do you want to borrow a sweatshirt? Maybe some pants? Get yourself warm?"

She shakes her head. "No, I'll just go sit by the fire if that's okay."

"That's fine. I'll be right over."

When she hops off the stool, I watch her walk over to the living room, where she takes a seat on the blanket I laid out. She removes my jacket and rests it across her lap as she scoots even closer to the fire. Her face is lit up by the flames, and I catch her profile—the plush of her lips and the gentle slope of her nose. She's beautiful. She really is.

Not that I had doubts, but her personality matches her

beauty. The joking, the quick wit, the teasing . . . hell, she's the whole package, something I've only discovered as she's loosened up around me tonight. *Perhaps I've only concentrated on the surface level with her too.* Although, learning more about her tonight has only intensified my attraction to her.

Once I finish up with the hot chocolates, adding a touch of Baileys, but not too much, I take them over to the blanket, where I set them on the coffee table right in front of the fire. I undo my vest and toss it to the side, giving myself more freedom in my movements since I like to get my suits tailored to fit me like a glove.

Reaching out, I hand her a mug, which she reluctantly takes with a shake of her head. "Thank you . . . for these breasts, and for the hot chocolate."

"You are welcome," I say while picking up my mug. I rub the nipples of my mug a few times and glance up at her.

"What are you doing?" she asks.

"This is all the action I'm getting tonight, so I might as well enjoy it." I pinch the nipple and let out a ridiculous moan that makes her laugh so loud that I mentally pat myself on the back for pulling that joy from her.

"I absolutely hate you for doing that."

"Nah, you love it." I hand her the fork and pop open the bakery box to reveal the pie. Topped in whipped cream and chocolate flakes, the crust is a light-blond cookie crust, and just from the mere sight of it, my mouth waters. "Shit, I'm not sure you're going to like what you see next."

"What do you mean?" she asks.

I don't answer. Instead, I dig my fork into the pie, scoop up a ridiculous forkful, and then shove it into my mouth.

Her eyes widen before she laughs. "Aw, you're about to demolish this pie in front of me, aren't you?"

"At least half of it," I say with a full mouth.

"Makes mental note to leave French silk pies around the stadium for you to find. I'm thinking a hidden camera show. Some pies are real, some are not."

"That's just cruel," I say after I swallow.

Smiling sweetly, she reaches up and swipes at the corner of my mouth. When she pulls away, she shows me a dab of whipped cream on her finger.

Without even thinking about it, I bring her finger to my mouth, where I gently lick off the whipped cream.

Our eyes connect.

The room falls silent.

The air grows stiff.

And before I can stop myself, I suck her finger into my mouth. I tug lightly on it with my lips, keeping my eyes connected to hers and making sure nothing is left on her finger. When I release her, she slowly lowers her hand and then averts her wide eyes while clearing her throat.

I recognize what she's been trying to mask all night. She wants me. I've seen hints of it, but right now, under the orange glow of the fire, I know for damn sure she's feeling the same way as I am.

So I take my fork, grab a smaller piece, and I lift it to her mouth.

She glances at it, and those gorgeous eyes turn on me, and I feel my stomach bottom out as she opens her mouth and sucks the pie right off the fork, staring at me the entire time.

And I go fucking hard.

"Don't look at me like that," I say.

"Like what?" she asks as she leans slightly forward.

"Like the pie isn't the only thing you want for dessert." I reach up to the buttons of my shirt and undo the top four, letting some air reach my now heated skin.

"I don't believe I'm looking at you like that," she says as she pushes my jacket off her legs. Her legs curl to the side as her dress rides up on her thighs. "Are you going to have another piece?"

I glance up at her, tearing my gaze away from how the fire bounces off the sheen of her smooth legs.

I clear my throat and nod. "Yeah." I take another bite, but

this time, it's more modest. But there is nothing modest about the way Penny is watching my mouth or the blaze in her eyes when I swallow.

Tempting fate, I stab a forkful of pie for her and lift it to her mouth. She stares at the pie for a moment before she parts her lips. Right before she moves her mouth over the pie, a droplet of whipped cream slips off and lands directly on her chest. We both glance down to find it resting on the swell of her breast.

Fuck . . .

My mouth waters as I say, "Let me get that for you." Before I move, I pause briefly to see if she protests. When she doesn't say anything, just breathes heavier, I know I have the green light. So I reach out and very slowly and very gently swipe my finger across her breast.

Jesus Christ.

Soft. Plump. Delicious.

Her breath hitches.

My cock hardens.

And the distinct swell in my pants causes me to push for more.

I lift my finger between us, offering it to her as a treat, so I can feel her mouth on me, and I can pretend she's not sucking my finger, but she's sucking so much more. I hold my breath as we both stare at each other, unwritten promises of pleasure being cast across the thick, lust-filled air. And to my utter fucking delight, she leans forward and takes my finger into her mouth.

She's gentle at first, just rounding over my finger, letting her tongue do the exploring, and then, when I'm not expecting it, she sucks hard . . . so fucking hard that my eyes start to roll in the back of my head.

Jesus Christ.

When she pulls away, my control slips. The armor I'm wearing is cracking, and anything Pacey has ever said to me about Penny fades in the dark. In my mind, the night went from innocent pie eating to *I'm going to fucking spread your legs and eat your pussy in a matter of seconds.*

I wet my lips and set the fork down in the pie pan before shoving it to the side.

"Are you done?" she asks.

"You tell me," I say as I wait.

"I could use another bite." I reach for the fork, but she stops me. "Off your finger."

Mother.

Fucker.

And with those three little words, I know my night is about to change. My fantasies will be fulfilled, and I'll finally get to have a piece of the very delicious Penny Lawes.

I swipe at the pie, grabbing some whipped cream and chocolate, and hold it up to her. After only a moment of hesitation, she gets on her knees and crawls over to me, sitting directly on my lap.

Yes.

Just where I fucking want her.

My hand falls to her backside as she takes my chocolate and whipped cream finger into her mouth.

Her lips float over the length of my finger, pulling me deep into her mouth where her tongue runs along the side, only for her to slowly drag her lips off.

I'm.

Fucking.

Gone.

In the blink of an eye, I roll her to the floor so her back is against the blanket, and I pin her hands to the ground.

"Tell me you want this," I say, my breath escaping my lungs faster than I expected.

Her eyes search mine. I can see her mind thinking, her brain churning with what to do. *Please don't fucking say no. I'm not sure I can take it.*

And just when I think my hopes are about to be crushed, she spreads her legs, allowing me in closer as she says, "I want this. I want this very much."

That's all I needed to fucking hear.

Tell me you want this.

I crash my mouth down on hers and finally take what I've wanted since I first laid eyes on her.

I take everything.

I take her mouth.

I take her breasts into my hands.

I press my hardened cock to her center.

I swallow her moans.

I fuck her on the blanket in front of the fireplace, and when she's about to come, when she's quivering in my arms, I pull out and bring her to my bedroom, where I kiss and lick all the way up her thighs and back down until she's clawing at me, begging for more. That's when I give us both a sweet release.

And I've never felt anything like it before.

Ever.

It felt like my body was ripping in half as I came, an immense amount of ecstasy spreading through me. This feeling, it was special to her. *To being inside Penny.*

Together, we pass out on my California king mattress, where she curls into me, and I hold on to her, hoping and praying I can have one more chance at the high she just gave me. A high I feel I'm going to be chasing for the rest of my goddamn life.

Did I skip the details of our night together? Of course I did. Because even though what we did was important—fuck, it rocked my world—it's what happens after that night that is the most important to the story.

When I wake up the next morning, she's gone. I'm left with the lasting pleasure still pulsing through my veins and a brief note.

Hornsby,

Happy Birthday, hope it was everything you hoped for. I borrowed a sweatshirt, will return it. Please, whatever you do, please make sure Pacey doesn't find out.

Penny

No *I'll call you.*

No *maybe we can try this again sometime.*

Just a plea for my discretion. There is no way in fuck I'll be telling anyone about what happened . . . ever. And not just because I like Penny and will honor her wishes. The last thing I need is for Pacey to find out. I made a promise to him, and I broke it. The worst thing about it all, though, is that I'd break that promise all over again.

Over and over.

Until I couldn't feel my limbs anymore.

Because that's how much I fucking liked being inside her.

How much I liked being around her.

When I head to my locker the next day, the sweatshirt she borrowed is there, folded . . . and it fucking smells like her. I bring the fabric to my nose several times, taking large whiffs, remembering what it was like to have her in my arms, to hear her moans vibrate through my ears, to watch her crumple with pleasure beneath me.

But that's when I realize the harsh truth.

Penny Lawes is done with me.

Even though I'm not remotely done with her.

Chapter Five

PENNY

Five weeks later...

"This is fake, right?" Blakely asks as she holds a positive pregnancy test in her hand. "Like you bought this at some crazy souvenir shop, and you're trying to be funny?"

"Why on earth would I ever think joking about being pregnant is funny?" I say, pacing the length of my living room. "Jesus Christ, not only is that wrong on so many levels, especially for those who struggle with infertility, but this is a fucking serious thing." I grip my forehead and try to calm my racing heart. It's been five weeks since I spent the night with Eli. *Five weeks. And now . . .*

"Wait . . . so this is real? This is a real pregnancy test, and you're pregnant?"

I pause, turn toward my friend, and nod.

"No." She shakes her head. "No fucking way." She points at my stomach. "There is a baby in there, right now? It's not just the two of us in your apartment, but the three of us."

I bite my bottom lip as tears start to form in my eyes. "Yes, there are three humans in this room right now."

"Holy . . . shit." Blakely collapses on my couch. "Who the hell is the father?" The minute the question falls past her lips, she shoots up to her feet again, eyes wide. "Jesus Christ, is it Hornsby?"

You know those tears that were welling up? Yeah, they're now cascading down my cheeks in droves as I nod.

"Oh my God, are you sure?"

"He's the only guy I've had sex with in the past year. So yeah, I'm pretty sure." I wave my hand in front of my face as I start to hyperventilate. "What am I going to do? I'm freaking pregnant."

"With Hornsby's baby!" Blakely begins pacing. "You know, Pacey is going to murder him. Absolutely destroy him into nothing. Like I hope Hornsby had fun playing hockey because his life is about to end."

"What? No." I shake my head. "Pacey is not going to find out about this."

Blakely pauses. "Oh." Her shoulders straighten as a thought crosses her mind. "Well, I mean, that's your choice. It's your body."

"What?" I ask. "No, I'm not . . . I'm not going to do that. I don't think I could."

Blakely looks confused as ever. "Then, uh, how do you expect Pacey not to find out?"

"I thought about that while you were driving over here. And the only thing I could come up with is that I start eating a lot around him. So much food that he possibly grows concerned. Whenever he's around, there's a burger in my mouth or ice cream, even an entire pizza. So when I start gaining weight, he'll just think it's because of this new eating habit I have."

Blakely taps her chin and nods. "Novel idea, absolutely brilliant." She holds her finger up. "One problem, though. After nine months of eating yourself into oblivion, you're going to have a baby. Dare I ask how you plan on explaining that?"

"Uh . . . random stranger dropped the baby off at my apartment door because she thought the flower wreath I hang year round is inviting, so they thought I'd do a good job raising a baby?"

She takes a deep breath. "I understand that you're pregnant, and that does weird things to your body and mind, but that suggestion is delusional. Pacey had a head injury, but it didn't knock the common sense out of him."

"Are you sure?" I wince.

"Positive," Blakely declares as we both go back to pacing my apartment. "Ooo." She stops. "Why don't we bring in Winnie? She could possibly help figure out a way to tell Pacey. She seems smart and has a good hold on your brother. She could be very helpful."

"True, but if I bring her in, I'd definitely have to tell Pacey because I wouldn't want her to have to keep a secret like that from him."

Blakely levels with me. "News flash, Penny. You're going to have to tell him no matter what. You realize that, right?"

"But do I?" I ask. "I mean, let's really give this some good thought. I could totally pull off the eating thing. Maybe slip in that I started a new foodie TikTok account. That's believable. And then when it comes to the baby, well, I obviously wouldn't bring it into work, so he would never see the child then, and it's not like he comes over to my place a lot. If he does, I'll just give you the baby. You know, the more I think about this, the more I realize that we can truly pull this off."

"Hold on a second." Blakely poses her hand to stop me. "You're my best friend, and I love you dearly, and you know that no matter what happens, I'll always be there for you, but"—she taps her crotch—"it's all vagina down here, no penis. And last I remember, I wasn't the one who got you pregnant. So when you say we, you can't possibly be including me in on that we."

"Uh, yeah," I say as if she's lost her mind. "This, you and

me." I motion between us. "This is a package deal. What I go through, you go through. You accepted those terms when you decided to be my best friend."

"I don't remember signing any contract."

I prop my hands on my hips in irritation. "It's a silent contract. Best friends are BOGOs. Buy one, get one. That's us. So my pregnancy is your pregnancy."

"Yeah, you keep saying that, and every time, it makes me want to take a step farther and farther away from you." She pushes her hair behind her ear. "I'm too young to be thinking about babies and all of that. Perry and I are still just having fun."

"Oh, my God, and you think I wanted this?"

She shrugs. "I guess . . . you play, you pay."

"Oh, my God." I pick a pillow up from my couch and throw it at her, pegging her in the leg and causing her to yelp. "I can't believe you just said that. That's something a disgruntled grandparent would say, not my best friend."

"Well, I don't know what you want me to do." She stretches her arms out to the side. "I'm trying to be helpful here, but your need to hide this pregnancy is absolutely ridiculous and will never work. You need to realize that. Unless you plan on terminating the pregnancy, which I know you don't want to do, hiding this child will not work. Pacey will find out, and think about his reaction if you don't tell him. The fury in that man's eyes will split you in two. And is that what you want, Penny? To be split in two?"

"Might make it easier. Responsible Penny can take care of the baby and hide while working Penny can provide for the family without revealing she had a child. Sooo, possibly this could work."

"You're acting insane!" Blakely throws her hands up in the air and heads toward the door.

"Where are you going?"

"To dunk my head in some snow."

I run up to her and stop her. "Please don't leave. I need you."

She turns toward me, and I can see the worry in her eyes. It snaps me out of my delirium. "You have to tell him."

My eyes water as I slowly nod. "I know."

"And you have to tell Hornsby."

I shake my head. "No way. I'm not telling him. Pacey will murder him. We've already established that. I'll just say this is some random hookup, and the guy is nowhere to be found."

"Why on earth would you do that? We don't get paid that much, Penny. And there are going to be a lot of expenses that come with a baby, so you *will* need Hornsby's help. And besides that, he has the right to know."

"Trust me, he won't want to know. We both made it quite clear that we didn't want anything serious. I mean, think about it. He doesn't ever date; he just hooks up. This is the last thing he wants. This is an anchor weighing down his fun-loving ship."

"Well, too bad for him," Blakely says with such strong conviction that I wish I could have her kind of sass at this moment. "I'm so sick of women—for the most part—taking on the brunt of the pregnancy. Sure, some great men out there are truly there for their partners, but in situations like this, it's more often than not that the woman deals with all the struggles when it should be both parents." She points her finger at me. "He doesn't just deserve to know. He needs to know. This is his responsibility too."

I agree with her. I do think it would be easier if I didn't have to go through this alone. But I barely know Hornsby, and what I do know about him doesn't really paint him as a father figure. And once Pacey finds out, I truly think he will kill Hornsby. Then what happens? I don't have a baby daddy at all.

A wave of nausea hits me all at once, and I reach out to hold my friend.

"Oh God, I have to tell him."

"You have to tell both of them. And do you know what my suggestion would be?"

"What?" I ask.

"I'd rip off the Band-Aid and tell them at the same time."

Is she insane? Telling them at the same time seems like a more ridiculous suggestion than hiding the baby.

I'm about to protest when I pause . . . well, would it really be that ridiculous? Ripping the Band-Aid off has always been a tried and true way to conduct truth-telling business. Telling them at the same time might not be too bad. I wouldn't have to say it twice. They could both just deal with the news together, and who knows, it might be a bonding moment for them. They very well might hug and congratulate each other on the wondrous news.

Ugh. Who am I kidding? We all know that is a far-fetched reaction that will never occur. I need to be prepared for the drawing of blood and fists.

"I'd need a buffer," I say, my mind actually thinking this is a good idea, despite how they might react. Telling them at the same time is easier on me, and that's what matters. "Someone who'd be able to protect Hornsby when Pacey unleashes the fear of God."

"That's a good idea," Blakely says as she walks me to the couch, and we both take a seat. "Because what if Pacey attacks Hornsby? You won't be able to get them apart, especially with a baby on board. So why don't you invite Taters?"

"Taters? Why him? He's an instigator. He'll only make matters worse."

"True." Blakely nods in agreement. "Then how about Posey? He's close with Hornsby. He's big, a bruiser. He could do some damage if need be."

"Posey could be a good option," I answer. "But won't that be awkward for him?"

"Probably," Blakely answers. "But I think it's necessary."

I worry my lip as I stare out my windows. It's a bright day, cold but sunny, the complete antithesis of how I feel at this very moment.

Because instead of being happy about bringing a new life into the world, I'm worried. Scared. Nervous. Still slightly in disbelief despite the four different tests I took just to confirm.

"Maybe I should wait until the season is over to tell them. I don't want to cause a rift. The team has been killing it this season. This will only divide them."

"By the time the season is over, you'll be showing, and it will be obvious. Might as well tell them now so they can get it out of their system and focus on the playoffs."

"Yeah, you're probably right."

Blakely loops her arm around my shoulders. "Who knows, maybe they will take it better than you think."

"I love how hopeful you are, but I think we both know that's never going to happen."

She lets out a heavy sigh. "I know. So when are you going to call them in?"

"Monday," I say. "I have some social media things planned. We don't have a game, so I'll have them come to my office and break the news after practice. I'll make them believe they're there for some sort of TikTok idea when, in reality, I'm about to change their lives."

"Hey, yours has already changed, might as well have company. And after, we'll get lunch, and you'll tell me every last detail. Because, girlfriend, you lied through your pretty little teeth when you said nothing happened between you and Eli Hornsby five weeks ago. I deserve to know." She had hounded me, but I'd denied everything. *Clearly.*

"Something to look forward to."

Chapter Six

ELI

"Where are you going?" Posey asks as he jogs up to me.

"Penny called me up to her office for some social media overview."

"Me too. Lawes is coming as well." Posey takes a bite of his bologna sandwich. "Hey, Lawes," Posey calls into the locker room. "You coming?"

"Yeah," he calls out and then appears at the door with wet hair while adjusting the hem of his shirt. When he spots Posey's sandwich, he says, "Dude, you realize there are much better things you could be eating or drinking after a workout, right?"

Posey takes a large bite. "It's a ritual, man. The last time I didn't eat a bologna sandwich after practice, I pulled my groin muscle. To hell if I'm going to let that happen again." He takes another bite.

"Don't even try to change his mind," I say to Pacey. "He's set in his ways."

"He's right," Posey says. "And there is nothing you can say or do about it." He then taps his legs. "These groin muscles are going to stay injury free."

"I can't with you today," I say.

"What's wrong with you?" Lawes asks. "Still got that headache?"

"Yeah." I press my fingers into my forehead. "Fucking brutal. After this meeting with your sister, I'm going straight home and passing out."

"What is this meeting about again?" Posey asks.

"Uh, some social media thing." Lawes shrugs. "Not sure. Probably something we're going to have to do that the fans want to see. I've already told Penny many times that I'm not doing some bullshit trendy dance. That's where I put my foot down."

"I don't mind the dances," I say.

"If I didn't have two left feet, I'd enjoy them, but I can't remember shit," Posey says with a mouth full of bologna.

"It's because you've been cracked in the head far too many times," Lawes says as we hit the elevator button to go to the third floor where all the offices are.

As they fight about dance moves, I dream of what the rest of my day after this meeting will look like. My head's vibrating with pain. A typical tension headache for me that will go away with some simple Theragun therapy, a caffeinated drink, some Icy Hot, Ibuprofen, and rest. But I have to make it through this meeting first, which could not have come at a worse time.

Not due to the headache, but because I've finally started to erase my birthday night from my memory. It was too fucking good. Way too good. And trying to have sex with someone else other than her has been next to impossible. Took me two weeks to even attempt to look at someone else, and when I went out to bars and flirted, I went home alone. By the end of the night, I simply wasn't interested.

Last week, I finally kissed someone in the hallway of a bar, which was a huge step for me, but it led to nothing. Absolutely nothing. Because her lips weren't plump, her moans weren't sweet, and the grip she had on my shoulders resembled nothing to the way Penny clung to me.

Which only means one thing: seeing Penny today and having to talk to her will be a setback in my process to move on from the best night of my life. I've done a good job so far avoiding her, only catching glimpses of her here and there, but being face to face . . . fuck. I just hope when I get to her office, that I don't feel the urge to pull her onto my lap and run my tongue up and down the column of her neck.

Wishful thinking.

My body is already humming with the thought of seeing her. *Settle that down, Hornsby. Her brother is standing right beside you.*

The elevator dings, and we all step out. Lawes leads the way down the hall, followed by Posey, and then me. A few staff members say hi as we pass, but the walk isn't very long, and before I know it, we're standing at Penny's door, walking in.

Keep it together, Hornsby.

"Hey, sis," Lawes says when we step in. I don't see Penny at first because Lawes pulls her into a hug, but when he steps away, I catch a glimpse of her hair pulled back into a high, tight ponytail. It swishes to the side, distracting me for a moment, just before her face comes into view.

And fuck . . . me.

Beautiful, tempting blue eyes sparkle against her long, thick lashes. Her lips are painted a pink that goes perfectly with her complexion and reminds me of that goddamn dress she wore on my birthday.

The dress that now haunts me.

That pink on her lips is like a punch to my chest and a flashback to a time when I have never been more satisfied in my life. Images of her dress being peeled off her body, revealing enticing black lingerie, play on repeat in my head, followed by the heady look in her eyes when I first entered her. The gasp of total satisfaction when I bottomed out. And then, I'm hit with the memorized sounds of her moans as she came all over my cock.

"Dude, take a seat," Posey says, snapping me out of my reverie.

My eyes immediately fall on Penny standing next to me, trying to shut her office door.

"Fuck, sorry," I mumble as I take a deep breath, trying to right my mind. But it's the wrong move because I'm assaulted by Penny's perfume. Fuck, that perfume. I've been savoring the smell of her perfume on the sweatshirt she borrowed that morning. The intimate scent spikes a wave of arousal in my veins, and before I know it, not only is my head pounding but so is my heart.

Jesus Christ.

I didn't think this would help, being near her, but I didn't think it would give me a full-blown attack of lust. An onslaught of human emotions that cause my legs to shake beneath me when we make eye contact.

I'm not keeping it together.

This was why I've avoided her. Because I knew the minute I got this close, my body would react in the worst and best way possible.

Holding on by a single thread, I offer her a simple smile and then quickly take a seat next to Lawes, who is relaxed in his chair, manspreading, and looking far too comfortable.

Of course he's comfortable. Why wouldn't he be? He's not the one who fucked one of his teammate's sisters and still craves for another night alone with her. There are not only cravings but bottles and bottles of need.

No, he met a random person in the woods, fell in love, and is sitting pretty, drama free.

I'm churning inside with yearning and anxiety. So much anxiety because what if I look at her wrong? What if I let something slip? What if, by chance, Pacey can feel that I fucked his sister? I could forget about fixing my headache because I won't have a head to fix.

Penny takes a seat in her black desk chair and scoots in, then places her hands on the top of her desk. For a moment, and only a moment, I truly allow myself to look at her. She's so goddamn beautiful. Wide eyes, pert nose, long-as-shit hair that is somehow as shiny as a Christmas ornament, and her tits . . . Christ. What I wouldn't give just to have one more night sucking on them, playing with them . . . fucking them.

"Thank you so much for coming up here. I know you guys have busy days."

"Not a problem. Couldn't pass up a moment to see my sister."

Jesus, Mr. Sunshine over there, cool it with the peppiness, bro.

Penny smiles, but it doesn't quite reach her eyes. Rather, it's washed away and replaced with a knit in her brow.

She clears her throat. "Well, I kind of have something to tell you, and this is hard for me, so just bear with me as I attempt to find the words."

Mr. Sunshine turns into a ball of concern as he leans forward and places his hand on her desk. "Is everything okay? Did they fire you? Who do I need to talk to?"

That would suck if she was fired, just because I know how much she loves this job, but on a positive—and I know this will make me sound like a total dick—that *would* mean that maybe I could get over this, well whatever this is that I'm feeling.

Call me a bastard, but fingers crossed she got fired.

"No, nothing like that," she says as she twists her hands together. Damn it.

And then, she quickly glances at me and looks away.

Shit, don't look at me. Why did she look at me? There's no need to look at me like that, like we have something hidden between us, which I know we do, but she doesn't need to make it known.

Wait . . .

Is that why we're all fucking here? Is she going rogue?

Is she . . .

Oh fuck, is she going to tell Lawes about our night together?

No, she wouldn't do that. Why would she? She didn't want

Lawes to know. There would be no reason for her to communicate that with him. Right? Plus, Posey is here. She wouldn't say something that intimate with Posey around, the bologna-loving brute.

"Then what's going on?" Pacey asks. "Did you post something that you shouldn't have? We'll defend you, don't worry."

She shakes her head. "No, that's not it."

"Then what is it?"

"Maybe if you actually let her speak, she'll tell us," I say before I can stop myself. I'm a goddamn bundle of nerves. I need Pacey to shut up so I can find out why we're here.

Lawes pins me with a seething gaze—he doesn't appreciate my outburst. I slowly melt in my chair, holding my hands up, not wanting to stir the pot any more.

"You know what, I don't think this was a good idea," Penny says while pushing away from her desk. "I'll, uh, I'll figure out a better time to do this."

Okay, fair enough.

She is not in the mood to divulge whatever it is she needs to say, fine by me. Let's pack up and get the hell out of here.

I start to rise from my chair when Lawes pushes me back down by the shoulder. "Penny, it's okay. We're cool. Whatever it is you called us up here for, we're here to listen. What's going on?"

Her eyes travel from Lawes, to Posey, and then land on me before she looks back at her brother.

On a deep breath, she finally says, "I called you here because I have to tell you that, uh . . ." She wets her lips. "I, um . . . I'm . . ."

"You're what?" Pacey presses her.

"Well, you see, it all happened so fast . . ."

Oh my fuck, what is she going to say? She is going to tell him. I can feel it . . . she's going to tell him about our night.

Why?

"What happened fast?"

I sink lower and lower into my chair, trying to cover my eyes. Maybe if I don't see Pacey, he won't see me.

"Uh . . ." she stumbles.

"Penny, just tell us."

"Fine," she squeaks. I wince, hold my breath, and then . . . "I'm pregnant."

Pre . . . pre-what? My body shoots up, I uncover my eyes, and my heart lodges in my throat as all of the blood drains from my head and pools at my ankles.

Did I just hear that fucking correctly?

Did she say . . . *gulp* . . . pregnant?

"Wait . . . what?" Pacey asks as he pulls on his ear. He chuckles and says, "Jesus Christ, I thought you just said you're pregnant."

Yeah, that's what I heard as well. Maybe I heard her wrong too.

Please, Jesus, I hope I heard her wrong.

"I did," she says, and once again, I've lost all feeling in my legs, my arms, every goddamn piece of my body as I attempt to comprehend what she's saying. "I'm pregnant."

"Pregnant?" Pacey asks, blinking a few times as if that will help him understand better. "As in there is a child in your stomach?" He points at her.

"Yes." She winces.

Pacey roars out of his seat and says, "You're fucking pregnant?"

When I say my dick just shriveled up into my scrotum, I'm not lying. Like goddamn roller blinds being sprung into place, my dick is gone, disappeared for possibly ever. Can't be sure during this moment of absolute terror.

"Y-yes," Penny confirms.

"How? How the fuck did this happen?" Pacey says as he looks around the room, pulling on his hair. When he spots us, it's as if something in his head clicks. "Why the fuck are they here?" He points at Posey and me.

I know why I'm here, but Posey . . . now that's a good question.

Before she can answer, he turns on us and yells, "Did you fuck my sister?"

Like a bullet out of a cannon, Posey scoots his chair all the way to the window and holds his hands up in surrender. "I didn't. I never went near her. I have no clue why I'm here. Please don't kill me."

And then that leaves me . . .

Pacey turns his throbbing, heaving, ready-to-murder body on me, and says through clenched teeth, "Did you fuck her?"

Shit.

What do I do?

Do I say yes and take whatever Pacey is about to hand me like a man? Or do I pull a Posey and flee like it's my job while claiming innocence?

I don't have a chance to react because Penny is standing next to Pacey now, pulling on his hand. "Pacey, stop." She puts her hand on his chest and sniffles. That's when I notice the red in her eyes and the dampness of her cheeks.

Fuck, she's crying.

Pacey sees it too, and the anger that's ripping through him eases slightly as he takes in his sister.

Through very clenched teeth, he asks, "Did you have sex with Hornsby?"

She swallows, glances at me, and with regret all over her face, she nods. "I did. On his birthday."

Jesus, we don't need to get into details.

Pacey's fists clench at his sides, and he turns toward me. "Are you telling me he's the father?"

The pause that she takes to answer that question is so fucking torturous. I'm pretty sure I know the answer, but confirmation would be great, on the slightest chance that somehow, someway she was oddly impregnated by Posey, who is still shaking over by the window.

This time, Penny looks at me and says, "Yes, Hornsby is the father."

I don't even see it coming, I don't have enough wherewithal

to even process what's happening, before a pain so severe ricochets through my jaw, and I'm tossed to the ground. Penny lets out a shrill cry at the same time I'm cloaked in two hundred pounds of pure muscle.

"Pacey, don't."

I look up just in time to see Lawes cock his arm back, only to be pulled off me and pushed to the ground by Posey.

"What the fuck are you doing?" Posey says, being a human shield for me while I gather my wits. Remind me to buy him two tons worth of bologna after this.

"I told you to stay away from her," Pacey says as he heaves with rage. "I told *you* specifically, I warned you because I knew something like this would happen. I knew you wouldn't be able to keep your hands off her."

When I sit up, I touch the side of my sore jaw as I say, "You say that as if I'm getting women pregnant all around the city. And it wasn't like I made her have sex with me. It was consensual."

"It better have been consensual," Pacey seethes.

"It was," I say, getting to my feet and standing tall. "And it wasn't planned. It just happened that one night. I haven't seen her since. I swear."

"Great, glad to hear that my sister is disposable like every other girl you've been with."

Shit, that didn't sound good.

"Not that I didn't want to do it again with her," I say. "We just agreed to one night."

"Do not fucking talk about having sex with my sister ever again." Pacey turns to Penny and asks, "Are you keeping the baby?"

When my eyes connect with Penny, she says, "Yes. I am. But I don't expect anything from Hornsby. I just thought—"

"The fuck you're not," Pacey says while moving in closer. "This is not your problem to deal with alone. He's just as much a part of this as you."

"Yeah, I can, uh, help," I say awkwardly because who the

fuck tells someone they're pregnant like this? With their brother and . . . a random teammate? Why did she do it like this? Better yet, why the fuck did she get pregnant? We used protection. We took all the precautions that we were supposed to. Yes, I might have fucked her really damn hard because being inside her felt like heaven, but that doesn't mean I'd get her pregnant, does it?

And pregnant, she's fucking pregnant . . . like, she's carrying my baby.

A baby.

There is going to be a baby in my life.

Holy shit, I'm going to be a dad.

Slowly, I sink back into my chair and grip my hair tightly as all of this finally pierces through my thick skull.

Penny is pregnant, and I'm the father. I'm going to be in charge of another human.

There is no way in hell I'm ready for that.

That's commitment.

That's the type of responsibility I don't think I ever wanted to take on.

"You know, before we make promises that we might not be able to keep, why don't we just all take this information in, and then we can talk later," Penny says softly.

"No," Pacey says while righting his chair that he knocked over. "We're going to sit down, and we're going to talk about every goddamn thing Hornsby is going to do for you."

"Uh, can I ask a question?" Posey says, holding his finger in the air. "Why exactly am I here, and do I have to stay? Because frankly, this is a really uncomfortable and awkward situation for me."

"I'm so sorry," Penny says. "I knew Pacey was going to react the way he did—"

"Because my best friend had sex with my sister when I specifically told him not to."

"I didn't do it out of spite," I say. "I've fucking liked her for a while."

"Is that supposed to make me feel better?" he asks.

"I thought it would. She wasn't some random to me."

Pacey folds his arms now and turns toward me. "So you're telling me you want to date my sister?"

Bile rises in my throat from the mere thought of dating someone. "No, I mean . . ." I look at Penny, who now is curling in on herself, which feels like a knife to my stomach. "Not that she isn't great because you are," I say to her now. "You're amazing, and I've thought about that night so goddamn much—"

"I'm going to murder you," Pacey says, lurching forward, but Posey saves me just in time, grabbing Pacey by the shoulders and settling him back in his chair.

"I think I'll stay a bit longer," Posey says quietly.

I let out a deep breath. "What I'm trying to say is that I enjoyed the night"—Pacey growls—"and, Jesus, calm down. I'm trying to tell her she's not like other girls, but I'm just not into the dating and commitment thing."

"Well, you better get used to it," Pacey snaps at me. "You're married to her now."

"Married?" I say, my mouth turning dry.

"Pacey, we're not getting married. I barely know him," Penny defends. Thank God, she's on the same wavelength as I am.

"The fuck I want you two to get married. What I mean is that you're metaphorically married. You're attached at the hip now. What you go through, he goes through."

"That's not necessary," Penny says with a shaky voice. "I know how Hornsby wants to live his life, and I don't want to disturb that."

"And your life isn't disturbed?" Pacey asks. "Why does he get to have a life, and you don't?" Pacey shakes his head now. "Fuck no, he has zero life now. All he's allowed to do is play hockey and be at your beck and call."

"You can't control my life," I say out of pure habit, honestly not thinking at this point.

"Test me," Pacey replies, his voice dripping with venom.

"Stop, both of you. This is getting absurd. This is why I

didn't want to say anything and just hide the pregnancy." Penny crosses her arms and sits on her desk. My eyes go to her legs because, apparently, I want to be a dead man.

"You wouldn't have been able to hide a pregnancy from me," Pacey says.

"I hid the fact that I slept with your best friend from you," Penny shoots back with some fire, and hell, it's sexy seeing her all fired up. "You didn't suspect a thing."

"Are you trying to make me angrier?"

"You know what, Pacey?" She hops off the desk and goes back to her chair, some fight sparking in her. "You are being a bad brother."

"How the fuck do you see that?"

"Because you're getting angry when you should be asking me if I'm okay and how you can help. I've been fretting over telling you and truly considered not telling you at all, but I thought you deserved to know." She looks at me. "You as well, Hornsby. But if you two are just going to act like children, then don't even bother. I can do this myself."

She then opens the bottom drawer to her desk, pulls out her purse, fits it over her shoulder, and picks up her phone from her purse.

"I'm done for the day. Don't come see me unless you decide to be supportive and drop all this alpha-male, brother bullshit."

With that, she rounds the desk and heads toward her door.

Because Posey always buckles under pressure, he calls out, "Congrats on the news. Let me know if you need anything." He smiles and waves.

Penny pulls her shoulders back and says, "Thank you, Posey." And then she takes off, leaving us all alone in her office.

I slouch in my chair.

Holy fucking fuck.

What just happened?

Here I was, worried that all these feelings for Penny were going to come rushing forward when I saw her. That should have been the least of my worries. Not only am I leaving this meeting with a heavier dose of wanting another round with her—especially after seeing her stick up for herself to Pacey—but I'm also leaving with the title: daddy.

———

"WHERE DO you think you're going?" Pacey calls out as I head to the garage where our cars are parked.

"Uh, home." Thanks to him and the news, my headache has intensified to blistering levels.

"Oh great, I'm going to your home too."

I pause mid-stride to my car and turn toward him. "What do you mean you're going to my home?"

"To help you pack." Pacey crosses his arms over his brawny chest.

I smooth my hand over my throbbing, aching forehead. "I don't have the energy for games, so just get to what you want to say, Lawes."

"You're going to move in with her."

"You've fucking lost it. I'm not going to run away from my responsibility if that's what you're worried about."

"I'm worried about my sister." Pacey moves in closer. "She lives alone, and the idiot who knocked her up is out of town for half of the season. She'll be going through this alone. As much as you like to think you're going to be the responsible one, she's still taking the brunt."

I hate that I didn't think about it that way. Then again, I haven't had much time to think about this at all. I'm still trying to comprehend that I'm going to be a father in nine months. But unfortunately, Pacey is right. I have no choice but to leave her by herself when we have to travel for away games.

"Moving in with her is not going to help," I say, denial wrapping around me in a solid chokehold. "It's not like I can carry the baby myself."

"I know that, you dipshit." Pacey pushes at my shoulder, and I bump into the wall.

"Watch it," I warn. "You might have gotten in a cheap shot at the office, but not now."

"Are you really threatening me?" Pacey asks. "You slept with my sister and got her pregnant. I'm pretty sure you should be thanking your lucky stars I haven't cut your dick off."

"She wasn't supposed to get pregnant." I don't know why I said that. Honestly, I can't think. My head is hurting way too fucking much.

"So you were just supposed to fuck her and leave her?"

"She wanted that too. A single night." I hold my arms out. "What the hell am I supposed to say?"

"You're supposed to keep your dick in your pants and send her home in a cab, ALONE! Jesus fuck, Eli." The sound of my first name coming off his tongue feels like a razor blade to the heart. We rarely call each other by our first names. "Do you realize how big of a hit this is to our friendship? I can't even . . . fuck, I can barely look at you. You, out of anyone, should know how hard it is to have one parent. Do you even remember how hard your mom worked before she passed away?"

My teeth grind together as his words sting my very soul. "I'm not going to be a deadbeat dad. Just give me a goddamn second to wrap my head around this. I've barely had a second to think about it."

Pacey slowly nods. "You know, you're right, you spend your time thinking about it. In the meantime, Penny will be carrying the baby and dealing with everything that comes with pregnancy, alone. But sure, take your time."

I scrub my hand over my face. "I don't know what you want from me, Pacey."

"I want you to step up and take care of her, or someone else is going to, and not only will they take care of her but they will take care of that baby too."

My eyes narrow. "What the fuck do you mean by that?"

"I mean, if you don't step up now, then don't bother, because you're only going to be an extra problem she doesn't need."

"I'm going to be a part of this baby's life," I say, my anger spiking from what he's implying. Pacey knows about my family life, about my history. We dove deep into it one night during the off-season. It was a starry night in Banff at Taters's cabin— where we spend a month during the off-season—we each had a beer in hand, and I told him about never having a dad and losing my mom when I was twelve. I told him that I had to move in with a distant relative. It was an emotional conversation, one where he got to understand me on a deeper level. "I'm not my father," I say, my throat rough from the thought of actually being like that man.

"Then prove it to me. Pack your shit and move in with Penny."

He's serious.

I don't think I've ever seen him this serious.

It seems I need to find some moving boxes.

Chapter Seven

PENNY

"I don't think I've ever seen Pacey that angry," I say to Blakely.

She came over after work when I texted her "911, my place now." She knew I was telling the boys today, so I wasn't surprised when she showed up with a gallon of vanilla ice cream, peanut butter cups, and fudge.

We didn't say anything to each other when she arrived. Instead, we went straight to the kitchen, where we made ourselves giant sundaes. With stomachs full, we sat down on the couch, unfolded a large blanket, and curled under it while facing each other.

"He actually punched Hornsby?"

"Yeah, knocked him over. Hornsby wasn't expecting it, and surprisingly, he didn't react and punch Pacey back. I've seen Hornsby get angry during a game before. He doesn't take shit from anyone."

"Probably because he knew he was in the wrong," Blakely says. "But it was a good thing Posey was there."

"I feel bad that he was there. He was so uncomfortable. I should give him a fruit basket or something. Treat him to a bologna sandwich. Maybe create a love post about him so he can relish in all the comments."

"All things he would appreciate." Blakely brings the blanket over her shoulder. "So where did you guys leave it?"

"They were being obnoxious idiots, and the stress of it all was too much, so I left. Pacey was more concerned with how it happened than what actually happened and how I was feeling. He was adding to the stress." I let out a huge sigh as tears well up in my eyes.

"What's wrong?" Blakely places her hand on my knee.

"I don't want to do this alone. My parents live all the way across the country. Pacey is in and out. Winnie, well, I feel bad for asking her for help because even though I love her, I don't think we're in a place where I can talk to her about the troubles of pregnancy and what I'm going through."

"You have me."

"And I appreciate that. I truly do. But you have a life too. I don't want to take away from anything between you and Perry. That would not be fair. You guys have lives. You don't need a baby mama in it."

"That's not true. You know we'll be there for you."

"I know, but it's not the same. No matter how much I like to believe I have you and Pacey, the truth is, I'm going to be doing this alone, and that's incredibly scary."

"You really don't think Hornsby will be there for you?" Blakely asks. "He's a player, but he's a good guy. One of the nicest guys on the team."

"He is. Winnie even said when she stumbled on the cabin, he was the first to greet her, welcome her in, and make sure she had everything she needed. But you should have seen the look on his face when I told him. It was as if he wanted to slowly melt away. Would it be great if he was a part of all of this? Yes, but I'm not going to force someone to do something they don't want to do, nor do I want to create animosity, you know?"

"You are being far too kind." Blakely sits up on the couch. "If it was me, I'd demand that he be at my beck and call. Hell, I'd make him move in."

"That's so weird. Pacey said the same thing."

Blakely taps the side of her head. "That's because we're smart."

"You're delusional."

I've played Hornsby's words over in my head several times since I left the office, and I still don't know what to make of them.

I've fucking liked her for a while.

She wasn't some random to me.

You're amazing, and I've thought about that night so goddamn much.

She's not like other girls, but I'm just not into the dating and commitment thing.

On the one hand, his words today matched those of five weeks ago. He's wanted me for a while . . . but he certainly hasn't shown any interest in me or sought me out since that night. He's probably been back out there hooking up. *Back to his normal MO.*

Continuing, I say, "Hornsby has his own schedule, and it's a bachelor's schedule. It works for him. There is no way he'd move in here. I think I'll be lucky if—"

Knock. Knock.

Blakely and I turn toward the door and then glance at each other.

"Bet that's Pacey," Blakely says. "I'm sure he has a litany of apologies to make."

He sure does, but I don't know if I have the energy to hear them tonight. Do I believe I went about telling him the correct way? Probably not. I was selfish in the moment and wanted to get it over with, so telling them at the same time seemed like the best option for me, but I should have told them separately. I should have pulled Hornsby to the side and explained everything to him, let it soak in, and then when he was mentally ready, we could have told Pacey. But fear and anxiety took over my decision-making.

I probably should jump on the apology train, too, because that wasn't fair to them.

Not at all.

"Do you want me to get the door?" Blakely asks.

"No, I'll get it. But depending on his mood, you should be prepared to leave or stay."

She chuckles. "Mentally preparing for both."

I shed the warm blanket from my body and then stand from the couch. The sharp movement causes me to rock back as I attempt to catch my balance. Dizziness beats through me, and before I know it, I'm collapsing back on the couch.

"Holy shit," Blakely says, coming up to me. "Are you okay?"

I blink a few times as the room spins around me. "Uh, yeah . . . wow, just really dizzy."

"Don't move." Blakely goes to the door, and I turn in that direction just as she opens it, revealing not only Pacey but Hornsby as well. At his side are two suitcases, one large one, one medium one, and his travel bag.

What on earth does he think he's doing?

"Hey, is Penny here?" Pacey asks just as he spots me on the couch. He pushes through the door, and Hornsby follows him, maneuvering his luggage into the small entryway.

"She just got really dizzy," Blakely says, which of course alarms Pacey.

He quickly sits on the coffee table in front of me and leans forward, placing his hand on my knee. "Are you okay?"

"Fine," I say, sitting up taller. "Just stood up too fast is all. Nothing to worry about."

Pacey's jaw clenches as he glances back at Hornsby and Blakely. "This is what I was afraid of. Something happening to you and not having anyone here to help."

"Pacey, I stood up wrong. It's fine."

"It's not fine." He pushes his hand through his hair, and I can see the worry deepening in his brow.

When I first moved out here, Pacey vowed to our mom and dad that he would watch over me and make sure that I was okay.

He's taken that promise very seriously. He always makes sure to check on me, have dinners together, and just hang out. Even when he came home with Winnie, he included me. He's made sure I've had everything I needed. I ran out of gas one day on my way to work, and he went out of his way to help me and was late to conditioning because of it. He's protective, and he always will be.

"Pacey, seriously, I'm fine." I stand, and this time, I don't grow dizzy—thank God. I move around the couch and eye Hornsby's bags. Pointing at them, I ask, "What's this?"

Joining us in the entryway area, Pacey says, "Hornsby is moving in."

"Oh, this is good," Blakely mutters to herself.

"What?" I shake my head. "No, he's not."

I know Pacey mentioned it, and Blakely had the same idea, but there is no way I thought it would happen. From the looks of it, Hornsby was handed marching orders rather than making this decision on his own. His usually broad, proud shoulders are turned in, his chin is lowered, and his hands are stuffed in his pockets, making him look more like a wounded puppy than someone who wants to take charge of the situation.

"Yes, he is," Pacey says. "And this dizzy spell is exactly why. You can't be alone. You need someone here, helping you."

"You guys are constantly traveling. It's not like he'd be here all the time anyway. So what's the point?"

"The point is, he would be here a lot of the time, and that's what matters the most. And when he's not here, Winnie and Blakely can check on you."

"Thanks for volunteering me," Blakely says. "But I've already told her that I'd be here, even if Hornsby chose not to be a part of this."

"I want to be a part of this," Hornsby says, his voice lacking its usual jovial tone.

"Oh yeah, really sounds like it," Blakely says sarcastically.

Hornsby turns to her. "Can you not start shit?"

"I'm not. Just making sure you're stepping up."

"Why the fuck do people keep saying that?" he asks, his voice now tainted in anger. "I'm not some deadbeat fuckup who doesn't own up to his mistakes." He motions to me. "What happened between Penny and me is between Penny and me, and I'd really fucking appreciate it if you would both leave so I can talk to her. Alone."

Without blinking an eye, Blakely is moving around my apartment, collecting her things while Pacey stands ramrod straight with his arms crossed at his chest. I can tell he's not going to move unless I say something.

So I walk up to him, place my hand on his shoulder, and say, "I've got this, Pace. Please let me handle it."

Turning toward me, he looks me in the eyes, and says, "I'm good with making sure this is seen through."

"Pacey." I let out a deep sigh. "Please leave. I'm asking you to please let me handle this myself. I'll call you later, okay?"

We exchange looks for a few beats before he finally gives in and pulls me into a hug. Tears well up in my eyes as I wrap my arms around him and hug him tightly.

Quietly, I whisper, "I'm so sorry."

"Don't," he says. "It's fine. We'll figure this out." He places a kiss on the top of my head and then gives me one last squeeze before walking toward the front door with Blakely. He holds it open for her, and together, they exit the apartment, the door softly clicking shut behind them.

And that leaves me alone with Hornsby once again, but instead of the electric excitement that bounced between us toward the end of our night together, there is an awkward, uncomfortable feeling suffocating us, pulling all the air from the space.

He can't be happy, and I don't blame him. I went about this all the wrong way, and I'm not ashamed to say that I owe him an apology.

"Do you want something to drink?" I ask him.

He shakes his head and when he looks up and his eyes

connect with mine, I can see it written all over his face. He's just as scared as I am.

"We need to talk." He walks past me and goes to the couch, where he takes a seat.

Okay, scared and angry.

Like I said, I've seen Hornsby angry before, but it's only been during a game. I've never seen him angry outside of hockey. He's always the jovial, good-time guy. So this side of him, it's new for me.

I follow him to the couch and take a seat as well, draping the blanket over my legs. Anything to add an extra layer of comfort for the conversation we're about to have.

"Listen," I say, pinning my gaze on him, "I need to apologize." His eyes connect with mine. "How I told you about the baby, that wasn't fair to you at all. I was being selfish because I was scared, and I figured telling you both at the same time would be easier for me. I didn't think about how you would take it, or how Pacey would take it. I'm really sorry. If I could do it all over again, I would. I'd offer you the respect you deserve as the father of this child and tell you alone. I hope you can forgive me."

His eyes soften. "I'm not mad at you, Penny. I know you did what you had to do out of self-preservation. Let's face it. I don't have the best background when it comes to women, nor do I have a childhood with positive parental influences. I seem like a flight risk, I get it."

"I didn't think that at all. None of that was taken into consideration," I say. "I don't even know about your childhood or anything like that. I was just scared, and I acted before I thoroughly thought everything through, and for that, I'm really sorry."

"Please stop apologizing. It's not necessary."

"It is for me," I say. "This has been weighing heavily on my chest, and I truly am regretful for how . . ." My throat chokes, and my eyes water. God, what is with the emotions? I suck in a deep breath as a tear springs free and drops down my cheek. "For how I handled everything. I'm sorry, Hornsby."

Silence greets us for what feels like an eternity, but when he finally speaks up, he says, "Eli. Please call me Eli."

"Oh . . . I'm sorry, Eli."

His lips rub together before he looks away. "I understand where you're coming from, and like I said, apology not needed, but I accept it either way." He grips his hands together, fingers lacing. "I know things are kind of weird right now. Pacey is on the verge of a heart attack or committing murder, you have got to be terrified, and well, frankly, I feel like everything is crumbling around me, and I have no control over it." He turns toward me. "And I say that just so you understand where I'm at."

I nod. "I understand completely. I've had the same feeling."

"And not to get too much into it, but I haven't had the best of luck growing up, so the idea of trying to raise a child when I can barely figure out how to mentally push past the feeling of abandonment that I live with on a daily basis, well . . . it's fucking with my head."

Abandonment? Who abandoned him?

Just goes to show how much I don't know about this man.

But from the strain in his eyes and the tension in his shoulders, I can tell that this news is not easy for him. It seems to have awakened the demons he's apparently living with, and that can't possibly be a simple thing to face. I'd hate to see him fall down a dark path, one that brings him pain, and despite being scared and afraid, the last thing I want to do is make this hard on someone who is already possibly suffering.

I have a solid support system, and I know if it came down to it, my mom would come out to help me if I truly needed it. But like Pacey said, I have him, I have Blakely, and I have Winnie. I'll be okay.

I'm not so sure Eli will.

Which only means one thing . . .

I wipe at my cheeks and take a deep breath. "Eli." His beautiful eyes meet mine. "I'm not sure what you're dealing with mentally. I can't possibly know because we barely know each other outside of hockey, but what I do know is I wouldn't want to put you in a position where you're fighting demons that have reawakened from your past. It's not good for you, and it's not good for the team. Hockey is your number one priority along with your mental health." I reach out and press my hand to his knee. "It's okay. I can do this."

His head slightly tilts to the side as he studies me, and after a few beats, he says, "Christ, you're a strong woman, Penny. But that's not what I was trying to say. I wasn't looking for an out, but rather, looking for an in."

Confused, I sit up. "What are you talking about?"

"I want to preface this by saying, your brother isn't forcing me to do anything I don't want to do. He's a strong, opinionated man, but if I wanted to take him on one-on-one, there's no doubt I would win." I believe it. Hornsby, oh, I mean Eli, is two inches taller than Pacey with probably ten more pounds of muscle. My brother is big, but Eli could easily take him. There is no doubt in my mind. "I don't want to be the person who walks out, like my dad. I don't want to be the unreliable person who doesn't understand the importance of bringing another human life into this world. I grew up without a father, and I'll be damned if this baby lives that same life." He shakes his head. "That cycle ends here." He reaches out to touch my hand. "You will not be walking this journey alone, Penny."

Probably because of the conviction in his voice and the sincerity in his eyes, tears I've been holding back cascade down my heated cheeks.

You will not be walking this journey alone, Penny.

It's all I can think about as he continues to speak. "I want to be here for every step of it, every part of this. I want . . . well"—he grips the back of his neck—"I want to get to know you better and build a friendship, so when our baby is born, he or she will know that there is no animosity between us. I want him to know we're friends."

"I would like to be friends," I say, knowing damn well he made a point of saying friends. Not that I'd want anything romantic to happen between us—I'm not even close to thinking about that at the moment—but from that comment, it's obvious where Eli stands. Friendship and that's it. *Even though he was attracted to me, pregnancy has totally eradicated that.*

"And I know this is asking a lot, but if you're okay with it, I'd like to stay here with you—"

"Eli . . ."

"Before you say no," he quickly says, "just hear me out, okay?" Sighing, I lean back on the couch now and nod. "This isn't just about helping you, which of course is one of the main reasons for doing this, but I also want to experience everything with you. I'm not carrying the baby, but at least I can be present, as present as my schedule will allow. I can be there when the baby kicks, they can learn my voice, and I can be there while they grow."

"And what happens when the baby is born? You can't possibly think we'll continue to live together."

"No, but I can always find a place closer, or we can both find apartments that are situated next to each other."

I let out a large guffaw. "Eli, your budget for an apartment is much different than mine."

"I'll help pay for it. Hell, I'll buy you a place. I don't care—"

"I don't want your money."

"Then it's something we'll figure out when the time comes closer, but for now, please just let me be a part of this."

Those imploring eyes nearly cut me in half.

"This is a one-bedroom apartment, Eli."

"This couch is comfortable," he says, patting the back of it. "I don't care where I sleep. None of that matters. All that I care about is being supportive to you and making sure I'm a part of this baby's life."

His eyes plead with me, and I swear, if I look closely, I can see them turning glossy, as he holds his breath, waiting for an answer.

How on earth could I possibly say no to him? To the hope that's pulsing through him. To the desperation he obviously feels.

I can't.

And I don't want to.

"Okay," I say.

"Okay?" he asks, sitting taller.

I nod. "Yeah, you can stay here. But you don't have to sleep on the couch. I have a king-sized bed. I don't mind sharing a bed with the obvious knowledge that nothing is going to happen."

He smirks. "Trust me, I learned my lesson the first time." He grips his jaw. "Your brother has a mean right hook."

I chuckle. "I wish I could say you're the first guy he's used it on when standing up for me, but you're not."

"I can only imagine what it was like growing up with him." He relaxes slightly. "I don't mind sleeping on the couch."

"I do," I say. "You need a good night's sleep, and I can't imagine what the team . . . and fans, for that matter, would think if you were sleeping on a couch. Hockey comes first."

He shakes his head. "That's where you're wrong, Penny. Hockey doesn't come first. You and this baby do." He scoots in closer and is about to take my hand when he thinks better of it. Instead, he laces his fingers together again. "There will be times when I don't have a choice other than to put hockey before you because of my obligations to the team, but just know, that isn't my choice. You and the baby are now more important than any of that."

"Eli, I'd never take you away from the sport. I grew up with a brother playing hockey. I've dated hockey players before, so I know the commitment that's needed at this level, and I'd never, ever hold that against you."

"I know you wouldn't."

"So, where do we go from here?"

He looks around my apartment, taking it all in, and then turns back to me. "Care to give me a tour?"

I smile softly. "I'd love to."

Chapter Eight

ELI

"How was last night?" Posey asks as he takes a seat next to me at our lockers.

The locker room is almost empty. Besides a few guys coming in and out from the training room, Posey and I are pretty much alone.

"Painful but it ended well," I answer. Before every game day, I come in an hour early before our morning skate, just to get my head on right, chat with the boys, and mentally prepare for the night ahead of us.

Today is no exception.

"So what happened?"

Stick in hand, I start taping it, carefully preparing it for tonight. I always start on the butt end, making sure the grip up top is to my liking.

"I moved in."

"You . . . you what?" Posey asks.

After everything that happened yesterday in Penny's office,

87

Posey almost looked more shell-shocked than me. He took off once he felt like Pacey wasn't going to be a threat anymore—not that I'd need the help, but I understood his concern—and when he got back to his place, he texted me to see how I was doing. I shot him a quick reply, telling him I was sorting things out, but kept it at that.

"I moved in with Penny."

"Uh, did Pacey watch over you the entire time?"

I shake my head just as the locker room door opens and Pacey walks in. His eyes land on me as he walks toward his locker, but he doesn't say anything. Instead, he grabs a hair tie for his hair from his locker and then heads back out toward the training room, where I'm sure he's getting his legs rolled out and prepped.

"Wow, that was fucking chilly." Posey smacks me in the chest.

"Hey, what the fuck was that for?"

"For clearly ruining the equilibrium in our fivesome. What were you thinking sleeping with Penny?"

"I wasn't," I say, now staring down at my stick. "I've wanted her since the first day I met her, and I kept that under control for two years. There was something that night with her, something that snapped within me, and no matter what I said to myself, it wasn't going to stop me." I look up at Posey now. "And she wanted me too."

"It was stupid and careless. Pacey has said on multiple occasions that she was off limits."

"I know," I groan. "There is no use talking about it now. It already happened. Can't change the past."

"But what are you doing to fix it now?"

"Taking responsibility," I answer. "I'll be damned if Pacey has to even think twice about whether or not I'm in this."

"Is that why you moved in with her? And she was okay with that?"

"Apprehensive at first, but she accepted my reasoning, and honestly, she looks just as terrified as I am. I don't think she wants to be alone, so she said yes. I offered to sleep on the couch, but she said I could sleep in her bed."

"Really?" Posey's eyes widen. "Are you, you know . . . starting something up?"

I shake my head. "No, neither of us want to be in a relationship. She made that really clear the night we hooked up. But we did agree on being friends."

"That's good. So you're friendly."

"Eh, not really." I snap the tape apart and smooth down the edge. "It was incredibly awkward last night. She showed me around, and then since it was late, we just got ready for bed."

"And how was sharing the bed?"

"Just as comfortable as you'd imagine it would be. I almost think I'd have gotten a better night's sleep on her sofa with my feet hanging off the edge. I kept waking up to make sure I wasn't on her side or hogging the blankets. I barely got any sleep at all. And then she woke up early this morning feeling nauseous, so I sat next to her while she held a bucket. We didn't really speak. It's a real fucking one-eighty from how our one-night stand went." Despite how awkward it started and how nervous Penny was, it had been the most fun I'd had with a woman in forever. I'd felt relaxed as if I could be myself without the expectation to be the super-god hockey player most women expect me to be. I was just Eli. But that's possibly too deep to share with Posey right now. I glance around to make sure no one is listening in and lower my voice. "I've been inside the woman, I've kissed her all over her body, yet being with her now in her place feels like I'm rooming with a complete stranger."

"Then maybe you find a way to get to know her better. You have a long way to go before that baby is born, so you need to find a way to make it work."

"I know. I just don't know how. It's like dating someone you have no intention of actually dating. The small talk, the get to know you crap, the sharing . . . it's not my strong suit."

"You share with the people you care about. Don't forget that," Posey says just as the door to the locker room opens and

Taters walks in with Holmes. When he spots me, a huge smile spreads across his face.

Oh hell . . .

"You know, for the longest time, I thought I was the one who was going to be the screwup of the group," Taters says. "It was bound to happen, but here I am, completely outdone by the resident nice guy." Taters claps. "Getting Pacey's sister pregnant. Wow, man."

"Can you shut the fuck up?" I hiss at him. "Jesus Christ, we're not telling anyone."

Halsey Holmes, the quiet but thoughtful one of our group, pushes Taters, and says, "I told you not to fucking say anything."

"I didn't listen."

"Clearly." Holmes takes a seat next to me, and asks, "You good?"

"Not really," I answer.

"Lawes is fuming," Taters says, pulling up a chair to close off our circle. "He's in the training room, huffing and puffing, making a show of it."

I scratch the side of my jaw and then pick up my tape again. "He doesn't need to be. I'm taking care of it."

"Really?" Taters asks. "So you're going to marry her?"

"What?" I nearly squeak. "No, we're just going to be friends, but I moved in to help her with whatever she needs."

"Friends?" Taters shakes his head. "Nah, I don't see that happening. You've been crushing on her forever, man. There's no way you'll stay friends."

"I don't want anything serious, and neither does she, so friends is the only option. And I'd rather be friends with my baby's mom than not even talk to her." I let out a huge sigh. "Okay, I'm done discussing this. I need to get my head on straight for the game tonight, and sitting here gabbing about my personal life is not going to do that."

"Yes, but your personal life just got very interesting," Taters says, the ever-present instigator.

"If you're that interested, go get someone pregnant yourself."

"Nah, I'm good. I just settled down from the crazy personal life. I don't need to rock the boat now."

Taters, or Silas Taters, also known as Potato, broke up with his girlfriend a little while back. They were together for a very long time, so long that Silas was considering proposing, and then, when we all least expected it, they broke up. We still don't know the reason. Taters never said why, but he took it really fucking hard, and it seems like he's finally out of the dark cloud of his breakup and now torturing me.

"Well, if you need anything, we're here for you," Holmes says before patting me on the back and going to his locker.

I know for a fact I'm not the only guy in the league who accidentally got a girl pregnant, but what I want to know is how they handle it because right now, as much as I try to focus on the game, my head keeps swinging back to Penny and what I'm going to do. If I'm going to be good enough.

If I'm going to follow through.

My dad never did.

I lost my mom at twelve.

My foster family, well, they were counting down the days until I turned eighteen. They didn't hate me, but I knew they didn't love me either.

So how the hell am I supposed to handle all of this when I'm not even sure how to be a parent? How to act like one this baby deserves?

Looks like I need to call my therapist. We have a lot to unpack, especially with playoffs around the corner. I need to focus if we're going to have a run for the cup this year.

THIS IS WEIRD.

Coming home after a game to a new building, a new hallway, and a new front door. None of it belongs to me, and none of it is familiar. None of it feels like home.

And home is important to me. It's my safe space, my

grounding zone, a place I know will never disappear on me. But that has all changed now.

I slip out the key Penny gave me, and I unlock the door only to quietly open it. I'm not sure about Penny's schedule. Couldn't tell you if she was an early-to-bed kind of girl or a night owl. I don't want to be too loud just in case she's sleeping, but it also takes me a few hours to wind down from the adrenaline of a game, especially after a brutal loss like we suffered today.

Four to one.

It was embarrassing.

You don't have to be in the know to realize something was going on between Pacey and me or that neither of our heads was in the game. Letting four goals go by is very unlike him. But it wasn't all his fault. I couldn't get my head out of the clouds fast enough to catch up to the offense and do my job, so it was almost as if Pacey was down a defenseman. You could only imagine how mad he is now.

It wasn't pretty in the locker room after the game, to say the least.

When I step inside the apartment, I'm surprised to see the lights on and my game day suits scattered all over the living room and kitchen. Every single suit I own.

I glance around the space and find Penny standing in the middle of the living room holding a steamer in one hand and the vest of my maroon three-piece suit in the other.

"Oh, I didn't think you'd be home so soon," she says, eyes wide. "I thought that maybe you'd take a bit longer."

"I skipped the weight room today and settled with just flushing my legs out on the bike." I set my bag down in the entry-way. "What, uh, what are you doing?"

She glances at the steamer in her hand and then the vest. When her eyes return to mine, she says, "Stress steaming your suits."

"Stress steaming?"

"Yes, well, you know, it was stressful watching your game tonight. I had to keep myself busy, so I unpacked your clothes, which I know is a huge violation of privacy, but I couldn't just let them sit there in your suitcase all crumpled up, especially your suits. And when I pulled them out, I realized they needed a solid steam, so I set up a system and started steaming. One suit led to another that led to another, and honestly, I'm glad you actually arrived because I'm pretty sure your boxer briefs were next." Her eyes widen. "Not that I noticed much about your boxer briefs. I mean, I did touch them but not in a creepy way, but in a *these need to be put away* kind of way. It was minimal touching of your private garments. They're shoved in a drawer." Her eyes widen even more. "Oh God, did you not want to be unpacked? I mean, that's really presumptuous to move you in like that and give you a few drawers in my dresser. It's not like a *you're my boyfriend* dresser drawer. I just thought you would be more comfortable—"

"Penny, take a breath." She collapses on the couch and drapes her arm over her eyes.

After a few seconds, she finally says, "You guys were atrocious tonight, and I know it's my fault."

Seeing where this is going, I move to the couch and take a seat, making sure to keep an appropriate distance. "We did suck tonight, but it was not your fault. It takes a team to lose a game, not a baby mama."

She glances over at me. "I hate that term. Can you not call me that?"

"Should I call you the woman carrying my child?"

"You can just call me Penny." She sits up. "Your head wasn't in the game, and neither was Pacey's. I knew this was going to happen. This is why I wanted to wait to tell you two, but then Blakely, with her horrendously thought-out ideas, came swooping in and convinced me to tell you now rather than after the season."

"After the season would have been too far out. It's probably best that you told us now."

"And ruin your chances at the run for the cup? Sure, that seems like a great idea."

"Penny, it was one game."

"Yeah, well, one game will turn into many, and before we know it, you're packing up your locker in May rather than getting ready for the next game. Everyone will hate this baby because you know the media will catch wind of it. It's bound to happen, and then what? All of Vancouver hates on little Jimmy John or Johnny Jim or Peggy Leggy."

"Peggy Leggy?" I ask, my nose curling. "Please don't name our child Peggy Leggy."

"You know what I mean. I ruined everything."

"You didn't. Stop saying that. We both made this baby. It was one game. We'll find our stride."

"Sure you will." She gets up and goes back to steaming my vest, continuing to work through the wrinkles. She doesn't say anything else. Her concentration is solely focused on the tweed fabric of my vest.

"You don't have to do that," I say, unsure of what else to do.

"It's fine." And she continues to work.

You could cut the tension with a fucking knife. It's thick. It's unruly, and it's extremely uncomfortable.

Normally after a game, I'd hit up the weight room with the guys, stop by my favorite late-night sub shop to pick up an Italian special with extra veggies and meat, and then go home and relax on the couch while tuning into the latest show I've been bingeing. After a few episodes, I usually settle into bed once the adrenaline has worn off.

Or . . .

I go pick up a girl after the game and wind down with sex.

Today, well . . . today my entire routine is off. Instead of my favorite sandwich, I settled for one of the to-go meals the team provides, scarfed it down in my car, and then drove here as quickly as I could to make sure everything was okay with Penny.

I'm not sure why I rushed now.

It doesn't seem like she wants anything to do with me.

Clearing my throat, I stand. "Well, at least let me help you get these suits out of the living room."

"That's okay. I have a process of where I'm putting them."

She glances past the hanging vest and says, "You can, uh . . . go out if you want. I know you like doing that."

Is she insane?

Go out?

When she's pregnant?

No, my random one-night stands have been terminated for the time being. The only action I'll be getting is probably in the shower.

"I'm not going out. That would be disrespectful to you," I say.

She scoffs. "We're not seeing each other, Eli. It's not like you can't date anyone."

"I'm not going to date anyone. You know I don't date."

Her eyes connect with mine. "I mean, you know . . . have fun with other women." She glances away, avoiding all eye contact with me. I'm not sure what's going on—if she's trying to push me away or attempt to fix a problem that's not there—but whatever it is, I'm not falling for it.

Instead, I say, "I'm just going to get ready for bed." Even though I'm not even close to being tired.

I grab my bag from the entryway and head back to the bedroom, where I unpack it, toss my dirty clothes in the corner that is currently my "hamper," and then I sit on the edge of the bed with my phone in my hand.

I type up a text and send it to the boys . . . well, minus Pacey. Not sure texting him about his sister would be the smartest decision at the moment.

Hornsby: *Things are really awkward over here. I don't know what to do. Help me.*

I rest my arms on my thighs as I check out the rest of the scores for the night, waiting for some responses. Thankfully, I don't have to wait long, and my phone vibrates in my hand.

Posey: *Describe awkward.*

Taters: *Yes, we need to know what we're dealing with before offering advice.*

Holmes: *It's probably not awkward. You're just feeling like it is.*

If only they knew. I slip my suit jacket off my shoulders and drape it over the edge of the bed before texting them back.

Hornsby: *I came back to Penny's and found her frantically steaming every suit I own. When I asked her what she was doing, she went on some rambling spree about the team sucking because of her, named our child Peggy Leggy, and then told me to go out and find a chick to fuck.*

That about sums it up.

I'm about to hit send when I stop. This is Pacey's sister I'm about to gossip about. If I had a sister, would I want all her quirkiness tossed around between my best friends? That would be a no. Not only that, but these guys have known her as long as I have, and they respect her, especially for how good she is at her job. I don't want them thinking she's a nutcase.

Fuck, but I need their opinion. And they know me. They know I'm a desperate fuck who is so far out of his comfort zone, I've forgotten what it looks like. And it's only night two.

I hit send and hope that the guys don't hate on me.

Holmes: *Yeah, that's awkward.*

Taters: *Peggy Leggy? What the fuck is that?*

Posey: *You know . . . Peggy Leggy could go either way. Charming or terrifying.*

Taters: *Nothing is charming about Peggy Leggy. She is the deranged doll in your grandma's attic that was never loved but somehow lost an arm anyway.*

Holmes: *Can't jump on board with Peggy Leggy. Sorry.*

Posey: *I don't think we're being fair about Peggy Leggy.*

Hornsby: *ENOUGH WITH PEGGY LEGGY!*

Taters: *Dude, you can't throw down a name like that without telling us you vetoed it. Can you imagine Peggy Leggy Hornsby? Woof.*

Posey: *Hey, don't you dare woof at Peggy Leggy. She might be a tattered shell of a baby, but she's still Hornsby's lineage.*

Holmes: *Did you veto the name?*

Hornsby: *Jesus Christ, of course I did. Peggy Leggy Hornsby is not happening.*

Taters: *At least he didn't lose his common sense, boys.*

Hornsby: *Can we get back to the advice? Christ.*

Holmes: *Let's remember this is Pacey's sister here and our colleague. Respect. Men. Did you tell her she doesn't need to steam your suits?*

Hornsby: *Of course I did. But she said something about a process. I don't know. After she told me to go out and find someone, I decided to call the conversation quits.*

Taters: *Hear you, Holmes. Let's pretend for a moment that we don't know her. Did she say you could go out and find someone in a nasty tone?*

Posey: *Oooo, good question. Tone is very important. And yes, I can pretend.*

Hornsby: *Thanks, Holmes. I don't want to disrespect her, either. As for the tone, she didn't. She said it in more of a nervous tone. Like she was unsure.*

Posey: *I'm secondary sweating for you right now. Sounds wretched.*

Taters: *Yeah, that's uncomfortable.*

Hornsby: *I KNOW! What should I do?*

Holmes: *I'd just go read a book, let her work through it herself.*

Taters: *You also don't have a life.*

Posey: *I don't think crawling into his own shell is the way to go on this, Holmes. Sorry. He has to live with her. Clearly, there's awkward tension between you two. Try to break it.*

Taters: *It pains me to say Posey is right, but he is.*

Hornsby: *How do you suppose I break it?*

Posey: *This is Penny Lawes, Hornsby. Not some chick you just met. She lives and breathes hockey, is a master of all things social media, and around anyone else on any other day, she is sweet, funny, and NOT awkward.*

Hornsby: *So the problem is me?*

Taters: *Yep, dipshit. But if you're still lost, it's called Google. Stock up on questions and ask some. And when she talks, actually listen rather than thinking where you can stick your dick in her.*

Holmes: *She really is sweet, and listening is key.*

Posey: *And the not sticking your dick in her is second to the listening.*

I'm about to text back when the bedroom door creaks open, and Penny comes in with three suits in hand. When she spots me on the edge of the bed, my shirt undone, she gasps out loud and spins toward the wall where she pins her head against the white surface.

"Oh my God, I forgot to knock. I'm so sorry. You must be horrified."

I'm really not.

"Penny, you've sat on my dick, and I've watched you bounce up and down on my lap. Pretty sure walking in on me with my shirt undone is nothing compared to that."

"Th-That was different," she says, still shielding herself. "You meant for me to see you naked."

I exhale loudly. "Can you please just turn toward me?"

Hesitantly, she turns around. That's when I stand from the bed, walk up to her, and take the suits from her grasp. "We need to learn to live with each other, and acting skittish is not the way to do it. You're going to see me without a shirt. I like to sleep with it off. Last night, I wore one because I didn't want to scare you, but it was uncomfortable. I'm sure you're going to want to walk around in a towel, or well, I don't know what women do, but I think if we're going to make this work, we try to act as normal as possible."

She swallows hard. "I don't know how to be normal around you without alcohol, and I can't have alcohol because of Peggy Leggy—"

"Jesus, please don't call her that."

"So this is the person you get. Awkward, weird, and someone who steams and cleans when they're stressed."

I press my lips together, attempting to figure out how to make this better. Holmes wasn't wrong. This is Penny. I've known her for a few years, and I've liked the fuck out of her for just as long. She said I make her nervous, so how can I stop that *without* alcohol?

"How can I make this better?"

"You can't. I'm just weird, and this is how I deal with things."

Right, maybe I can try just talking about all things hockey another night. Tonight is not that night.

"Okay, then, I guess . . ." I look around. "What, uh, what else can we steam? Did you do all of my suits?"

"You don't want to steam things."

I really don't.

I want this nightmare to be over.

I want to be at my house with my favorite sub watching the latest season of *Ozark*. But instead, I'm in a completely new-to-me apartment trying to navigate the clumsy waters of sharing a space with someone I barely know.

"I don't have experience in steaming." Or cleaning, for that matter. "But you can show me. I have some jeans we can steam."

"You don't steam jeans."

"Okay, well, you mentioned my boxer briefs. Do you want to steam those?"

That pulls a smile from her lips, and she finally relaxes her tense shoulders. "I'm actually pretty tired. I think I'm going to get ready for bed."

"Same." I clasp my hands together and look around. "Should we, uh, take care of my suits then?"

"Yes." And then she walks toward her closet, where I hear her hang the ones she just took from me. Without another word, she walks out to the living room and grabs more. Shit. *And this is my new fucking normal.*

Chapter Nine

PENNY

"Can you stomach a bagel?" Blakely asks while sticking her head through the doorway of my office.

Looking up from my computer screen, I'm relieved this morning's nausea has subsided, leaving me ready for food.

"Yes, I could really use one right now, actually."

Bagel bag in hand, she takes a seat across from me in my office, doling out the bagels on the napkins and then setting out the cream cheese and knives. "After your text this morning of suffering over the toilet, I figured I'd grab some food in case you were hungry when you got here."

"Just dry-heaving again, but I wasn't able to stomach anything, so this is perfect timing."

We break apart our bagels, slather them in cream cheese, and then each take a bite. I lean back in my chair. "Thank you so much."

"You are more than welcome." She pauses. "So tell me how

things are going. Do you miss Hornsby now that the boys are on an away trip?"

No.

Not even in the slightest.

And not because he's a bad house guest or because he's messy. He's none of those things. He's actually quite tidy, and he doesn't do anything to ruffle my feathers. He walks around the apartment, trying to go undetected. The first night after the horrible game when the boys took a huge loss, Eli tried to have a conversation about snow, and it fell flat after his comment about liking how white it was.

The second night, he asked me if I liked bread. I said yes. And then he nodded, and that was that. It's made me wonder if the only language Eli speaks with women is *flirt*.

I was happy for the reprieve last night, that was until he called me . . .

"I was. I mean, he's been nice and all, but I can't tell you how massively uncomfortable this entire arrangement is."

"Still not the conversationalist he is when trying to hook up with somebody?"

"I can't necessarily blame it on him because I'm not great either. I don't know what to say to him, and it's clear as day he doesn't know what to say to me as well. Where has all the charm from the bar and his apartment gone, Blakely? We got on so well, laughed, had sex, and now we have no clue how to be around each other? I mean, I shrieked the other night when I saw him with his shirt undone." I lean in and whisper, "I licked his nipples, Blakely, and now I'm clutching my pearls over seeing a little man-cleave? What is wrong with me?"

She chuckles, and when I give her a not-so-happy glare, she stops. "I'm sorry, I know this hasn't been easy for you, but you have to admit it's slightly comical."

"I find nothing comical about this. It's so bad, Blakely. Never in my life have I been so clumsy and tongue-tied for words before. When he's around, my mind just goes blank. And then last night, he, uh . . . he called me."

"From the hotel?" Blakely's eyes nearly pop out of their sockets.

"Yup. Said he wanted to check on me and tell me he planned on staying in the entire night. I told him I'm not his nanny so he doesn't need to check in with me. He then proceeded to tell me in a strange voice that he knew I wasn't his nanny."

"Define strange?"

"Uh . . . like he ate a tablespoon of cinnamon and was slowly choking on his own dried-up saliva."

"That is a very detailed yet odd description, and even more odd, I can hear it in my head. What happened after that?"

"A long pause that felt positively deafening. I was fidgeting, wracking my brain for anything to say. All I could think about was how my nipples have been tingling lately, and to hell if I was going to say that. So instead, he told me about the pack of free pretzels he got in his room. And all he said was they were salty and free."

Blakely, to my disdain, lets out the loudest laugh while waving her hand in front of her face.

"This is not funny."

"I'm sorry." She wipes under her eye. "But oh my God, this is the most dysfunctional yet hilarious coupling I've ever seen, and I hate to admit it, because I know you're going through an ordeal, but I'm kind of living for it."

I take a large bite of my bagel and chew while staring out the window of my office. "I think I'm going to ask him to move out. We're not doing each other any favors here. We tried, we failed miserably, so let's move on."

"What in particular did you try?"

My phone buzzes with a text.

"Try to be cordial and live with each other, but it's just an absolute nightmare. We don't know how to act around each other. We don't know how to talk. We're both being far too polite not to bother the other . . . I can't possibly survive the next eight months like this."

I lift my phone and see that it's a text from Eli.

Great.

I swipe my phone open and read it.

Eli: *I just ate an apple.*

I wait to see if there is more to his text, but when the little texting dots don't appear, I realize that's all he had to say. I shouldn't be surprised. This is to be expected at this point.

"Is that him?" Blakely asks.

I nod. "He just told me he ate an apple."

"That's it?" I nod again. "No freaking way. Let me see." I flash the screen toward her, and she squints while reading, then leans back in her chair. "Wow, you know, I'd expect a text like that from someone like Halsey Holmes. He's so introverted and quiet that an 'I ate an apple' text feels very fitting. But from the outgoing ladies' man of the team, I never would have guessed. What do you even say to that?"

I type him back and press send. I show her my screen.

Penny: *Was it red?*

"Was it red? Oh, my God." She laughs again. "Okay, I can see what you're talking about."

"See?" I groan and slouch in my chair. "It's like we're trying to force something that's not there. I truly believe we had one hot night, and that's it. There really is nothing between us, friendship-wise. I'm not sure we even have much in common at all. What do you think? Would he be mad if I asked him to leave?"

"He might be relieved."

"I think he might be too."

My phone buzzes, and I lift it to read it.

Eli: *Green.*

I flash my phone to her, and she covers her mouth, cackling. "This has to end."

⊂══⊃

ELI

"POSEY, I need your goddamn help right now. Emergency," I say, barging through his hotel room. We just got back from our morning skate, and this is about the time when a lot of the players take a nap, but I'm at DEFCON 1 right now, and I don't care if Posey needs his beauty sleep. I need him.

"Dude." He lifts his eye mask up—it's one of the ones with the googly eyes on it. He saw it on *Ellen* and thought it was funny as shit, so he got himself one . . . as well as the rest of the team. "You know I need to sleep before the game."

"I know, but this is important."

"What could be so important that—"

"I told her I ate an apple."

His brow creases in confusion. "What?"

"Penny. I was trying to come up with something to say to her, you know, to start a riveting conversation, and all I could think to say was that I ate an apple, and it's just been disastrous from there."

He sits up a little taller. "That was your conversation starter? You ate an apple? What happened to googling some questions to ask her?"

"I did that, but they all seemed unnatural like I was interviewing her, so I've been trying to come up with some more everyday conversations."

"So you told her you ate an apple?"

"At least it seemed better than telling her I like snow because it's white."

"Jesus Christ," he grumbles while throwing his blankets off and walking over to me. "Hand me your phone."

"Why? What are you going to say? Don't say anything stupid."

"Any more stupid than I ate an apple?" He quirks one brow at me.

"You know what I mean."

He shakes his head in annoyance and then starts typing away on my phone. I try to look over his shoulder, but he turns away from me, blocking me from seeing the screen. "What are you writing? Hey, I can't see. Did you send it? Don't send it without my approval, and don't say anything inappropriate like 'I like your ass.'"

He glances over his shoulder. "Do you like her ass?"

"Of course, it's hard not to like everything about her body."

Another raise of an eyebrow, and this time, he fully turns toward me. "Eli Watkins Hornsby——"

"That's not my middle name."

"I know you crushed on this girl, but from the way you've been acting and your abundance of paranoia, I'd say that you actually care. You're acting almost like you . . . like her."

"Enough with that shit. I don't like her in the way you're saying. I mean, yeah, is she hot? Of course. You'd be dumb to think otherwise. But I barely know her. And the things I do know about her I wouldn't say would tip me over the scale to liking her like that." Even though I do kind of like the rambling. It's funny. It's one of the reasons I pressured her to spend my birthday night with me. I had one of those perpetual, stupid smiles on my face from her rambling that night.

"Then why does it matter to you what I say to her?"

"Because she's still the mother of my baby. I don't want to come across all clingy and horny."

"Are you horny?"

Yes.

It's been seven weeks since I've had sex—my longest dry spell ever—and the last person I had sex with is now my awkward counterpart.

"I don't need sex all the time, you realize that?"

He snorts. "Okay." Then he goes back to typing on my phone.

I pull at his shoulder. "Seriously, what are you saying?"

"Chill, dude. I'm just asking her how she's feeling."

I pause. "Oh . . . that's probably a good idea."

"You are such a fucking idiot." He hands me my phone back and then launches himself on his mattress.

I glance down at my phone to read the text he sent.

Eli: *Sorry about that last text. I meant to send it to Posey. How are you feeling today?*

I glance up at him, and he's smiling smugly at me. "Simple," he says, holding his arms out wide. "You're overthinking it."

I take a seat on the edge of his bed and then lie back on the mattress as well. "I fucking hate this. I feel like ever since my birthday, things have not felt the same, and it's freaking me out."

"What do you mean?"

Closing my eyes, I say, "I can't stop thinking about her, and now that we're living together, I can't seem to screw my head on right."

Posey props himself up on his arm. "Dude, I think you like her."

I shake my head. "No, that can't possibly be the problem."

PENNY

"BLAKELY," I whisper as I turn into her office.

She glances up from her computer. "What? Why are we whispering?"

I close her office door behind me. "He wrote back."

"Is this really what's going to happen? I have to be present for your text messages? You know, I have a job to do, right? These VIP tickets aren't going to sell themselves."

"I know, but I don't think he wrote this text message."

Blakely's eyes grow with interest as she reaches her hand out and twiddles her fingers at me, looking for the phone. "Things just got interesting. Hand it over."

I give her my phone and then round her desk to look over her shoulder.

She reads the text out loud. "Sorry about that last text. I meant to send it to Posey. How are you feeling today?" She looks up at me and smiles. "Yeah, he didn't write that. Not after what you've told me your conversations have been like."

"Who do you think wrote it?" I take a seat in one of her chairs and cross one leg over the other.

"My guess would be Posey since he used his name in there. Hornsby is probably freaking out because he looks like an utter fool in these text messages and doesn't know how to handle you."

"Handle me? What is that supposed to mean?"

"Come on. Out of everyone on the team, who is the most extroverted?"

"Eli," I say, not even questioning the answer.

"Exactly. He's the one who should have no problem striking up a conversation, but for some reason, interacting with you is crippling him into a fumbling mess. It's kind of funny to observe from the outside. But I think it's safe to assume that he's probably freaking out like you are and asked Posey to help him, just like you're asking me to help you."

"Okay, so then . . . what do I say?"

She rolls her eyes so hard I'm afraid they might fall out of her head. "Tell him how you're feeling. My God, woman. What is wrong with you?"

"The baby," I say. "It's sucking all of the intelligence out of me."

"I'm not sure that's how pregnancy works."

"How would you know? Are you pregnant?" I challenge her with a wave of arrogance.

"No, and I don't plan on finding out." She points at my phone. "Now message him back. Tell him how you feel."

"Okay, I can do that."

On a deep breath, I text him back. When I'm satisfied with my reply, I press send.

"Done."

"What did you say?"

I read my text message out loud. "Feeling kind of weird, you know, with everything. So I thought that maybe when you come back from your away trip, you should move out."

"What?" Blakely's eyes shoot open. "You sent that?"

Panic ensues. "Wait, what do you mean? You told me to tell him how I felt."

"Like . . . physically, not mentally. Oh, my God, I can't believe you told him you want him to move out right before a game."

My mouth shrivels up into a small pea-sized "o" as my eyes widen in horror. "Oh God, why did I text that?"

"I don't know!"

"Maybe he didn't read it, or better yet, maybe he's relieved . . ."

ELI

"HOLY FUCK, Posey, wake up. Wake up." I shake my friend, who was mid-snore when I charged through his door again.

He whips his mask off his face. "I am going to murder you."

"This is bad." I sit on his bed and hold my phone up to him. "She wants me to leave. You texted her, and now she wants me out of the apartment. What the hell am I supposed to do with that?"

"What?" He rubs his palm over his eye. "What did you say to her?"

"Nothing. I said nothing. I didn't write anything after your text. Dude, if she wants me to leave, that's bad. Pacey will not like finding out that I'm not helping her. He already won't talk to me. Now this?" I pull at my hair. "What the fuck do I do?"

"I'm still trying to figure out how this escalated so quickly. That was a simple question."

"Do you see what I'm dealing with?" I say, my voice an octave higher than normal. "I should have just kept it simple and told her the apple was juicy. Which is better than saying it was moist. What the hell was I thinking letting you take charge?"

"Give me the phone." He swipes it from my grasp and reads the text message while scratching the side of his face. "Huh."

"See. How can I possibly figure out how to talk with her—"

My phone beeps, halting my sentence and freezing me on the spot as the recognizable sound of a FaceTime call rings through the room.

"What the actual fuck are you doing?" I ask Posey as he holds the phone in front of me.

"Getting to the bottom of this."

"I don't want to call her. Give me the phone. Give me the goddamn phone . . ."

PENNY

"BREATHE, BREATHE," Blakely says while I breathe into the bagel bag from this morning. "It will be okay."

I shake my head, the bag crinkling next to my ears.

"Yes, it will. I'm sure he didn't even read—"

My phone buzzes in front of us, and my eyes meet the image on the screen. I tear the brown bag off my face and, in a panic, scream, "He's FaceTiming me!"

"Oh, dear God," Blakely says while reaching for the phone. I quickly swipe it away.

"What the hell do you think you're doing?"

"Answering it?"

"What? Why?"

"Because he clearly wants to talk to you after what you wrote."

"And that's what text messages are for, so you can reply through text, not FaceTime. Who in their right mind FaceTimes

109

someone in the middle of a text conversation? That's unheard of. That's . . . that's breaking social etiquette."

"Well, he's probably freaking out because you told him you want him to move out. That warrants a phone call."

"I'm not answering." I clutch my phone to my chest, but in some wizardly way, Blakely rips it from my grasp. I then swat it from hers just as I hear the sound of the phone being answered.

I gasp and clasp my hand over my mouth while Blakely stares at me wide-eyed.

Silence falls over the both of us, echoing through her office as a distant voice says, "Hello? Penny. Are you there?"

Nostrils flared, I stare at my friend. Mouthing to her, I say, "Don't say a thing."

She gestures harshly at the phone and whispers, "Answer it."

I shake my head vehemently.

"Penny, is everything okay?" Eli's voice rings through.

Blakely and I stare at each other. I'm telling her to zip her lips, and she's drastically trying to convey with her eyes that I need to answer the phone.

Neither of us moves until . . .

She reaches down and grabs the phone and points it at her face. She fluffs her hair and says, "Oh, hey Eli, how's it going?"

"What are you doing?" I hiss-whisper at her.

"Is everything okay?" he asks, worry clear in his voice.

"Yup, everything is fine. Oh look, here's Penny."

"What are you—" She points the phone at me, and I smile. But it's not a normal smile. It's as if each side of my mouth has been hooked, and two people are pulling straight back, baring my teeth in a mid-hiss-snarl.

Just know, it's extremely unattractive, and I don't blame him when his facial expression turns from concern to an appalled wince.

"Uh . . ."

"Say hi," Blakely mouths when I look at her for help.

Turning back to the phone, I lift my hand and say, "Hi."

Seeming just as uncomfortable as me, he lifts his hand as well. "Hi."

And then . . . silence descends upon us.

I glance at Blakely, and he glances at whoever he's with, who I'm going to assume is Posey, unless Pacey is there, wielding a hockey skate, ready to slice Eli's neck.

"Oh, for fuck's sake," I hear someone say before they take the phone away from Eli. I let out a sigh of relief just as Posey's face comes into view. "You two need to get it together. You're having a baby. Find a way to communicate without telling each other you ate an orange."

"It was an apple," Eli corrects in the background.

"Either way, I'll not be a part of this anymore." Posey looks at me on the phone and says, "Penny, you know I adore you, but you can't kick Hornsby out. You and I both know that. Not only does he deserve to help you, but he will be absolutely murdered by your brother if he moves out."

"I know," I say as guilt swarms me. "I just . . . everything is just so uncomfortable. Like I know he truly doesn't want to be there, and the tension is high, and I can't take it."

"I want to be there," Eli says, but it's still Posey I'm technically talking to. "But you're weird."

"I'm weird?" I ask. "You're the one telling me the only part of a horse you like is its mane."

Posey turns away and asks, "You said that to her?"

"It was a weak moment for me. I didn't know what else to say."

"Jesus." Posey pinches the bridge of his nose as Blakely comes into view.

"For what it's worth, she's not being a helpful conversationalist, either."

"Thank you," Eli says, and I can see one of his hands flap in the air.

"How the hell did you two even hook up?" Posey asks.

"Alcohol," both Eli and I say at the same time.

"Well, that makes sense," Posey says. "But since we can't use alcohol this time, we're going to need a solution that works so Blakely and I are not pulled into these text messages. I don't care how uncomfortable it might be. You two need to talk. Even if it's about apples, for fuck's sake."

He then tosses the phone at Eli, who catches it in his lap—I can tell from the angle of his jaw—and then he brings the phone up to his face. His eyes connect with mine, and he quietly says, "Uh, do you think we can talk after the game? That's if you're still awake."

Blakely is nodding, encouraging me to say yes.

I roll my teeth over the corner of my lip, and I say, "Yeah, that would be fine."

"Okay, I'll text to see if you're awake."

"Sounds good."

"Okay. I should go."

"Have a good game."

His lips tilt into a small smile. "Thanks."

And then we hang up.

I collapse into one of Blakely's chairs and drop my phone to the floor as I let my tension-filled body relax for the first time since he sent me that text about his apple.

"Wow, that was . . . that was something I never want to experience again," Blakely says. "I don't know if I should thank you for including me or demand you grace me with a present after having to deal with that."

I gently close my eyes. "Maybe a little of both."

Chapter Ten

ELI

"Good game," I say to Pacey as we make our way into the locker room. "You had some pretty brilliant saves."

He looks my way for a moment before turning toward his locker and muttering, "Don't suck my ass."

Ohh-kay.

So, we're still not on talking terms. That's fair.

At least we won tonight.

And at least we both played marginally better than the night before. I still felt off, though, like my skates weren't entirely listening to what my brain was telling them to do, but it was better.

Posey claps me on the shoulder, and we both take a seat at our lockers. He whispers, "He'll come around. On the other hand, I'll tell you right now, if you ever fuck up my nap again, I'll murder you myself."

"Noted." We both take our skates off and leave them in front of us as we tug off our jerseys. Some of the guys enjoy the time in the locker room of dressing and undressing—not because they enjoy watching each other, but because it's a time to bond. I don't mind getting ready for the game, but undressing, no fucking thank you. I wish the entire jersey and equipment was a zip-up suit that I could easily shed afterward.

What's crazy to me is that some of the guys, two of our biggest bruisers on the team, change their underwear between every period.

Do you know what it takes to change your underwear between periods? A lot of goddamn work that I'm not interested in.

"Are you going to call her when you get back to your hotel?"

"If she's awake," I say while shedding my absolutely drenched shin pads.

"Do you have any idea what you're going to say to her?"

"Sort of. I think I'm just going to be honest and tell her how I feel."

Posey pats me on the back. "Wow, what a novel idea."

"Don't be a dick."

"Hey, I heard of this bar in Vancouver that we need to check out. When we get home in a few days, you game?" Taters asks as he takes a seat next to me. He's usually the last to arrive in the locker room after the game—only if we win—because he hangs out with fans, signs some things, and takes pictures. He's been known to give away more pucks than anyone on the team, which is impressive because Posey will hand out pucks for candy, and the fans know this. There will be signs lined up along the Plexi, asking Posey to trade a puck for a Milky Way. He goes for it every time.

My eyes float to Pacey, who's staring daggers at me.

"Uh, no," I answer. "I'm probably going to be staying in for the foreseeable future."

"Oh, because of the—"

"Don't say it." I don't want him to clue in the other guys with what's going on. The last thing we need is to start more fighting within the team. "But yes, I have some things I need to take care of."

"Look at you growing up," Taters says. "I mean, you've always been the responsible one, but this is rather mature of you."

"Can you not make a big deal about it?"

Posey leans forward and whispers, "He's still having a hard time learning how to communicate with her. He told her he ate an apple today, and that was it. That was his text."

I shed my pants. "Can we not hash it out, please? I have it under control now."

"Didn't seem like it this afternoon," Posey mutters.

"Why are you going to Posey for girl advice when I'm clearly the one you should be asking?" Taters asks.

"Why are you the one?" I ask. "No offense, but you're not currently attached to anyone, and the last person you dated . . . well, it's unclear what happened between you two."

"Not all of us are a tell-all autobiography for the world, Hornsby. Some people like privacy."

Smiling, I say, "Well then, take this as a hint. Give me some fucking privacy."

I take off toward the showers. We have a flight to Denver we have to catch tonight, and I want to get on the bus as quickly as possible so I can call Penny.

I've seen the guys on the team with families hustle up after a game because they want to call their wives and their kids before they go to bed. It's odd to think I'm joining that club now.

Not quite sure how I feel about that other than I don't really have a choice in the matter.

⸺

PENNY: *Yes, I'm awake.*

Damn. I kind of hoped she'd be sleeping or at least pretend to be sleeping. But maybe she needs to talk just as much as I need to. And when I say talk, I mean just tell her how I wish everything was normal between us.

I grabbed a bowl of chili and a to-go box of cornbread for dinner from the players' table and then practically sprinted to the bus with the rest of the family men. Needless to say, a few of them were shocked to see me.

I settle myself toward the back and up against the window, set my food and bag down, and then slip my earbuds in before taking a deep breath and hitting her name in my phone.

It rings two times, and then she answers, "Hey."

I swallow as a wave of butterflies shoots up my stomach. I know it's not the kind of butterflies people get when they see the one they love or their crush walk by. This is nerves. All fucking nerves.

"Hey, Penny." My voice comes out all gravelly, so I take a quick sip of my water. "How, uh . . . how are you doing?"

There you go, a solid start to a conversation.

"I'm doing okay," she answers, and I can already feel the tension. It's obvious that neither of us wants to be in this current situation—on the phone, forcing ourselves to communicate—but we have to make the most of it, which means we need to learn to talk to each other.

"Okay? Are you having any symptoms?" Symptoms? *Symptoms of what, you idiot?* Jesus Christ. You're not her goddamn doctor. But unfortunately for me—and her—it's the first thing that comes to mind.

Thankfully, there's a light chuckle on the other end of the phone, and that eases some of the embarrassment from my idiotic question. "Just tired at the moment."

"Oh, should I, uh, should I let you go so you can get some sleep?"

"No, I think we need to talk."

We need to talk.

Hell, nothing good comes from those four words. Usually, they're accompanied by a breakup or a confession like . . . I'm sorry, but I cheated on you. Weirdly, though, none of those scenarios apply to us.

"Yeah, you're probably right. Do you want to go first?"

"I guess so." And then she's silent, and I wish I could hear what she's thinking. I'm sure it would be a world of information that would make cracking her shell so much easier. If only she would talk to me like she talked to me that one night, so free and open. But circumstances are different now. Finally, she sighs. "I don't know why I'm so awkward around you. Well, I mean, I sort of know why, but still, for some reason, I either ramble on for too long or don't know what to say at all. It felt so easy the night we were together."

Yeah. Same.

"If you recall, it took you a bit to warm up that night as well," I say, trying to help her out.

"True, but you were incredibly chatty that entire time. Why have *you* changed?"

This time, I chuckle. "I think I'm freaked out. I did something I shouldn't have done, which was pursue you, got in trouble for it, and now I'm trying to figure out how to navigate these murky waters. I don't want to stress you out by being too . . . in your space, and I don't want you to feel uncomfortable, especially in your own home, nor do I want you doing this alone. I'm trying to find that balance. My mom raised me by herself before she passed away, and even though I don't understand completely how hard being a single mom is from a little boy's point of view, I do remember her telling me fairly often how sorry she was that her money wouldn't stretch as far as I'd wanted it to. I don't want that for you. So, my usual fun attitude is slightly askew at the moment."

"I can understand that. I feel the same way about trying to make sure you're comfortable."

"No need to worry about me. But for you, I'll try harder. Can I ask you something, though?"

"Of course."

"I need to know why you're so nervous around me. It might help me relate better."

She doesn't answer right away but gives it some serious thought, which I appreciate. "I think the intimidation is still there. It was easy to forget when we were buzzed, but now that we're just normal human beings under no influence at all, I feel . . . out of place."

"Not that shit again," I say in a joking tone. "Come on, Penny. I think you can set that aside by now. I mean, I've pretty much touched every part of your body. There has to be a level of intimacy between us that pushes away that feeling of being out of place."

"You have to remember, Eli, when we hooked up, it was a big thing for me to do, and I had some liquid encouragement to help me. First of all, I wasn't going into that night with the most confidence in the world. The last guy I was with really tore me down romantically, told me I was bad in bed—"

"I can one hundred percent tell you right now that guy was fucking wrong. Trust me, Penny, he was really, really fucking wrong."

"Well, uh . . . thank you."

"I'm serious." I lower my voice. "I don't think I've ever come that hard." And that's straight-up facts. I still fucking think about that night.

She pauses. "Uh, well, we don't need to get into the details, but I appreciate your reassurance."

"Anytime you need it, let me know, but continue."

"Okay, so yes, I wasn't very confident that night, and it was a big deal for me to allow myself to do that with you, out of all people. And I know I act differently at work, but when I'm doing my job, I can be outgoing and extroverted with the guys, but that's because it's a job. I have a checklist of questions and conversation pieces I know I can cling to when I'm talking to all of you. The pressure to impress isn't there. But one-on-one, it's harder. I'm more of an introvert who likes to curl up on the couch and watch *Ozark*—"

"You watch *Ozark*?" I ask. Finally, something we can actually talk about.

"I do . . . do you?"

"Oh, yeah. Fucking love Jason Bateman. I met him last year at a charity event. Dude is fucking cool as shit. More of a baseball fan, though, but he respects the game."

"Wow, I didn't know you met him. What season of the show are you on?"

I settle into my seat and pop open my chili. Guys filter soundlessly onto the bus. We all respect each other and know this is when the guys with families and loved ones like to make their phone calls, so we all stay quiet and eat our dinners.

And even though I don't acknowledge what she said about her job and being an introvert, I file it away. Finding something in common to talk about rather than fixating on why we're weird together seems like a better way to have a conversation. That's why I jumped on the discussion about *Ozark*.

"I'm on the current season, episode two. What about you?" I ask.

"Season three. Darn, that could have been something we did together, you know . . . to make things less torturous when we're together."

"I wouldn't call it torturous, well . . . maybe slightly." She laughs, and I realize I really like the sound of her laugh. I remember liking it the night we hooked up, but hearing it again just reminds me why my will slipped that night, and I allowed myself to taste her. I had to. "But I don't mind rewatching with you."

"You don't have to do that."

"I know, but it could be good for us. We've already started talking more just because of one thing we have in common."

"True." She lets out a deep sigh. "God, what you must think of me."

"I think you're pretty legit, Penny. I've thought that for a while," I say, finally starting to find my voice. "Ever since Pacey introduced you, I've only had good thoughts. Even now, when I come home from a game and find you rambling and steaming my suits, I still think you're pretty damn great."

"Thank you," she says quietly.

"This is where you tell me how great I am."

She chuckles. "And you're pretty great too, Hornsby."

"Eli, call me Eli. Do I have to keep telling you that?"

"Probably. I'm so used to calling you by your last name because of Pacey and all the guys, well . . . and fans. It's out of habit."

"I get it, but I don't think I want my kid calling me Hornsby, you know?"

"He wouldn't call you Eli, though, either. He'd call you Daddy. So, if anything, I should call you Daddy."

She walked right into that one.

"That works for me. Call me Daddy all you want."

She pauses. "I'm blaming that one on pregnancy brain."

As I laugh out loud, I catch Pacey walking onto the bus wearing a scowl across his face. Pretty sure that scowl has a name, and its name is Eli Hornsby. He moves right past me and doesn't even bother to acknowledge me. He sits in the very back where I know he spreads out and calls Winnie. If anyone can put him in a better mood, it's her.

Turning my attention back to Penny, I ask, "Have you had many pregnancy brain moments?"

"No, I think they've been more like blonde moments, which I have from time to time. But I'm glad I can blame them on the baby now."

"You're a human incubator, so you might as well get as much from it as you can."

"I guess so." She yawns, and I look at the clock, realizing how late it must be for her.

"I should let you get some sleep. You must be exhausted."

"Yeah, pretty tired. I've been waking up at four with nausea, so the fatigue is really kicking in."

"Have you thrown up?" I ask, feeling guilty as shit that I'm not there.

"No, just nausea. It's nothing compared to what some women go through. Blakely brought me some ginger ale to have in the morning, and that's helped a lot."

"I'm sorry I'm not there to help."

"You don't need to apologize. You have a job that requires you to be away. I get that, trust me. I'm just glad I have Blakely. And Winnie stopped by the office yesterday as well to see how I was. So I'm really okay."

"You'll let me know when you're not? I feel like we broke through that awkward bubble tonight, so maybe we can move forward from here?"

"That would be nice, you know, as long as you don't say weird things like I just ate an apple."

"A low point in my life I wish we could move on from."

She laughs. "As long as we're friends, I'll never let you live that down."

"Calling us friends now, Penny?"

"Well, we're on our way to being friends, but I think we can get there and kick this co-parenting thing in the ass."

For some reason, that irks me. *Co-parenting.* The term makes me feel like we did something wrong. Like we weren't able to work something out, so we're settling for co-parenting. Not that it's a bad thing. A few guys on the team are co-parenting with an ex, and they're killing it. But with Penny, it just feels weird because we never even gave anything a shot. Then again, we both agreed to be friends, so I don't know why that bugs me.

It just does.

"We will," I say, not bothering to bring up my thoughts. I'm honestly not sure I'd be able to articulate them in a way for her to understand. Instead, I say, "Thanks for this phone call. I know you were probably dreading it, but it's almost like we shook off the stink."

"Ew, what a horrible term."

"You know what I mean. Like in running, the first five minutes are absolutely dreadful, but then you get into the flow of it, and it all seems pretty easy after that, right?"

"I prefer Pilates or barre."

"Help me out, Penny."

She laughs. "I know what you mean, and I agree. I feel much better, and if you call or text tomorrow, I'm sure it won't be as bad as it was today." As if she just realized what she said, she quickly backtracks. "But don't feel obligated to call or text tomorrow. I know you have a life and all—"

"Penny, and I mean this in the most non-romantic way possible, you are my life now. So yes, I'll talk to you tomorrow, okay?"

The relief in her voice flows easily through the phone. "Okay. Talk to you tomorrow."

"Get some good sleep and text me in the morning to let me know how you're feeling."

"I will. Good night, Eli."

"Night, Penny."

I hang up and set my phone on my lap as I stare forward at the chair in front of me. The feeling I have floating through my chest is odd to explain, almost like I'm as light as a feather. The pressure building in my ribs and constricting my lungs has been released.

I can breathe.

I just hope that Penny is feeling the same relief. The same . . . peace.

Chapter Eleven

PENNY

"I brought smoothies . . . and Winnie," Blakely says while charging through my office door, holding up a tray of drinks. Winnie follows her, looking as cute as can be in a pair of high-waisted jeans and a tucked-in V-neck long-sleeved shirt.

"Ta-da," Winnie says while giving me jazz hands.

"Hey, what a great surprise." I stand from my desk and give her a hug. "You look amazing."

"Thank you." Winnie smiles. She's curvy and beautiful and so freaking perfect it's nauseating. But I love her. She's sweet and has the kindest heart, and she makes my brother extremely happy, which is all that matters in the long run. "This is a leotard, can you tell?" She plucks at the maroon fabric.

"I wondered how you got such a good tuck," Blakely says. "How does it ride in the crotch area?"

"High and tight. I believe a one-inch piece of fabric barely covers my vagina. But there's something to be said about walking around, wondering if the next step will be the final step of giving yourself a frontal wedgie."

I chuckle. "What a way to live life. So exhilarating."

"Living life on the edge over here," Winnie says.

We all take a seat, and Blakely hands out the smoothies. "Yours is the pregnancy special," Blakely says. "I'm not sure what's exactly in it, but they told me it is full of the nutrients you need, and it tastes good, so it checked off my boxes."

I take a sip, wary at first, but when the flavor combination of strawberries and bananas hits my tongue, I'm pleasantly surprised. "Wow, it's good."

"I'm glad because that was a real guess on my end." She sips her green smoothie along with Winnie.

"So how are you feeling?" Winnie asks.

"Pretty good. Still nauseous, but not throwing up. I hate the feeling of being sick to my stomach, but at least I'm not heaving over the toilet every morning. I'm grateful for that."

"Was your mom the same way?" Winnie asks.

Ooof, wouldn't know.

"I, uh . . . I haven't told her yet. I really haven't told anyone. I have a doctor's appointment today to check things out. Maybe after that, I'll tell them." I set my drink down. "I feel like they're going to be so disappointed in me."

"It was an accident," Blakely says. "You guys used protection. Sometimes this just happens, and at least you're doing your best given the circumstances. That's all they can ask for."

"And I have a pretty good feeling they're going to be excited about a grandchild. I know they're always pestering Pacey about when he's going to have kids."

Blakely leans toward her. "And when is that going to happen?"

Winnie smirks. "Not anytime soon. I want to be married and for us to own a house. A few things need to be done before that is even an option. So until then, I'm on birth control, holding down the fort."

"Does Pacey want kids?" Blakely asks.

"He does." Winnie meets my gaze. "He probably doesn't want me saying this because, you know, he has to act like the strong, angry brother who has been wronged by one of his best friends, but last night, he said he was kind of excited to meet the little one."

"He said that?" I ask, completely dumbfounded. I just assumed Pacey has been angry ever since he found out and can't seem to get over the idea that Eli got me pregnant.

"He did. But I'll swear to my death that I never told you that. Do you hear me?" She pins me with a threatening look that is actually non-threatening because it's Winnie. I'm not sure she has a sinister bone in her body.

"I won't say a thing to him, I promise. But I'll tell you that makes me feel a little more relieved."

"He'll get over the anger at some point. He just feels really betrayed right now. But he's working through those emotions. Give him a little time."

"It isn't all Eli's fault," I say. "I was an equal partner in what happened."

"And, uh, what exactly happened that night?" Blakely asks. "You've skimmed over all of the good stuff."

"The good stuff will remain skimmed," I say as my phone buzzes on the desk. I glance down quickly to see that it's a text from Eli. I don't open it even though I really want to see what it says.

"Is that from Hornsby?" Blakely asks.

"How can you tell?"

"Your face turned pink," Winnie points out.

I raise my hands to my cheeks, feeling just how heated they are. God, how embarrassing.

"It's just hot in here," I say as both of them laugh, seeing right through me.

"I take it your conversation with him last night went well?" Blakely asks and then turns to Winnie. "You should have been here yesterday. What an absolute disaster. They were trying to communicate with each other, but it was the most uncomfortable thing because neither knew how to act normally. They were talking about horse manes and apple eating. It was a total fail."

"Horse manes?" Winnie asks with a cute scrunch to her nose.

"Not my doing."

Blakely points her smoothie at me. "You were not helping. The guy was trying, and you were responding with one-word answers. Of course conversation would result in talking about eating apples. He didn't know where to go from there."

"Either way, it was better last night," I say. "We both spoke about how we've been uncomfortable and found some common ground with *Ozark*."

"Love Jason Bateman," Blakely says.

"Eli has met him, and I'm so jealous. But honestly, it's better between us, at least as best as it can be. Before last night, there seemed to be an elephant in the room hogging all of the air. But now that we are actually finding the ability to communicate, I think it will be okay."

"And he's living with you?" Winnie asks.

I nod. "Yeah."

"How is that? You know I love Pacey with everything in me, but Eli is quite handsome. When I first walked into the cabin in Banff, I was honestly struck by how attractive he was. I can't imagine what it would be like living with him."

"Oh, don't worry," Blakely says, placing her hand on Winnie's shoulder. "Nothing romantic will happen between them."

Winnie chuckles. "Do you really believe that, Penny?"

"Of course. We're not looking to start anything. That would just complicate things. We decided on being friends, and that's good enough."

"Wait until she gets to the horny phase of pregnancy," Blakely says. "When my sister was pregnant with my niece, she'd try to sit on my brother-in-law's face every chance she got."

"I could not even imagine having sex right now," I say as I press my palm to my stomach. "Everything feels weird and out of place. I'm terrified I'd throw up, so any sort of intimacy is completely off the table."

"Just you wait." Blakely smiles while taking a sip of her drink. When she's done, she asks, "What did Hornsby say to you anyway?"

Wanting to get off the topic of sex, I lift my phone and open his message. I read it to myself first.

Eli: *Good morning. Just checking on you < - - see, I can be pretty good at this talking thing.*

I chuckle and then text him back, forgetting that two pairs of eyes are staring at me.

Penny: *Good morning. Everything is good now. I have an appointment with the doctor later. I'll let you know how it goes.*

When I set my phone down, I lift my drink just as I see both of my friends looking at me with annoying grins on their faces.

Blakely turns to Winnie and says, "Surrrrre, nothing is going to happen between them." They both chuckle together. "This should be a lot of fun to watch as it unfolds."

"Agreed. Get me some popcorn. I think there might be some romance in the air."

I roll my eyes because they have completely lost it. There's no romance anywhere. Nothing about our situation is romantic at all. Maybe if we were married and in love, then yes, this whole experience would possibly be romantic. But we're not married. We're practically strangers. Therefore, we're just trying to make it day by day.

There's absolutely zero romance.

None.

Zilch.

⌐⌐

ELI: *Thinking about you. Are you at the doctor's office right now?*

Penny: *Yeah. I had to change into a gown and take my underwear off. Errr, is that too much information?*

Eli: *Nah, I think the more honest we are, the better. It will keep us from*

127

saying stupid shit like I like snow because it's white. The more honest, the better.

Penny: *Then should I tell you that my nipples tingle?*

Eli: *LOL. Yes, please tell me that. And what kind of tingling are we talking about here? A good tingle or a bad one?*

Penny: *An interesting one. Not sure how I feel about it.*

Eli: *Anything else tingling that I should know about?*

Penny: *No. Just my nipples. Is there anything tingling on your body?*

Eli: *Not at the moment, but when Posey takes his shirt off in the locker room, my whole body is tingling and humming.*

Penny: *ROFL. Gives me an idea to put heart eyes on your face and then flash to a video of Posey walking toward you. I think it could be a really good post.*

Eli: *Or of him bending over and stretching with his stick.*

Penny: *OMG, even better. Oh hey, the doctor is here. I'll let you know how this all goes.*

Eli: *Okay. Sounds good. Tell him about the tingling nips.*

ELI: *Are you awake?*

Penny: *I am despite being totally exhausted.*

My phone rings, and I answer and put it on speaker before laying my phone on my stomach. In bed and comfortable, I don't feel like holding my phone up to my ear. "Hey, congrats on the win tonight."

"Thanks," he says, his voice sounding just as exhausted as mine. "Just waiting on a few guys, and then we're heading to the airport. I'll be home pretty late. Want me to sleep on the couch so I don't disturb you?"

"No. I'm sure once I fall asleep, I'll be out cold."

"Okay." He pauses for a second. "How was the appointment?"

"Good. Confirmed that I am, in fact, pregnant, but we knew that."

"Did you tell him about the, uh . . . the tingling?"

"Yes." I chuckle. "He said it was normal and to expect many more changes to come. He also told me to take prenatal vitamins and set what he thinks is a due date."

"What is it?"

"November eleventh."

"Right after the season starts back up again." I can hear the concern in his voice. "I need to check on paternity leave and see if we even get anything. I know it's not mandated by the league, but maybe the Agitators have their own policy."

"I don't think it's something you need to worry about right now. We have a long way to go. I'm still in a timeframe where my pregnancy could go either way."

"What do you mean by that?" he asks.

"You know, I could still have a high chance of a miscarriage. That's why the doctor always tells you to wait until you start telling people. Once we hit twelve weeks, then we can start telling people, and you can check on paternity leave."

"How far along are you now?"

"Almost eight."

"Why does it feel like it's been longer?"

I sink further into my pillow as I say, "Probably because the first week we found out, it felt like paint was drying while trying to have a conversation."

He chuckles. "Yeah, that could be it. I'm glad we can joke about it. Does that mean you're starting to feel more comfortable around me?"

"I think so. Maybe by tomorrow, I'll actually be able to look at you and not have the incessant need to clean."

"Glad that seeing my face makes you want to clean."

I let out a low laugh. "Are you still thinking you want to live here? Because honestly, you don't have to if you don't want to. It all seems kind of silly at this point."

"Is this your roundabout way of kicking me out?" I can hear the teasing in his voice, but there is also a slight edge to it.

"No, not at all. But everything happened so fast, and I know

Pacey is breathing down your neck. I don't want you to feel obligated. I can handle Pacey."

"I can handle him too. I appreciate your concern, Penny, but I'm going to need to fight my own battle with Pacey. As far as the apartment is concerned, I'd truly like to stay with you, just so I can be there in case anything happens. I know I'm out of town a lot, but at least when I am in town, I can be there."

"If that's what you want, then that's fine."

He's quiet for a second and then grows serious when he says, "But what do you want, Penny?"

I stare up at the ceiling, giving that question some thought. In this uncertain time of my life, I could really use the comfort of someone going through the same thing as me. And sure, Eli might not be the one carrying the child, but he's still about to become a parent in November, and that's some scary shit. It might be nice to go through that together.

"I don't want to be alone while going through this. And I know this might sound silly, but I truly want to get to know you, more than just the hockey player, but the man who you are so when our baby does arrive, I can make sure to tell them what a great daddy they have."

When silence falls over the phone, I wonder if we've been disconnected.

"Eli, you still there?"

"Yeah," he croaks. "I'm here."

"Oh okay, did you, uh . . . did you hear what I said?"

"I did, and Jesus, it kind of knocked the wind out of me. I want the same thing. I think we're going about this the right way. Getting to know each other so when the baby is here, we can always be on each other's side, rather than fighting over the child."

"Exactly."

"You know, I'm pretty sure you're the most laid-back pregnant woman. There have been a few guys on the team who have come and gone, been traded or retired, and I've heard nothing but horror stories with getting someone pregnant."

"Well, you don't need to worry about that with me."

"I'm glad to hear it. Hey, they want to get moving, so I'm going to hang up since it will start to get loud in here."

"Sure. Safe travels. I'll see you later."

"Thanks. I'll be quiet when I get in. Bye, Penny."

"Bye."

I hang up the phone and smile softly. Now that we've shaken off all of the awkwardness, I truly think I can do this with him. Have a baby, raise a kid. I mean, if I were to choose anyone on the team to do this with, it very well might have been Eli, just because he's so easygoing, him and Posey. But Posey's fetish with bologna sandwiches would most likely bother this pregnant stomach.

I'm just glad I have someone who wants to do this together. I could be way worse off.

My phone beeps with a text message, and I have a feeling I know exactly who it is. I bring my screen into view and catch Eli's name.

Eli: *What's your favorite breakfast?*

I roll to my side and hold my phone out in front of me as I text him back.

Penny: *Like of all time? Restaurant and everything or just generic breakfast food?*

Eli: *Generic breakfast food.*

Penny: *Hmm, well, given that breakfast is my absolute favorite meal of the day, I'd say I have many favorites. I love bagels, especially with a mound of cream cheese. I enjoy a good yogurt parfait as long as the fruit isn't all mushy and gross. And of course, the classic cinnamon bun is never wasted on me.*

Eli: *If you had to pick one, your last breakfast ever, what would it be?*

Penny: *Slightly morbid, but I'll go with the questioning. I'd probably have to choose a cinnamon bun.*

Eli: *Have you ever been to Denver?*

Penny: *No. Are they known for their cinnamon buns?*

Eli: *Lol, not that I'm aware of, but there is a place here that Posey and I go to called The Denver Biscuit Company, and they serve these giant* *cinnamon buns that are impossible to eat by yourself. If I had known this was your favorite breakfast food, I'd have brought one home to you.*

Penny: *My mouth is watering.*

Eli: *Next time we're here, I'll grab one for sure.*

Penny: *Why do you ask?*

Eli: *Just a good thing to know. Get some sleep. I'll see you in the morning.*

Chapter Twelve

ELI

I roll out of bed quietly, making sure not to wake Penny, and I head out of the bedroom, closing the door behind me.

I've been up ever since Penny woke up at four with a bout of nausea. She dry-heaved into the toilet a few times, but that was it. I sat next to her the entire time, unsure of what she really needed, so instead of talking, I just made sure she knew I was there for her.

When she was feeling better, I helped her back into bed, and as she drifted off to sleep, I lay awake until my phone buzzed with a notification from my Uber Eats driver, letting me know that the food I ordered was delivered.

I move to the entryway of her one-bedroom apartment, across the semi-creaky floorboards, and over to the front door, where I quietly open it to find a paper bag of food on the doormat.

Perfect.

I scoop up the bag just as my phone buzzes again. I glance at the screen and see a text from Penny.

She's awake?

And why is she texting me? Maybe she needs something. With the bag in one hand and my phone in the other, I bring my phone into view and read the message.

Penny: *Oh my God, Blakely. I've had to fart so bad, and Eli finally left the room. Why is this happening to me?*

I snort so hard, droplets of snot fly out of my nose. Oh shit, she's going to be absolutely mortified when she realizes she sent the text to the wrong person. And we just moved past the awkwardness. I have a feeling this might set us back.

But . . .

I chuckle.

Why didn't she just get up and go fart somewhere in private? Why did she have to wait for me to leave the room?

Something I'll probably never know because no way in hell am I going to bring it up.

Nope, I'm going to pretend I read nothing. Ignorance is bliss.

I take the food to the kitchen just as my phone buzzes again. A grin spreads across my face as I reach for my phone and read it again.

Penny: *I just farted again. I've never felt so light in my life. Do you think all the gas I've been having lately is the reason for the nausea? I think I'm going to ask Dr. Big Pecs.*

Dr. Big Pecs?

Who the hell is that?

She never mentioned her doctor having big pecs, but then again, why would she mention that to me? And I know I shouldn't care if she thinks her doctor has big pecs because that's none of my business, but . . . how big are we talking?

Bigger than mine?

I have some decent pecs. I know I look good with my shirt off, so could they be bigger than mine? They have to be if that's his nickname. So what is a doctor with big pecs doing sniffing around women's vaginas? In my head, her doctor was some crusty old man who has to push his glasses up on his nose every few seconds because he never thought about getting them fitted properly. Where is Dr. Old Man? Also, is Dr. Big Pecs single?

I know I said ignorance is bliss, but . . .

Now I'm itching to have a conversation with her to get more information on this doctor, but then again, that would probably make her want to crawl in a hole and die of humiliation. I don't want to humiliate her, but God . . . I want answers. Are his pecs real? Has she touched them? Has he offered to let her touch them?

Can I fucking touch them?

Jesus Christ, one mention of big pecs, and I'm losing my goddamn mind.

No, this isn't about me. It's about Penny, and even though it's painful to set aside my big pec paranoia, I'm not going to make this about me—offer me praise, everyone—and I'm going to let it go.

I pull out the three boxes from the bag—two cinnamon buns and an assorted fruit medley that will be plenty for us to share. In addition to what I ordered, I make myself a quick protein shake because even on my day off, I need to be smart about how I treat my body.

After scouring the cabinets for plates, cups, and silverware, I pull the food out of the boxes, arrange them on the plates, and then set everything on the table. I considered making Penny some sort of warm beverage, but I'm not sure what she likes or what she can have, so I can always make it when she comes out here.

Which, by the way . . . when is that going to be?

She's awake, I know that.

Could she be in the bathroom again? Could she be . . . airing out? *winces* Don't want to disturb that process.

But what if she's feeling sick again?

Maybe I should go check on her.

Errrr, but what if she's changing or something? Or taking a shower?

Walking in on her doing anything like that might absolutely abolish any of our forward progress, especially after the fart text. I'd better just stay put and wait for her to emerge.

Checking highlights from yesterday on my phone, I note that the Polar Freeze are doing annoyingly well this year, and they are a force to be reckoned with. They arrive in a few days for a game, and I know there will be bloodshed out on the ice. I'd say they're our biggest rivals because many of us have a history with the players on the team.

Me in particular.

I played with a guy in the American Hockey League, Remi Gasper. Fuck, I hated him so much, and the feeling was . . . *is* mutual. We have never gotten along.

Hell, I haven't told anyone this ever, but the night Holden Holmes passed away, Halsey's twin, we were out at the bars enjoying a few beers when Remi walked in. Seeing him immediately made me turn red. The guy plays dirty on the ice and will try to get away with everything. That night was no exception. He was making cheap shots at us, saying some bullshit things about our skills, and having no ability to let the insults roll off me, we got into it. Words were said, fists were thrown, and before I knew it, we were kicked out of the bar. Holden wasn't a part of it, though. He kept away from the fight and ended up staying at the bar. A few short hours after, he got in his car accident. Had Remi and I not fought, there's no doubt in my mind that Holden wouldn't have chosen to drive home that night . . .

Fuck.

Just thinking about it makes me sick as Holden and I were pretty close. I still live with the guilt over that night, another feeling I work on with my therapist.

After that, I was hoping Remi would have some career-ending injury, but instead, he's a defenseman for the Polar Freeze. Every time we're on the ice together, cheap shots are thrown, and a guaranteed fight will break out. The fans, of course, eat it up. I fucking dread it.

I'm knee-deep in checking out highlights from the Freeze's

game last night when I hear a throat clear from down the hall. I look up from my phone and spot Penny wrapped up tightly in a fluffy, floor-length robe, long plaid pants, and from what I can barely see, a high-neck shirt. The only skin showing is her hands and face. Even her feet are covered by black slippers. We're a long way from that hot-pink dress.

"Hey, how are you feeling?" I ask.

"Fine." She pushes her toe into the floor, not making eye contact with me. "I, uh, I see that you have your phone."

Oh shit, she figured it out.

"I do," I say. How should I navigate this? Should I tell her I read the texts? Should I act like they never happened? I know one thing is for sure . . .

Don't.

Fucking.

Laugh.

No matter how hard you want to. Do not laugh.

Also, don't ask about Dr. Big Pecs.

"I see." She moves a step forward. "Have you, uh, have you had your phone all morning?"

"I have," I answer.

"Sure, of course you have." Another step forward. "Did you happen to receive any text messages this morning?"

Now what should I do? Play dumb? Or tell her I read everything from the blasting of farts to the man with the pecs? The thought of ignoring it all is really appealing, but I don't think she will believe me. Plus, we said we should be honest with each other. So I guess we'll be breaking the ice this morning.

"I did receive some text messages. Some informative ones."

Her lips purse together as her hands join in front of her, fidgeting.

"Did they happen to be from me?"

Solemnly, I nod. "I'm afraid they were."

She closes her eyes and lets out a harsh breath. "Excuse me, I need to go stick my head in the toilet and wish this never happened." She turns to head back to the bedroom, but I'm out of my chair in no time and stopping her from moving forward.

"Hey, you have nothing to be embarrassed about. Nothing that you should be sticking your head in a toilet over, that's for sure."

Her eyes meet mine. "Really? You don't think anything was embarrassing at all about those text messages?"

The corner of my lips pull, tugging, desperately attempting to make me smile, but I don't allow it. Keep it the fuck together.

"No," I squeak out. "They were regular text messages."

Don't fucking laugh, man. She will never, ever be able to look at you if you laugh. She will never forgive you. Remain neutral.

She crosses her arms over her chest and juts out her hip. "You're telling me that my, err, my text about an immense amount of flatus was a regular text?"

Why did she have to use the word flatus? I was doing fine keeping it together until she used that word. Now I can feel the grin spreading across my face.

Trying to tamp it down, I say, "Everyone has gas."

She studies me, her eyes moving back and forth, and then finally she says, "I don't like what's happening."

"What do you mean?"

"You're trying to act like everything is fine when, in reality, let's just call a spade a spade, Eli. I texted you something I'd rather jump off a cliff than you find out."

"Listen, it's fine. If you want me to forget about it, I will."

"Oh please, this is something you will always remember. The day the mother of your child texted you that she waited for you to leave the room so she could fart. That is a moment in a man's life that he will remember until the day he dies."

I let out a heavy sigh. "Fine, yes, you're right. This moment will stick in my memory for a long time, but that's a good thing."

"How on earth is that a good thing?" she asks. "Do you really think I want to be recollected in your mind as the girl with the farts?"

"Because we crossed a line. Now you don't have to wait for me to leave the room. If you want to fart, you can just fart."

Her eyes narrow, and her finger reaches out and pokes me in the chest. "Over my dead body will I ever fart in front of you." She then turns toward the kitchen, where she stops and sees the food on the table. She tosses her hands up in surrender and then turns back to me. "Look at what you did."

Nervous that I did something wrong, like use her mother's fine dining ware when I shouldn't have, I look over her shoulder at the table setting. Everything seems to be in order, but I tread carefully. She seems to be highly emotional at the moment between the nausea and the farts. "Uh, is something wrong? Did I use the wrong plates?"

"Did you use the wrong plates?" she asks, her voice a next-level shrill. "No, you didn't use the wrong plates, Eli. You freaking got me breakfast? Do you know how that makes me feel?"

Errr . . .

Can anyone help me out here?

I wet my lips and very carefully say, "Uh, bad?"

"Why on earth would that make me feel bad?" Tears well up in her eyes. "Getting breakfast, ugh, that was nice of you."

Okay, so not in trouble?

But she's crying?

Which, of course, makes me shrivel up like an old prune. I don't do well with crying women. I don't know how to act. Do I pat her on the shoulder, tell her "there, there, you'll be fine"? Do I give her a hug and not say anything? Do I offer her a tissue?

What's a man supposed to do in this situation? We went from farts to tears because I got her breakfast. This is way past my comprehension level.

So I decide to approach with caution. "I figured since I don't have to skate until ten this morning and you have the day off, it might be nice to have breakfast together. I hope that's okay. Honestly, if you want me to sit out on the balcony, I can do that."

She nods. "Yup, that was thoughtful." Tears stream down her

face. "Very thoughtful. And here I am, acting like a grotesque human, telling you about my farts and Dr. Big Pecs."

Yes, she fucking mentioned him. Here is my in.

Sure, it might not be the best time to bring him up, given the one-eighty in conversation we just had, but I'm dying to know more.

"How big of pecs are we talking?" I ask, trying to add a jovial tone to my voice.

She walks over to the kitchen, grabs a napkin, and dabs at her eyes. "I said I was grotesque, and that's what you want to know? The bra size of my doctor?"

Something is happening. Something I don't think I'm mentally prepared for. I'm pretty sure from what I've seen in movies and on TV that the professionals would refer to this as hormones. The ups and downs. The crying over something that doesn't seem that terrible at all. If I could put my finger on it, that's what I'd guess. Now if only there was an easy map that showed me how to navigate through said hormones.

"You're not grotesque. You actually . . ." I study her. "You're actually quite pretty in the morning."

She stops dabbing her eyes, and they laser in on me. "Am I not pretty at night?"

Oh, shit.

"What? No, you are. You're very pretty at night."

She dabs her eyes again. "But you said only in the morning."

Christ. Sweat trickles down my back. *Reel it in, Hornsby.*

"Well, that's because not everyone can wake up as beautiful as you, especially after dry-heaving for as long as you do. A head in a toilet doesn't scream beauty, but wow, you really show up with the prettiness . . . all the time. All the time pretty."

There, that should do it.

"Is that a compliment?"

Uh, it was supposed to be.

Clearly, it was not a satisfactory one.

"I assumed it was, but judging by the disgusted sneer on your face, I'm going to say you didn't take it that way. Okay, how about this. In case there is any kernel of doubt in your mind, I think you look nice, very pretty. No matter where you've been or what you've done, you're always pretty. I don't think you're the least bit grotesque, or anything you do is grotesque. Not to mention, everyone farts, it's a natural thing that occurs, and if you didn't fart, well, that would be weird and grotesque. So congrats on what you called the flatus. Well done." I offer her a thumbs up. "Now, I hope you join me for breakfast. I got cinnamon buns, and I know how much you like them."

She glances at the table and then back at me, and once again, her eyes well up and tears leak down her cheeks. Please let those be happy tears. I'm clenching my ass cheeks so hard, I'm not sure how much longer I can hold on. "I'm sorry." She wipes at her eyes. Oh, thank fuck. "Things are just weird for me right now. And I don't know how to control my emotions."

Well, at least she recognizes that.

"It's okay. No need to apologize for anything." I walk over to the table, and I pull a chair out for her. "Take a seat, and I'll get you a drink. Do you want coffee or tea?" The faster we can move past the circle of hell we just experienced, the better.

"Water is fine." She sits down and scoots her chair in. I quickly fill up a glass for her and then set it in front of her before taking a seat.

"I wish these were from The Denver Biscuit Company," I say, "but they will have to do for now. They're pretty good. Gooey in the middle, which is all that matters."

She pulls her cinnamon bun apart with her fingers and lifts a chunk to her mouth before taking a bite. Her eyes slowly close, and she leans back in her chair while moaning. "These are so good."

Well . . . that's, uh . . . that's a sight.

The moaning.

The relaxed position.

It's almost as if she just had an orgasm right in front of me, but I had nothing to do with it other than purchasing the cinnamon bun.

And I hate to sound like a fucking creep, because that's how it's going to come off, but hearing her moan like that takes me back to my birthday, to that night, the way she writhed on top of me right before I made us switch positions.

It's hard not to think about that night, especially when I can honestly say it's the best I've ever had.

And I don't know if it's because I'd wanted her for so long, or if it was because it was my birthday . . . or if it was because it was just her, but either way, sitting across from her in that buttoned-up robe outfit, I find myself wanting her all over again.

"Are you going to eat your cinnamon bun?" she asks, pulling me out of my reverie.

"Oh yeah, uh-huh," I say as I dive into the bun with my fork.

"So what are your plans for today?"

"Reading probably," she answers.

"Cool. What are you reading?"

"A pregnancy book. You know, just so I know what to expect."

"Oh, yeah. Do you want me to read it too?"

She vehemently shakes her head. "I'd rather you not know what's happening to my body. Call me old-fashioned, but I want to keep that a secret."

"It might help me better understand moments like we had this morning."

She bites down on her cinnamon bun, leaving a dollop of icing on her finger that she licks off. Like the goddamn pervert that I am, I watch her intensely as she drags her tongue over her finger, envisioning what it would be like if it was my cock instead.

"I'll give you the CliffsNotes," she says. "The first trimester, I'm going to be an emotional wreck. I won't be able to control any of my hormones, so if I'm laughing hysterically one moment and then crying my heart out the next, just know, it's the little alien baby inside me that's controlling my every move." I chuckle at that. "And I'm also supposed to not feel great during the first trimester, which, check, I've got that covered." She makes a check mark in the air. "In addition, I'm supposed to experience severe heartburn, feel incredibly bloaty, and as you might have guessed it from this morning, I'll be quite farty. So that will be an utter joy for you . . . and me."

"I mean, we can make the most of it. Do you want a designated fart zone? Somewhere where you can take care of business, thus an area I know to avoid?"

She stares at me blankly. What? I thought it was a good idea. When her nose curls in disgust, I know she disagrees.

"I'd rather accidentally let one out in front of you than have you know I'm going to a designated fart zone to let loose. Jesus, that would be humiliating. Could you imagine? Me entering a taped-off zone in the living room that you should never go near in fear of . . . God, I can't even finish the sentence." Her eyes connect with mine and pin me with seriousness. "There will be no zone. Nothing. Do you hear me?"

"Got it. No zone." I hold my hands up. "That was a completely useless suggestion, and I should never have brought it up."

"Well, you don't have to say it like that. I know you were trying to be nice, and I appreciate it, but if we can just move on from all that stuff this morning, that would be great."

"Fair, we can do that for sure. I just have one more question."

In a deadpanned tone, she says, "Is this about Dr. Big Pecs?"

"I just need to know how big."

"Ugh, you're annoying." She takes another bite of her bun and answers, "They jut out a few good inches past his chin."

"A few inches?" I ask incredulously. "Seriously?" I glance down at my chest and then back at Penny. "Do my pecs extend past my chin?"

She picks up her glass of water and takes a sip. "Not like Dr. Big Pecs." She shrugs and then goes back to her cinnamon bun.

"Do men experience crazy hormones as well?" I ask. "Because I'm feeling pretty emotional and inferior about Dr. Big Pecs."

She rolls her eyes dramatically. "His head is too small for his broad shoulders. He has a whole Beetlejuice shrinking head thing going on, so you don't want his pecs. You are perfect as you are."

My brows raise in surprise before I lean forward on the table. "Perfect, huh?" I waggle my eyebrows, which only causes her to shake her head at me. "Tell me more about that."

"You're perfect, Eli, but you could afford to learn how not to snore at night."

I sit taller, appalled. "I do not fucking snore."

And once again, with a grin on her face, she just shrugs her shoulders and continues to eat her cinnamon bun.

What-the-fuck-ever . . . I do not snore.

⊏▭⊐

"HAVE YOU EVER HEARD ME SNORE?" I ask Taters as I close my notebook. We skated for an hour this morning, grabbed some food, and then sat down to review some videos. It was nauseating having to watch Remi skate around like he's some sort of god on ice.

"What?" Taters asks as he stands from his seat.

"We used to share a hotel room. Did I ever snore?"

"Why do you want to know?"

"No reason," I answer casually even though I feel the least bit casual about it. I need to know. After Penny's comment, I can't be sure if she was teasing me or not, and when I went to ask her again, she just went into the bathroom to take a shower.

It was infuriating.

Taters studies me as we make our way toward the parking lot. "She told you you snore, didn't she?"

"Yes." I sigh. "But I can't tell if she was saying it just to piss me off or if she meant it, and now I'm feeling self-conscious."

"And we can't have you feeling self-conscious. That would be an absolute detriment to your ego."

"I know," I say, causing him to laugh. "So did I snore?"

"Like you were sawing wood for an entire colony."

"What?" I nearly shout. "Are you fucking serious?"

"Bad, man. Really bad. I considered telling you, but you were struggling that season, so I didn't think I should pile that kind of blast to the self-esteem. But yeah, you snore, and loud."

What the actual fuck?

Taters pats me on the back. "You got the pretty face and the talent. Something had to be wrong with you." And then he pushes through the door to the parking lot and throws up the peace sign. "See you tomorrow."

I tuck my notebook under my arm and go straight to my car, where I take a seat and pull up my phone. I spend the next half hour researching ways to stop myself from snoring. To hell if I'm going to be a hindrance to Penny's sleep.

―――

"I JUST DON'T UNDERSTAND why they have to make the show so blue," Penny says as she stands and stretches her arms above her head. My eyes immediately fall to the small patch of skin that comes into view as her shirt gently rides up her stomach. "It's so hard to see. Don't they watch the show themselves? Shouldn't they be like, oh, that's a heavy blue filter, maybe we should change that?"

I release my gaze from her exposed skin and stand as well. "I think they're going for a psychotic vibe with the filter."

"Well, job well done." She shivers dramatically and wraps her arms together. "God, after sweating all day, I'm freezing now."

"Do you want me to make you some tea?"

She shakes her head. "No, that's okay. I think I'm just going to get under the covers."

"Okay."

When she starts toward the bedroom, I follow closely, and just as we reach the door, she looks over her shoulder. "You don't have to go to bed as well."

I shrug. "Nah, I'm tired."

"Okay. You can use the bathroom first. I'm going to change into some warmer clothes."

She takes off toward the dresser, so I go to the bathroom, where I take care of my business and brush my teeth. We just spent the past two hours watching *Ozark*, and I found myself glancing over at Penny from time to time, watching her reaction. She's very much into the show, emotionally invested. She clutched a navy-blue throw pillow the entire time and commented with little oohs and ahhs every once in a while. It was cute.

She's really become more animated around me, which I appreciate. It makes hanging out with her easier and actually really fucking enjoyable. She has a funny personality, and when she's not freaking out about a text message she accidentally sent and is relaxed, I feel this need to get to know her even more.

I walk out of the bathroom to find Penny sitting on the bed in a pair of long johns and a thermal-wear long-sleeve top.

"Ready for your trip up to Alaska?" I ask her with a teasing grin.

"We aren't that far from it." She stands and moves past me. "I foresee myself shedding these clothes in the middle of the night. Please don't freak out if my shirt whacks you in the face, it's just the hormones."

"Take off all the clothes you want."

Once again, she rolls her eyes at me and then retreats to the bathroom. That's when I go to my side of the bed and reach under it, pulling out my *Breathe Right* strips. There won't be any snoring tonight. I fix one over my nose, and just as I'm getting it in place, Penny steps out of the bathroom and sinks herself into the bed, under the sheets.

With my strip in place, I turn over just as she turns toward me, and the moment her eyes land on the *Breathe Right* strip, she tilts her head back and lets out such a loud laugh that I feel myself wince.

"You know, it's not kind to laugh at somebody who is trying to make a change," I say, dabbing at my strip, keeping it in place.

"Oh my God, is that for the snoring?"

I nod. "Yeah, and if this doesn't help, I found a doctor who can help me."

Another guffaw.

A clutch of the blankets and then . . .

Tears of joy stream down her cheeks.

She's laughing so hard that she's actually crying. Talk about a fucking blow to the ego.

"Wow, you sure know how to make a guy want to off himself."

She laughs even harder and holds her stomach now. "Oh my God, that's the best thing I've ever seen."

"It's a fucking *Breathe Right* strip. It's not like I'm wearing a Darth Vader mask to help me breathe better at night."

She waves her hand in front of her as she attempts to catch her breath. "It's not that."

"Then what is it? They don't make these in a nude color. They really should because white is just so obvious."

"No." She swipes at her eyes, collecting her tears. "It's that you actually went out and got them."

"Uh, yeah, because I don't want to keep you up at night. It's bad enough you wake up with nausea."

She laughs some more, and between her giggles, she says, "I was . . . kidding, Eli. You don't snore."

"What?" I say, lifting to a sitting position on the bed. "You were fucking kidding?"

"Yes." She laugh-cries some more, her handle on the humor slipping further and further as she attempts to gather herself, but it's not working.

I snag my phone from the nightstand and shoot a quick text to Taters.

Eli: *You fucker! I bought Breathe Right strips.*

I rip the strip off my nose and toss it to the ground as my eyes water from the pull of the adhesive just as my phone dings with a response. While Penny continues to laugh, I read the message.

Taters: *HAHAHAHAHA. Oh fuck, that made my night.*

Eli: *Go fuck yourself.*

I plug my phone back in and turn toward Penny, who's finally starting to settle down. "You are an asshole."

She chuckles and then lifts from the bed and pulls her shirt over her head and drops it to the side, leaving her in only a tank top. It's a loose tank top, so it doesn't cling to her top half. Rather, it gently molds around her hard nipples.

"Oh, I'm hot now. See, I told you I'd be taking my shirt off."

Yeah, I only wish there was nothing under it.

"Glad I could once again make you hot and bothered." I lie down and turn toward her, tucking my pillow under my head.

"Are you referring to the night we were together?" she asks.

I nod, and since she left her nightstand light on, I maneuver over her and turn it off, shrouding us in darkness. There's just enough light coming from the city for me to see her face.

"Yes, I'm referring to that night."

"I'm pretty sure I'm the one who made *you* hot and bothered."

"What night are you remembering?" I ask. "I had you eating out of my palm."

"Are you delusional?"

"Are you?" I ask.

"No, I remember it like it was yesterday. We were eating pie, and I sucked on your finger. In your head, you pictured it as your penis in my mouth." I chuckle because that's incredibly accurate, and we never discussed this. She just knows guys. "You practically squealed with delight, and then I sat on your lap, and the night was history after that."

"I didn't squeal."

"I heard your mental squeal."

"Telepathic, are you?"

She nods with a smile. "Totally, specializing in hearing guys moan in their minds."

"Wow, quite a gift you have. But that wasn't when the hot and bothered portion of the night began."

"Oh, you think there was a different moment?"

With a cocky grin, I say, "I *know* there was a different moment."

"Oh please, enlighten me. I have to hear this."

"It was when we were at the bar."

"Trust me, nothing but awkward tension happened at the bar."

I shake my head. "Nope. Something happened."

"What was it?"

Grinning, I reply, "When I leaned over and nibbled on your ear."

She goes to respond, but then she shuts her mouth and gives it some thought. When her eyes dart away from me, I know I'm right.

"See, told you. I'm the one who got you hot and bothered, and you just followed suit."

"So what you're saying is you're the reason we're in this predicament right now? Sharing a bed as friends and nothing more while I run through the gauntlet of emotions and internal body temperature?"

I shake my head. "No, the blame rests on the condom company. For if they'd done their job, this never would have happened. In fact, I believe we should start a slander campaign to dismiss them from their duties they are clearly not accomplishing."

"They have warnings on the box."

"I'm quite aware of the warnings."

"And you should have doubled up on protection with one more condom, then maybe we wouldn't have been in this situation."

"If I'd doubled up, I'd have felt absolutely nothing."

She shifts her pillow under her head. "Trust me, from the way you were pounding away, you would have felt something."

I chuckle. "Pounding, huh?"

"Please, spare me. I can't afford to offer you another compliment. Your ego is already big enough as it is."

"You say that as if it's a bad thing."

"Because it is."

"Ego is not a bad thing, it's confidence." I stare into her playful eyes and realize this is exactly what I've been looking for with her. The same fun, teasing behavior we've shared before. It's what made me attach to her that night. Sure, the dress was the main show, but the joking with her, that was icing on the cake. Girls flirt with me—*throw themselves at me*—wherever I go. But it's because I'm Eli Hornsby, Agitator defender. Not simply because I'm Eli. A guy who doesn't want to be fawned over, but likes a good laugh.

"There's a huge difference between being confident and having an ego."

"I can agree to that, but don't you think it's almost a requirement to have an ego as a professional athlete?"

She shakes her head. "No, take Holmes for instance. He is very humble and doesn't parade around like a buffoon searching for compliments, and he's one of the best in the league. Some might say he's paving his way to the Hall of Fame."

I'd be shocked if Holmes wasn't considered for the Hall of Fame whenever he retires. He has a while until that happens, but it just goes to show how great he is.

"You think I act like a buffoon?"

She smirks. "Sometimes."

"Yeah, well . . . you slept with me."

That makes her laugh out loud. "That's the best comeback you can muster?"

"Unfortunately, it is. My brain is only partially functioning at night."

"Well"—she tucks a strand of hair behind her ear—"that would explain all the late-night hookups."

"Haven't had one since you," I admit, which of course wins her undivided attention.

"You haven't had sex since the night we were together?" she asks in such a stunned tone that I almost find it mildly insulting.

"I haven't."

"Seriously? Wow, I mean, I've hooked up with at least eight guys since then, all of them far more endowed than you."

"Is that so?" I ask. "And when you say you've hooked up with eight guys, do you mean eight flag poles? Because that's the only thing bigger than me."

She howls out with laughter and shakes her head. "Guys are so predictable. You mention penis size once and they claim they have the biggest penis in the hemisphere."

"What can I say, I'm not all that different from the rest, other than my obvious good looks, addicting charm, and killer skills on the ice."

"To name a few." She scratches the side of her nose. "We all know what you're good at, so why don't you tell me something you're not good at, or something you're insecure about?"

"If you're looking for a flaw, you're going to need a magnifying glass, because you won't find one without."

She makes a gagging noise. "If you need help, I'm more than happy to offer my opinion."

"Oh, you think I have flaws? Please, delight me with what's wrong on my person."

"Are you sure? I don't think you'll be able to handle the truth."

"Try me," I challenge her.

"Okay, well, besides the snoring . . ." I roll my eyes and she giggles. "I'd have to say your strength in skating backward is average at best."

"Excuse me?" I say, sitting up on my elbow so I can look down at her. "Okay, I thought you were going to say something like I make weird noises when I eat, but you're going to lie there and insult my skating?"

"I warned you." Her smile stretches across her face. It's adorable. It's refreshing. It makes me believe that we're going to be just fine. That we could very much be good friends.

"There's no way I believe you, not unless you have concrete evidence. I fell for the snoring, but I'm not going to believe you when it comes to my skating."

"You do realize I grew up helping Pacey get to where he is, right? I spent many weekends out in the driveway shooting slapshot after slapshot at him until it was too dark to see anymore. I've also dated a few hockey players in the past, not to mention I'm an avid fan. I wouldn't second-guess my knowledge. I know a lot more than you probably think."

Uh . . . now I'm starting to think she's actually serious.

Quietly, as if I say it too loud, the hockey gods might hear me, I say, "Wait, are you being serious? You really think my skating needs work?" When she just gives me a slight shrug, panic swirls in my chest. "Is it my weak calves? I fucking try to build them up as much as I can, but I can't seem to make much of a dent without causing issues with my ankles. Do you think that's it? Fucking weak-as-shit calves."

She slowly brings the blanket up to her mouth, covering it from view. Why is she blocking her mouth? Why are her shoulders slightly shaking? Wait . . . is that a smile I see?

I tear the blanket away from her mouth to see a grin spread so far over her face that I actually gasp. I gasp way too loud, as if I just caught my lover cheating on me. But instead of a lover, it's a new friend trying to shit on my hockey skills.

"I swear to God, woman, if you're joking, I'm going to make sure your life is a living hell."

She laughs now and brings the blanket up and over her head, shielding herself from my deathly glare. My eyes attempt to burn holes through the white sheets, but I fail miserably despite my brain playing tricks on me, making me think I see the start of some smoke.

"Penny Lawes, lower that blanket at once."

"I don't want to."

"Penny . . ."

"May I remind you, I'm pregnant, with child, your child, and things I might say could be out of context. I can't control the emotions." She peeks over the top of the blanket. "You do have smaller calves."

Nostrils flared, I slowly say, "I suggest you take that back, Miss Lawes, or you're not going to like what happens next."

"And what perchance is going to happen next?"

I give it some thought. Normally, if we were romantically involved, I'd do something like pin her down and claim her mouth, but we're not going down that path, therefore, I need to hit her where it hurts.

"You know how there's a whole cinnamon bun in the fridge?"

Her eyes widen with surprise. "You wouldn't."

I shrug. "I have no problem doing the dirty work. You know, unless you want to take what you said back . . ."

She rolls her eyes while lowering the blanket. "Fine, I was only kidding. But you do realize that you are quite perfect, and it's annoying. Therefore, I need to find fault somewhere, even if it's a lie."

I lie back down and stare at the ceiling. I might seem perfect from the outside. I'm not going to lie here and say I'm not attractive. I know that I am—that's not being conceited, it's just facts. And my hockey skills are clearly good enough to warrant a starting position on a professional hockey team. And I'm a decently nice guy as well. But there's a lot about me that is not perfect. I have my flaws, and I know them quite well.

But just because I have them doesn't mean I need to bring them to Penny's attention.

I loved my mom dearly, but growing up before she passed away, all I heard about was my father's inadequacies and her frustrations with him. Penny seems like a good person, and I don't think she'd do the same, but either way, I don't want to feed her fodder.

I'd prefer to remain perfect in her mind.

"Well, keep looking for faults," I say in a teasing tone. "I doubt you'll find any."

Chapter Thirteen

PENNY

Penny: Am I sending this text message to Blakely? Just triple-checking before I state what I need to state.

Blakely: Confirmed, you are texting Blakely, your best friend. You may proceed with all embarrassing things.

Penny: What is the secret password to receive all embarrassing text messages?

Blakely: Penis breath

Penny: And the pin number?

Blakely: 3003 < - - boob

Penny: And your mother's maiden name?

Blakely: Honker Hoo Hoo < - - made up for our benefit

Penny: Lastly, the last four digits of your social security number.

Blakely: 4398

Penny: Processing . . . processing . . .

Blakely: *crosses fingers*

Penny: We have confirmed that you are, in fact, Blakely. Please wait for incoming embarrassment.

Blakely: *pins and needles*
Penny: I threw up in Eli's shoe.
Blakely: WHAT? How?

Penny: He was in the bathroom, taking a shower, and I was in the closet trying to pick out an outfit for the day that didn't touch me in a weird way. Recently, I've been feeling every thread in my clothes, and it's really starting to drive me nuts.

Blakely: It's an odd pregnancy side effect. I'll agree to that. But please, back to the shoe.

Penny: I was attempting to pick out an outfit when a bout of nausea hit me. Since I haven't thrown up since I started having morning sickness, I didn't think much of it, but then I started to sweat.

Blakely: The sweats, nothing speaks more like a warning flag than the sweats.

Penny: And I wasn't about to barge through the bathroom door, because he was naked and in the shower. I felt something coming up soon, so I found the closest vessel I could find, and it happened to be Eli's shoe.

Blakely: Please describe the shoe.

Penny: Black loafer that he wears often with his suits, bedazzled in my regurgitated food.

Blakely: I know precisely what pair you're talking about.

Penny: I threw up in it, and then I realized I threw up in a shoe and then threw up again. Strangely, my accuracy was impeccable.

Blakely: What did you do with the shoe?

Penny: That's the worst part. Eli was looking for those particular shoes to wear to the arena today. He said they're his lucky shoes against the Freeze.

Blakely: Did you give him the puke-soaked shoe?

Penny: No! Are you insane? I couldn't tell him I just puked in his shoe.

Blakely: Then what did you do?

Penny: *winces* Threw it out the window.

Blakely: WHAT?

Penny: I know, I know. I panicked. When he left, I retrieved the shoe, but it needs a solid cleaning, and I'm not sure how to get puke out of a shoe.

Blakely: Is that why you're not at work right now?

Penny: *Correct. Puke shoe is in the bathroom sink, and I'm pacing, trying to figure out how to fix this.*

Blakely: *Do you have any of that OxiClean stuff? I heard it works well.*

Penny: *Will it bleach the shoe?*

Blakely: *I don't think there's bleach in it . . . is there? Uh, I don't know.*

Penny: *Not helpful . . . wait, oh God! He's home. HE'S HOME!*

Blakely: *Plot twist!*

Penny: *You're not helpful.*

Blakely: *FaceTime me, I want to see his reaction.*

Penny: *You are dead to me.*

"Penny, are you here?" Eli's voice calls through the apartment. The rumble of his voice is normally soothing, but right now, at this moment, all it does is send a frightful chill up my spine.

What the hell is he doing here?

Shouldn't he be at the arena doing hockey things? Getting ready for the game? Pumping some iron—I've never said that in my entire life—or perhaps taping up a stick? Why is he here? In this apartment, in the middle of my puke shoe crisis!

Does he have a radar that tells him when I'm in an embarrassing, compromised situation, prompting him to report to my side immediately?

"Penny?"

Panic consumes me as his voice grows louder. Oh God, he's not going to go away. He can't see me like this, all frazzled, and he sure as hell can't see his shoe!

"Penny?" AHHHH! His voice is growing closer by the second. Think . . . think.

Paused in the middle of the bedroom, I look to the left, look to the right, think about burying myself under the bed . . . wait, that could work, but the shoe is in the bathroom . . .

And his footsteps are growing closer.

Me or the shoe.

Me . . . or the shoe.

I don't have time to react. I don't even have a moment to stick half my leg under the bed to hide before the bedroom door parts open.

He's here.

Fear creeps up the back of my neck.

My stomach churns in a nasty shade of green, revisiting the nausea from this morning, but this is different. This is the being caught red-handed kind of nausea.

He's going to see the shoe.

He's going to see my panic.

He'll smell the puke . . .

I can't avoid the inevitable, but I can come up with one hell of a story.

That's right. I can lie through my teeth.

Cracks knuckles Let's get down to business. *Come up with the most elaborate story of your entire life.*

The door fully opens, and when Eli comes into view, immediate relief floods through his eyes right before confusion hits them. "Are you okay?" he asks. "You weren't at the arena. I went to your office to see if you needed anything, and one of the girls up there said you didn't come in this morning. I wanted to check to make sure you were okay."

Ugh, duh, of course he'd check on me the one day I didn't go into work. Since we have to work nights and weekends, we have a pretty flexible schedule, so no one really bats an eyelash when someone doesn't show up in the morning. But Mr. Nosy Nelly over here was worried.

Trying to act as casual as possible, I say, "Oh, yeah. Fine. You know, flexible hours and everything." I smile, but it turns out to be more of a flat smile rather than one that reaches my eyes. Anyone would be able to discern this attempt of feigned casual behavior. Eli being no exception.

"Then why are you wearing your dress inside out, and your hair is half curled?"

Inside out? Really?

I glance down at my dress . . . and would you look at that. It is inside out. God, would I have gone out in public like this? I want to say I would have realized, but then again, I used my lotion as toothpaste the other day, so I can't be sure.

But no need to show him that I'm on the verge of completely losing my marbles, so I say, "The pressure of dressing oneself can be very overwhelming. Mistakes are bound to happen." I move toward him and attempt to direct him away from the bathroom. "Now if that is all, we should probably move you along, you know, so you can get back to your busy schedule."

Despite not having his lucky shoes, he's wearing a forest-green suit with a black button-up, the top two buttons undone—because that's what he does. He likes to flash his man pecs to the world and when I say flash, I mean barely give us a glimpse. It's maddening. Either show it all or don't show anything at all. Instead of his beloved shoes, he's sporting a green, velvet loafer with gold embellishment that not every man would be able to pull off. But Eli, well, with those ankles, he can pretty much wear any shoe.

His style is absolutely impeccable. I'm not sure when it happened, how he came to be so stylish with such raw, sexual magnetism while wearing a freaking suit, but it happened and he's perfected his work to the point that he makes grown women —and even grandmas—weep when he walks by. And here I am, hair half curled and my dress inside out, with a faint glistening of sweat still on the back of my neck from my morning nausea. Not to mention, I have a heinous zit on my chin that has claimed squatter's rights for the undesirable future. I think my nose has grown, can't be sure, but it doesn't look right, and I plucked a black hair from my cheek today. A black freaking hair! I can safely say I feel like a grisly ogre with one tooth hanging out of its mouth, especially next to this handsome, smooth, suave man.

God . . . it makes me want to just kick him in the nose.

"Why are you being weird?" he asks as I push at his back, trying to shove him out of the bedroom, but he remains unmoving.

Attractive and strong . . . so very strong.

"I'm not being weird. You're being weird," I respond like the mature adult that I am.

"I'm not being weird." He turns to face me. "You're acting like you're hiding something." And then as if the answer crosses his mind, his eyes go wide, and he says, "Oh shit, do you . . . do you uh, have someone here?"

He can't possibly be serious. What would I even do with a man right now? Introduce him to my witch zit? Tell him I've never in my life had an actual third eye on my face before. Ask him to braid my cheek hair? Or would I show him how bloated my stomach is, give him a little shimmy of my protruding stomach from what I can only assume is gas, since it's too early to be showing baby just yet. Maybe introduce him to the farts. Or better yet, give him a detailed tour of exactly where I threw up this morning and maybe a reenactment.

"You have absolutely lost your mind if you think I'd even consider having a man here," I say. "I am in no state of mind or body to welcome any gentleman lovers into this." I motion to my body up and down. "Do you understand the kind of nausea I sit through every morning? Or the throat-burning indigestion I suffer through at night? Or how about the constant tingling of my nipples that is in no way sensual and every bit annoying? This sex shop is closed. So you can get that right out of your mind. Plus, why would I want to date anyone in this condition? Pregnant with another man's child doesn't necessarily say single and ready to mingle."

He grips the back of his neck, pulling on it tightly. "Yeah, but you know, if you wanted to—"

"Did you just hear what I said?"

"I did. I really did, but just throwing it out there."

"Don't bother. I don't even want to think about men or dating or sex or anything romantic at all. I don't even want to see a couple holding hands. That's how repulsed I am by it all. This vessel"—I motion to my body—"is sailing some rocky seas right now. No one wants to come near it. And I sure as hell don't want anyone clogging up any holes of mine, if you get what I'm saying."

"Loud and clear." He glances to the side, his eyes traveling the room, clearly wanting to abort *that* conversation. "Then what's going on?"

"Nothing, okay? Just weird pregnancy things that I don't care to talk to you about. A little bit of privacy is not going to kill you." I push him again. "Now, excuse me while I attempt to finish my hair so I can look somewhat presentable at work."

He pauses and looks me up and down. "I know you're not going to believe me when I say this, but you look nice."

I take a calming breath and close my eyes. Speaking through very clenched teeth, I say, "My dress is inside out, Eli. How on earth do I look nice?" Do not lose it on him. He's clearly lost all ability to read the room. It's not his fault he's an idiot. Sometimes, you're just made that way.

I give him another nudge, and to my delight, he starts walking out of the bedroom. Thank God for small miracles. "I mean, it would be nice if the other half of your hair is curled, but if you don't go that route, I think you can pull it off."

I pause. What did he just say?

"Are you really going to say something like that to an emotional wreck of a woman?"

"I guess not."

"Do you hear the psychosis in my voice, Eli?" He nods. "Then choose your words wisely."

His nostrils flare as he nods. "Noted, don't mention appearance or that you have toothpaste in the corner of your mouth."

What?

Heat enrages me, and I point at the door, shouting, "Out!"

"Yup, saw that coming." He starts to leave just as he snaps his fingers in the air and says, "Oh shit, can't forget my deodorant."

And before I can grasp his arm and hold him back, he moves past me and straight into the bathroom. The word "noooooooooooooo" is on the tip of my tongue as I watch him pause at the sink.

He looks back at me and then points at his shoe. "Why is my shoe in the sink?"

For the love of God, why?

Why are you doing this to me?

Especially on a day like today when I look like Shrek's ugly friend Elmira with the third eye.

WHY?

I'll tell you freaking why because my luck, when it comes to dignity during this season of my life, has absolutely run out. Actually, I don't think I've ever had any dignity since Eli fertilized me. Nope, it was stripped away from me. Apparently, it is not only my responsibility to carry this child but to suffer wild embarrassment the entire time as well.

Fine.

I accept it.

What's next, universe? Do I pee my pants in front of the man?

Oh God, I take that back. I didn't put that out there. Please, please don't let that happen. I'd never survive. Farting, sure. Puke in the shoe, okay. But peeing my pants . . . No, there's no coming back from that.

I'm blasted right back to the present when I hear, "Fuck, what's that smell?"

My vomit.

That is my wet vomit you're smelling, you beautiful nimrod!

"What smell?" I ask, playing nonchalant. Be cool, Penny, be cool. This is your moment to shine. Story time. *Mentally rubs hands together* We are taking back our dignity! "If you're smelling anything, then you're probably smelling the beginning of athlete's foot. You don't wear socks with loafers, so mold and creep are bound to accrue. Maybe consider a different shoe, something less showy and instead, more practical."

Oooo, good one! Not only did you deter, but you insulted the ridiculously gorgeous grossed-out man in front of you.

I move away from the bathroom, happy with my response

and hoping he follows, but when he doesn't, I know there's a slight possibility that my story is not settling well in his head.

"That is not athlete's foot." I glance over my shoulder just in time for him to look closer. His eyes shoot to mine, and he asks, "Is that vomit in my shoe?"

What is he, Inspector Gadget? Jesus.

Seems as though there are brains with the beauty.

"You know, I think I'm just going to throw my hair up in a bun and get to work. If you will excuse me—"

"Penny, why is there vomit in my shoe?"

Hands on my hips and back turned toward him, I say, "I don't know, Eli. Maybe you should check within yourself to see why there's vomit in your shoe."

I start to walk away, but the nimble beast scoots in front of me, halting me from my retreat. He places his large hands on my shoulders and bends in the knee so we're eye to eye. With serious but also compassionate eyes, he asks, "Penny . . . did you throw up in my shoe this morning, then hide my shoes so I wouldn't notice?"

"Ha." I guffaw so loudly, I startle the both of us. "What a far-fetched, entirely factitious thought."

"Penny . . ." He pins me with a glare.

What's the use?

Honestly, I've been caught red-handed, so just deal with the consequences.

I throw my hands up in the air and surrender, my white flag waving in chagrin.

"Fine. Yes, I threw up in your shoe, and you should be happy it wasn't one of your suit bags. Because that was a close second. And before you get all mad because that's your lucky shoe, I would highly recommend taking a step back to realize that I am carrying child, and anything I do for the duration of this preg-nancy can't be held against me." I fold my arms over my chest and raise my chin high. There, he has been told.

I prep myself for him to be mad. For him to moan and groan about his favorite shoes being tarnished with my technicolor—

winces—upchuck. My mind forms comebacks, resting them on the tip of my tongue, ready to be fired off in defense. Like a stockade, ready to banish any emotion on his end, I mentally get in my stance, tongue ready to lash. *I shall take you down, dear sir, do not mess with these hormones.*

His hands move closer to my neck, and I immediately sense where this is going. There's no doubt in my foggy, dense-filled brain what's about to happen. That's right, folks. He's about to put me in a good old-fashioned chokehold for tarnishing his shoes. Gasp, I know. But I can feel it. Sense it. He's mad about his shoe. He's about to choke me. I can see it in his feral eyes. Too bad for his manhood, I'm two steps ahead of him. He's going to wring my neck, but not before I get a good swift kick to the crotch ready.

Unprotected strike zone, that's your problem, man.

And before I can stop myself, I whip my leg back and then toss it forward, right into his junk. "Don't you dare try to choke me over a shoe," I yell out as a war cry.

A loud gurgling sound echoes against the walls, followed by a slow descent to the ground. His knees hit first, and then his body as he cripples over on his side.

Huzzah!

Thou shall not battle the holy one in gestation.

She might be nauseous, and she very well might have enough indigestion to burn down a thousand buildings at night, but she is mighty, and she knows how to pack a solid blow to the very nutsac that put her in this position.

"Holy . . . fuck," he groans, cupping his sensitive niblets. "Why?"

"Why?" I blink down at him. "Uh, I wasn't about to allow you to choke me over a shoe."

"Choke . . . you?" he asks, still groaning. "Fuck, Penny. I was going to ask if you were okay. Why would I choke you?"

Um . . . what was that?

Blinks

He was going to ask if I was okay?

Hmm . . . where did I go wrong?

"Fucking Christ," he groans some more, now covering his eyes with his arm.

Well, now I feel kind of bad.

With my toe, I nudge his shoulder. "You okay, sailor?"

"Does it look like I'm okay?" he shoots back, rage and pain lacing his every word.

"Not really, but I wasn't sure if you were dusting off your acting chops."

Red in the face, neck muscles bulging, he looks up at me and says, "I'm not fucking acting."

I nod continuously as my hands twist together. "Okay, noted. Not acting. Got it. Well, then. I guess this was all just a silly misunderstanding." I attempt a laugh, but it comes out strangled.

He takes a few deep breaths and then slowly sits up, but still clutching his crotch. "Fuck," he mutters before one more deep breath. After a few seconds, he looks up at me. "Why would I want to choke you?"

"Uh . . ." I toe the ground. "Angry about the shoe?"

"You think I'm going to choke a pregnant woman over a shoe?"

"I don't know!" I toss my arms up in the air. "Who knows the kind of anger levels you might have. I'm still getting to know you, and honestly, from what I've seen on the ice, you have a temper. How do I know it doesn't carry into the household? These are things we need to learn about each other, Eli."

He pinches his brow, clearly still suffering in pain. "Penny, for your future reference, please know, I'll never . . . ever try to choke you or physically harm you in any way. Got it?"

I tap the side of my head. "Yes. Logging that nugget in. Good to know."

"Jesus." He takes the next minute to stand to his feet, moving entirely too slow if you ask me. Does it really hurt that bad? Or are men just weak? After another deep breath, he looks me in the eyes, and the anger has disappeared as he says, "Penny, you threw up in my shoe. Are you okay?"

You okay, sailor?

MEGHAN QUINN

"It's just a shoe, Eli. It's not like I threw up on your dog . . . wait . . ." I tilt my head to the side and say, "Did you ask if I was okay?"

"Yes." He lessens the space between us despite the evident pain he's still in. "You threw up, and you haven't done that yet. I want to make sure you're okay."

He's not concerned about his shoe?

He doesn't think I just tainted his bad luck?

He doesn't want to choke me?

He actually cares about me more than his shoe?

That's . . . well . . . that's just the nicest thing.

Tears well up in my eyes and cascade down my cheeks in seconds. "I'm more important than your shoe," I say.

"Hell, of course you are, Penny." He lets out a frustrated breath. "Why would I think my shoe is more important than you?"

"It's your special shoe that you like to wear when we play the Freeze, and I took that away from you. And not only did I take it away but I also did inconceivable things inside said shoe."

"It's just a shoe." He reaches up and swipes away my tears with his thumbs. "I'm more concerned with how you're feeling."

Of course he is, because not only is he beyond gorgeous, but he's considerate as well.

Great. Just freaking great!

More tears.

I can't stop them. I can't control them. I can't even tell myself that everything is okay. It's as if I have lost any authority over my body.

"I'm embarrassed," I reply. "I wish I wasn't crying right now and that this was all some sort of nightmare I haven't woken up from yet."

"No need to be embarrassed," he says while pulling me into a hug. He wraps his strong, comforting arms around my shoulders, but I stand there ramrod straight, not sure if I should touch him or not. He smells so good, like yummy man. Not the best description, but that's all I have. Yummy man. And I know if I

166

wrap my arms around him, I might not let go, as this has all been so scary, so different, so challenging. The comfort of his arms very well might make me melt. "And I believe the crying is bound to happen when you're pregnant. At least from what I've read."

That makes me shoot off him, putting at least two feet of distance between us.

I swipe at my cheeks as panic sears through me. "What have you read?"

My panic mirrors his as we both stare at each other. "Uh . . . just an article."

"What kind of article?" I ask him.

"You know." He swallows. "The kind that is sent to me every week to tell me what you will be experiencing and how I can help you. And before you get mad, I know you told me not to read anything, but I can't just sit back and not know what you're going through. This is helpful to me."

"So do you just look at me and say, oh, that's her being emotional because her hormones are out of whack?"

"Yeah, kind of, but it's better than me thinking, wow, she's a complete psycho."

"Do I look like a psycho?" I ask, pointing at my chest, and I can see him searching for the right words to answer.

"You look like you're scared and are unsure of everything that's happening to you right now, so I think it's good that I educate myself so I can help you along the way."

Well . . . would you look at that. He knows just what to say . . . . that's . . . that's really nice.

And once again, my eyes well, and I break down in tears.

"I'm such a mess," I say as he pulls me into a hug. This time, I wrap my arms around him and rest my cheek on his black shirt, very much aware that he'll probably have to change it before he leaves. "I'm sorry."

His hand falls to the back of my head. "Don't apologize. It's okay."

"I'm losing it."

"You're going through a lot, and that's okay. That's why I'm here, to help you through it."

I glance up at him. "So this is the Hornsby Winnie was talking about."

His brow pinches together with humor. "What does that mean?"

"She said when she first got to the cabin last year, you were the nicest one at first and were the reason she felt she could stay for the night. This is the guy."

"What guy have I been to you?"

"Flirty at first, followed by alpha in the sheets—that's how we ended up having sex. Then awkward. Uncomfortable. Nervous. And now I'm seeing the kind."

"Only took me a bit." He chuckles. "But this is who you'll get from now on." He gives me a good squeeze. "Promise."

Then I guess I'm a very lucky girl.

Chapter Fourteen

ELI

"Those aren't the shoes you wear when we play the Freeze," Taters says while we both head to the locker room in preparation for game time.

"I'm well aware."

"Are you trying to jeopardize our chances tonight?"

"My shoes were incapacitated for tonight."

"What the hell does that mean?"

I consider telling him everything that happened this morning, from the vomit to the kick to the cock, but I realize it's probably not in my best interest to share what Penny's going through. She was embarrassed enough as it is. The last thing she needs is for the rest of the Agitators to know what's going on between the walls of the apartment.

"Nothing you need to worry about." I nudge him with my shoulder. "Are you ready for tonight?"

"When am I not ready?"

"The other day, you weren't. You actually sucked."

"Coming from the guy who couldn't check a duster in the boards if his life depended on it."

"I'm going through some things right now," I defend.

"Yeah, well . . . you're not the only one."

"What does that mean?" I ask just as I hear footsteps behind us.

"Wait up, you guys," Posey says, jogging after us. I glance over just to see him reach me with a bag of gummy bears in hand. He presses it against my chest when he catches up, and he says, "To refill your stash. Can't have you not have your lucky bears before a game." He glances down at my shoes. "Hey, those aren't the right shoes."

Groaning, I say, "I know. Enough with the shoes, okay?"

"What did I just walk in on?" Posey asks, hands held up.

"Apparently, his shoes are incapacitated," Taters says.

"And apparently, Taters is going through something emotional right now."

"With Sarah, I know," Posey says haphazardly and then winces while quickly making eye contact with Taters. "Uh, I mean . . . I don't know what you're talking about."

I pause in the hallway and turn toward Taters. "Are you seeing her again?"

"The other night," Posey answers, only to receive a death glare from Taters. "Uh, you know, I'm actually going to jog ahead of you guys. Warm up the legs a bit." And then he takes off.

"I don't want to hear it," Taters says, moving forward as well.

"Dude, she's fucking with you."

"You don't know that," he answers. "You have no fucking clue what we talked about."

"Then what did you discuss?" I ask.

"Why don't you worry about Pacey's sister who you got pregnant and stay out of my personal life." Before I can stop him, he picks up his pace as well and heads down the hallway.

What the actual fuck? When has he ever not told me anything? He shares everything with me. What's changed?

Gummy bears in hand, I start down the hall and realize I don't want to head to the locker room just yet, not after that "delightful" conversation, so instead, I move toward the offices. I'm going to check on Penny one more time before I can't because I'm strapped to the ice for our game.

⸺

"GOOD LUCK TONIGHT," someone says as I walk through the hallway. I wish I knew everyone's names who works for the team, but unfortunately, I don't spend enough time here to grow familiar. Instead, I offer a fist bump and keep moving toward Penny's office.

"Looking good," one of the guys from marketing says as he moves past me. "Hey, where are the lucky shoes?"

Note to self, don't designate wardrobe anymore. It only creates a hassle in the long run.

"Got them dirty," I say. "These will work, though." I offer the guy a wink, which feels odd, but I don't know what else to do, and make the right at the hallway toward Penny's office.

When I reach her door, I give it a slight knock and then let myself in, only to stop dead in my tracks when I see another man in her office.

But not just any man . . . Remi Gasper.

What the actual fuck?

"Gasper," I say, straightening up. "What the hell are you doing here?"

He stands from the chair situated across from Penny and buttons his suit jacket. "Just saying hello to an old friend," he answers, with that aggravating grin of his. "Good to see you too, Hornsby."

Penny stands, and the worried expression that crosses her face snaps me out of my tunnel vision of wanting to chuck this guy through her glass door. "Well, you said hi, now you can move along."

He smirks even wider and then walks around Penny's desk,

where he pulls her into a hug and drops a kiss on the top of her head. "Think about dinner, okay? Would love to spend more time with you."

Dinner? Over my dead fucking body.

He lets Penny go and moves toward me, where his shoulder bumps into mine. "Still see you believe gummy bears will help you. Laughable, dude. See you out on the ice," he says before moving out of the door and shutting it behind him.

"Hey, Eli—"

"How the hell do you know him?"

Her eyes draw into concern. "What do you mean? I grew up with him. He was good friends with Pacey. They played together for a long time."

For some reason, that rings a bell. Pacey's never said too much about Gasper because he knows how much everyone on the team absolutely hates him, and for good reason. If only he knew Gasper was behind why I wasn't there to help Holden. Something makes me think Pacey wouldn't want to be friends with him much longer.

"Is there something going on between the two of you?" I ask.

"Are you serious? Eli, I just told you this morning I don't have time or energy for that. Can you not understand that? And what does it matter? It's not like you and I are together. You don't have claim over me."

"I don't want that fucker around my baby."

"*Your* baby?" she asks, folding her arms, preparing for battle.

"I mean our baby," I attempt to correct myself. "He's a shit person."

"No, he's not," she defends, which of course raises my anger to the next level. "Do you even know him?"

"Yeah, I fucking do. He's the reason at least three guys on our team have been blasted in the backs of the knees by his stick. He plays dirty and will do anything to win, even if that means doing something that's possibly career-ending. And you're friends with him?"

"He is aggressive but not purposeful with what he does."

"Are you really defending him right now?" I hold my arms out, one hand still gripping the stupid five-pound bag of gummy bears.

"Are you really in my office yelling at me?" she asks.

Bringing my arms back, I take a deep breath. "You shouldn't be hanging out with him, and you definitely will not be going out to dinner with him."

"Excuse me? Are you now telling me what I can and cannot be doing?"

"I'm trying to educate you."

From the way her eyes light on fire, I can immediately tell that was the wrong thing to say.

"I don't need you to *educate* me," she says through clenched teeth. "I know Remi. You only see him during the games. I know him outside of hockey. And he's a good man. He's been very helpful toward our family over the years and cares about the same things we care about. He's helped Pacey with his charities and has given a lot back to our hometown. Sure, he can get excited during a game, but that doesn't define him."

"The way you act on the ice is a direct depiction of who you are as a man," I say. "And there's no honor in his body." Not wanting to discuss this anymore, I turn toward the door, ready to walk out when I remember what I came up here for. Gripping the doorframe, I ask, "How are you feeling?"

"Go to hell, Eli," she says, and I take that as just fine.

"DUDE, your vibe is not really settling me right now," Posey says next to me as we warm up. "You're all charged up."

I am.

I'm fucking ready to go.

My eyes haven't left Gasper since I got on the ice. I've watched him skate around, stretch, and even joke around with a few of the guys on both teams. Three years ago, we were playing game seven in the playoffs that would grant us a spot for a try at the cup. Game was tied. It was the third period. He took a cheap shot at Holmes and knocked him to the ground. The ref ignored the attempt to take out our center, blatantly favoring Gasper. Holmes was out with an injury, and they ended up taking the win. That was the moment I started hating this guy.

What solidified my hatred for him . . . well, we all know that by now.

"Just ready for the game," I say, gripping my stick tightly.

"Okay, because it doesn't quite look like you're ready for the game. It looks like you're ready to murder."

Yeah, that too.

"Did you have some gummy bears?" he continues. "Because I can have Hank run back to the locker room and grab you some."

"I'm fine." I pat him on the shoulder and skate to the bench, where I pick up my water bottle, giving it a good squirt into my mouth.

The teams are rounded up, and we get ready for the national anthem. We all line up, and as we parade through the beginning ceremonies, I keep my mind mentally set on one thing and one thing only—making sure Gasper has one hell of a shitty game.

I'm fired up.

I'm ready to take him out.

And nothing, and I mean nothing is going to stop me.

Once the national anthem is over, we all skate into our positions. The refs are huddled together as Gasper skates up to me. That fucking grin on his face makes me want to shove my elbow into his teeth.

"So, you and Penny, huh?" he asks, and I know what he's trying to do. He's trying to goad me like he always does.

I don't answer him, but instead, I grip my stick tighter and get into position, ready for the puck to drop. Taking the hint that we're not here to have tea and gab, he does the same. He presses his shoulder against mine and slaps his stick on the ice.

"I'm surprised Pacey even let you near her." He's just loud enough for me to hear him over the roar of the crowd and the announcers. "I thought I was the only hockey player he trusted around her."

My teeth grind together as my hands grip my stick so tightly I'm afraid I might snap it in half before the game even starts.

"Seems as though things have changed, though. At least what I gathered. You looked protective. You like her, Hornsby?"

I keep my mouth shut and stare at the ice, willing the refs to hurry the fuck up so I can do some damage . . . undetected.

"Don't want to talk about it? I get it," he says, his voice dark . . . sinister. "Hard to talk about Penny Lawes without wanting to talk about all of her attributes."

Don't do something stupid. Keep it together. He's poking you for a reason, to get you to react, to get you to hurt the team and make this win an easy one for him.

"Fucking great tits, right?"

And . . .

I explode.

You can't talk about my goddamn Penny like that and get away with it.

I turn on him so fast that he's not expecting it. I drop my stick, and I clock him right in the helmet before shucking my gloves and helmet and barreling into him, bringing him down to the ground where I straddle his body.

But he's quick and well-trained, and he rolls me over and blasts me in the face with a punch before I roll him over and swing, clocking him in the nose. That's as far as we go before we're pulled away from each other by our teammates.

"What the fuck?" Posey says, holding me by the arms while Pacey stands between Gasper and me. His eyes pierce me.

"He's saying shit about your sister," I say, spitting out blood before I'm taken to the bench where I know I'll be serving a ten-minute misconduct penalty.

"The game hasn't even started, you fuckhead," Taters says, coming up to me as well. "You're giving us a disadvantage."

"He was saying shit about Penny."

"To get under your skin." Taters tosses my helmet at me, which I catch. "Jesus fuck. We did not need that right now."

"I'm not going to let him—"

All hell breaks out on the ice again, but this time, it's Pacey who's in the mix of it all, pulling Gasper's jersey over his head while throwing uppercuts. I hop off the bench, scale the boards, and then skate out to the ice along with our teammates as we get into a five-minute brawl with the Polar Freeze.

Needless to say . . . we lose the game.

But the fans were entertained.

—

PACEY: *What the fuck did he say?*

I'm sitting in my car, outside of Penny's apartment, not excited to go inside out of fear of what she's going to say to me. After the loss, we received a blistering speech from our coach, who threw a few hockey sticks at a table in the middle of the locker room, knocking over some food. He apologized to the staff, helped them clean it up, and then we quietly all went our own ways. We were never able to recover after losing Pacey and me for ten minutes, and the loss did not come at the best time since we are racing to the finish line to make it to the playoffs.

I'm to blame for the loss.

I still have no idea what came over me. Like Penny said, we're not dating, I have no claim over her, yet today I acted like a jealous boyfriend, a title I've never worn in my entire life.

Staring down at my phone, I text Pacey back.

Eli: *You don't want to know.*

The only bright side of this entire night is that Pacey actually looked at me after the fight. In the locker room, he gave me an appreciative nod. And right now, he's texting me. It might not be what I want to discuss, but it's an open door that I'll take.

Pacey: *If I didn't want to know, I wouldn't have asked.*

Fair enough.

Eli: He was goading me about Penny, and then right before I clocked him, he talked about her tits.

Pacey: I'm going to fucking murder him.

Eli: Easy, killer. Wait until after the season. I shouldn't have reacted tonight. He cost us the win.

Pacey: No one talks about Penny like that and gets away with it. You did the right thing. Thank you.

And just like that, as I stare down at the text from Pacey, the weight that I've been carrying around for the past few weeks over my broken relationship with one of my best friends slides off my shoulders. In the heat of the moment, I wasn't thinking about the consequences of sleeping with his sister, and even after, I didn't think much of it because neither of us was going to say anything. But it's been painful not having him to talk to since he found out. Not hanging out with him. Basically living in a Pacey-induced exile. I can only hope that things will change now. Or at least start to change.

Eli: You may not believe it, but I do care about her, dude.

Pacey: In what way?

Eli: Just as a friend.

I text him quickly back so I can clarify my intention. I feel like I might be on the verge of patching things up with him. The last thing I need is to spoil that.

Pacey: Good. She needs someone reliable in her life, not a hockey player who is in and out every week.

Someone reliable? Did I not just get penalized for ten minutes today because I stood up for his sister? Have I not been living with her for a few weeks, making sure she's okay? And I haven't said a goddamn thing about it because it's my responsibility. That seems pretty reliable to me.

Eli: I'm taking care of her.

Pacey: And I appreciate that. But you and I both know you're not the settling down type and that she needs someone who will treat her like she's the center of their world.

I mull that over, as it doesn't sit well with me. He's not wrong. Penny does deserve someone who will make her the center of his world. And sure, we've said time and time again, we're friends, that's all we'll ever be, and we both don't want to get involved romantically. But given all of that, I don't like someone telling me I'm not good enough. That is shitty. That doesn't feel good.

And maybe, I'm not. Maybe in the grand scheme of things, he's right. I very well might not be good enough for her. I might be good for her now, given the situation, but . . . would I be good for her later?

My phone buzzes in my hand again.

Pacey: You two aren't meant for each other. Learn how to co-parent now because that's all it will ever be.

Okay, yes, that's all I want. We both want that. We don't want to start anything serious. But in the back of my mind, I can't help but be consumed by the insult that rattles through my prideful chest.

Eli: Don't worry, there's nothing romantic going on. She's the mother of my child. That's it.

His response is nearly immediate.

Pacey: And that's what it should always be. Respect me and my wishes that much.

Irritated, I shove my phone in my pocket, grab my bag, and head up to Penny's apartment. Just from the outside, I can see that her lights are off. Not sure if she's tired or just ignoring me, but there's only one way to find out.

I make my way up the stairs, and when I reach the front door, I unlock it and slowly let myself in, trying not to make too much noise in case she's asleep.

The apartment is pitch-black, but when I turn on the entryway light, I'm greeted by a pillow and blanket neatly folded on the living room couch.

Hmm, wonder where I'll be sleeping tonight?

Fucking great. I can't help recall the words I said to Penny earlier today.

"The way you act on the ice is a direct depiction of who you are as a man." And then she saw me go apeshit on *her friend*.

Yeah, I'm fucked.

I set my bag down in the entryway and move to the couch, where I toss the pillow to the end and then unfold the blanket haphazardly. When my "bed" is set up, I head toward the bedroom so I can use the bathroom. That's when I see a sliver of light under the door.

She's awake.

Unbuttoning my suit jacket, I make my way to the bedroom door and slowly turn the handle, wincing the entire time and hoping that it isn't locked. When I realize it's not, I push open the door only slightly and poke my head in. I see her lying in bed. The nightstand light is on, and she's reading a book.

I push the door farther open and take a step inside.

"Hey," I say while removing my jacket.

Her eyes don't leave her book as she says, "Did you see the blanket and pillow?"

"Yup, got your suggestion loud and clear. Just need to brush my teeth and change, and I'll be out of your way." I walk toward the closet and strip down to my briefs which are fresh from my shower. I slip on a pair of shorts and then make my way to the bathroom. I catch her eyes on me for a moment, so I pause and say, "For what it's worth, he said some stupid shit about you. That's why I punched him."

"I don't care what he said," she fires back. "Do you really think I want our child seeing that?"

I'm about to enter the bathroom, but I stop and turn toward her. "You realize I play hockey, and that's what we do. Your brother was part of the fight too."

"And he knows how unhappy I am. I don't want this baby coming into the world thinking it's okay to punch someone whenever they feel like it. How do you think I'd explain that if our son or daughter saw it? Oh, it's just hockey, no big deal."

"He was talking about your tits," I say. "What the hell was I supposed to do?"

"Ignore him," she shouts at me. "That's what Gasper does. He's an instigator. He was trying to get you riled up, he

179

succeeded, and they ended up winning the game because you lost control of your temper."

"Because of what he said about you. Don't I get any credit for being valiant?"

"I don't need a white knight, Eli. I need someone I can depend on."

"And clearly, just like your brother, you don't think I can be that person."

"Not after what I saw tonight. Seriously, you let him get under your skin, and you have a loss and a fat lip to show for it." She slow claps. "Wow, great job, Eli."

"Well . . . maybe if you didn't throw up in my shoe, none of this would have happened," I counter back because I'm the biggest moron on the face of the earth.

She sits up now. "You're really going to blame my morning sickness for this? Is that the road you want to take?"

I scrub my hand over my face. "No, that's not what I want to do. But . . . hell, Penny, he acted like you two have fucked in the past, and I didn't like the way he was talking about it."

She stands and closes the space between us so she's only a few inches from me. She's wearing a silk shirt that clings to her hardened nipples, and the shorts she's paired them with match exactly with a lace trim at the hem. And she smells fresh, good, like she just got out of the shower. Combine that all with the fiery spirit igniting through her eyes, and I feel that yearning for her all over again, that burning desire that's never stopped since my birthday.

"First of all, Remi and I have never done anything like that, ever. Second, it shouldn't matter if we have because we're not on that level. You and I are just trying to co-exist with this child. And thirdly, you are not in charge of me, nor are you in charge of defending me. I can hold my own, I don't need you stepping in."

"So I should have just let him say shit about you? Is that what you want?"

"I want you to realize that what you did was reckless, and something could have happened to you. And then what do I do?

How do I explain that to a child who might be watching you on TV? How do I tell them that kind of behavior is unacceptable, yet Daddy can do it? I can't." She pokes me in the chest. "So that means you need to get your shit together."

"You act like I fight all the goddamn time."

"Once is enough to know you can't be doing that anymore."

"It's part of the game, Penny," I bemoan.

"It was a personal attack, and you know it. The puck hadn't even dropped. You were just waiting for him to say something to justify your reaction."

"Are you really defending him?" I ask.

"You're impossible," she says while attempting to walk past me, but I snag her by the waist, keeping her close. Her hair brushes over my bare shoulder, like silky strands enticing me. I push her hair behind her ear slowly, and I lower my head so I'm speaking close to her ear.

"I wasn't putting up with shit that came out of his mouth about you, and I'm going to tell you right now, I won't be putting up with it in the future. No one speaks about you like that, even if you're just my friend. Got it?"

Her breath catches as her eyes travel up to mine. Intense, locked. They stay on mine for a second, then two, then three. I watch as she swallows carefully, her breath vibrating against my hand just as she looks away. Without a word, she slips into the bathroom and shuts the door behind her.

Looks like I'll be waiting to brush my teeth.

Chapter Fifteen

PENNY

"Pizza is here," Winnie calls out as she barges through my door. "And some side salads of course because fiber is something we all need."

"You can just bring it over here and set it on the coffee table," I say. The game is on. They haven't started yet, but the announcers are talking about Pacey and how he's been holding down the team lately despite the lack of defense from Eli.

They've compared his play from earlier in the season to recently, and it's obvious that he's having trouble, and it's probably because of me.

"They talking about Hornsby again?" Winnie asks while taking a seat next to me and flipping open the pizza box.

"Yeah, basically about how he's sucking. They think he should go down to the second line."

"Ooof, really? That would be an absolute blow. Not to just him but the team morale." She stares at the TV and smiles as they show Pacey warming up his legs. "He's so bendy. Look at him go."

I chuckle. "He is quite bendy. He's been doing special stretches for as long as I can remember."

"What was it like growing up with him? Was he a total douche?"

That makes me laugh out loud. "He had his douchey moments for sure. But he was actually a good big brother. He always included me, and when we weren't playing hockey together, he'd ask me what I wanted to do, which was usually to see a movie in the theater. Those were some of my favorite memories because he made a day of it. We'd purchase two giant buckets of popcorn, Raisinets, and drinks, and then we'd spend the day movie-hopping."

"What's that?" Winnie asks while handing me a salad.

"It's when you go see a different movie without paying. You just slip into another movie theater after the one you paid for is over. There was one day when we saw three movies in a row. And of course, we had unlimited popcorn and drinks. It's one of my favorite memories with him."

"That's so sweet and illegal."

I laugh and move my fork around the salad. "Yeah, probably not the best choice, but it was fun then. I'd probably never do that now because the feeling of being fearless, like we'd never get caught, doesn't sit well with me."

"For some reason, when I was ten, I didn't think gravity existed, so I'd test it and fall off rocks to see if I was pulled down or not. After a dozen tries to float, I realized maybe gravity was real."

"I really wish I knew you when you were little."

"Trust me, you don't." She bites into her salad and asks, "So are things better with Hornsby?"

"Define better?"

"Have you spoken since the fight?"

"Barely," I say.

"Barely? It's been two weeks. What have you two been doing for two weeks?"

"Avoiding one another." I twirl my fork around, never biting into my salad, just pushing the lettuce around. "I feel like we're right back at where we started. But this time, it feels worse. He's sleeping on the couch—"

"This couch?" she asks, surprised. "How on earth does he fit on it?"

"Not very well. His legs hang off, his neck is all scrunched, and I've heard him drop off the side a few times. He can't possibly be comfortable. I told him he could sleep on the bed, but he refuses. So yeah, it's been fun, to say the least."

"Have you talked about the fight at all, or is it just the elephant in the room?"

"We talked about it that night, but ever since then, it's been like he's shut down. He only ever asks how I'm doing and if the baby has been bothering me. The other night, I was leaving to get a milkshake, and he stopped me before leaving and went and got it for me instead. But when he got home, he handed me the milkshake and went back to not talking. That is pretty much the extent of our interactions."

"God, I'd be an absolute wreck. I don't do well with confrontation. You must be happy that they're away right now."

"More than you know." I finally take a bite of my salad just as the puck is dropped and the game begins.

"Are you going to throw him a bone and talk to him?"

"I'm not even sure what to talk to him about."

"Well, what were you guys doing before the fight?"

I think back to two weeks ago and shake my head in disbelief. "I threw up in his shoe that morning. He was telling me it was okay. It was one of the first times I saw his compassion. He was sweet and kind and didn't make me feel like a fool. Nor was he angry. I wish we were there again."

"Then reach out to him. I'm sure he's not saying anything to you because he's the one who screwed up. He's probably looking for forgiveness in some weird way. Maybe texting him might make him feel better and open up more. I'm pretty sure the last thing you want is to be fighting with the man who's the father of your child. You want to keep things peaceful, so reach out to him."

"You really think that will help?"

"Guaranteed. I'm sure you two will be back to normal in no time."

"I'd really like that. I mean, I was really mad about the whole fight thing, but I don't want it to drive us apart. I just wanted it to be a lesson."

"Then you need to reach out. Trust me, this will work."

I sigh and glance at the TV just in time to see Eli check somebody into the boards and shoot the puck over to Posey, who passes it to Holmes. Winnie is right. I need to close the gap between us, and if that means sucking up my pride to say something, then I will.

PENNY: *Good game tonight. You guys looked great out there.*

I stare at the text message as my stomach churns with nerves. Reaching out to him like this feels awkward. I'm not sure he's even going to respond. I wouldn't blame him if he didn't. Two weeks is a long time to share a living space and not talk. But they're on a long road trip this go-around, so it might be good to try to patch things up now when we aren't necessarily face to face.

Yes, that's the immature way of thinking, but listen, I've been thrown for a loop here. I'm juggling this pregnancy with trying to keep things calm with the father of my child. If I want to hide behind text messages to make things better, then so be it.

No judgment!

Lying in bed, I open the team's TikTok app to scroll through fan messages and comments when at the top of my screen, a text comes through from Eli.

Bracing myself, I click on it and read.

Eli: *Thanks. It was a needed win. How are you feeling?*

His go-to question. It's what he asks almost every single day but doesn't extend the conversation after my typical answer of "okay." I'm worried he might do the same thing here.

Penny: *Okay. Didn't have much to eat even though Winnie came over and brought salad and pizza.*

After I press send, I quickly exit the text thread because I'm too worried I won't see him responding. That I won't see those three dots pop up, telling me that he is engaging. I talked about pizza. That's opening up the conversation, right? Let's see if he takes it.

But when he doesn't answer right away, panic sets in.

God, why is he taking so long to respond?

Is he going to respond?

I'm tempted to go back to the thread to see if it shows him typing, but instead, I decide to distract myself and open TikTok again just as my phone buzzes and a text comes through.

"Thank God," I whisper.

I click over to the thread.

Eli: *Were you not hungry or was the pizza shit?*

I chuckle and text him back.

Penny: *Been uneasy lately, so my stomach has been in knots. Haven't been super hungry.*

This time, I can see him typing back right away. I settle into my mattress and curl up to my pillow as I wait for his response.

Eli: *What have you been uneasy about?*

He took the bait, and now I need to just be honest like we said we would be. On a deep breath, I text him back.

Penny: *Us. We were in such a good place before the fight with Remi. And I don't know how to fix it.*

I toss my phone to the side and cover my eyes as I take a few deep breaths. God, why is this so hard? Why do I feel like a teenager all over again trying to communicate with a boy? It shouldn't be like this. It should be easy. I should be calm and relaxed.

My phone buzzes, and I pop up and grab it.

Eli: Me neither. But I want to.

Relief floods me. This is exactly what I wanted. Open communication. His willingness to patch things up along with mine. I need to tell Winnie how smart she is.

Penny: How about this? I'm sorry about what happened. I was upset about how you acted, and I should have spoken to you rather than yelled at you.

Eli: I'm sorry, too. Not for what I did, defending you, but for how I did it. I understand what you mean about getting into fights. I wouldn't want our kid to do the same.

Penny: Thank you for apologizing. I really appreciate it.

Eli: Are things cool with us?

Penny: You tell me.

Eli: I've been giving you space because I know how upset you were. I didn't want to push my luck.

Penny: I was giving you space.

Eli: Lol, how about next time, we just talk to each other when we're not as heated.

Penny: Hopefully, there won't be a next time.

Eli: Wishful thinking. There will be a next time. 100 percent certain. We're moving to uncharted territories for the both of us, so there are bound to be some bumps along the way. But we're not going to go through two weeks of not really talking to each other. Got it?

Penny: Got it. *sighs* Thank you for texting back. I was nervous you weren't going to.

Eli: Seriously? I was just sitting here, hovering my thumb over your name, trying to think of something, anything to say to you to open the conversation.

Penny: You could have told me something like . . . oh, I don't know, something like you ate an apple.

Eli: Yes, because the first time was a real conversation starter.

Penny: LOL. It would have made me laugh, and that would have started the conversation.

Eli: Noted, so whenever you are mad at me, I'll be sure to throw it back to the apple day, and let you know that, in fact, I ate one.

Penny: It's a brilliant tactic. I might use it if needed.

Eli: *I can guarantee you, if you texted me tonight, "I ate an apple" I would have 100 percent thought everything was good between us.*

Penny: *Well, I'm glad we have established that.*

Eli: *Very glad . . . so where do we go from here?*

Penny: *I sort of have an idea, but if it's stupid, you need to tell me, and we can think of something else.*

Eli: *Let me hear it.*

Penny: *Let's simply ask questions as if we're new friends.*

Eli: *So we tell each other something the other person might not know?*

Penny: *Sure. You start.*

Eli: *Okay, I have to have five gummy bears before every game, home or away. Posey makes sure I'm always fully stocked up.*

Penny: *Is that why you had that bag with you when you came to my office?*

Eli: *Yeah, Posey brought it to me.*

Penny: *When did you start doing it?*

Eli: *When I was young before my mom died. The last game she saw me play, she gave me gummy bears before the game, and I had one of the best games of my childhood.*

Penny: *Why the number five?*

Eli: *Five was her favorite number.*

Penny: *That's really sweet, Eli.*

Eli: *Yeah, I keep it pretty close to me. Please don't use it as something to promote the team.*

Penny: *Anything you say to me outside of the stadium is personal. Please know that. I'd never take your personal life and spread it to the fans without your permission.*

Eli: *You don't seem like that kind of person, but I figured I'd say it anyway. So what's your thing?*

Penny: *When I helped Pacey with his practices, I used to purposely shoot the puck at his crotch because I thought it was funny when he'd miss, and it would hit him. I enjoyed watching him crumple despite having protection.*

Eli: *LOLOL WHAT? You'd try to hit him in the dick on purpose? Seems like a recurring theme with you.*

Penny: *Of course. Isn't that what little sisters are supposed to do?*

Eli: *Is that why they were created? To wreak havoc on their brothers' junk?*

Penny: *Yup. Aren't you glad you don't have a little sister?*

Eli: *For the sake of my balls . . . yes. Were you always a terror?*

Penny: *I want to say no. I want to tell you that I was the picture-perfect little sister, but that would be lying. I wasn't even close. I made Pacey's life hell. Sure, I helped him with hockey, but when we put the sticks down, I made it my mission to make him miserable.*

Eli: *If my relationship with him wasn't so rocky, I'd ask you for tips on how to drive him crazy.*

Penny: *Things still bad with him?*

Eli: *I wouldn't say bad, just not the same. I'll say this, defending you on the ice won me some points. He at least talks to me now. Thinking about taking him out for a beer tomorrow night. What do you think? Should I ask him out?*

Penny: *Not sure you're his type.*

Eli: *Maybe if I find a long blonde wig, something that looks like Winnie's hair, he might give me a chance.*

Penny: *Now there's an idea. If it helps, he barely talks to me too.*

Eli: *That doesn't help. I don't want him mad at you.*

Penny: *It wouldn't be the first time. We always work through it.*

Eli: *Not the first time you've slept with one of his teammates?*

Penny: *No, I've never done that. You are the first and only. I meant the first time we've been in a fight. When it came to Pacey and his teammates, I've always been off limits. He never wanted to mix the two. Plus, he always said hockey players are horny assholes and I deserved better.*

Eli: *We are horny, and we can be assholes. He might be onto something. The horny, though, that comes from adrenaline. After a game, it's hard to shake that high off, you know?*

Penny: *Unless I'm completely naïve, what have you been doing to shake it off now? (assuming you're not having sex with anyone)*

Eli: *You're assuming correctly. I'm not doing much to shake the adrenaline. And the last person I had sex with was you, and if I were being completely frank, it's because you rocked my world that night, and it was hard to forget.*

Penny: *You were drunk.*

Eli: *I wasn't.*

My teeth roll over my bottom lip as I stare at his text. His confirmation.

I rocked his world?

Me?

Penny Lawes.

The girl who was told she was bad at sex?

I haven't had much experience in the bedroom. I mean, I've had moments, but I add "rocks people's worlds" to my sexual résumé. I'd say average with an occasional moment that borders spectacular.

But to rock Eli Hornsby's world? That just doesn't seem possible.

Eli: *Did I say too much?*

Penny: *No, sorry. I was just . . . well, I guess I'm not good at taking compliments, and I wasn't expecting you to say that. But I guess . . . thank you. Seems weird to say thank you, but I don't know what else to say.*

Eli: *How about we say good night? I'm sure you're tired, and, uh, I need to shake this adrenaline off somehow, and when I say that, I mean staying in my hotel room and finding something to do. Like I said before, you don't have to worry about me sleeping around.*

Penny: *If you need to, it's fine.*

Eli: *I don't want to, Penny. Okay. It's just not in me anymore.*

Penny: *Okay . . . well, good to know. This might be the little sister in me coming out with a dumb question, but were you alluding to the fact that you're going to go, you know, pleasure yourself now?*

Eli: *Yes, it was. LOL. I'm becoming reacquainted with my friend the right hand.*

Penny: *Is it weird we're talking about masturbation?*

Eli: *You tell me.*

Penny: *Sort of, but I guess I enjoy the honesty. So . . . have fun whacking off.*

Eli: *I never should have told you.*

Penny: *You probably shouldn't have. This will live in my mind forever.*

Eli: *Fantastic.*

—

PENNY: *How was your night? Romantic?*

    Eli: *I really shouldn't have told you.*

    Penny: *It's all I could think about last night and not in a creepy I'm picturing you and your orgasm face kind of way, but more fascinated in the process.*

    Eli: *I don't have an orgasm face.*

    Penny: *Ha . . . okay.*

    Eli: *I'm not even going to ask.*

    Penny: *It's best you don't.*

    Eli: *And what do you mean by the process?*

    Penny: *Well, you know. Did you light a candle? Use lotion? Set up the tissues? Play some romantic music? Strike up a conversation with your hand before you brought it down south . . .*

    Eli: *Are you always like this? Is this the real Penny and you've been hiding her all along?*

    Penny: *I'm afraid to answer that.*

    Eli: *If the answer is yes, I don't mind her. I just need to mentally prepare myself for what to expect moving forward.*

    Penny: *Then yes, this is me in all of my glory. Awkward, weird, asks uncomfortable questions, and doesn't tend to have a filter when rambling.*

    Eli: *I accept this. And if you have to know, it was in the shower. Easier that way.*

    Penny: *Fascinating. Okay, I can go on with my day now.*

    Eli: *Glad I could assist.*

—

ELI: *Have you ever gotten stitches?*

    Penny: *Are we just asking questions now without any lead-in? Nothing like how's your day going? Just straight to the point?*

    Eli: *Penny, how is your day going? Have you ever gotten stitches?*

    Penny: *It's okay. I dry-heaved into my waste basket while in the middle of a meeting with an intern and told him I had bad shrimp the night before. He turned a hideous shade of gray, and I'm pretty sure he'll pray to* the Lord up above to never have to work with me again. Other than that, great. Feeling good. And yes, I've gotten stitches before.

Eli: I thought the morning sickness was easing.

Penny: It is. I think it was because this kid's cologne was next level. Nearly gagged me. But I wasn't about to tell him that.

Eli: Okay. But you're doing okay?

Penny: Yesssssss, Eli. I'm fine.

Eli: Don't appreciate the sass, but we'll move on. Where were the stitches? And why did you have to get them?

Penny: My palm. I was cutting a bagel and ended up slicing right through my hand. The bagel was later used to help sop up my blood.

Eli: Were you allowed to cut bagels after that?

Penny: Funnily enough, the next day, there was a bagel-cutting device in the kitchen. Pacey will deny it to this day, but he passed out in the car when I showed him my flapping skin. He said he was tired, but we all know the cut was too gruesome for him.

Eli: Logging that away for future teasing when we're back to normal.

Penny: Did you do the thing I told you to do?

Eli: Pin him against the wall and give him a noogie?

Penny: Yeah.

Eli: No, because that was terrible advice.

Penny: How do you know? You didn't try.

Eli: I ran it by Posey. He said if I was looking to get an uppercut into the ribs, then go for it.

Penny: Hmm. I thought guys liked to play around with each other like that.

Eli: That's like me assuming you and Winnie had a pillow fight the other night when she was over.

Penny: How do you know we didn't?

Eli: Did you?

Penny: No.

Eli: Exactly. Trust me, it was not good advice.

Penny: Do you want me to run the scenario by him and ask him what he would do if you did that?

Eli: Jesus, no.

Penny: Are you sure? I don't mind texting him.

Eli: For the love of God, don't text him.

Penny: I just did. Waiting on a response.

Eli: You what? Penny! Come on, seriously?

Penny: No, but hearing your whining was fun. And before you get mad, please note, I'm pregnant and don't get to do a lot of fun things at the moment due to nausea. So give me this little thing.

Eli: You know I'm never going to be able to trust you with the number of times you've tricked me.

Penny: I think that's fair.

———

PENNY: *Are you excited to only have two more games on this away trip? It's been a long one.*

Eli: I'm excited to be reacquainted with my good friend, the couch.

Penny: You realize you can sleep in my bed, right? I told you that before you left.

Eli: Yeah, but you said it with a snarl to your lip, so I wasn't sure I should attempt to lay a foot in your bed. Is the snarl gone?

Penny: There was no snarl.

Eli: There was a snarl. It twitched and pulsed, and frankly, it would scare the sugar off a lollipop.

Penny: Umm . . . the sugar off a lollipop? Dare I ask where that horrible comparison comes from?

Eli: Scarily enough, it was the first thing that came to mind.

Penny: I fear there's a hint of a sociopath in the depths of your being, and that's unsettling. Maybe you won't be allowed back in the bed.

Eli: Don't play with my heart . . . or back muscles.

Penny: Are you a sociopath?

Eli: Can't say that I've ever been called one before. I can offer some references.

Penny: References work.

Eli: Please refer to Levi Posey and Halsey Holmes.

Penny: They aren't reliable.

Eli: Not even Holmes?

Penny: *Partially. I'd need him alone and not under the influence of your stare.*

Eli: *I can arrange such an event.*

Penny: *Good. Now, I have to ask, what did you eat for dinner? You look different on the TV from what I'm used to, and I'm wondering if it's something you ate.*

Eli: *Different good or different bad?*

Penny: *Don't let this get to your head, but different good.*

Eli: *Is that so?*

Penny: *Ughhhhhhh, never mind.*

Eli: *Tell me how good.*

Penny: *Good night, Hornsby.*

Eli: *It's Eli.*

Penny: *Not when you act like that, it's not.*

Chapter Sixteen

ELI

Hair mussed, wearing sweatpants, a long-sleeved Agitators shirt, and my slide-ons, I shuffle through the conference room door where the hotel has set up breakfast for us. I stayed up late last night reading into the second trimester and what to expect from the incredibly unpredictable Penny Lawes.

Things I learned: she'll start to show, and we'll be able to find out the sex of the baby which, to me, is pretty exciting. I'm not sure where her head is at when it comes to wanting to find out. If she wants to wait, I'll painfully wait with her, but I'm kind of hoping that she wants to find out.

Lifting my head from my phone—where once again I'm checking on scores—I spot Pacey in the back corner, hovering over a plate of eggs with his phone in hand. He's the only one in the room besides me. Normally, I wouldn't even think twice about sitting next to him, but now that things are rocky between us, I walk over to the buffet, where I pick up a plate and contemplate whether to sit next to him or not.

I pile on eggs and bacon to my plate, along with a fruit cup and a bran muffin. It's always the same thing at every hotel. The team likes to keep things easy on us, not having to make too many decisions, and keep us fueled with all the right things at the same time. Occasionally, the hotel will throw in their own spin like a baked good, but everything is pretty much the same.

After my plate is full, I grab some water and then turn toward Pacey's table. His back is to me, and I'm not even sure he realizes I walked into the room.

This is it. Either I could sit somewhere else and let there be a break between us, or I could close the gap and continue to mend my friendship.

On a deep breath—and a hope and a prayer he doesn't kick me across the room—I head over to his table. I leave a chair between us, so we're not shoulder to shoulder, but not too much room so it looks like I'm avoiding him.

When I set my plate and water down, his eyes glance away from his phone, and he meets my gaze. I steel myself for him to tell me to fuck off, but instead, he sets his phone down and leans back in his chair.

"Did you see the Freeze lost one to five last night? Clemens apparently forgot how to goaltend."

Is he . . . uh, is he talking to me?

I want to look behind me to make sure no one walked in when I wasn't paying attention, but then again, his eyes are on mine, which means he must be talking to me.

Play it cool, man.

Don't mess this up.

"I did," I answer. "An absolute upset that works in our favor."

"Not just an upset, a blow to the ego." He leans forward. "They lost to the Rockets, the second-worst team in the league. And not just lost, but lost bad."

I chuckle. "Karma is a real bitch, isn't it?" I allude to what Gasper did, hoping it's not going to stir trouble, but when Pacey laughs and nods, I know we'll be just fine.

"Yeah. The dickhead can't quite hold his head high at the moment, can he?"

"Not so much." I scoop a forkful of eggs, and before I bite into them, I say, "Your sister threw up in my shoes."

His brow raises. "What exactly are you talking about?"

I swallow and lean in closer. "I'm not supposed to tell anyone because, well, she threw up in a shoe, but I feel like I need to explain to you why we probably lost that game to the Freeze. Because I didn't have the right gameday shoes, because your sister threw up in them. And before you start worrying, it was the one and only time she's thrown up, and I made sure she was okay."

The corner of Pacey's mouth twitches.

His finger drums on the table.

And then he chuckles.

He actually fucking chuckles.

The vise that's gripped my chest loosens once again. The clouds start to part, the fog lifts, and for the first time since we found out Penny was pregnant, I feel like I can see my friend again.

He lifts his water to his lips and says, "Good for her."

"Good for her?" I ask incredulously. "You're happy she threw up in my shoe?"

"Seems like something you deserved."

"Dude." I level with him. "Those were the game-time shoes. No one deserves that kind of abuse."

"You got her pregnant, which in return is the cause of her throwing up. Therefore, I'm pretty sure you deserved it."

I lean back in my chair, water glass in hand. "Well, when you put it like that."

He laughs some more and then grows serious. "How are things with Penny? She hasn't spoken to me much, and I don't blame her. She hasn't spoken to our parents much either because I'm pretty sure she's avoiding telling them. I fear she's alone, and I know I created that for her with the way I reacted." He scrubs his hand down his face. "About that." He winces. "Winnie has been a persistent voice in my ear about how you can't take time with those you love for granted. And how I wouldn't want an unresolved rift between us . . . you know, should something happen. And, now that I've cooled off, I realize how badly I've handled the entire thing." His eyes meet mine. "Even with you." Winnie would know, having lost her mom not long ago.

"Dude, don't worry about me. We're cool. I probably would have had the same reaction as you. I'm just glad we're looking at each other. I missed staring longingly into your eyes."

"You are so fucked in the head."

I laugh and then say, "She's not alone. I talk to her several times a day. I'm sure you know Winnie is hanging out with her a lot, and when Winnie isn't there, Blakely's there. She's very much taken care of. She hasn't said anything about being alone, and honestly, she's in very good spirits."

Pacey's lips twist as he studies me. "You talk to her several times a day? What kind of talking?"

I hold my hand up. "Nothing like you're thinking. Just friends. Trust me, I learned my lesson."

"Okay." He still eyes me. "Would you want something more?"

I shake my head. "I'm not in that kind of headspace right now. I'm focused entirely on making sure Penny has everything she needs, preparing for what's to come, and making sure I'm mentally prepared to become a father."

Gently, Pacey asks, "Have you been speaking with your therapist?"

I nod. "I haven't told Penny that because I don't want to freak her out, but yeah, I've been speaking with him."

"Why would it freak her out? There's nothing wrong with seeing a therapist."

"I don't want her to worry that I'll be an unfit partner in this parenting journey, you know? It's bad enough I'll be gone a lot because of hockey. I want her to know she can depend on me. Not wonder if I'll be a flight risk."

"You won't be. Not just because me and the rest of the boys

will murder you if you are but also because you're someone who breaks the cycle. You won't be like your father. You don't have that kind of bone in your body."

I glance down at my plate and push a few eggs to the side. "You mean that? Because when we were in Penny's office——"

"I know what I said was out of line, and I'm sorry. There's no excuse for saying something like that. Or for saying half of the shit I've said to you. You deserve better, but I'll be honest when I say, I think you will be there for her, but I don't necessarily trust you to be there romantically for her."

I slowly nod. "I agree with you. I don't trust myself either, and that's why I'm not going there."

Pacey lends out his hand, and I take it, giving it a good shake. "I appreciate it, man. And I appreciate you stepping up. A lesser man wouldn't have done the same thing."

"Thank you." I release his hand and say, "She's actually kind of funny. Really weird at times, but she has a good sense of humor. The more I get to know her, the more I can see us being good friends."

"She is. She's also a hellion, an instigator, and stubborn. Very stubborn."

"Shy and awkward," I add.

"But very loving and thoughtful." He lets out a sigh. "She's a catch, and I just wish things were different for her. I feel like she's doing this all backward, and I'm worried what her future will be like."

"Well, I'll try to make it as easy on her as possible."

"It's all I ask." Pacey claps me on the shoulder and then stands from his chair. "A few more games, man. So close to the playoffs."

"We got this," I say as he walks away. I turn back to my plate with a smile on my face.

Didn't expect that this morning, but fuck, does it feel good.

PENNY: *Did you need to get stitches?*

Eli: *Just five.*

Penny: *When I saw your helmet fly off, I pulled a blanket over my eyes and cringed.*

Eli: *I honestly still don't know how it all happened. All I can remember was fighting for possession of the puck against the boards, an elbow to my head, my helmet is gone, and then, blood is running down my face.*

Penny: *It was a stick that got you. To the fans, you looked like a badass with the blood.*

Eli: *What did you think?*

Penny: *I thought you looked like something from a horror film. Let's just say you've had more attractive moments. That was not one of them. Also, what's with the thick stubble? Are you growing a beard?*

Eli: *Haven't shaved on this away trip. For an avid hockey fan, you think you'd know that's tradition for the last away trip before the season ends.*

Penny: *I never paid that much attention to you.*

Eli: *Ouch.*

Penny: *LOL. It's true. Sorry.*

Eli: *Well, for future reference, every last road trip, I don't shave until we get back.*

Penny: *Does that include your arms and legs as well?*

Eli: *I don't ever shave those.*

Penny: *Huh, okay.*

Eli: *I'm not falling for it, Penny. Not this time. You trying to trick me into whatever is scheming in your head.*

Penny: *I'm not scheming anything. I have better things to do with my life, like grow a child, than try to trick you. Honestly, Eli. Oh, which reminds me, I got a phone call from the doctor's office. They asked about the microchip and if we want to put one in the baby when it's born.*

Eli: *Microchip. Like what they put in dogs?*

Penny: *Yes, exactly. I told him I'd talk it over with the baby's father and come back with an answer. I think it might be a good idea.*

Eli: *Wait, this is a real thing? They really put tracking devices in kids?*

Penny: *Yes, but don't worry, after ten years, they dissolve. So it's not like we're still tracking him when he's twenty. It's just so we can make sure* *we know where they are when they're young. Especially toddler age. They get into everything at that age.*

Eli: *It dissolves? I haven't read anything about this.*

Penny: *Want me to send you the website with all the information you might need?*

Eli: *Yeah, that would be great. If I'm going to make an executive decision about this, I'll need all the information. And you're leaning toward yes?*

Penny: *Seems like a great idea. It works for dogs. Why not for babies too?*

Eli: *Just seems weird, you know? Does the tracker come with an app?*

Penny: *The more expensive one does. And the app also tells you when the baby is about to pee and when it is going to poop within ten minutes. Very accurate so you can prepare yourself for what's to come. And then the obvious sleeping stuff, which is nice. But that one's $2,000. Seems pricey.*

Eli: *It predicts poop? That might be nice, actually. And money is not a thing so don't worry about that. I still want to look at the information, but it all seems like it could be good.*

Penny: *Not a problem. Here is the website: ICan'tBelieveYouFellForThat.com*

Eli: *I. HATE. YOU.*

Penny: *HAHAHAHAHA DYING! Oh my God, did you seriously think that was a thing?*

Eli: *You know, it's not nice to fuck with me. I'm a sensitive guy. I could cry. Is that what you want? For me to cry?*

Penny: *You and I both know that would never happen.*

Eli: *You don't know that. I could be crying right now.*

Penny: *Send me a picture. I want to see your tears.*

Eli: *Who's the sociopath now?*

Penny: *Hahaha.*

Eli: *Did you just text me to goad me? Or was there a reason for these texts?*

Penny: *Checking on your eye. Remember, I was nice at first.*

Eli: *So this is more like a toxic friendship then. Luring me in with sweetness only to gaslight me after.*

Penny: *If you think some innocent teasing is gaslighting, then I don't think we can be friends.*

Eli: *Now I feel like you're extorting me.*
Penny: *Do you even know what these terms mean?*
Eli: *Generally.*
Penny: *Glad your eye's okay. Good game out there. I'm going to bed.*
Eli: *Night, Penny.*

———

ELI: *You got my shoes dry-cleaned? Seriously?*
Penny: *I felt like it was the right thing to do.*
Eli: *I didn't even know you could do that.*
Penny: *Trust me when I say I did a lot of research and found a place in Vancouver that was pretty confident they could restore them to their natural state. They did say the shoe that didn't have puke in it was more smelly from foot contact. They asked about athlete's foot.*
Eli: *I'm sure they did. *insert eye roll* But thank you. You didn't have to do that.*
Penny: *I felt like I owed it to the fans. I thought about making a TikTok on how they've been found and returned to your feet, but I'm not sure if it's too much.*
Eli: *I'm more than happy to have you slip them on my feet like Cinderella if that's what you want to do.*
Penny: *That seems like something Posey would enjoy, not you.*
Eli: *He's rubbing off on me.*
Penny: *I can see that.*
Eli: *We come home tonight. Are you excited to see me?*
Penny: *Eh.*
Eli: *Come on, there has to be at least a shred of excitement.*
Penny: *I've had my place to myself, my bed to myself, and I've been able to do whatever I want without your judgmental eye looking in on me. Does it sound like I'm excited to have you home?*
Eli: *Positively riveted. Maybe this will change your mind: I got something for you.*
Penny: *For me? Like a present?*
Eli: *Yes, that's usually what it's called when someone gets you something.*

Penny: *Why?*

Eli: *Lol. Because I saw it and thought of you. Are you going to be mad about that?*

Penny: *Not at all . . . God, why am I feeling emotional right now? I hate these stupid hormones.*

Eli: *Are you crying?*

Penny: *. . . No. *wipes at face**

Eli: *So you're telling me, beneath the sarcastic sociopath, there's a sensitive side to you?*

Penny: *I thought we established you were the sociopath.*

Eli: *Either way, I like it. You don't have to be so tough all the time.*

Penny: *Is that what you think I am? Tough?*

Eli: *Yeah, I think you sort of have a wall up. I'm getting to know you, but there's still a defensive barrier, and it's your humor and teasing.*

Penny: *Weren't you saying I have all different sides to me? Well, here is another one. Apparently, I cry at the mention of a gift.*

Eli: *Well, keep your expectations low because it's not that big of a deal.*

Penny: *I think you could give me an old rabbit's turd, and I'd be happy.*

Eli: *Well, it's not a rabbit's turd, so get that out of your head.*

Penny: *Sad, could have been a lovely gift*

Eli: *You are so strange. I don't know which one of your many personalities is going to show up.*

Penny: *So you're saying it's been a fun roller coaster so far?*

Eli: *Yes, that's exactly what I'm saying. Shy at first, then a fucking fire in bed, then shy and extremely awkward, then teasing, then angry, now fun and charming. Anything else I need to worry about?*

Penny: *Nope, I think that just about covers it, but I suggest you don't sleep on a new side of me. You never know what might appear.*

Eli: *Got it. Okay, see you tonight, or in the morning. I'll try not to wake you up when I get in.*

Penny: *Don't worry about it. Good luck tonight. Bruise someone's ribs.*

Eli: *Haha. I'll try.*

Penny: *Oh and Eli? I am excited to see you tonight.*

Eli: *Ditto.*

Chapter Seventeen

PENNY

The front door clicks shut, followed by the sound of the lock being put into place. I glance over at my nightstand clock and see that it's nearly one.

I've drifted in and out of sleep for the past few hours but woke up the moment I heard the front door open. The boys won tonight, bringing them that much closer to a spot in the playoffs. Unfortunately, with how rough their second half of the season has been, they're not going to win the division, but they're a possible shoo-in for the wild card. I'm sure it's not their preferred way to make it to the playoffs, but at least there's a chance.

Eli's feet shuffle down the hallway, and he slowly opens the door, peeking in.

"Hey," I say so he doesn't think he has to be super quiet.

"You're up. It's late, Penny."

"I've been in and out of sleep." I press my hand to my chest. "Been dealing with some serious heartburn lately."

"Really? You said everything was good," he says in a

concerned voice as he comes over to my side of the bed and takes a seat.

"It's heartburn, Eli. It's not like I'm bleeding from the ears."

"Well, do you need anything?" He glances behind me. "I read about how heartburn can hit you hard in the first trimester and leading into the second. You should be propping yourself up on pillows. Also, do you have any yogurt? That might help. Or some sugar-free gum. Want me to go grab you some? There's a convenience store around the corner that's still open. I can run to it if you want."

I place my hand on his arm and shake my head. "No, that's okay, really. I'm fine."

"Are you sure?"

"Yes, but thank you. You must be tired."

He pulls on the back of his neck. "Adrenaline's still kicking me. It was a battle tonight."

"I saw that. Congrats on the win. You're a clear favorite to win the wild card."

"Three more games and we'll find out." He lets out a deep breath. "It's been a fucking year. I know I shouldn't be saying this, but I'm ready for it to be over. I kind of wish we could just win the cup now and then go up to Banff. I could use the relaxation."

"You have quite a journey to win the cup. Have you forgotten the two-month-long process of the playoffs?"

"Don't remind me," he groans. "We have a long way to go, but it will be worth it." He lifts his duffel bag on the bed and says, "Now that you're awake, do you want your gift?"

"Uh, obviously."

He chuckles. "Okay and remember, not quite rabbit turd, but not much better."

"Expectations are at an all-time low." I hold my hands out in front of me.

He unzips his bag, reaches in, and then places something in my hands. When I look down, I see a candy bar, but not just any candy bar, a Snickers bar, limited edition cinnamon bun flavor.

"I have no idea if it's good, but when I was getting myself a Gatorade in the hotel gift shop, I saw it and thought you had to try it. I truly hope it's good."

"This was so thoughtful," I say as I lean forward and wrap my arms around him. One of his arms goes to my back, and when I give him a squeeze, he does the same. It's brief, and there's absolutely nothing romantic to the hug, but for that moment, when the palm of his hand is stretched out over my back, and his fresh soap scent is flooding my space, I have this pang of awareness. The same type of awareness I had when I first saw him at the bar on his birthday. This masculine, charming, amazing smelling man is talking to me. Well, not just talking to me anymore, but giving me gifts because when he saw it, he thought of me.

It's so kind.

It's so crazy.

It's not something I'd ever expect, so when I pull away, I feel an overwhelming sense of emotion start to tighten my throat.

Don't cry.

Please don't cry.

Not over a candy bar. I've already humiliated myself enough.

Keep it together.

But when I look up at him, and our eyes lock, I know there's no way I can stop it from happening.

My eyes well, and immediately, he takes my hand in his.

"Don't cry. It's really just a stupid gesture. Nothing to get emotional about."

"Too . . . late," I say as I wave my hand in front of my face. "God, this is humiliating. I honestly can't control it."

He lifts his other hand to my face and gently wipes away the tears that have fallen down my cheeks.

"I'm sorry. I know this must be uncomfortable for you."

"It's fine," he says.

Trying to make things not so awkward anymore, I hold up the candy bar and say, "Want to try it?"

"Right now?"

"We're both awake. Why not?"

He cutely shrugs. "Sure. But don't feel like you need to share it with me."

"I'm not going to sit here in my bed, feeling more bloated than ever, and eat a candy bar in front of you without letting you have any." I tear open the packaging and give it a sniff. The smell makes me wince. "Maybe it tastes better than it smells."

"Does it smell bad?" I hold it out to him, and he sniffs. "Jesus, that doesn't smell appetizing. How is that possible?"

"I don't know, but only one way to find out." I break off a piece for both of us. I hand him his chunk, and I hold up mine. "Here's to the playoffs." We clink our chunks together, and then both put them in our mouths.

I chew.

He chews.

And then we both stare at each other in horror.

I sprint to the toilet, where I immediately throw up while I hear him behind me. He spits into the trash can and then bends down next to me, where he holds my hair back for me.

"Christ, I didn't know it was going to be that bad. I'm so sorry."

I'm going to tell you right now, throwing up into a toilet is probably the least attractive thing you could do, let alone in front of hockey's Prince Charming. Yet I can't stop myself as I heave wave after wave until nothing is left inside me. And he sits there, listening to every last part of it. He continues to hold my hair with one hand while gently rubbing my back with the other one.

"Are you okay?" I nod and rest my head on my arm that's draped over the toilet seat. Don't worry, with my nausea lately, I've been swiping it with a Lysol wipe after every time I use it for this exact reason.

"Yes," I say before slowly lifting up and wiping under my eyes. "I'd, uh, like to say, the candy wasn't throw-up worthy, and the scene that just unfolded was more of a pregnancy reaction rather than a normal human reaction. Just need to make it clear, I'm not this dramatic about food."

"So you don't throw up when something doesn't taste good to you?"

"Nope, not a normal occurrence."

He slowly nods. "Good to know." Then he turns fully to me and asks, "Are you seriously okay? The last thing I wanted to do was make you throw up."

"I know, and the gift was super thoughtful. I think we blame this one on the Snickers, not on you."

"I can take that." He stands and then lends out his hand to help me up. I take it slow, just making sure I'm okay, and when I don't feel my stomach roil, I walk over to the sink where I load my toothbrush with toothpaste.

He does the same.

And together, we brush our teeth.

And it feels . . . familiar. Like we've done this at least a dozen times when, in fact, we have not. We've never brushed our teeth together. We've always taken turns in the bathroom.

I glance at him in the mirror and find him studying me. Through a mouthful of toothpaste, I ask, "What?"

He smirks over his toothbrush. "Just can't believe the first thing I do when I come home from a long road trip is make you throw up. What kind of friend am I?"

I spit out my toothpaste into the sink. "Clearly, not a good one." I rinse my mouth, and so does he. We set our toothbrushes in the holder, and then I turn to him.

I don't know what takes over me, call it the hormones or the fact that someone is here, and it feels comforting, but I step up to him and once again, loop my arms around his waist. This time, he returns the hug with both arms, and we stand there, in the bathroom, hugging each other. For quite a few seconds before I pull away.

"It really was thoughtful. Thank you."

"You're welcome. Sorry it made you puke."

I shrug. "A lot of things make me nauseous, might as well add that to the list."

And then I move past him and back to the bed. He goes to

the bathroom and finishes getting ready. By the time he's plugged his phone into the charger, I feel the heaviness in my eyes.

He scoots under the covers and faces me. His body heat warms the bed, something I've actually missed.

"You're tired," he says.

I nod. "The sleep is taking over me. Are you still pumped up with adrenaline?"

"Had a mild spike with that whole throwing-up situation, but I've calmed down. You sure you're good with me sleeping here?"

I nod and yawn at the same time. "It's nice. You make the bed all toasty and warm. Missed it while you were gone . . . and well, not really talking to me."

"Hey," he says softly. "You were the one not talking to me."

"I think we both weren't talking." I snuggle into my pillow. "But we're talking now."

"We are." And then he reaches out and pushes a loose strand of my hair around my ear.

My eyes part just in time to connect with his. His finger drags across my cheek tenderly, and he says, "Good night, Penny."

Almost breathlessly, I answer back, "Good night."

And then he closes his eyes, leaving me with an elevated feeling as my pulse picks up.

What was with that touch? Did he mean to do that? Was it a loving touch or a pity touch because I threw up?

No. We're here for the baby. Plain and simple.

Nothing else. My pregnancy brain needs to take a time-out and go to bed.

Everything will be just fine in the morning.

⊏⊐

"HEY," Eli says, poking his head in the bathroom where I'm carefully straightening my hair. Day off means I get to spend time doing something I wouldn't normally do in the morning when I have to go to work.

"Hey, I didn't think you'd be home so early from your morning skate."

"We're trying to rest our legs more." He nods at me. "What are you doing?"

"Straightening my hair." I give him a once-over. "Why are you wearing jeans?"

He chuckles. "What should I be wearing?"

"I don't know, sweatpants? That's what you normally wear. Are you going to go run some errands? Do professional hockey players even do errands? Pacey never talks about it, so I can't be sure. Do you have an assistant who does everything for you?"

"I run my own errands. But that's not why I'm wearing jeans."

I glance down at them again and then nod in understanding. "Ah, a new pair, wearing them in around the house."

He presses his hand to his forehead. "Why are you like this?"

"Like what?"

"Why do you assume I'm doing everything other than what I actually want to do?"

"I don't know." I shrug while combing one of the final sections of my hair to straighten. "I ramble and talk a lot. You should know that by now."

"I do." He lets out a heavy sigh. "I'm wearing jeans because I was hoping I could take you to lunch."

I pause and turn toward him, hair in the straightener. "You want to take me to lunch?"

"Unless you have other plans."

"I don't. But why do you want to take me to lunch? Do you need to tell me something, and breaking the news over a soup and salad combo seems like the better thing to do? If so, please don't take me out in public to break the news to me. You know how emotional I am right now."

He places his hands on his hips as his head falls forward. "I just want to spend some time with you as a friend. That's all. There's nothing behind the request, just wanting to take a friend out to lunch."

"Oh." I chuckle and then face the mirror again. "Well, if that's all, you should have just led with that instead of creating all of this nonsense."

"You were the one creating nonsense. I didn't even have a chance to get a word in."

"Well, lesson learned for you." I finish up and then set the straightener down and turn to him. "Ready. Where are we going?"

"That would be up to you, the puker."

"Hey." I hold my finger up to him. "Don't call me that. It's not my fault this spawn you inserted inside me is making me sick."

"Pretty sure I didn't insert a spawn in you."

"Fine." I roll my eyes. "Leaked a spawn in me."

"Ew, come on."

I laugh out loud and move past him to my dresser, where I spritz myself with perfume and then slip on my boots. "I was planning on going to the bookstore. Think we can stop there as well?"

"Sure, oh, you know, there's a deli right around the corner from the bookstore on Commercial Drive that's really good."

"I can't have deli meat," I say.

"Oh shit, that's right, I read that somewhere. Uh, then what are you in the mood for?"

"Soup," I answer. "And bread. Can we get that?"

He smiles softly. "Soup and bread, it is. I know the perfect place. A French café if that works for you."

"That seems charming. I'm in." I head into the main living space, where I grab my brown leather jacket that's draped on the back of my chair and zip it up. Eli is standing at the entryway, leaning against the wall, eyeing me. "What?" I ask as I fluff my hair out of the collar.

"You look cute."

I quickly glance at my black jeans, brown boots, and now covered-up white sweater. "This is nothing to write home about."

"Just take the compliment, Penny."

My cheeks flame with embarrassment. He's right. I should. "Thank you." And just to toss one his way, I say, "You, uh, you always look nice."

He chuckles and shakes his head while walking over to me and looping his arm around my shoulders. "Come on, let's get going."

⊏▭⊐

"IF YOU HAVE something you want to look for, you can go peruse. No need to follow me," I say when we enter the bookstore.

"I don't need anything."

"Are you sure? Because I'm just going to be looking at pregnancy books. You know, boring stuff."

"Oh great, I'll look with you."

Not exactly what I wanted, but I have to give him credit for being interested. I'm not sure how many non-romantically attached fathers would be walking into the pregnancy section of a bookstore excited to peruse.

"Is there anything I can help you look for?" he asks as he walks side by side with me.

"Uh, not really. Just searching for a journal sort of thing."

"What kind of journal?"

"One where I can write down my feelings and such as I move through the pregnancy. My mom kept one when she was pregnant with both me and Pacey. She just used a notebook, though. I know there are some out on the market that guide you. So, you know, just looking for that."

"That's pretty cool. Do you have yours from when your mom was pregnant with you?"

"Yes, I do. She gave it to me when I graduated high school. I really enjoyed looking through it, so I thought it might be nice to have one for our kid."

"That is nice." He's silent for a second. "Have you told your parents yet?"

I shake my head as we round the corner to the pregnancy section. "I honestly have no idea how to break the news to them. I don't know what they're going to say. I'm pretty sure my dad just assumed I've never had sex and wants to keep it that way in his mind."

"Do you want to tell them together? That way, you have someone to fall back on in case it doesn't go well?"

"I know it won't go well. I love my parents, but I don't think they expected to be grandparents without a wedding beforehand. And they're pretty chill about a lot of things, but I think this might be a hard one for them to accept."

"Either way, I'll be there for you. Like we said from the very beginning, this pregnancy isn't for you to shoulder alone. We're in this together. Just let me know when you want to tell them, and I'll be there."

"That means a lot to me, thank you."

"Of course." He glances at the stack of books and pulls one off the shelf. "*The Big Fat Activity Book for Pregnant People.*" This seems like fun. He flips it open and starts laughing. "Oh, this is good. Look, you can draw pictures of the people who annoy you while you're pregnant."

"Isn't that charming?"

"Ooo, and it has quizzes."

"Uh, that doesn't really seem like what I'm looking for."

"Well, I'm sold," he says while leaning against the shelf and flipping through it.

"Sold as in you're getting it for yourself?"

"Yeah."

"But you're not pregnant."

"I'm not?" he asks, staring down at his stomach. "Are you sure?"

I pat his stomach, his rock-hard stomach, and swallow hard. Wow, that's a lot harder than I remember. Not that he was flabby by any means on his birthday, but that's quite the flat stomach he has. "Uh, no . . . no baby in there."

"Odd, I thought I was pregnant."

"Stop it." I poke him this time, which makes him laugh. "You don't need that pregnancy book."

"Uh, hell yeah, I do. I might not be carrying the child, but I'm still experiencing things. Plus, it will be entertaining. Something to do when I'm in my hotel room by myself. Or when I'm waiting for you to be done in the bathroom. Which, by the way, you take a long time. If we were at my place, we would have our own bathrooms, and that wouldn't be a problem."

"I would not be comfortable in your place."

His brow scrunches together. "Why not?"

"It's big."

"It's a two-bedroom. I wouldn't call that big. You should see some of the places the other guys have. My apartment is incredibly modest."

"And the fireplace would just taunt me, chanting over and over this is where you had sex, this is where you got pregnant."

"You think it was in front of the fireplace? I thought it was in my bed."

"Why do you assume the bed?"

"Well"—he tucks the book under his arm—"for one, we didn't penetrate much in front of the fireplace. If you recall, we went from there to the wall, where you came first, and I followed closely after."

My cheeks heat immediately as I glance around to make sure no one is listening.

"And then after that, we went to my bedroom where, as you put it, I jack-hammered into you. You said the pounding was so hard. That's how the condom broke."

"I didn't." I lower my voice and whisper, "I didn't say it like that."

"Along those lines, you did. So I don't think it was the fireplace. It was definitely the bed. That's where you had the biggest orgasm too."

My cheeks are so hot right now that I actually feel like you could fry an egg on them. And not only are they heated with embarrassment, but the image of Eli pulsing into me also floats through my brain. I have this strange pulse developing between my legs, an awareness, a yearning that I didn't think I needed or wanted since I found out I was pregnant.

But it's there, reminding me of that night, of the best sex I ever had. The feel of his strong body, taking charge, demanding from me, but also making sure my needs were taken care of. The feel of his long, hard length in the palm of my hand. How soft but firm he was. The way his teeth dragged over his lip when I smoothed my hand down to his balls. Or how he slowly moved inside me, allowing me to adjust to his size, but then took no mercy when he was fully inside. Pound after pound after pound . . .

The sweat that beaded between us.

The grasp of his hands on my hips, indenting to the point of pleasurable pain.

The delicious moan that vibrated from his chest . . .

"Are you okay?"

"Huh?" I ask, my eyes shooting to his. Oh my God, how long was I daydreaming?

"Your face is all flushed. Do you need some water?"

"Water?" I croak out

"Yes." His eyes grow concerned as he bends at the knees to look me in the eyes. His hand falls to my shoulder, and it feels like a total lightning bolt of lust zapping through me.

I immediately step away. "Uh, I can get my own water. Be right back. Stay here. Don't come and get me."

"Penny, wait, what's going on?"

"I just have to pee. You can't assist me with that, so stay put."

"But do you need water?" he calls out.

I wave behind me. "I'm fine." And I take off toward the bathrooms, where I pull my phone out and lock myself in a stall. I send a quick text to Blakely because something is happening to me, and I don't like it.

Penny: *SOS! Something just happened to me.*

Within seconds, Blakely's name is scrolling across the screen. "Hello?"

"Are you okay? What's going on?"

Talking quietly, I say, "I'm in the bathroom at the bookstore."

"What are you doing in there?"

"Hiding from Eli."

"Ohh-kay. Why are you hiding from Eli?"

"Because something really weird just happened to me, and I didn't want to be around him while I attempt to settle myself down."

"Oh God, was it some sort of discharge? Do you need me to bring you pants?"

"What? No. Ew, gross, Blakely."

"Girl, if you think that's gross, just wait. When my sister was pregnant, so many things came out of her. Discharge is the least of your concerns. You should happily welcome some minor discharge."

"Can you please stop saying discharge? Nothing like that happened. It was more of a full-body reaction."

"Hives? What have you eaten in the last few hours? Did you step on a bee? My parents' dog once stepped on a bee and had an awful reaction. They had to take him to the emergency vet at three in the morning because he wouldn't stop scratching. Absolutely terrible. Is your tongue swelling? Your voice sounds normal."

"Oh my God, now I know how Eli feels when he's trying to tell me something. Just stop talking for a second, and let me tell you what's going on."

"Okay, fine, you shall speak, but make it quick. I have pins and needles here."

"I'm at the bookstore with Eli. He asked me to lunch—"

"Aw, really? Like on a date?"

"No, as friends. Remember, we're not going there."

"Right, right. Okay, proceed."

"So we're looking for a pregnancy journal for me, and somehow, we got on the topic about where we conceived the baby. And then, it hit me, this wave of heat followed by vivid, and I mean . . . *vivid* images of that night. And just like that, I became all panting and needy and . . . horny. It was so bad. Then he leaned down to be eye level with an extremely concerned look on his face. It was mortifying."

"Oh my God, you told him you were fantasizing right there, in front of the how to birth a melon books?"

"Good God, no! Are you insane? I told him I had to pee and fled."

"Smart move."

"Did your sister ever experience something like this? For weeks, I've been so disgusted by the mere thought of a penis or any sort of affection that I feel absolutely out of sorts right now that a penis doesn't seem so repulsive anymore."

"Are you saying penises offer affection? Because it's more like a pounding—depending on who you're with, but affection? The penis doesn't have that kind of bone in its sheath of skin."

I'm silent for a second and then say, "I honestly hate you right now."

"I'm just spitting out facts."

"Just tell me if your sister experienced this or if I need to talk to my doctor."

"Oh, she did," Blakely says, her voice full of innuendo. "And frankly, I've been waiting and hoping this would happen to you."

"What would happen to me?"

"The horny phase. It doesn't happen to everyone, but when the second trimester comes along, that libido shoots through the roof, and I'll guarantee your nipples will harden at the sound of a wrapper opening, thinking it's a condom. You are in for a world of fun. Especially sharing a bed with Eli . . . oooo, this is where you cash in."

"What the hell are you talking about?"

"You're going to want sex, and badly. Eli is clearly good at it, so enjoy it."

"I told you, we're not doing that."

"Okay." She chuckles.

"I'm serious."

"Yes, sure, I know you are. Talk to me in a week or two and

let me know if it still stands. Because if you're already having these vivid thoughts, then it's only going to get worse. And Eli likes you. If anything, you guys can have no-strings-attached sex. He helps you. You help him with the backup. It's a win-win."

"That's not going to happen. We are not hooking up. That is off limits."

———

HAVE his lips always been that full looking?

No . . . we are not thinking about his lips or his biceps or his hair and how it looks so full that I want to lose my fingers in it. Nor are we thinking about his boxer briefs, what's underneath the boxer briefs, and what can be done when said boxer briefs are removed. Seriously, Penny. Get a freaking grip.

I shake my head and stare down at my menu. Food, you want food.

Not him.

Food.

"Do you like French onion soup?" Eli asks. "It's fucking incredible here."

Onions.

That's exactly what I need.

I need a big fat onion to sit on my tongue and fester because nothing screams mood diffuser like a festered onion.

"I'll have that," I nearly scream, scaring Eli back into his chair. Clearing my throat, I calmly say, "French onion soup sounds good." Gently, I rest my menu down and then pick up my water to take a sip.

Studying me with a curious eye, Eli asks, "Are you okay? You've been a little jumpy ever since the bookstore."

"Do you realize you must ask me if I'm okay a dozen times a day?"

"Well, because I want to make sure you're okay."

"How about this? You assume I'm okay unless told otherwise."

Just then, the server comes over, and Eli, the gentleman that he is, orders soup, a bread basket, and a side salad for each of us. The server, of course, asks for a selfie—which Eli kindly obliges —and then he takes off with our order.

When he's out of earshot, Eli speaks lowly and says, "It's my duty to make sure you're okay, so if I ask, it's because I care." He winks. "Deal with it."

"Deal with it?"

"Yup." He grins. "Now, tell me, are you excited to fill out our pregnancy journals together?"

I twist my water glass on the table and shake my head. "I can't believe you got one too."

"I want the full experience."

"Oh, do you now?" I smile. "Then does that mean we should hook the stim machine up to your undercarriage and reenact what childbirth will feel like? I've seen many influencer couples do that. Seems like fun."

He shrugs. "If you want. My threshold for pain is quite high."

"You say that now."

"I mean it," he says, his voice completely serious. "I once played a game with a torn ligament in my ankle. I can make it through pretty much anything."

"Are you challenging me?"

"Let me put it this way, Penny. You're carrying my child, which means I'll do what you ask of me. If that means strapping a stim machine to my junk so I can experience a sliver of what you'll be going through, fine, I'll do it. If you want to strap a watermelon to my stomach and make me do everyday activities around the house, then that's fine too. Whatever you want, you get."

"It's annoying how accommodating you are."

He laughs out loud. "I'm sorry, would you like me to be more unaccommodating?"

"No, because then that will only irritate me more."

It's my duty to make sure you're okay.

"Glad you're honest." He lifts his glass of water. "Tell me another thing I might not know about you."

I give it some thought, and tell him the first thing that comes to mind. "I had a pregnancy scare in college. And I know how that makes me look—"

"It doesn't make you look like anything. There's such a shit double standard in this world. If a guy has sex, then he's the man, but if a girl has sex, she's looked down upon. That needs to change. Don't apologize for being a human with normal sexual needs."

His comment doesn't surprise me. Eli seems to be the kind of guy who roots for everyone. An open and honest man with good morals. But the seriousness, the irritation in his voice, now *that* surprises me. It almost sounds like he's fed up and can't take the negative talk anymore.

"Well, thank you for saying that. I appreciate it. So, pregnancy scare. I was dating a guy, Jamie. He was pre-med and very focused but also very sweet. He made time for me in his busy schedule, which I know was hard for him. We dated for a little over a year when I thought I missed my period. I was freaked out, of course, because we were juniors in college and having a baby at that time isn't ideal. When I told him, he immediately, without even blinking, told me to get an abortion. Demanded it. I didn't even know if I was pregnant yet. I was just hoping for him to hold my hand and take me to the store to get a test. But he wouldn't even look at me. He got up and left. I never took a test because I was so nervous it would be true, and then three days after, I got my period. When I told him, he tried to pull me into a hug, but I ended things with him. During a scary time of my life, he abandoned me. I couldn't forgive him for that."

"Wow." Eli drags his hand over his mouth. "What a fucking tool." And then his eyes grow soft when he says, "I'm sorry that happened to you. No woman deserves such inconsiderate treatment, especially during such a sensitive and unknowing time. Where's the loser now?"

"I think he's a family practitioner in Pennsylvania somewhere. Last I saw, he was still single."

"Shocking," Eli says sarcastically.

"Well, I'm still single. What does that say about me?"

"You're not single. You have me, babe." He winks, and my
heart performs a rather messy somersault.

"We're not a thing, Eli."

"No, but you still have me, and that's all that matters."

Just then, our soup, salad, and bread are brought out. Eli
thanks the server with a very welcoming grin and then picks up
his spoon to smash through the crouton top of the soup.

"Are you going to share something with me?" I ask.

He lifts a spoonful of his soup, blows on it, and then takes a
mouthful. When he dips his spoon back in his bowl, he says,
"When my mom passed away, I was sent to live with her cousin,
Marge. She had three children as well, all girls. Because they
didn't trust me, a twelve-year-old boy who just lost his mom, they
made a room for me in their barn. It was insulated, so I wasn't
freezing during the winter, but it was lonely. Mom had got me
started in hockey when I was about nine, and even though she
didn't make a lot in her job, somehow, she made sure I got to
play hockey. Have new skates, equipment. All that stuff. I thought
I was going to lose hockey like I lost my mom. It was shit. But I
earned money for ice time through chores. I got up early to feed
the animals, help with the cows, and after practice and school, I
helped Tobias with anything he needed. I learned a lot, but I
wasn't loved. There was no affection shown toward me, and
there were many nights when I just went to my barn to watch
hockey. Study it, live it."

Tears are streaming down my cheeks when he glances up
at me.

"Shit," he says as he moves his chair around the table. He
picks up my hand and strokes my knuckles with his thumb. "I
didn't tell you that to make you cry. I just wanted you to know
that I know what it feels like to feel abandoned."

"But that's so awful. You were so alone for six years. How is that fair to you?"

"It wasn't, but it was the hand I was dealt. I had hockey, and the hard work around the farm grew me into the man I am today. They weren't abusive—"

"Making you live in a barn by yourself because they were afraid you'd be a sexual predator is abusive, Eli."

"I guess in a certain way, it is. But they never hurt me. I spent Christmas with them. They bought me simple presents, but they were more of a fostering family than anything. I barely knew them, and they were put in a situation they didn't ask for."

"But you step up when put in that kind of situation." My mind keeps thinking about a twelve-year-old version of Eli with bright blue-green eyes, just looking for anybody to love him, and it splits me in two. Before I know what I'm doing, I throw my arms around him and bury my face into his chest, clinging tight. "I'm so sorry you went through that."

"You don't need to apologize. I pay a therapist a lot of money to help me sort through all the bullshit in my head. But I appreciate your compassion."

I still hold him tight, not sure I'll be able to let go right away.

He rubs my back softly as he says, "Penny, it's really okay. I'm okay."

"Are you sure?" My voice is wobbly, and snot drips from my nose.

"Yes." He chuckles. "I'm sure."

When I pull away, I reach for my napkin, and I quickly blot at my nose. Eli's hand remains on my back, ever the protector. "How about after this, we go get some ice cream?"

I nod. "I'd like that."

⊏⊐

"STOP, you did not draw naked women for money," I say as I sit across from Eli at home. We decided to pick up ice cream at the store and make sundaes. I will not be telling Blakely because I believe this would be considered cheating on her.

"Sure did. I needed the cash. Hockey was expensive, so I did anything to make a buck."

"Are you good at drawing?"

"Fuck no." He shakes his head. "But I convinced the guys at my school they needed my drawings. They went for ten bucks apiece."

"Ten dollars? For someone else's drawing, that they could probably do themselves?"

"Yup. My signature was pointy nipples. The guys loved them. Every girl had really pointy nipples, and it worked for me. I made around five thousand dollars on those things."

"Wait, what? Five thousand dollars? That means you had to draw five hundred pictures of pointy nipples. When did you have the time?"

"I made the time. Luckily, school came easy to me, so I didn't have to spend hours upon hours studying. When I was alone in the barn, I'd just start drawing. I'd replicate a lot and sometimes do different variations, but yeah, it was a great moneymaker for me. I have the horny guys in my school to thank for supporting my hockey career."

"Would you ever get special requests?"

He smirks. "I got a few, but I didn't stray far from what I knew."

"Did Marge or Tobias ever ask where you were getting the money from?"

"Not really. They didn't pay close attention. I used the money for new gear and gas for the people who drove me when I needed a ride. Simple shit like that."

"Did you ever keep pictures for yourself?"

He lifts his spoonful of mint chocolate chip ice cream. "A few."

Chuckling, I ask, "Did you ever get a boner drawing them?"

This time, he laughs and nods. "A few times."

"Wow, just wow." I wipe my mouth with a napkin. "I never would have pegged you for an erotic artist."

"You have to make a living somehow. Thankfully for me, I found my niche and ran with it."

"Did anyone ever try to copy your business model?"

"Oh, yeah. There was this guy who thought he'd try to undersell me, but his stuff wasn't nearly as good as mine. I learned shading in my art class and used that to my advantage."

"Do you draw still?"

He shakes his head. "Not really. And honestly, I think if I did, all I'd draw is topless women because that's all I know how to draw. Then what do I look like at that point? Not someone trying to make money for ice time. I'd just look like a twenty-eight-year-old creep."

"You're right about that. Oh, I can only imagine what the guys would say if they caught you drawing on the bus."

"Let's not even think about it." He finishes the last mouthful of his ice cream—which he took three giant scoops of. I'm not here to judge, but it was a lot of ice cream, and he ate it with no problem. "Ever step into the realm of drawing penises?"

"Only the basic silhouette on a random person's notepad just to—no pun intended—dick around with them."

"Were you a troublemaker in school?"

"Depends. When it came to class and school, I was a respectful student. I never wanted to get in trouble, and if I knew I could kiss my teacher's ass for a better grade, I'd do it. But with my friends, I was a bit of a troublemaker. I had so much fun pranking Pacey, so I found ways to get under my friends' skin as well. I was a tease."

"Ah, kind of like the mild torture I've been through since I've been here?"

"Exactly." I smile at him. "And I appreciate your use of the word mild because, let's be honest, half the stuff I've done to you is barely a blip on the things I could be doing."

"Oh? Are there pranks you want to pull on me?"

"There are things I could be doing, but I'm also a smart

225

woman, and I know you probably have a vengeful side in you. I know you wouldn't just let my pranks go unanswered. There would be retaliation."

"You can bet your cute ass that I'd retaliate. And you wouldn't know when or how."

"Exactly why I don't go there. Well, besides the whole baby chip thing, I couldn't help myself. It was too easy. Plus, I needed that laugh."

"Glad I could assist in making your day brighter."

"You did. There have been some rough days, so that was definitely a bright one."

"When you speak of rough days, are you talking about when we weren't talking?"

"All of it," I say while I absentmindedly twirl my spoon in my bowl. "Finding out I was pregnant, telling you and Pacey, and the fallout from that. The awkward phase we went through, and then, of course, the fight between you and Remi and the ramifications from that." I let out a deep sigh. "I feel like I hopped on a roller coaster unwillingly. But today has helped a lot. Today has been one of the best days I've had in a while, so thank you."

"It has been a pretty great day." He smiles back at me. "Now, how should we end it?"

"Maybe we watch some *Ozark*?"

"Sounds perfect." He stands from the table and takes my bowl. "I'll clean up. You go get in your pajamas, and I'll meet you out here for some *Ozark*."

And then he walks into the kitchen with our bowls, leaving me feeling warm and . . . anchored. And after such a crazy last month or so, that's a good way to feel.

Chapter Eighteen

ELI

"Penny?" I whisper.

"Hmm," she mumbles against my arm

"You fell asleep."

"Mmm," is her response but she doesn't move.

I can't say when, possibly twenty minutes into the show, but she slowly lowered her head to my shoulder, and her body became limp. I looked over and saw that her eyes were closed, and I didn't have it in me to wake her up. But now that the show's over, she's not going to want to stay here the entire night. That's just asking for pain in the morning, and I know her body must be sore from all of the changes it's going through.

Not wanting to disturb her, I carefully maneuver both of our bodies until I have her in my grasp, carrying her like a baby as I stand from the couch. Lifting her feels like nothing, and I carefully walk her to the bedroom while turning off the lights. She already brushed her teeth when she put on her pajamas.

With all the finesse I can muster, I lay her gently on the bed and then unfold the blankets so I can cover her. She doesn't move from her position on the bed. Completely and utterly passed out, she is the depiction of someone who needs rest.

Her blonde hair fans out against the cream silk of her pillowcase, and her rosy-red lips part ever so slightly as she breathes.

Devoid of makeup and completely natural, she's easily the most gorgeous woman I've ever met. A true beauty with soft features that I haven't been able to get out of my head since my birthday. Because now that I'm getting to know her, I feel myself opening up, wanting to tell her more, wanting her to tell me more. I want to know about her childhood, not just as Pacey's sister, but as the girl she was back then. I want to hear her laugh when I say stupid shit, and I want to see her cheeks blush when I say something laced with innuendo.

I want to be privileged to her charm, to her teasing, to the way she ever so slightly flips her hair over her shoulder only to pin me with that striking blue gaze.

I desperately want to climb into this bed, and instead of lying on my side where I'd lie stiff as a board, trying not to touch her, I want to pull her soft curves into my chest and bury my head in her hair. I want to feel her against me, wake up with my arm around her.

What's so fucking crazy to me is I'm not *that* guy. I don't think about this kind of shit. I don't cuddle. I don't revel in the feel of a woman resting on my shoulder. I don't have it in me to explore these deep-seated feelings that develop into more.

I still remember asking Marge for a hug on one of the bad days not long after my mom passed away. I'd nearly cried at school because I missed my mom so much. I'd seen Marge hug her girls, and I desperately craved a hug. Mom had been the best hugger. But Marge had turned to me, looking . . . horrified. I can still hear her quiet yet firm words. *"I'm not your mom, Eli. I can't . . . well, I shouldn't give you hugs. You're a boy and don't need them."* She then sent me away to the barn. I'd felt . . . banished. Disciplined. Simply for asking for affection.

I think that was the moment I first believed feelings equated to weakness. That it was weak to look for affection. As a defense mechanism, I guess I shut those thoughts down, avoided looking for affection, and I've done a good job of it so far.

Until Penny cried for me today.

I turn away from her and head back to the living room. *Is that what this is?*

I need to go for a walk to clear my mind. That will help. I can't search for something I decided I didn't need many years ago. *Fuck.* Things just got intense today with sharing, that's all.

Nothing else.

I'm not falling for her.

I'm not wishing for her affection.

Nope.

———

"YOU'RE LATE," Taters says as he joins me on the bikes, where I'm warming up my legs.

"Had a therapy appointment today that I couldn't miss," I answer.

"Couldn't miss? You say that as if you needed it."

"I did," I say as I push a little harder on the bike.

Taters's voice grows with concern. "Everything okay?"

"Yeah." I slow down the bike and glance over my shoulder to ensure we're the only ones in here. All the guys are already in the locker room getting ready for our last home game of the season. With a wild card berth already assured for us, we'll take it easy tonight. "Just had to talk through some things. The other day, I told Penny about my mom and growing up. It opened some wounds that made me feel confused, and I wanted to work through that shit."

"Confused in what way?"

Instead of pedaling, we're both just sitting on the bikes now, talking. I push my hand through my hair and say, "Well, after we spoke, I started to have these feelings toward Penny, the type of stuff I don't think about. I had this overwhelming urge to hold her, cuddle into her, protect her in a way I've never thought of before."

"Because you like her," Taters says, causing me to blow out a heavy sigh.

"You see, that's the thing. I think I was just feeling that way because she's a female figure in my life, and I want to protect her."

"Is that what your therapist said?" Taters asks.

"It's what we concluded."

"Uh-huh, and did you tell him that you can't stop thinking about her sexually?"

"Dude, I don't think about her like that."

"Bullshit, you said you couldn't get her out of your head, and that's why you haven't hooked up with anyone else."

"Well, yeah. I mean"—I lean in and whisper—"she was the best sex I've ever had. It's going to take a second to recover from that."

"Did you tell your therapist that?"

"No, he doesn't need to know that."

"Uh, yeah, he does. You're giving him half the story, man. He's going to think that you're having some mom complex when the reality is, Penny Lawes is rocking your goddamn world, and you have no clue how to deal with it."

"I don't like her like that."

"Bull . . . shit," he says. "You can deny that all you want, but the fact is, you slept with her because you thought she was hot. Now you're getting to know her on a deeper level, you're starting to realize how amazing she is, and you don't know how to handle that."

"That's so not fucking true," I say. "And even if it were true, Lawes looked me in the goddamn eyes and told me not to go there with her. That I wasn't the guy she needed. Do you really think I'm going to go against what Lawes has said after everything that happened? Fuck no."

"Funny thing is, Lawes might be her brother, but he doesn't get to dictate your life. If you like her, go for it."

I shake my head. "I don't think I can provide her with what she needs. I'm not in the right mindset to even think about a relationship. I'm not sure how to even have one. I'm sure as hell not going to try to figure it out while navigating this pregnancy. It's a bad fucking idea."

"Okay," Taters says while he starts to pedal again. "But I'm going to tell you right now, the minute another man snatches her up, you're going to regret everything you just said to me."

I want to believe he's wrong, but a small part of me thinks that he might be right.

⸺

"GOOD GAME TONIGHT." Penny's voice cuts through the dark of the night.

I pause mid-stride to the bathroom. "Jesus, I didn't know you were awake."

She rolls to the side and flips on her nightstand light, illuminating her beautiful yet sleepy face. "I was in and out a bit." With her palm, she rubs her eye. "Coach was smart not giving you too much playing time."

"Yeah, he's saving us for the first round. I'm glad we're in the playoffs, but the wild card blows—"

"Because you have to play the top seed," she finishes for me. "Yeah, that sucks. But I think you guys have it in you to beat Washington."

"Thanks. Well, I'm going to get ready for bed and then hang out in the living room to cool off a bit."

"Want me to join you?"

"No, get your rest. You're fine."

I move through the bedroom and bathroom as quietly as I can, and when I'm done getting ready, I retreat to the main living space, where I grab myself a glass of water.

My body is sore.

Everywhere.

Even though I didn't play too much today, the season is

catching up to me, and I can practically feel every last muscle in my body telling me that it's ready to be done with the abuse it's been put through.

Happens every year.

My ribs get to the point where sometimes, it hurts to breathe from all the battered blows they've taken. My legs feel like noodles, and the only reason I'm able to skate on them is because of the impeccable training staff we have who revitalize me every day. And my brain is mentally exhausted. The hockey season is a long-ass season, not to mention the playoffs on top of that.

My mind is already thinking about the quiet peacefulness of being in Banff, surrounded by trees, and not having to worry about what I eat, conserving energy, and who the hell we're playing next.

I've never been this mentally checked out of the playoffs before, but I think it's from the emotional journey I've been on these last few months. It's been difficult, to say the least, and I'm ready for it all to be over.

For a moment of peace, where I can take a deep breath and focus on the things that matter—preparing for this baby and how I'm going to handle being a father and a hockey player come next season.

From the kitchen, I go to sit on the couch but stop from the figure standing just outside the hallway.

"Jesus," I breathe out. "You scared me, Penny."

"Sorry, I was thirsty."

I walk up to her and hand her my water. "Here, take mine."

"Thank you." She takes a sip before lowering the glass. "What are you going to do out here?"

I shrug. "I don't know. Think. I just don't want to lie in bed when I know I'm going to toss and turn until I can calm down."

"Want company?" The way she asks, standing there in her matching pink flannel pajamas, she looks so goddamn cute, it would be hard to turn her away.

"Not if you're tired. I don't want to keep you up."

"You won't," she says as she takes my hand in hers and moves me toward the small couch.

I forgot just how small she is up until this moment, when my palm connects with hers, my hand eclipsing hers. She fits . . . perfectly.

We both take a seat on the small loveseat that she calls a couch, and whereas I sit down with my back to the back cushions, she leans against the armrest and stretches her legs over my lap. It shows how comfortable she is with me now.

"Is that okay?" she asks.

"Yeah, you're good," I say. "Do you want a blanket?"

"Sure," she answers before taking another sip of water.

I grab the draped blanket from over the arm of the chair, unfold it, and place it over our laps.

"Good?" I ask.

"Yeah." She smiles and hands me the water.

Still thirsty, I take a drink, then hold it between my two hands.

"I know this is normal, you know," she says. "Being wired after a game. Needing to release some of the pressure and adrenaline. I have been around hockey for years."

"Well, I've never truly found a way to calm down that works for me other than . . ." *fucking.* But I am not saying that.

"Other than what?" But, of course, she won't let that go.

I let out a heavy sigh and say, "Other than sex."

"Oh." She chuckles. "Well, as I said, you're welcome to go take care of that need."

"And as I said, that won't be happening."

"So that's why you're wired right now, trying to find a new solution to the energy?"

"Exactly," I answer. "Calmly sitting is what I'm going with tonight."

"Sounds riveting."

"Maybe a conversation might help. If you want to join in, we could get into some heavy stuff that will make us both not want to sleep," I joke.

"I think I'm good with not talking about the heavy stuff at the moment, especially since I'm half awake." She rests her head on the back of the couch. "Tell me what you'd be doing right now if you weren't stuck sharing a blanket with a pregnant woman."

I shake my head. "You don't want to know what I'd be doing."

"I really do." She smirks. "Give me the dirty details. I want to hear all about it."

I scratch the side of my jaw and figure, why the hell not? We've been honest about everything else between us, so why not this?

"Well, I'd be dressed in a suit still, not comfortable five-year-old sweatpants. And I'd probably be at one of my favorite bars, the one where I saw you on my birthday being one of them. I'd either have Posey or one of the other guys with me, and I'd be looking for someone to take home."

"I just don't see Levi as someone who trolls the bars looking for someone to sleep with."

"He's the most deceiving one out of all of us. He has this innocent, goofy, outward appearance, but he also has a real dirty side to him. He's gotten blow jobs in the locker room before."

"What?" Her eyes widen in surprise. "You're talking about sweet, bologna-eating Levi Posey?"

"Yup," I answer. "He has everyone on the outside fooled, but the guy is a real player. And I mean that in the nicest way possible because he's super respectful, but the guy gets a lot of action. You just don't hear about it at all."

"No, you only hear about your action." She smirks.

"Which has been absolutely abolished thanks to you." I squeeze her leg so she knows I'm teasing.

"Took you off the market without technically taking you off the market." She conducts a mock bow. "You are more than welcome."

"Yes, thank you for that." I take another sip of the water. "But I actually don't mind the quiet nights in. I think I spend so much time moving around from state to state, game to game, that I forget to just take a second to breathe. I've always wondered why the guys on the team who are either married or have significant others retreat so early, but I can see the appeal. Coming home, slipping on some comfortable pants, and just sitting back. It's nice."

"Oh my God, Eli Hornsby, are you becoming domesticated?"

"I very well might be. All thanks to that little nugget in there." I motion to her stomach. "Have you thought about the baby much? I've focused on more than just the pregnancy this week. I've actually thought about how you will be having a baby. My therapist and I have been talking about it. He said I need to face the reality that I'll be in charge of a human."

"I have thought about it." She plays with the edge of the blanket as she speaks. I finish the rest of the water and then set the empty glass on the coffee table in front of me. With nothing to hold, I just rest my arms on the top of her legs. "I have considered how I love this apartment, but I think it might be too small for a baby and me. I've started looking around for something a little bigger. I inquired to see if anything was opening up in this building. I love this area, and it's close to work but not too expensive where I can't afford it. And I feel safe here."

"Which is important." I look around, and as I've thought before—and mentioned—my apartment could work. It has two bedrooms. The last time I brought it up, Penny quickly shut that idea down. But . . . "It is small here, and I'm sure you'd want a second bedroom." *Like my place.*

"Yeah. The baby needs his or her own bedroom, and not that I've done a lot of research, but I do know babies come with a lot of things. Lots of gadgets and large items, and even though this apartment feels like home, I know it won't be able to house all of the baby things."

"How many large things?"

"A lot."

"But the baby is so small."

"That's the crazy part." She chuckles.

"I don't know if you've given this much thought, so tell me to shut up if you don't know yet, but are you going to hire a nanny for when you're at work or drop the baby off at childcare? Assuming you're going to keep working."

"I have to keep working, Eli. I need money to pay for everything."

"Technically . . ." I drag my hand over the soft fabric of the blanket. "All you have to do is file for child support, and given my salary, you'd make a living off that."

When I glance over at her, I can see the stunned look on her expression. "Do you really think I'd do that?"

"No, but hell . . . how do I say this without coming off like an ass?" I scratch my chin. "If you wanted to stay at home with the baby, just know, I can cover things. And I don't mean that in a chauvinistic way. I just want you to know you have options with whatever way you choose to go."

"Well, I appreciate that, but I truly love my job and don't foresee giving that up. The Agitators actually offer childcare at the arena. So I'd probably just use that. That way, I could still go see the baby while at work. A lot of parents do that. They spend their lunch break with their kids."

"Really?" I ask. "I had no idea they offered that. Do the players use it?"

She nods. "Yup. Zalapski sends his kids there a lot since he's a single dad. They also offer a shuttle service for kids who need rides from school. They're pretty good like that."

"Wow, I had no idea. So that means I could go visit the baby too, right?"

"Yeah. There are even smaller rooms meant for players to sneak away with their kids. Plenty of games and puzzles and toys as well that are, of course, all sanitized. It's a great resource."

"I see that you've thought about that."

"Only a little."

"Have you thought about the sex of the baby?" I ask as I shift slightly closer to her so her legs are more comfortably draped over me.

"I have. And I mean this when I say, I'll be happy either way, but if I had to pick, I'd want a boy."

"Interesting," I say slowly.

"Why? Oh my God, do you want a girl?"

"Yeah, I kind of do. I just know the boy will be a little dickhead like me, and I'm not looking forward to that, whereas the girl, I really hope she's like you."

That makes her smile. "Like me?"

"Yeah. Smart, sweet, kind heart, a touch sassy, and, of course, beautiful."

She pauses, and her eyes grow soft when she says, "That's really sweet, Eli. But you realize a boy could have the same personality as me and a girl could have the same personality as you. Think about that for a second."

My eyes widen in horror. "Fuck . . . I'm not sure either of us could handle that."

"Definitely not," she answers and then yawns.

"Do you want to go to bed?"

She shakes her head. "No, I like talking to you."

"I like talking to you, too, Penny." And I mean that. This might be a complete change from what I'm used to doing after games, but I really like it.

"Tell me about any names you might like," she says.

"Now, that's something I haven't thought about at all. But . . . you know, if it's a boy, we could call him Puck. That would be cool, right?"

"Wow, you just guaranteed yourself no right to naming our baby. Good job."

I let out a loud laugh. "You don't like Puck?"

"No one likes the name Puck. Honestly, Eli. What happened to just a solid name?"

"Like Peggy Leggy?"

That makes her throw her head back and laugh so hard that actual tears spring from her eyes. "Oh God, I totally forgot about that. What were the other names . . . Jimmy John, or Johnny Jim?"

"Both solid options. But I think I'm leaning toward Johnny Jim."

She nods. "Oddly, I was thinking the same thing."

"Then it's settled. We are either having a Johnny Jim or a Peggy Leggy."

She holds her hand out to shake on it, and I take her hand, giving it a light squeeze, but for some reason, I don't let go. Instead, I keep my hand clasped with hers and rest it on her legs. "It's a deal, but the last name, that has to be mine."

She smirks. "Everyone is just going to love Johnny Jim Hornsby. What a name."

"Couldn't agree more."

Chapter Nineteen

PENNY

"Do you have everything you need?" I ask Eli as I sit cross-legged on the bed, watching him pack for the first game of the playoffs. Since they're the wild card, they don't get home advantage, so they'll be flying to Washington in a few hours.

"I think so." He scratches his bare chest as he looks around the room, making sure he hasn't left anything. He's grown more and more comfortable with me, and it shows as he stands in front of me in nothing but a pair of sweatpants that hang incredibly low on his waist. So low that it sits below his Adonis belt, so all I've seen this afternoon are his perfectly defined abs, thick pecs, and loads and loads of muscular skin. It's been hard to keep my eyes off him. "I have the dry-cleaned shoes, which actually look better than ever."

"Maybe you should do it more often because . . ." I waft my hand in front of my nose and make a disgusted face. "Pee-yew."

"Fuck off, they weren't that bad."

I laugh. "They made me puke."

239

"You made yourself puke."

I eye him with my most scornful glare. "The baby you inserted inside me made me puke. Therefore, you made me puke."

He chuckles lightly. "The visual with that sentence." He zips up his suitcase. "You know, you've never watched me pack before. Does this mean you're going to miss me?"

"Miss you? Pfft, no way." I passively wave my hand in front of me. "I couldn't be happier about your departure. Quite thrilled, to be honest."

"Mm-hmm." He takes a seat on the bed and leans toward me. He points at my eye. "I can see a tear, right there. You're sad."

Tear?

What tear?

I quickly swipe at my eye. "There's no tear."

He chuckles. "Ahh, but it was fun for a second making you think you were crying over me."

"Ugh, you're irritating. You wish I was crying over you, then you could ride off on an airplane, chest puffed, knowing you have some girl back home pining after you. Well, I'll have you know, Eli Hornsby, there is no pining here."

"You sure know how to gut a guy."

I smirk. "My specialty."

"Okay, so you're not going to miss me. You're actually thrilled I'm leaving."

"Thrilled and thriving when you're gone, that's my motto."

He slowly nods while he looks away. "In that case, I guess I won't bother calling you at night, you know, since you're thrilled and thriving and all."

"Good," I say. "Wouldn't want to have to sit through your snooze fest of a diatribe. Thank you for doing me a favor."

Now he turns to me, and with a shake of his head and a glint in his eyes, he says, "You know, you're a real smart-ass."

I flutter my lashes at him. "Aren't you positively ecstatic you get to have a baby with me?"

"Oh, yeah." He stands from the bed and moves over to his suit that's strewn across the chair in the corner of the bedroom. Without even thinking twice, he slips his sweatpants off, revealing his black boxer briefs, and reaches for his black pants.

"Wow," I say, holding my hand up to my eyes. "What do you think you're doing there, fella?"

"Uh, getting changed. I have to wear a suit, you know that."

Eyes still covered, I say, "There's a perfectly fine bathroom right over there."

"Yes, and you've seen me completely naked. In fact, my dick has been inside you. Therefore, you seeing me in my boxer briefs is G-rated at this point."

I hear the telltale sound of a zipper, so I lower my hand and glance over at him. He's facing the wall, so I'm granted a view of his backside. His taut back muscles seem to tighten as they move closer to his ass, which, of course, is the perfect round shape from all those years skating up and down the ice. And his legs, which are thicker than the average man's, are encased by his tight suit pants.

He slips his black dress shirt over his upper half and then turns toward me, and my tongue nearly falls out of my mouth from the sight in front of me. He's hunched over ever so slightly to button up the shirt, causing his abs to ripple in the most delicious way possible.

When he looks up at me, I'm met with a devilish grin. "Getting a good show?"

Yes.

But he doesn't need to know that.

I chuck a pillow at him and then fling myself back on the bed. "You wish. Nothing I haven't seen before."

"Uh-huh, and that's why you were covering your eyes a moment ago."

"Because I'm a lady, and I'm sorry if I don't want to be blinded by your man-thigh."

"My legs aren't that white."

"Okay, sure, they're not *that* white, Hornsby."

I hear him walk over to me, rounding the bed until he's just above me, tucking his shirt in. "It's Eli."

I gulp.

Because the way he just said that, all deep and serious, while wearing this black ensemble, makes me swallow my tongue and want to beg for more.

Trying to mask the overwhelming thudding of my heart, I say, "Oh, here I thought it was Elijah."

Once again, he shakes his head at me. "Smart-ass." He puts his shoes on and a deep blue velvet jacket with black lapels.

He adjusts his cuffs and then holds his arms out. "How do I look?"

Really.

Fucking.

Good.

Lickable.

Suckable.

Fuckable.

I plaster on a smile and offer him a thumbs up. "Matching."

"Matching?" He raises a brow at me. "That's all you have to say? I'm matching?"

"Takes a noble man to be able to mix textures like you." I offer him a golf clap. "Well done, dear sir."

His quizzical brow grows higher. "You're acting weirder than usual. What's going on?"

"Nothing is going on," I say over the roar of my escalating pulse. "Everything is normal over here."

He still eyes me. "Why don't I believe you?"

"Trust issues, perhaps?" I hop off the bed, and I reach for his bag to help him, but he's quickly at my back, taking the bag from me. "Hey, I can help."

"You're pregnant. You're not lifting anything."

"Uh, I lifted a donut to my mouth yesterday. Where were you then, huh?"

"You are something else right now." He moves down the hallway toward the living room, where he sets his bag down and turns toward me. "I'm slightly nervous about leaving you in this sort of state."

Hands crossed at my chest, I ask, "And what sort of state would you be referring to?"

He gestures up and down my body. "This insane state where you're clearly losing it."

My fingers drum along my biceps as I maintain my crossed position. Head tilted down, I say, "Has anyone ever told you not to call a pregnant woman insane?"

When I glance up at him, I can see the panic in his eyes, which, of course, makes me laugh. And for some reason, I can't seem to stop myself. I close the space between us, and I wrap my arms around him while chuckling.

"Don't worry, I'm not about to bite your head off before you leave."

I press my cheek to his chest, and stiffly, he returns the hug. "Well, that's good." He's coming off as awkward, and it's probably because I'm holding him, and we don't normally hold each other.

But I can't seem to let go. The baby is forcing me to do this, to keep my hold on him.

The baby is soaking him up.

His strength.

His delicious smell.

His stiff but warm embrace.

After a few more seconds, he finally pulls me in tighter. I relish in the feel of him holding me tightly. I haven't really given it a lot of thought before this moment, but being held by Eli reminds me that I haven't had much human touch through the whole thing. As much as I love living on my own, I often miss human contact.

This, right here—hugging him—it feels right.

It feels comforting.

Needed.

He rubs my back and quietly says, "Are you going to be okay?"

"Yeah," I say. "Just needed a hug."

That causes him to pull away just slightly so he can look me in the eyes. "If you needed a hug, you should have asked."

"I'm going to awkwardly take it instead."

"That works too." He squeezes me close to him again. "We're both going through something incredibly different. If that means you need a hug, then don't hesitate to ask."

"Okay. Thank you."

He continues to rub my back until I realize I'm going to make him late, so I let go of him and take a step back.

"You good?" he asks me.

"Yes, I'm good. Thank you."

He nods. "Okay, I'll call you when I get to my hotel room." He reaches out and tilts my chin up. "I'll talk to you later."

Why do I feel so needy right now? I don't want him to leave. I want him to sit on the couch with me again, my legs draped over him, just talking about everything and nothing. I want to listen to his deep voice as he tells me about his upcoming hockey game, and I want to watch the way he tugs on his hair when I compliment his skills. I want him to stay here, with me, close to me . . .

Tears well in my eyes, and I curse my godforsaken hormones for not being able to keep it together.

"What's wrong?" he says, immediately picking up on the walking disaster in front of him.

I swipe at my eyes. "Ugh, hormones. I'm fine."

He makes a strangled noise in his throat and then pulls me back into a hug. "Please don't cry. I already feel guilty leaving you. You crying is just going to make it worse."

"It's not me crying. It's the baby unfairly controlling how I feel. You put the baby in there. Blame yourself."

He chuckles and kisses the top of my head. "I'll fully take the blame for this." He lifts my chin when he pulls away, and our eyes connect.

Mine watery.

His full of concern.

"I'll call you later."

"Okay."

"Make sure you answer."

"I will."

"Okay." He heaves a sigh and then picks up his bag. "Let me know if you need anything." He offers me a wave, which I return.

"Kick some ass, Hornsby." When he pins me with a glare, I chuckle and say, "Kick some ass, Eli."

"Better."

And then he leaves, the door softly clicking behind him.

I fall back on the couch and drape my arm over my eyes. God, I'm in so much trouble.

Because I can't decide if I like Eli or if it's the hormones. Either way, my body is reacting to him in a way that I can't control, and I know it's only a matter of time before this tight hold I have on my emotions and needs will slip.

———

THE COOL, sweet feel of a pint of Cherry Garcia rests on my chest as I delight in the comedic styling of Melissa McCarthy rolling around on a car. I love her so much. If I could be friends with a celebrity, I'd choose her. She's not only funny but also down to earth and very kind. I feel akin to her in a way that is so strong I have the temptation to message her on Instagram and ask her if she wants to be my friend.

Would she accept?

I smooth the ice cream off my spoon and give it some good thought.

"I'm a good time," I say out loud to no one. "Possibly strange at times, but who doesn't like a little odd behavior in a friendship? Keeps things alive and slightly unpredictable, which is key to maintaining longevity in a relationship." I pause and then say, "Am I really talking out loud to myself?"

Knock. Knock.

I quickly turn to the door. Who the hell is that?

It's clearly not an appropriate time for a visitor. It's past eight, which to me is the time when everyone crawls into their homes and strips down to troll status. Hence why I'm wearing my pajama pants and don't mind the ice cream stain on my shirt.

I strip out of my blanket cocoon, set my ice cream down, and walk to the door, where I look through the peephole to see a large bouquet.

Oh. Flower delivery.

I open the door, and instead of taking a bouquet from a delivery person, I'm bombarded by the happy glees of my mother and father.

What.

On.

Earth.

"Penny!" Mom shrieks as she passes the bouquet to Dad and pulls me into a large hug. "Oh honey, we are so happy to see you."

Uh . . . what are they doing here?

Am I missing something? Did I miss an email? Correspondence that they were coming? Was Pacey supposed to tell me they were on their way and forgot to mention it to me?

Either way . . . THANK GOD the boys are on an away trip because that would have been incredibly uncomfortable to explain to them why a six-foot-four hockey player, shirtless—because God forbid he wear a shirt—lived with me.

And then a bolt of sweat forms on the back of my neck as I remember said six-foot-four beast moved in with me. What if there's evidence of his residence here? As my mom hugs me and my dad looks at us lovingly, I desperately scan the living room to see if he left a sock or a man item around the apartment.

I can't tell from this angle, but that's not to say I'm in the clear.

"Oh, you feel so frail. Have you been eating?" She pulls away and spots the ice cream stain on my shirt. "Well, I guess you have."

"Take these, Tina," Dad says as he gives her the bouquet and then pulls me into a hug, jostling me around. "Oh, my baby girl, how are you?"

Frantically trying to see if there's any evidence of my live-in baby daddy.

"Surprised," I answer as my dad traps me in a giant bear hug. My face is buried in his chest, making it impossible to look around. "Did you guys say you were coming?" I muffle into him.

"Nope," Mom answers with pride. "This was done on a whim. We thought we'd surprise you. Hopefully catch a game when the boys return, but until then, we'd love to spend some time with our girl. And before you freak out, don't you worry, we have a hotel room."

Look at that. Miracles still do exist.

"Oh, well, what a surprise," I say when Dad releases me. I straighten my shirt and give the apartment one more scan. Nothing seems to be screaming "hockey man lives here." "Sorry that I'm not properly dressed."

"Oh, please." Mom waves her hand dismissively. "No need to dress up on our account."

"And you brought me flowers." I take the vase. "How kind."

"We didn't." Mom waggles her eyebrows at me. They didn't? "They were at your doorstep when we arrived."

Hmm, I thought I heard a knock when I was going to the bathroom but just chalked it up to the noises of living in an apartment building.

"Who could they be from?" Mom asks, following me into the kitchen while Dad shuts the door and takes his shoes off.

Who could they be from? Great question. No one sends me flowers, so I honestly have no idea.

Wait . . . they can't be.

They wouldn't be.

Eli would never send me flowers.

There's no reason to.

And we don't do that, romantic gestures like flowers.

Would he send me flowers?

"There's a card," Mom says as she reaches for it, and out of pure survival instincts, I swat her hand away and rip the card out of the holder and hold it against my chest.

"No one," I say with panic. "They're, uh, they're from me." That sounds believable. "Yeah, you see, I read this book that you should treat yourself to certain things you don't normally get, so yeah, I sent myself flowers. Sounds kind of lame, but trust me when I say, my spirits were just lifted seeing how much I care for myself." I toss the card on the counter. "Anyway, do you guys want any ice cream? I think I have a quarter of a pint I can offer you."

"The card says it's from E. Who's E?"

I whip around to see my mom reading the card. What on earth? Isn't privacy a thing for old people?

"And why is this E telling you thanks for the hug?"

He wrote that? What would possess him to do such a thing?

"Err, well E, is me." I nod and smile manically. "E stands for the E in Penny. Have to come up with a nickname, you know. That was part of the blog post. Nickname yourself. Clearly, I'm not very creative. Anywho, I hugged myself earlier, long and hard, and boy, oh boy was it a great one. So great that I decided to send myself flowers." I sigh. "So, yeah, about that ice cream." I motion toward the freezer.

Dad is now on the couch and holds up my phone. "Are you calling yourself too? Seems like an Eli is trying to get in touch with you."

Jesus Christ!

Panic swells in my chest as I run up to the phone and snatch it out of my dad's hand before he could do something completely asinine like answer it himself.

"Eli?" Mom coos. "Ooo, who is this Eli human?"

"Telemarketer," I screech as I hurry down the hall. "Excuse me for a moment."

I find the first door I see, open it, and shove myself into the hall closet, bumbling over my vacuum and dodging empty plastic hangers. When I answer the phone, I whisper, "Hello?"

"Penny? Is everything okay?"

"No," I hiss at him. "Everything is not okay. My parents are here."

"They're . . . what? They're there, at the apartment?"

"Yes, and they are questioning who the flowers are from. Which are gorgeous and thank you, but why did you send flowers? And you said thank you for the hug? Now my mom thinks I nicknamed myself E, and I send myself flowers and hug myself. Do you know what kind of loser status my parents must think I'm at right now? I'm pretty sure they're questioning all of their parenting decisions at this very moment."

"Why would they think you sent yourself flowers?"

"Because that's what I told them when they asked who they were from. I am panicking. Can you hear that I'm panicking? Because I am. I haven't told them about the baby yet and then all of a sudden, while I'm trying to enjoy freaking Ben and Jerry's and watch a movie to get my mind off the fact that I miss your company, my parents come barging in with your flowers. Eli, this is not good. They're going to be able to smell it."

"Smell what?"

"My pregnancy," I hiss again. "Keep up."

"Uh, I'm still trying to comprehend that you hate the flowers but miss my company."

"I didn't hate the flowers, but I have ice cream on my shirt. I didn't think I'd be seeing anyone. If I knew I'd be entertaining tonight, do you think I'd be doing it so unpolished? At least I would have put some ChapStick on or something. But then they stop by, unannounced, and I have ice cream on my shirt." My throat chokes up as tears start to form. "I don't want my parents to see me like this, a frozen dairy treat stuck to the fabric threads of my shirt, telling them self-love stories of how I enjoy my own damn arms wrapped around me so much that I send myself flowers. It's not a good look, Eli."

"Okay, slow down for a second. Did they actually see you hug yourself?"

"THAT'S what you're going to pull from what I said? What is actually wrong with you?"

"I don't know. I don't know how to help. Maybe, just be cool, you know? Try to act like everything is normal. Or tell them about the baby. It might help."

"Tell them that I'm pregnant and have no intentions of getting married to the man who inserted the baby?"

"I didn't insert—" He lets out a large sigh. "Listen—"

"And what if they ask about the sex of the baby or the name. For Christ's sake, Eli, we are naming our child Peggy Leggy or Johnny Jim Hornsby. They'll commit me to an insane asylum."

"They're not going to commit you to an insane asylum. They won't even know unless you say something and only say something if you're ready. How long will they be there?"

"At least through to the third game of the series."

"Okay, so I'll be back. Why don't you just hang out with them, have fun, and when I get back, we can tell them together so I can be there to support you and field questions."

"You'd do that?"

"Of course I would—"

The closet door opens, revealing my parents. Arms crossed, nostrils flared, they stare down at me with twin glares that I can actually feel my skin start to melt off my body.

"Uh, can I help you?" I ask them with a forced smile.

Dad holds up a book. "Why do you have this?"

My eyes narrow in on the pregnancy book I've been reading.

Oh, God.

That's more revealing than a damn man sock!

"Uh, Eli, I'm going to have to call you back." Before he can say anything, I hang up and slowly extract myself from the closet.

Okay, don't panic. This will all be okay. You've gotten pretty far on the whole loving yourself lie, so why not stretch it out a bit? They don't know what's going on with your friends. For all they know, it could belong to someone else.

Like Blakely.

YES!

It belongs to Blakely. She's in a relationship. She's sexually involved. She's the perfect scapegoat.

"It's Blakely's," I shout and then turn to face my parents, whose arms are still crossed. "She left it here at my apartment the other night. Yeah . . ." I slowly nod. "Poor girl is knocked up, but you know, at least she has Perry, right?"

"Call her," Mom says.

"Um, what?" I blink a few times.

"Call her. We'd like to congratulate her." There's a challenge in my mom's eyes, the kind of challenge that scared me right out of my socks when I was young. And if I was wearing socks now, they most likely would have shot across the room.

"You know, it's late," I say as casually as possible. "I don't want to disturb her."

"Call. Her," Mom says, her words so forceful that I find myself searching for my friend's name on my phone.

"I don't even think she's awake, you know. Because of the baby and all. Makes her tired. She just sleeps all day, every day. Sleep. Sleep. Sleep. So, don't be surprised if she doesn't answer. Maybe we should just—"

"Put the call on speaker."

Ugh, my mom is being a total pill.

I put the phone on speaker and think of a way to communicate to my friend that she needs to cover for me. If she's quick enough on her feet, she'll be able to handle this. I know she can.

"Hello?" she answers.

"Hey, you," I say as casually as I can. "So I just wanted—"

Mom jostles the phone out of my hand like a ninja and then walks toward the kitchen, out of grabbing distance. "Hello, Blakely dear. It's Mrs. Lawes. How are you?"

"Oh hey there, uh, I'm good. How are you? Visiting, I'm guessing?"

"Yes, we are." Mom looks up at me and says, "Just wanted to celebrate with our daughter."

Oh no . . .

Ladies and gentlemen, this is what a master conversationalist

251

looks like at her best. Tina Lawes was once the PTA president, a woman celebrated for her ability to communicate so well that local businesses feared her as she walked around, searching for donations. She is a manipulator but will do it with a smile, so you never truly realize what Tina Lawes has done to you until you're recovering, thinking over everything, and slowly understanding that you've been stripped from your dignity by only her words.

And that's precisely what she's doing right now.

"Celebrating, oh that's fun," Blakely says.

Blakely, if you can hear me, you're pregnant. You have absorbed my child, and you are now the one with indigestion, onion cravings, and the need to bury your head into a pair of testicles because that's how horny you are.

Can you hear me?

"Yes, such exciting news about Penny, right?"

Damn it!

"Blakely, don't—"

I start to shout, but Dad slips his hand over my mouth, halting me. Did I mention Joseph Lawes is Tina Lawes's evil henchman? He performs the dirty work, as you can see.

"Aw, about the baby? And here she thought you guys were going to be angry." Oh Blakely, what have you done? "I told her anyone would be happy to be grandparents."

"Thank you, Blakely. You've been incredibly helpful." And then, like the freaking mob boss that she is, she hangs up and slowly lowers the phone onto the counter.

"Care to explain?" Mom says.

"Uhh . . . sure." I step away from my dad and slowly make my way to the living room area, near the windows. "You see, when she said baby, she was talking about the puppy I'm going to adopt. Surprise." I raise my arms up in the air. "We call it a baby."

"And what are these?" Mom holds up a bottle of prenatal vitamins.

You see, this is EXACTLY why people should tell you they're coming *before* they arrive, not just show up willy-nilly. It makes it impossible to hide all evidence of a pregnancy!

"I read that it's healthy to take prenatals before adopting a dog. Something about the dog can feel your nerves—"

"Penny!" Dad shouts, startling the ever-loving shit right out of me.

With my hand clasped to my chest, I turn toward my dad and say, "You almost made me pee myself."

"Tell the goddamn truth, right now."

I've been caught.

And here I thought I was truly doing a good job at covering it up. *I'm lying.* My parents are not idiots, and I knew I'd have no real chance of lying myself out of this one.

I slump on the loveseat, exhausted. "Ugh, fine. Yes, the rumors are true. I had sexual intercourse." I hold my finger up. "*Protected* sexual intercourse, I'd like to add, and five weeks later found out I was pregnant. I didn't tell you because I didn't know how to tell you, and frankly, the entire situation has been an absolute nightmare because I don't want to like Eli. Still, I do like him, and we're not supposed to like each other because we're just friends, and he sure as hell doesn't want a relationship with this brand of crazy. But the flowers are from him because I gave him a hug. It was a friendly hug on his part, not so much on my part, and I smelled his chest, and I *liked* it."

I reach over and grab my ice cream, scoop up a large ball, and shove it in my mouth. The cold is so severe that I feel my brain freeze immediately, but I don't care. I keep powering through and shoveling the sweet goodness in.

"And he's living with me. Eli, that is. Yup. We share living quarters and a bed." I lick the spoon. "He sleeps in my bed, but there has been absolutely no touching. Zero touching. Not even a gentle brush of a hand or an accidental erection in the morning. No moaning. No groaning. Nothing. Sure, we said this was platonic, but if you ask me, I think he's too scared to even go near me in fear of getting me pregnant again before this first child is born. Which I know can't happen, but with my luck, somehow, someway, I'd get pregnant in my shin, and that would be that. One baby in the uterus, one in the shin. Call it a medical marvel." I twirl my spoon in the air.

"Honey—"

"And of course, I have to get pregnant by a hockey player—"

"Wait . . . Eli *Hornsby*?" Dad asks.

"Oh yeah, Dad. Eli freaking Hornsby." I lick my lips obnoxiously. "The one and only. Yup, we did it. Sorry to throw it out there like that, but in fact, we canoodled in bed . . . naked. Technically, it started in front of his fireplace, then the wall, then his bed. And we were so naked, the most naked of all the nakedness. Private parts touched. And all it took was one time to seal the deal, and I told him and Pacey at the same time, and oh my God, Pacey clocked Eli right in the face. An old one-two pow pow." I jab the air with my ice cream carton. "And then threatened Eli with his life if he didn't live with me. I thought it was ridiculous until I realized I was doing this all by myself, and how could I do this by myself, take care of a baby, if I still have trouble ordering my own food off Door Dash? I say no plasticware, yet they still give me plasticware. I'm having this delivered to my place of residence. What person doesn't have eating utensils? Stop killing the earth with all this godforsaken plasticware to a freaking place of residence. What more does a person have to do to avoid all of the PLASTICWARE?"

"Honey." My mom is at my side now and slowly lowers my ice cream and spoon. She hands it to my dad and then pulls me into a hug. When her hand hits my hair, I start sobbing into her shoulder.

"I don't want plasticware, Mom."

"I know, honey. I know." She rubs my back, and all I can think about is how when she rubs it, it isn't nearly as nice as when Eli does it. "Joseph, why don't you make us all some tea, and we can talk."

"Sure." Dad starts to move but then he comes over and places a kiss on top of my head. "It'll be okay, sweetie. We'll work through this."

Chapter Twenty

ELI

I pace back and forth in front of the hotel door, wondering why the fuck he hasn't opened it yet. I raise my fist to pound once again just as it parts open, and Pacey's one eye shows through the crack.

"What the actual fuck?"

I push through the door, knocking him back, and start pacing his room. "Dude, have you heard from—" I glance at him and notice he's naked, holding a pillow in front of his crotch, and that's it. "Uh, what the hell are you doing?"

"What the hell am *I* doing?" he asks. "I'm trying to have some privacy with my goddamn girlfriend."

"Winnie is here?" I ask, confused.

"No, you moron, I'm FaceTiming her."

I look over at the nightstand, where I see a phone propped up. "Oh . . ."

"Yeah. Oh. So tell me what the hell you want before I shove my foot up your ass."

"Your parents. They surprised Penny and are with her right now."

His anger quickly morphs into concern. "Oh, shit." Pillow still covering his crotch, he walks over to the nightstand where I get the perfect view of his ass—nothing I haven't seen before—and picks up the phone. "Hey, babe. I need to handle this."

"Okay. Love you. Call me later."

"Love you." He hangs up the phone and then walks into the bathroom, where he slips on a pair of pants.

When he comes back out, he still has the pillow covering his crotch as he sits down on the bed.

"Boner?" I ask.

"Yeah, and I'd rather you not be able to stare at it."

"You're confusing me with Taters. He's the one who likes to compare."

Pacey drags his hand down his face. "Just tell me what the fuck is going on."

"I don't really know. I sent her flowers, because she was feeling weird earlier, and I thought they'd cheer her up. When I didn't hear from her, I called, and she answered in a whispered tone. Told me her parents were there and then started talking about how she was telling them she nicknamed herself and sent her own flowers. Honestly, I couldn't fucking follow, and then I heard her parents, and she hung up. I came here because I wasn't sure if you'd heard anything."

"Nothing. Should I call my parents?"

"Can you?" I ask in desperation. "I've tried calling Penny several times, and she's not picking up. I've also tried texting. It's been silent." I push my hand through my hair. "She's been terrified to tell your parents, man. I'm worried she's not doing well."

Pacey is already scrolling through his phone, looking for his parents' info. He presses a button and then turns it on speaker. It rings a few times, and then the phone is picked up. My heart jumps in my chest.

"Hey, son," a male voice says over the phone.

"Hey, Dad," Pacey says nervously. "Uh, how are you?"

"Doing okay, just listening to your sister have a nervous breakdown is all. You? Get to your hotel, okay?"

"Fuck," I mutter as I start to pace.

"Yeah . . . Eli told me that you guys were there. I'm assuming you found out?"

"We did. We found out a lot of things. I forgot how much your sister can ramble. I've heard some things a father should never hear about his daughter. Is Eli with you right now?"

Pacey looks over at me. "He is."

"Ahh, tell him I don't think I'll be able to look him in the eye after the monologue your sister gave us about his birthday night."

Jesus fuck!

I grip my hair with both my hands now. "Is she okay?" I mouth.

"How is she, Dad?"

"Uh, still crying. Mom is holding her. We've been back and forth with emotions. I think your mom is going to stay with her tonight, and I'll head back to the hotel. She seems to be going through a lot."

"Yeah, Eli was saying she was scared to tell you. Are you . . . mad?"

He pauses and then says, "No. This sort of thing happens. You're all adults, and sometimes you can do everything right, and something still goes wrong. I'm just more upset that she's taken so long to tell us. She just started her second trimester. That's a long time to go through something of this magnitude alone."

"She hasn't been alone," Pacey says quickly. "Eli has been there." Color me shocked, he's defending me. I know we're on our way to reconciling, but I didn't think I'd be hearing him defend me anytime soon. "And Winnie has been filling in as well as Blakely."

"Which I'm very happy to hear, but she should have told us. Mom could have helped her with some things. Been someone to talk to who has been through it before. You should have encouraged her, Pacey."

Guilt washes over Pacey as he says, "Yeah, I haven't necessarily handled everything in the best way possible. Anger sort of took over, and it's taken a lot of conversations with Winnie to realize I was being a tool."

Looks like I owe Winnie a present.

"But I promise, I'm better now."

"Good. You know you two can come to us with anything, right? We don't want you to fear us."

"I think she was more embarrassed than anything," Pacey says.

"Nothing to be embarrassed about. She's carrying a child, and even if it's not the way we would love to see it, she's still having a baby, which means we'll be grandparents. That's exciting to us."

The ball of tension in my chest slightly eases.

"Well, I'm glad you know because I know it's been weighing on her."

"Seems that way. I'm going to help Mom, okay?"

"Can you tell him to ask her to call me or text, anything?" I say to Pacey.

"I heard him," Joseph says. "I'll make sure she reaches out. Good luck tomorrow, boys."

"Thanks, Dad." After a few more goodbyes, Pacey hangs up and then tosses the phone to the side. "Man, that was not what I was expecting to do this evening."

"Sorry," I say while taking a seat next to him on the bed. "I just wanted to make sure she was okay."

"No, I appreciate it." He pats me on the back. "You're really stepping up."

"Just don't want to be like my dad," I say.

"You're not. And when I said that——"

"I know, dude, I know." I let out a huge sigh and stand. "Well, I'll let you get back to whatever it was that you were doing with Winnie, and I'm going to wait painfully next to my phone for your sister to call."

"Thanks, and hey, you did the right thing coming here. I

know things have been weird between us, but I appreciate you pushing through it to make sure my sister is okay."

"No need to thank me. I care about her and will do anything to make sure she's okay."

———

FUCK, I've never been this out of sorts before in my entire life. It's been an hour since I went to Pacey's room. It's fucking late here, and we have a goddamn playoff game tomorrow, but the only thing I can think about at the moment is Penny.

Should I just try calling her again? Shoot her a text? Remind her that I want to hear from her?

Sitting on the edge of my bed, I stare at my phone as my leg bounces up and down, willing it to ring. But it doesn't. It stays dead silent, so instead of waiting, I text her again.

Eli: *It's late here, I know, but I need to know that you're okay. Call or text. I'm awake waiting to hear from you.*

Once I press send, I start to pace my room again. Was that text wrapped up in a tidy bow of desperation? Yup. Do I care? I don't give one single fuck.

Since I already brushed my teeth, got ready for bed, and laid out my clothes for tomorrow, I have nothing to keep me busy. Therefore, I traverse this hotel carpet—

Buzz. Buzz.

I nearly toss my phone in the air from the excitement of a text message.

Please be from Penny.

Please be from Penny.

I glance down at the phone, and instant relief hits me as I see that she texted me back. I take a seat on my bed and open the text message.

Penny: *Sorry. Been an emotional night. Everything is good.*

I text her back immediately.

Eli: *Can I FaceTime you?*

I don't know what possessed me to ask, but I need to see her face. I need to make sure she's okay.

Penny: *I look like a wreck.*

Eli: *I don't care. Please, Penny?*

I wait for a response, worried that she's going to say no when my phone buzzes with a FaceTime call.

Thank. Fuck.

I accept the call and hold the phone out in front of me as Penny's tear-soaked face appears on the screen.

"Hey," she says with a sheepish smile. She's lying on her bed, curled into her pillow, looking like she needs a goddamn hug.

"Hey." I exhale harshly and then push my hand through my hair. "You're probably sick of me asking, but how are you?"

"Better. I'm sorry I didn't text or call. I thought you'd be asleep by now."

I shake my head. "Nah, been waiting to hear from you. So, is everything okay with your parents?"

She nods. "My mom was going to stay the night with me, but I told her I was fine and she could go to the hotel with my dad. They just left."

"How do they feel?"

"Honestly? Excited." The lightest of smirks pulls at her lips. "After the shock of it all, they were very excited and already started talking about possibly finding a place in Vancouver so they can split their time between here and Minnesota. They want to be as helpful as possible. They understand your schedule and want to be a support to both of us."

"Wow, that's . . . that's pretty awesome of them."

"They also want to have dinner with you when you come back. I told them to wait until the playoffs are done."

"No, I can have dinner when I get back from Washington. I'd like that, actually."

"Are you sure? I know you have more important things to do—"

"Penny, you are the most important thing in my life right now. I'll have dinner with them when I get back. That's not a problem at all. I just ask that we do it at your place and order in or something. We'll be disturbed too much if we go out, especially right in the middle of the playoffs."

"I think they'd enjoy something more intimate." She snuggles closer to her pillow. "Thank you."

I lie back on my bed, holding my phone up. "It's my pleasure." I stare at her tear-stained eyes and say, "You look beautiful, Penny."

"Oh my God, you're sleep-deprived."

I shake my head. "I'm not. You truly are. You look so real and so natural. You really are beautiful."

"You're going to make me cry again."

"Well, we don't want that. Tell me more about this farce you were running about sending flowers to yourself."

She chuckles and then turns on her bed to the other side. "It's what sheer panic will do to you. The number of lies I sputtered was astronomical."

And just like that, we spend the next half hour laughing and talking about how she attempted to trick her parents when they first arrived. We laugh so hard together that tears spring to our eyes, and we're both gasping for air. It's the most real and honest conversation I've ever had, and every time she pushes her hair behind her ear or snuggles into her pillow, all I can think about is how I wished it was me she was resting on, or how I wish I was the one fixing her hair.

To put myself in that sort of frame of mind is a scary thought, but the more we talk, the more we hang out, and the more I realize that I wish things were different for the both of us because I like her.

I actually fucking like this girl.

—

THE PAST FEW days have been one blow after the other. We ended up losing our first game, two to one. We looked lethargic and distracted out there, and our coach called us on it. When it came to our second game of the series, we ended up losing again, this time three to one. It was fucking painful.

None of us have our heads in the game. And all for different reasons.

Taters is caught up in the drama that is his ex-girlfriend.

From what I heard, Posey has a crush on a girl he can't even fathom asking out. Not sure why, but that's all I've heard.

Pacey and I have been recovering from what happened between us earlier.

And the playoffs are always hard on Halsey because of his brother.

You're looking at five guys who can't get their heads out of their asses.

But now that we're home, we're looking to turn things around. It's a seven-game series. We have some work to do, but we aren't out of it yet.

With my bags over my shoulder, I make my way up to Penny's apartment, and I take my key out of my pocket to unlock the door.

Once again, it's late, so I'm not expecting her to be up. I'm just glad to be back. I thought I'd miss my apartment more than I have, but I'm starting to realize that it's not the place I go home to, but having someone there when you arrive.

I walk through the door and lock it up behind me. The living room is dark other than the one accent lamp she left on for me. I turn it off and make my way to the bedroom, where I slip through the door, trying to be as quiet as possible. When I spot her in the bed sleeping, I gently set my bags down and go to the walk-in closet, where I strip out of my suit. In the dark, I sift out my toothbrush and tiptoe to the bathroom, where I brush my teeth, leaving the light off the whole time. She must be tired if she isn't stirring. I spoke to her every night, and she said she's been apartment hunting, working on a list with her mom of things she's going to need for the baby and, of course, working. I've noticed how tired she is in her eyes.

I slip out of the bathroom and don't worry about plugging in my phone since we could charge it on the airplane. Instead, I quietly move to my side of the bed just as she shifts. She rubs her eye and says, "Hey, you."

"Hey, I'm sorry I woke you up."

"It's fine. I have to pee." She throws the blankets off her, revealing a silk pajama set that I haven't seen yet. A thinly strapped tank top and matching shorts that barely reach her upper thigh. It's, uh . . . it's really fucking sexy, especially when her hair is all mussed up like that. "How was your flight?" she asks as she walks up to me.

My eyes are glued on the way her tits sway against the silk fabric of her shirt. Is it me, or have they gotten bigger?

"Uh, it was good," I say just as she puts her arms around me. I sink into her embrace and hug her back, moving one of my hands up to the nape of her neck. "Glad that I'm back," I say truthfully.

"Me too," she says as she presses her cheek against my bare chest. "It's not the same without you."

And then she releases me and goes to the bathroom, leaving me in a state of bewilderment. I wasn't expecting her to say that, nor was I expecting the welcoming hug.

Nor was I expecting the warm feeling spreading through my veins from both her words and her embrace.

I'm glad for technology like FaceTime. But it doesn't compare to being here in person. I miss so much while I'm gone. It hasn't sat well with me that I've missed every single doctor's appointment. And now I also missed being her shoulder to lean on when she told her parents about us. *About our baby.*

And this is only the beginning. How much more will I miss when the baby is actually born? Yet this beautiful, sleepy woman greeted me with a hug, telling me she missed me. *She is fucking awesome.*

Clearing my throat, I walk to my side of the bed and get under the covers. The bed is warm, and the silk of her sheets comfort me as I sink into her mattress. I used to love my bed when I'd get home from an away trip. I sought it out, looking for that bit of home after being gone for so long, but now, this bed is what feels right. A little lumpy in spots but cool to the touch and warm from the person next to me. I sleep my best here. And that's a scary realization because I know being here is only short term. Things will change once the baby is born, and the unknown is starting to make me panic.

Penny emerges from the bathroom and slips under the covers as well, facing me. From the distant light of the moon, I can catch glimpses of her beautiful face.

"Good?" I ask her.

She nods against her pillow. "Yeah."

"How has it been with your parents?"

"Okay. Mom said I looked frail, which didn't bode well for me."

I frown. "Have you been eating?"

"Not as much as I used to, but now that I'm feeling better, I'm able to stomach some things. My mom also said I have a little bump."

"Really?"

"Yeah." She grabs my hand and places it on her stomach. "You probably won't be able to tell, but there's something in there." She smooths my palm over her stomach, but all I feel is her warm skin. "I'll try to show you in the morning. I think it just looks like I'm bloated."

"I'm sure it doesn't." Instead of moving my hand, I keep it in place, holding her stomach gently.

"I'm tired." She yawns.

"Then let's go to sleep." Reluctantly I move my hand off her stomach just as her eyes drift shut.

"Can I ask you a favor, Eli?" she says quietly.

"Anything," I answer.

Her eyes open again and connect with mine. "I know we don't do this, and it might be crossing the line, but after the past few days, I could really use the comfort."

"What do you need?"

"Will you cuddle with me? Just once," she says quickly. "And I won't ask again. I just need to feel . . . protected."

I don't even hesitate. I'd do anything she asks of me, but I'm also so goddamn desperate to be near her. I haven't been able to shake the feeling of her warm body pressed against mine since she hugged me before I left for our away trip.

So her request is an easy yes for me.

I scoot in close to her back, rest my head right next to hers, and then drape my arm over her waist. The moment I'm settled, she melts into my embrace, and it's the best fucking feeling I've ever felt . . . well, besides the moment I sank into her. This is a close second.

She's so goddamn warm, and soft, and feels like she fits perfectly against me. Like she was meant to be spooned by me all along. I move in so close that I share her pillow and bury my head in her hair.

"Are you comfortable?" I ask her, my palm splaying across her stomach.

"Very," she whispers. "Thank you, Eli."

No, thank you, Penny.

"You're welcome," I answer as my eyes drift shut and my breathing evens out. I hadn't realized how much I love being able to hold a woman in an embrace like this. Perhaps it's simply that I haven't had this sort of . . . affection for the past sixteen years. *Nor been needed.*

This bed, these sheets, this woman. *She feels so right.* And before I know it, I'm drifting off to sleep, my mind a complete haze as I soak in being next to Penny and holding her like I'd have hoped to.

Chapter Twenty-One

PENNY

"Mmm," I mumble as a hand moves across my breast, fingers toying with my nipple. "Right there," I whisper.

My entire body is lit up, pulsing, throbbing, as the fingers circle my nipple over and over again until . . . a pinch.

"Ohhh," I moan and shift my pelvis, bumping right into a very stiff erection behind me. Yes, that's exactly what I want.

That's what I need.

Relief.

Desperately, I move against the erection behind me, the crack of my ass gliding up and down his ridge, searching for more.

"Yes, fu-uck."

I pause.

That wasn't me. That was a male voice.

A familiar male voice.

And the desperation in that one "fuck" encompasses exactly how I feel.

His hand cups my breast and squeezes, sending me into a

tailspin of need. Who cares if the voice is familiar? Whatever he's doing is working for me on so many levels. I arch my back into his touch and lean into the strong masculine chest behind me.

"More," I whisper just as my hand grips the top of his and guides it slowly down my stomach.

There is one thing on my mind . . .

I want him between my legs.

I need him between my legs.

"Touch me," I whisper. "Make me come."

"Fucking hell," he says, and I pause his hand one more time.

Why do I know that voice?

I release his hand and reach behind me, connecting with a strong chest, a body built for protection. His hips thrust into my backside, reminding me how hard he is, and that's when my eyes blink open, and the sun coming in from the window momentarily blinds me.

It takes me a few seconds, but when I finally gain my bearings and feel a hand at my stomach, toying with the hem of my shorts, I turn around to find Eli sleeping.

"Oh God," I say loudly, causing him to fling his eyes open.

He assesses what's going on, and when he realizes his hand is almost down my pants, he springs backward, flying right out of bed and onto the floor.

When he stands, he dives his hand through his hair, and together, as if there is a giant neon sign pointing south, we both look at his crotch and take in his massive erection.

And I mean . . . massive.

"Fuck." He drops his hands in front of him. "Shit, I'm sorry, Penny. I didn't, fuck, I was dreaming. I'm sorry."

"It's okay," I say while I adjust my top to make sure everything is covered. "I, uh, I was dreaming too."

Only, right now, I kind of wish I didn't wake up.

His teeth roll over his bottom lip as his eyes glance down at my hardened nipples, and at this moment, I don't think I've ever seen anything sexier in my life. Eli Hornsby, hair all a mess, chest muscles rippling as his hands attempt to cover his erection, while his eyes blaze. *At me.*

Silence falls between us as we both attempt to catch our breaths, our eyes staying connected.

Look at him. What I wouldn't give for him to lower his hands, walk over here, and finish what he started.

I'd savor the moment, begging and pleading with him to please take away this unbelievable heaviness that rests between my legs.

"Uh, I should probably go . . . take a shower." He nods toward the bathroom.

Ughhhh, noooooo.

Come over here.

Rip my shirt off.

Run your tongue all over my body.

Let me feel you inside me . . . one more time.

"Yeah, a shower sounds like a good idea. I'll just, uh, lie here."

Good one, Penny. He doesn't need the play-by-play.

"Okay." Hands kept in front of him, he moves around the bed and into the bathroom, where I hear the shower turn on immediately.

I throw my head back on the pillow as my body attempts to calm down from what I just went through. I thought it was a very realistic dream, yet it felt so real because it was real. It was his hand caressing me, pinching my nipple. It was his hard-on behind me and his breath on my neck. It was all real, and God, do I wish I was in that shower with him.

More than that, I wish he was still in this bed, finishing what we started.

I drape my hand over my eyes and take deep breaths. You're fine.

But I'm really not.

I'm fired up.

I'm needy.

My desire for this man is so strong that I can taste it.

It's why I couldn't stop myself from hugging him before he left for his away trip. It's why I couldn't stop reading the card he sent with the flowers. It's why when I watched the game, I begged and pleaded with the cameras to focus on him, to show me any glimpse I could get. And late at night, it's why I watch TikToks on the team's account that focus mainly on him.

It's why I couldn't wait for him to come home. Win or lose, I just wanted him. And when he did come home, I wanted so much more than a hug, but I knew it was all I could ask for, so I took it, relishing in the way my cheek felt pressed against his bare chest.

And then my vulnerability took over, and before I could stop myself, I asked him to cuddle me. I thought he'd say no. I thought he'd deny me, but he didn't. Instead, he wrapped himself around me, and I curled into his large body. I've never felt so comfortable in my life, and I fell asleep before I could even take my next breath.

When I woke up this morning to his hands all over me, he almost gave me exactly what I needed. It's branded in my brain, the way his hand cascaded down my stomach and almost beneath my shorts. The feel of his dexterous fingers toying with my nipple, and the way he pressed his pelvis into me, showing me how turned on he was. God . . . why couldn't we finish?

My teeth roll over my lip as I slowly lower my hand between my legs to feel how aroused I am. So, I start moving my fingers over my clit. My legs spread even wider, and I bring my other hand to my breast, trying to recreate how he played with my nipples.

In the distance, I hear the shower spray against the tile, and I envision him naked, droplets of water cascading down his rock-hard chest, all the way to his length where his hand is pumping vigorously, seeking that release I'm seeking as well.

A groan escapes me as I wiggle against my hand, searching . . .

Sweat forms on my upper lip as my body tenses, the motion of my fingers bringing me to a much-needed apex. And that's when I hear it, his guttural groan from behind the closed bathroom door and then a hand slap to the wall.

He's coming.

In the shower. Right now.

He's coming to the thought of us, to what we did, in this bed.

That's all it takes. The image of him hunched over, spilling himself onto the shower floor.

My muscles tense, and a delicious, much-needed orgasm rips through me. My back arches, and my fingers fly over my clit over and over, pulling every last ounce of pleasure from my bones until I'm completely sated and out of breath.

I remove my hand and melt into the mattress.

Although I took care of my present need, I know it wasn't what my body wanted or desired.

I want him.

His cock.

His mouth.

His body writhing and pulsing over mine.

And then it hits me . . . very clearly, something that's been building for a while.

I'm not sure how much longer I can keep my distance.

And right now? I have no idea why I should.

⊏⊐

"KNOCKITY, KNOCK, KNOCK," Blakely says from the doorway of my office. She's holding a takeout bag from our favorite salad place and a drink carrier with lemonades—a drink I've never truly cared about until this pregnancy. Now, all I want is lemonade.

All the time.

"Hey," I say while looking up from my computer. "Let me finish this email real quick."

"Sure thing. Want me to shut the door?"

"Yes," I say, my voice laced with desperation.

"That yes has some meaning behind it, and given the fact

that the boys got home last night, I'm guessing there has to be something in that beautiful brain of yours that you need to tell me."

"You are correct."

While I finish typing, Blakely shuts the door and sets up lunch for us at my desk before taking the seat across from me. We both ordered the southwestern chicken salad with extra guacamole. It's a go-to for us that we nearly get it once a week.

I press send, and then I turn toward her. "He felt up my boobs this morning."

"What?" Blakely shouts and then catches herself and leans forward. In a whisper, she repeats, "What?"

"Technically, we were both sleeping, but he still felt them up and had a huge hard-on, and I might have rubbed my ass against it and guided his hand down to my shorts."

Blakely fans herself. "Seriously? Were you sleeping still?"

"Yes, and we both woke up before anything serious could have happened, but oh my God, Blakely, I've never wanted anything so bad in my entire life. He, of course, sprang out of bed and muttered some apologies before retreating to the shower."

"Oh, he totally masturbated."

"Yeah, I heard him when he came, and it was so fucking sexy. I, uh . . . I might have done the same."

"Jay-sus. To be a fly on the wall in your apartment this morning." She pours her dressing over her salad and then mixes it around with her fork. "What happened when he came out of the shower?"

"I took a shower, we both had a bagel, and then I came to work."

"Did you talk about it?"

"Nothing other than more apologies." I groan while I squeeze a lime over my salad. "It was as if he was totally humiliated that he even touched me. He could not have gotten out of bed faster."

"Oh please, I bet you if he'd had his own way, he'd have finished what he started."

I shake my head. "No, he doesn't see me like that. I can tell. He's very standoffish around me. Sure, he gives me hugs——"

"And sends you flowers and calls you every night and texts Winnie and me to check on you."

"Because he's concerned about the baby."

"No, because he's concerned about *you*. Why can't you see that?"

"Because that's not how we are. From the beginning, we said this was all going to be a friends thing. Sure, there's attraction there, and of course, I couldn't be hornier at the moment, thank you, hormones, but he doesn't see it that way." *Doesn't see me like that anymore.*

Blakely just shrugs as she forks some salad into her mouth.

"What is that?" I ask. "What's that shrug for?"

"I think there's more to it."

"I don't think——"

There's a knock on the door, and I call out, "Come in."

The door parts open and Eli sticks his handsome face into my office. Freshly showered from his morning skate, his hair still looks wet, and he's wearing a black long-sleeved Agitators shirt and black jogger capris. The man can more than pull off the look.

"Hey, am I interrupting?"

"Nope," Blakely cheerily replies. "We were just talking about your *rousing* morning."

Oh my God!

Eli's eyes flash to mine, and I'm sure my expression resembles a deer in headlights as I look at my friend.

"Heard you got a good feel in."

"Blakely," I hiss at her. "Shut the hell up."

She just laughs as I watch Eli's face redden.

I don't believe I've ever seen the man blush . . . ever, but there he is, standing in the doorway of my office, red cheeks and all. It is a sight to behold.

He clears his throat and says, "Yeah, kind of got lost in my sleep."

"Find what you were looking for in Penny's shirt?"

"I'm going to murder you," I whisper to her before looking up at Eli. "Ignore her. She forgot what social decorum is."

"My boys would probably do the same," he says while scratching the side of his cheek. "And it's true, I did find something in her shirt, a hard nipple."

And that's the Eli I know, right there, the one who can turn embarrassment into a joke.

"Ooo, a hard nipple." Blakely pops the collar of her shirt out and looks down it. "Haven't seen one of those in a while. Good for you on finding one."

"Thank you." Eli chuckles and then turns back to me. "Uh, dinner with your parents is tonight, right?"

"Only if you're up to it. Seriously, you don't—"

"I want to." He smiles. "Just wanted to see if they had any allergies. I was going to make some lasagna. It's the only thing I really know how to make."

"Oh, you don't have to make anything. I don't want to put you out."

"Would it be okay if I made something?" The vulnerability in his voice is so heavy, it nearly weighs me down right then and there. "I like your parents, Penny. And besides, I want to show them that I'm more than just a talented hockey player with a credit card."

Wow, okay . . . not sure my heart can handle such a statement.

I swallow deeply and say, "Of course you can make something if that's what you really want. And my parents don't have any allergies other than my dad can't have cashews, but I doubt you'll put any cashews in the lasagna."

"Not so much." He stuffs his hands in his jogger pockets. "Okay, I'm going to run to the grocery store then. Do you need anything?"

"Um, I think I'm good. I can pick up a dessert on the way home when I'm finished here."

"Don't worry about that. I got it covered." He smirks at me. "Picking up some ice cream." And then he winks, and I swear to God, I can feel my heartbeat between my legs. "Text or call if you need anything."

"Okay. Thanks."

"Catch you later, Penny." And then he leaves, shutting the door behind him.

Blakely, mouth ajar with humor in her eyes, turns toward me and says, "Oh, he wants you."

"Oh my God, can you stop with that? He doesn't."

"He does, and I say go for it."

"You have completely lost it. There is no way. He's just a nice guy."

"Okay, keep telling yourself that." She takes a mouthful of her salad and leans back in her chair. "Mark my words, you two will be married in a year."

"Ha." I guffaw. "Wow, okay, sure, Blakely." Eli Hornsby has made it very, very clear that marriage is not on his radar. She'll be eating her words.

———

HAVE I told you how much I hate my friend?

Because I hate her.

Tremendously.

Since lunch, all I can think about is Eli and the slightest chance he possibly likes me. Which I know is not the case, but now that she's put that in my head, it's all I can think about. He sent me a text a few times at work about random things, nothing serious, and I kept thinking, is he texting me because we're friends or because he wants more?

The logical answer is because we're friends.

The horny, hormonal answer is he wants me.

He wants me so bad that he wishes he could smell me through the phone. That's why he texts so often.

Yup, my mind went to teleporting smell through a cellular service.

And then it graduated from there.

Teleporting scents was just a blip on the radar.

My mind went so far to think that as I'm walking through the door of my apartment to the tangy, tomatoey smell of lasagna, he's waiting on the counter, stretched out completely naked with an oven mitt on his ding-dong, waiting for me to rip it off and start sucking.

Yes, sucking.

That is where we're at, folks. Sucking a man on a countertop.

And what's even worse, when I actually walk through the door and look toward the kitchen, I'm devastated to see that there isn't a man spread across my kitchen counter with an erection pointing at the ceiling with my name on it. Instead, he's leaning on the counter, looking at his phone . . . dressed.

Sure . . . he looks great and all in his light blue sweater and dark jeans with his hair styled to the side that says, I'm meeting the parents tonight. There is nothing about him screaming, "suck my cock, bitch," and it's incredibly disappointing.

He glances up from his phone, and when he sees me, he smiles. "Hey, how was the rest of work?" He sets his phone down and grips the counter, but the damn sweater he's wearing reveals nothing. Not even a slight flex.

"It was fine," I say while hanging my purse on my purse hook in the entryway. "Nothing super great."

He frowns as he studies me. "Are you okay? You seem like you're in a bad mood."

I am, because you're not asking me to take my top off the minute I walk through the door.

"Tired," I say while offering him the best smile I can muster.

Tired . . . not so much.

Sexually charged . . . one thousand percent.

Something has happened to me. Sure, I've been craving intimacy lately. But ever since this morning, since Eli tweaked my nipple, it's almost as though he turned on a light switch in my body, and I can't seem to turn it off.

And my best friend, the one who's supposed to help me, did nothing but throw fuel on the fire.

Instead, she put unrealistic thoughts in my head and then sent me articles about how my "genital sensitivity" has increased drastically and how I should take advantage of it.

She didn't have to tell me that. I already noticed, thank you very much.

"Should we reschedule for a different night?" Eli asks as he walks up to me.

"No, I'll be good. I think I'm going to go take a quick bath, my shoulders are tense, and then I'll get dressed."

"Okay. If you need me to rub your shoulders, just let me know."

His hands all over my body is the last freaking thing I need. I can only imagine my reaction to that.

Panting.

Sweating.

Moaning.

No, thank you.

Do not come near me unless you plan to do so naked.

"I'm good," I say as I slip by him. "Uh, smells good in here, by the way. Real magical."

His brow creases. "Are you sure you're okay?"

"Quite right, quite right," I reply in a British accent, which only causes his brows to rise higher.

I don't blame him.

I'm just as confused as he is.

And there is absolutely no use in explaining any of this to him because I wouldn't know where to begin, so instead, I turn toward the hallway and leave the confused man behind me.

Just take a bath and walk it off, Penny. You have to get it together for dinner tonight.

Chapter Twenty-Two

PENNY

"Wow, that's, uh . . . that's a dress," Eli says as he moves his hand over his mouth, surveying me.

"If I ever learned anything from Rachel Green, it's that I have to wear things that I won't be able to wear when my pregnant belly gets too big." I smooth my hands down my skintight black dress. Yes, it might be too much for dinner with my parents, but when I slipped out of the bathtub, I was feeling really sexy, and I wanted to keep that feeling. So I slipped on this little number.

"Well, you look, uh . . . really good," he says, his voice breaking.

I smile and squeeze his forearm. "Thank you."

While in the bathtub, I relaxed, took care of business—if you know what I mean . . . with the showerhead—and then spent a very long time lotioning my body so I smelled like heaven.

His eyes are still scanning me when he asks, "Is there anything I need to know about your parents?"

"You've met them before. No need to be nervous."

"Yeah, but I didn't meet them under these circumstances."

I adjust the straps of my dress and grumble, "These boobs of mine are making things difficult. I think they get bigger by the minute."

Eli clears his throat just as there's a knock on the door. "Do you want me to get that?"

"No, I got it," I say while shifting my boobs one last time. I give Eli a quick smile and then open the door to reveal my parents. My mom has chosen one of her many floral vest-turtleneck combos, while Dad is wearing the classic Agitators polo that Pacey gave him one year for Christmas. He now has four and rotates through them whenever he's in town.

"Oh my, look at you," Mom says, pulling me into a hug. "You look fantastic."

"I feel fantastic," I say, speaking the truth. The nausea has disappeared for the first time in a while, and I actually feel like I'm glowing. I know people say that about pregnant women, but I actually feel that now.

Dad steps up to Eli and holds his hand out. "Eli, good to see you."

"Good to see you, Mr. Lawes," Eli says, his voice sounding nervous.

"Joseph is fine."

Mom then pulls Eli into a hug and says, "Ooo, I forgot how tall you are. And before you call me Mrs. Lawes, Tina will do."

He chuckles. "Good to see you, Tina."

When Mom pulls away, she sniffs the air and says, "Did someone cook?"

"I did." Eli raises his hand and then sticks it back in the pocket of his jeans. "Hope you like lasagna."

Dad pats his stomach just like a dad would and says, "Always room for lasagna."

"Good, I made a large pan of it."

Dad claps Eli on the back, and together, they walk into the kitchen while Mom hangs back with me.

Whispering, she says, "He made dinner? That's impressive."

Quietly, I say, "He wanted to show you guys he's, as he said, more than a talented hockey player with a credit card."

"He's so adorable." Mom watches as Dad talks to him about the series. Always hockey on his brain. "And my God, honey, is he handsome." Tell me about it. "Are you sure you two are just friends?"

"Positive," I say just as Eli looks up and our eyes meet. He smirks at me and then goes back to cutting up the garlic bread in the kitchen.

"Are you sure? Because that look he just gave you doesn't really say friends."

"Please, Mom, not you too. Blakely won't let up about this nonsense either."

"Well, forgive us if we see something you might not see."

"You're coming up with things in your head."

"Mm-hmm, so this dress you're wearing has nothing to do with him?" She looks me up and down.

"Can't I wear a nice dress?"

"Penny dear, you know I love you, but the dress you're wearing isn't necessarily something you'd wear while having an intimate dinner with your parents. That's more of an intimate one-on-one dress, if you know what I mean."

"Mom, fashion advice from you, the turtleneck queen, won't necessarily be on point."

She chuckles and takes my hand. "So you're telling me those second trimester hormones haven't kicked in?"

I gulp.

"I, uh, I don't know what you're talking about."

She just smiles. "Okay, honey."

And then we walk toward the dining room, where Eli is setting down the breadbasket, and Dad is bringing over the salad.

Like the gracious host he is, Eli asks everyone to take a seat before pulling out my chair and helping me take a seat. My mom eyes me suspiciously, but I just ignore her. It doesn't help that Eli drags his hand over my shoulder before walking away. Doesn't help at all.

He takes the next few minutes to retrieve drinks for everyone, rejecting all help and telling us to just relax. He moves around my kitchen effortlessly, serving everyone lasagna with poise and ease, and he waits until everyone has taken a mouthful of their dinner before he starts his own.

"Wow, this lasagna is incredible," Mom says. "I might have to steal the recipe from you, Eli."

Eli winks, and my ovaries flutter. "I'll be sure to write it down before you leave."

"Is this beef?" Dad asks, jabbing at the meat with his fork.

"Yes, sir."

"Delicious," he says before taking a forkful into his mouth.

"And he didn't burn the garlic bread. He's a keeper," Mom says while picking up a piece of bread.

Chuckling, Eli asks, "How long are you both in town for?"

"We leave after tomorrow night's game," Dad answers. "We can only catch one game. Unfortunately, I have a knee replacement surgery in a few days I have to prepare for."

"Oh wow. That seems pretty serious? Old injury?" Eli asks.

"I used to play some hockey back in my day, and I took a stick to the back of the knee during an exhibition game. I have post-traumatic arthritis as a result, and the operation should provide more mobility and less pain. So we're taking care of that."

"Pacey mentioned you used to play."

"Yes, that was back when we didn't have all the protective gear you have now. We were real men on the ice."

Mom guffaws. "More like real idiots."

Eli and I both chuckle at the same time, which of course causes us to glance at each other, and the warmth I see in Eli's eyes puts a smile on my face.

"What about you two?" Mom asks, butting into something she shouldn't. "Have you thought about what you're going to do when the baby gets here?"

"Not really," I answer. "Still taking this all day by day. Because of the hockey season schedule, Eli hasn't been able to go to a doctor's appointment. Granted, I've really only had a few, but it's all still new."

"Do you have any ultrasound pictures?" Mom asks.

I wince. "I did."

"You did?" Eli asks, looking surprised.

"Yes, but, uh . . ." I take a deep breath. "God, this is humiliating. I was at the park, looking at the pictures while eating a pretzel, and mind you, I hadn't really had anything to eat all day because of nausea, and the pretzel was really hitting the spot. A gust of wind hit me, and the picture blew out of my hand and into the bay."

"What?" Eli chuckles. "You never told me that."

"Well, for one, it's embarrassing. How great of a mom will I be if I can't even keep pictures safe? And two, I didn't want to disappoint you, so I didn't mention it."

Eli turns to me and places his hand on mine, his large palm covering my hand completely. "Penny, you're going to be an amazing mom." My mom audibly sighs. "And if you think about it, you kept the pretzel safe, which is most important, because of nutrients for the baby."

"Wow," Dad says. "Way to spin that, son. Well done."

Eli keeps his eyes on me and says, "I mean it. You're going to be amazing."

Okay . . . well, slap me in the ass because I believe heart eyes are beaming out of me, right in front of my parents, over a plate of lasagna. My body and my mind are spewing all the love and affection for the man sitting right next to me. If it wasn't for my parents sitting across from us, my hand would currently be down his pants, ready and willing to show him how incredibly grateful I am for him.

ELI SETS a bowl of ice cream in front of me, fudge and cherry chunks included.

Is he trying to make me weak in the knees? Because he's doing a really good job at it.

"I know it isn't super fancy," he says, "but Penny has been craving ice cream, so I figured I can't go wrong with this."

"Very thoughtful," Mom says while picking up her spoon. "When I was pregnant with both kids, I craved Ruffles dipped in a milkshake. Joseph dry-heaved every time he watched me devour a bag with a large milkshake."

"It was a sight to behold," Dad says. "I'd turn away for one second, and when I turned back, she'd have milkshake lining her lips and chip crumbs clinging to her milky mustache." He shivers. "Never been more attractive."

Mom playfully nudges him. "At least I had an excuse. I was pregnant. What's your excuse for getting cheese stuck in your beard every time we have French onion soup?"

"Poor manners," Dad says, causing Eli to laugh out loud. "Laugh now, son, just wait until you're older and have lost all self-respect. There will be cheese in your beard as well."

"Can't wait." Eli grins.

"Do you plan on settling down at some point?" Dad asks, and just like that, the tension in the room skyrockets.

"Dad," I say, leaning forward. "I told you guys, we're just friends."

"I understand that, but a father needs to have his concerns, and isn't that what tonight is about? Airing those?"

"It is," Eli says with a nod.

"Then I'd like to know, seeing as though you have a reputation, is there any immediate thoughts on what your personal life will look like now that you'll have a child?"

Eli pats his mouth with a napkin and then says, "I understand the concern. I'm not going to sit here and tell you what you hear is a lie because it's not. I had a reputation, but that's slowly dwindled since I've been with your daughter. Right now, my main focus is helping her and making sure the baby has a safe environment to grow up in. I had a bit of a mixed-up childhood. There were some great times and some really tough ones. I'm not sure Penny has mentioned this to you, but my dad wasn't around, and my mom passed away when I was twelve. There were times in my life where I felt truly loved and times where I have never felt more alone." The honesty in his voice, the shakiness as he tells the truth, I can't help it. I reach out and take his hand, and to my shock, he squeezes hard on our connection and doesn't let go. "I want to make sure this baby never feels that way. No matter what's in store for us in the future, my top priority is to always make sure the baby feels safe and loved."

Dad nods in approval. "Very admirable, son."

Mom, of course, dabs at her eyes. "I had no idea, Eli. That must have been so hard, growing up without parents to lean on."

"It taught me some valuable lessons, like hard work and goal-setting. I know I probably wouldn't be here today unless I learned resilience at such a young age."

"And your plans are to always support Penny, no matter where the future might take you?" Dad asks.

"Correct," Eli answers. "I've actually spoken to my therapist about our situation, and I know in order to raise a child in a healthy environment, my relationship with Penny has to come first. It's why I'm here now, to show her that she does matter to me, that I care about her well-being, and that no matter what, I'll be here for her. I want there to be an unbreakable trust between us, a bond that we can carry on as we co-parent."

Dad nods as Mom continues to look between us, her eyes bouncing back and forth between Eli and me and our connected hands resting on the table. I know what she's thinking. I don't have to be inside her head to understand because it's written all over her face. She thinks there's more between us.

Ha, if only that were the truth.

"I appreciate your honesty," Dad says. "And since we're being honest with each other, I'll say, I was quite surprised to hear Penny was pregnant, for obvious reasons, but I was wary when I found out it was with you."

"Dad," I say out of embarrassment.

Eli squeezes my hand. "It's okay. Your dad is just telling us how he feels. And given my reputation, I don't blame him."

"But I'm glad we had this dinner," Dad continues, "because I can see that you really have made all the right choices, Eli, the kind of choices that puts a father's mind at ease. Now, do I wish this was all coming about under different circumstances, just to ensure that Penny's life will be easier? Of course, but I do believe you're making the most of the situation, and I truly appreciate that."

"Thank you," Eli says. "And I promise you, Joseph, you have nothing to worry about. I'll make sure Penny and the baby are the priority."

Dad gives him a curt nod before he dips his spoon into his ice cream bowl.

"Well." Mom claps her hands together. "Does this mean we'll get to see you for the holidays? I sure hope so. We always say in the Lawes household, the more, the merrier."

"If I'm welcome, I'll be there."

Mom smiles sincerely. "Eli, you are the father of our grand-child, our first grandchild. You will always be welcome."

"That means a lot to me," Eli says, and then he digs into his ice cream right before looking over at me and smiling. The boyish charm in his eyes, paired with the gratefulness in his grin, all hits me like a Mack truck to the chest, knocking away my breath.

I press my hand to my stomach and say, "I, uh, I think I'm pretty full. I'll get started on the dishes."

I stand from my chair, and so does Eli, still holding my hand. "You okay?" he asks.

"Mm-hmm," I answer. "Good. Enjoy. Tell my dad about your fight with Gasper. I'm sure he'd enjoy that."

"Oh yes, I tried to sneak details from Pacey, but he was close-lipped. Tell me, did you get him good?"

Eli chuckles, and as he sits back down—after one more thoughtful squeeze to my hand—I bring my bowl to the kitchen as Mom follows me. I stand at the sink, staring at my dad animatedly talking to Eli as Mom stands right next to me.

"Honey, I can see it all over your face. You like him."

"I do," I say quietly and then turn away. "But he doesn't like me like that."

"I beg to differ. There's more than friendship between the two of you, and I think you need to figure out just exactly what that is."

"Mom——"

"Penny, look at me." I turn toward her, and she grips my chin. "There is something there. Despite what you might have said to each other, there is more, and you would be doing your baby a disservice if you don't figure out what it is." When tears start to well in my eyes, she softly says, "I've never seen someone look at you so intently, the way he looks at you. He speaks so honestly, so sincerely, about and to you. Reminds me of how Pacey looks at Winnie, if I'm honest. Give Eli a chance, give you a chance, and at least see if anything is there."

I smooth my lips together and glance away.

"You won't regret it."

Just then, Dad and Eli erupt in laughter, and when I look over my shoulder at them, Eli has the largest grin on his face, a smile so wide that it stretches all the way to his eyes.

What would it be like if I gave us a chance? If I told him how I felt, how I've been feeling?

What's the worst that could happen?

He could reject me. That's the worst that could happen.

But what would happen if he said he felt the same way . . .

That's the question that's burning a hole in my twisted-up stomach.

What if he feels the same way . . .

———

ELI CLICKS the door shut and locks up before turning to me. Cutely, he pulls on the back of his neck and says, "I think they

285

like me."

I chuckle and nod. "Oh yeah, they're pretty much in love. I'd say it was a successful dinner on your end."

"I think so too. And hey, thanks for doing the dishes, you didn't have to do that. I planned on doing them after your parents left."

"It was good for you and my dad to have some talking time together. I didn't mind."

"I appreciate it. I really like your dad. I mean, I've known him through Pacey, but I've felt that made us more mates, than anything. It didn't give us a father and son relationship. This might be stupid to say, but he kind of encompasses what I think a dad should be—tough but loving. And the way he called me son . . ." He smiles softly. "Hell, it felt good, Penny. It felt really good. Thank you for tonight."

I never thought what it might be like for him, someone who doesn't have parents or siblings, being included in a family dinner with a close-knit family. I didn't notice when my dad called him son, but I guess that's not something I'd generally take note of. But I can genuinely sense his appreciation, the way he feels accepted within my family, and it reminds me to thank my parents later for treating him like one of our own.

"No need to thank me, I should be thanking you."

"For what?" he asks, stepping closer and taking my hand in his. The subtle move makes my pitter-pattery heart skip a beat. Maybe Mom was right. Maybe there is something more between Eli and me. Maybe he does look at me a certain way and has just been hiding his feelings in the hope of keeping the peace between us.

And now that he takes another step closer, all I can think about is . . . should I attempt to see if she was right?

"I'm saying thank you for being so open and honest with my parents. I know they needed the reassurance that everything is going to be okay."

"And do you believe everything will be okay?" he asks as his fingers gently brush a strand of hair behind my ear.

I wet my lips, and his eyes follow the movement as I slowly place my hand on his chest. I'm not sure what's pulling us together, I'm not even sure if I'm dreaming this up, this connection we have, but I'm letting myself fall into it.

Between the absolutely sexy vulnerability he showed tonight and how his smile lit up the night, the whirlwind of emotions is messing with my heart and mind.

"With you by my side, yes, I do believe everything will be okay."

"I'm not sure you know how much that means to me."

"Well, it means a lot to me what you said tonight."

He reaches up and touches my cheek. "I meant it all." And then he says, "Should we watch some *Ozark* to end the night?"

"I'd like that." And I'd like so much more. I slide my hand nervously up to his shoulder and then behind his head. His eyes remain fixed on mine as I quietly ask, "Can you, uh, unzip the back of my dress for me?"

I watch as his Adam's apple bobs right before he nods. "Sure," he answers in a gruff voice. And then his hand slides around me. He grabs my zipper and slowly pulls it down for me. His fingers drag along my skin as it's exposed.

"Thank you," I whisper.

When I should move away to go change, I don't. I stay fixed on him. On his grateful eyes. On his strong jaw. On his enticing lips.

Just kiss him, Penny.

What could go wrong?

He's holding you close. His hands are on your hips. This means something. This proximity.

Just dive in.

See if there's more.

You won't regret it. I know you won't . . .

A blast of courage tears through me, and before I can stop myself, I wet my lips again and sift my fingers through his hair just as I stand on my toes and press my mouth to his.

I kiss him.

I kiss the mouth that I've missed for the past few months. The mouth that has sent me into a tailspin of unrequited desire. The same mouth that scoured my body and made me come harder and faster than any mouth ever has before.

I take what I've wanted.

Unapologetically.

And for a moment, his lips caress mine. He kisses back. *Yes, he wants me.* And his grip on me grows tighter . . . right before he pulls away, putting a good foot of distance between us.

Breathing heavy, hand digging into his hair, he shakes his head. "Fuck . . . I . . . I can't, Penny."

He can't?

My heart plummets as I feebly ask, "You can't what?"

He motions between us. "I can't do this."

The hope. The belief that there might be something more, the idea we could be a couple, all blows up in smoke. Poof. Gone. Right in my face.

I was proven wrong.

My mom and Blakely were wrong.

All this time, I thought he possibly thought more of me, but it *was* all in my head.

"I'm s-sorry," I say, taking a step back. "I, uh, I just thought, well . . . never mind what I thought." I take another step back.

"Penny—"

"No, it's fine." I smile at him, but I can feel just how fake it is. I take a step toward the hallway. "I got caught up in the moment. You know, hormones and all of that." I nervously laugh and move backward again, but in my retreat, my heel snags in the entryway rug, and I tip backward, landing flat on my ass. Embarrassment washes over me as the top half of my dress falls off my shoulders.

"Jesus," he says, quickly coming to my rescue and attempting to help me up, but I ignore his help and stand on my own. "Are you okay?"

Yes, he wants me.

"Fine," I answer. My cheeks are flaming as I adjust the top of my dress. "I'm fine." I then muster up a yawn. "I'm actually just going to go to bed. Pretty late night."

"Penny, let's talk about this."

To my absolute horror, a tear slips down my cheek, and I quickly swipe it away. "I'd really rather not."

"I don't want you to be upset."

Too late for that.

"I'm really fine. Okay. Just . . . just let me do my thing."

His eyes are full of compassion. "I don't want to mess anything up."

Too late.

"It's fine, Eli. Okay. I'm just going to change. Do what you want to do. You know if you want to go out with the boys or something."

"You know I don't want to do that."

"Well then, just do something," I say, moving down the hall-way. "Good night."

When I reach my bedroom, I shut the door behind me, then quickly grab my phone on the nightstand and take it into the closet, where I collapse to the floor, tears streaming down my cheeks.

I don't think I've ever been more embarrassed in my life.

He doesn't want me.

He doesn't want me at all.

I call Blakely and bite my lower lip while I wait for her to pick up, tears continuously flowing down my cheeks.

"Hello?"

"Hey," I say, my voice choked up.

"Penny, what's wrong?"

"I . . . I kissed him, and he told me to stop."

"What?" she says in outrage. "Wait, where are you?"

"In my closet, hiding from him."

"Okay, I'm actually right around the corner. Want to meet me at the coffee shop?"

"Be there in five."

⊏⊐

BY THE TIME I ARRIVE, Blakely is sitting at a table with two drinks and a cookie. When she spots me, she immediately stands and pulls me into a hug.

I welcome her embrace and cry into her shoulder, thankful for her friendship.

When I hung up, I quickly changed out of my dress and into a pair of sweats and a long-sleeved T-shirt. I threw my hair up in a bun and then took off. Told Eli on my way out that I'd be back. He's texted me five times since I left. I haven't answered them.

When Blakely releases me, we both take a seat, and she hands me a drink. "Chai latte."

"Thank you." I grip the warm drink between both of my hands.

"So what the hell happened?"

Great question. Still trying to figure that all out.

"It was a good night." I recount how the dinner went with my parents and everything my mom said, confirming exactly what Blakely said about Eli. "And I don't know, we were holding hands. He wet his lips. I wet mine. I couldn't think of a more proper time to kiss him, so I did. And then he pulled away and said he can't."

"He can't?" Blakely asks with a raise of her brow. "Hold on. He can't, or he doesn't want to?"

"He can't. Blakely, it was so humiliating. I put myself out there, and he turned me down. I really . . ." More tears. "I really thought he wanted me."

"Wait, hold on." She presses her hand to mine. "Penny, he said he can't. Do you understand the difference between can't and doesn't want to?"

"It's kind of hard to understand anything at this point," I say.

"Let me ask you this, did he kiss you back?"

"No—" I pause and give it some thought. "Well, actually, yeah, I guess he did. There was a moment when he kissed me

291

and gripped me tighter. We actually kissed deeper for a second, and then he pulled away."

"So he did kiss you back, which means something is holding him back from moving forward with you."

I press my fingers to the bridge of my nose. "Or maybe, he just wants to be friends like he's said this entire time. Between you and my mom, I falsely believed that this guy actually wants me. He probably just wants some peace in reality."

Blakely shakes her head. "No, something's holding him back. From seeing how he dotes on you, how he had his hand up your shirt, and now to this kiss. He wants you, Penny. But there is a roadblock, and you just need to move it."

I let out a large sigh. "I'm tired, Blakely. I'm a vulnerable mess right now. I don't want to play a guessing game about what he's *possibly* thinking. All I want is a man to want me, to comfort me, to hold me, and to want to have sex with me. Eli is not the man. He made that quite clear tonight."

"Has he texted you since you bolted?"

"Yes."

"Have you looked at them?"

"Been too afraid."

She lifts her cup then says, "Read them to me."

"They're probably just stupid texts asking where I am."

Pinning me with her stare, she repeats, "Read them to me."

Too tired to fight with her, I pull out my phone and unlock it. I click on my messages and on his name. Clearing my throat, I say, "Penny, I'm so sorry. Can you come back so we can talk about this? Where are you? I'm worried. You fell, and I want to make sure you're okay. I want to make sure we're okay. Please text me back, Penny. I'm really fucking sorry." I glance up at my friend and say, "See. He's predictable."

But to my surprise, Blakely is sporting an evil grin as she slowly nods her head. "This is perfect."

"What's perfect?"

"We have him right where we want him."

"And where exactly is that? That's the same sort of thing he always texts. Sorry to say it, but we need to face the facts. I put myself out there, and he rejected me. We need to move on and figure out how to mend this hole that's burying deeper and deeper in my chest."

"Sure, he rejected you, but not because he wanted to. There is something . . ." Her eyes widen. "Hold on a second, I have a thought." She pulls her phone out and starts typing away.

"What are you doing?"

"Getting to the bottom of this."

"What does that even mean? Are you texting him? I swear to God, Blakely—"

"Cool it. I'm not texting *him*." When she's finished typing, she says, "I have an inkling about why he stopped that kiss."

"Oh, yeah?" I cross one leg over the other. "And what exactly is that inkling? You've been *sooo* intuitive thus far."

"It's obvious that he wants you. I think we all established that." Still delusional, okay, good to know. "Clearly, he kissed you back and wanted more by the way he gripped you."

"He could have been falling backward, possibly off-balance from my unwelcomed mouth to mouth. That's why he gripped me tighter."

"You and I both know that's a lie, so cut that out. And from his panic texts, he obviously wants to patch things up with you. We just need to get to the root of all of this." Her phone chimes with a text message, and she holds her finger up to me. "Hold, please."

She reads her text and smiles.

"What is it?"

"Bingo," she says, turning the phone toward me.

Winnie: *Yeah, Pacey threatened him not to go near Penny again.*

"What?" I seethe, grabbing the phone from Blakely and looking at it closely.

"Just what I thought. All the signs were there. We just had to figure out what was stopping him, and it's Pacey."

Humiliation is quickly replaced by rage.

"Where the hell does he get off saying that to Eli?" I ask.

293

"Well, he's always said that, but I'm pretty sure he reaffirmed it with Eli once you told him you were pregnant."

I set the phone on the table. "So what you're telling me is that my needs aren't being met because of my brother?"

"Yup." Blakely smugly breaks off a piece of the cookie that's on the table. "And now that we know the issue, we set out to break Eli."

"What do you mean?" I ask.

"It's time you get what you want, and that means you drive that man nuts. He wants you. Therefore, make him wish he had you."

"You mean . . . flirt with him?"

"No, not just flirt, Penny. You need to be comfortable in your own skin, if you know what I mean."

A light bulb goes off in my head. "Oh . . . I do know what you mean."

She chuckles. "Show him what he's missing out on. Accidentally touch him when he's least expecting it. Have your hand graze him at night. Give him a freaking show."

The embarrassment I was feeling only moments ago quickly washes away as I think about exactly all the things I could do.

Blakely is right—a scary thing to say. In that small moment, I felt the same level of need from him as I felt on the night of his birthday. The same . . . passion. Desire. If only fleeting. Is Blakely right? *Does Eli just need a little—passive-aggressive—nudge?*

"This could be fun," I say.

"Oh, please . . . please make it fun." She chuckles over her drink as I reach for a piece of the cookie.

Oh, yes, I'll be making this fun for sure.

Chapter Twenty-Three

ELI

I hate myself.

I really, truly hate myself.

Well, if we're hating people, I'm going to throw some hate toward Pacey as well because he's the goddamn reason my lips aren't currently on Penny's. Why she ran out of this apartment, and why she isn't returning my texts.

He's the goddamn reason I took a step back and told her I can't, even though I want to so fucking bad. Jesus Christ, just tasting her delicious mouth all over again took me back to the night I haven't stopped dreaming about. The night I wish I could play over and over and over again.

Her mouth on mine felt like a goddamn whirlwind of emotions and flashbacks, and I'm still reeling.

Pacey specifically told me not to go near her.

Not to touch her.

To keep things platonic.

And like the dumbass that I am, I'm honoring that request.

All because I broke his trust the first time, I'm trying not to do it a second time.

But fuck . . .

The door to the apartment opens, and I crank my head to the front door, where I see her walk through. She shuts the door behind her, locks up, and then takes off her shoes and puts them in the entryway closet.

Here we go . . .

I stand from the couch and stick my hands in my pockets, really unsure of what to do at this moment.

"Hey," I say.

She looks my way. "Hi." She smiles and then moves toward the kitchen.

She's smiling?

Not only is she smiling but there's also a cheeriness in her voice that raises the hair on the back of my neck. *Warning. Warning. Proceed with caution.*

If you're thinking, *you should be scared, Eli*, you're right. Given her past hormonal changes, this could be a real doozy.

And I don't know how to react to that other than in fear. My belly button's all puckered up, shrinking as she moves around the kitchen, grabbing herself water. With every cabinet that's shut, my belly button winces, turning into nothing but a divot of dust.

"Uh, do you . . . do you want to talk?" I ask.

She looks up at me. "I'm good, Eli. Seriously." She smiles again, and I nearly wince from the flash of her teeth. "Everything is okay between us. Okay?"

"Uh . . . oh-kay," I say, uncertainty beating through me at an uncomfortable, rapid rate.

"Great. So, do you want to watch some *Ozark?*" She walks over to the couch, reaches for the remote, and turns on the TV as she takes a seat and curls her legs under her.

I stand there, awkwardly, still very much confused.

And slightly frightened.

Is something going to happen to me if I take a seat next to

her? Did she not just go in the kitchen for water? Did she slip a knife under her shirt, and I didn't see it?

What happens if I don't take a seat? Will she lash out? Start crying? Act normal?

I really wish there was a how-to guide on how to handle this current situation. A situation where I got my best friend's sister pregnant, moved in with her platonically, and then kissed her again when I shouldn't have but then pulled away and made her cry.

Where is the goddamn how-to book for that?

"Why are you being weird? Sit down." She pats the couch.

I'm being weird? *Me?*

Uh, last I knew, she was crying and upset, and now, she's acting as if nothing had happened. Where did she even go? A place that erases memory? Is *Men in Black* real?

Carefully, I take a seat, making sure to keep a good distance between us, just in case. And then she starts the show. She watches intently while I keep one eye on the TV and one eye on her.

Maybe this is a pregnancy thing, like a hormone switch. But she seems so cool and calm. It's just . . . alarming.

I'm tempted to text Posey and ask him for advice, but I also don't want her to think I'm texting about her since I never text while we watch *Ozark*. So instead, I just sit there and watch, hoping that she's right, that everything is going to be okay, while still keeping one eye on her . . . you know, in case there *is* a knife under her shirt.

"HAVE YOU SEEN MY LOTION?" Penny says as she comes out of the bathroom after getting ready for bed.

I think God hates me. I really do. I did something wrong in this lifetime, and I'm being punished for it because standing right in front of me, in a skintight, white tank top—no bra—is Penny, and I can fucking see everything.

EVERYTHING!

The curve of her breasts.

Her areolas.

Her . . . nipples.

Not to mention, she's wearing underwear that cuts high on her hip instead of shorts. Not quite sure where her pajama sets went, but this . . . uh, this is not what I'm used to. And under any other circumstance, I'd be welcoming the outfit, pulling her down on my lap and sucking on her taut little nipples through the thin fabric.

But I'm in a state of purgatory, where I can't do anything like that. I just have to sit in my desires and never act on them.

"Oh, there it is, on my nightstand." She chuckles. "The other day, I found it in the fridge. That's pregnancy brain for you."

Also, let it be known I'm still frightened with her easygoing attitude right now. Sure, there was no knife under her shirt, but that doesn't mean she's not planning an attack.

She pops open the lid and squirts some lotion in her hands. From where I stand, I can smell it, and God, it smells so good, like a delicious flower. She usually puts it on her hands before we go to bed, but tonight, she's rubbing it over her shoulders. Does she know I fucking live for the smell of that lotion? That I so look forward to the smell of it at night that I actually bought myself a travel-size bottle. *And I'm so pathetic that I rub it on my hands at night before I go to bed when I'm away.*

I hope to fuck she doesn't know that.

"I think I need to go buy new bras tomorrow."

Gulp.

She lifts her shirt up, showing off her stomach, and rubs lotion on it.

"I think they've gotten bigger. What do you think?" She tugs on the fabric of the shirt, pulling down to reveal her breasts, but allowing the straps of her tank top to cover her nipples and only her nipples.

Holy . . . shit.

My dick grows hard. Difficult not to when she's practically standing in front of me, naked, asking me to look at her tits.

And I do.

I fucking stare.

I beg and plead for the straps of her tank top to grow smaller, to slip up, to show me just a little of her nipples.

But then she releases the fabric, letting it bounce back into place, and she climbs on the bed, where she kneels. The outfit, her hair, her goddamn pose, she looks like a sexy pin-up model.

"Come here." In some sort of a trance, I walk up to her just as she says, "Feel. I really think they're bigger."

Before I can respond, she lifts my hand and places it on her breast.

Jesus Christ.

My thumb slowly closes around her round, pert tit out of habit, gently squeezing her. Fuck yes, they've gotten bigger.

"Are they bigger?"

They're fucking soft. They're round. They're everything I fucking remember but slightly bigger.

Clearing my throat, I say, "Uh, yeah, they seem bigger."

I go to remove my hand, but she stops me and places her hand over mine. "Squeeze them. They're big, right?"

I couldn't stop myself if Pacey was standing right here, watching. It's instinctual. My body is made to react to this woman, to do what she tells me and feel her when presented with the opportunity.

Together, we squeeze. Her chin slightly lifts, causing her chest to fill my hand better, and I find myself losing self-control as I give her another squeeze and then another . . . and then I slide my hand over her nipple.

Fuck, what I wouldn't give to tear her shirt off right now.

Or to pull down the neckline and suck her into my mouth.

To push her back on this bed and make love to her tits until she came.

"Yeah, they're bigger," I confirm, almost asking her if she wants me to test them in my mouth for her.

"That's what I thought." She pulls away, and the smallest groan pops out of my mouth in protest. She eyes me. "You okay?"

"Yup," I squeak out and quickly slide under the covers to hide my crotch from view.

"Bigger boobs and increased libido, that's what it says in the books. I was telling Blakely the other day, that I'm wearing out my vibrator with the number of times I use it."

Ummm . . . what?

Blinks

Blinks again

She's, uh . . . *clears throat* she's wearing out her vibrator?

"And the weirdest thing about it is that I come so fast now because of the increased blood flow in my vulva that you would think I don't need a new vibrator so quickly, but, God, I'd really love one with a clit stimulator. Have you ever seen those?" She hops into bed and twirls her hair onto the top of her head, exposing the feminine slope of her neck.

"I have," I choke out.

Her eyes light up. "Have you ever used one on a woman?" She leans forward, her breasts push together, her cleavage on full display.

Like a moth to a flame, my eyes fall to her cleavage, where the neck of her tank top dances dangerously low. All I'd have to do is lightly tug on the neckline, and I'd find her sexy nipples in my fingers.

"Have you?" she asks again, pulling my attention back to her eyes.

"Huh?"

She smiles. "Have you ever used a clit stimulator on a girl before?"

"N-no," I answer. But fuck would I like to use one on her.

"Oh darn. I was hoping you could have given me some pointers." She reaches over to her nightstand, turns off the light, pitching us into the dark, and then rests her head on her pillow, facing me.

I guess it's time for bed. Don't mind me with the half-hard cock over here.

I lie down as well and turn toward her but keep my distance for more than obvious reasons.

"Hey, Penny?"

"Hmm?" she asks as her feet find my shins.

I gulp. "Are you, uh, are you sure we're okay?"

Her eyes open, and she smiles at me before placing her hand on my cheek. Her thumb caresses it before slowly lowering down my neck and across my chest, just above my nipples. So much for trying to get my cock to calm down.

"We're good. I promise. It was a lapse in judgment, and I respect your choice to keep things platonic between us. I actually appreciate it."

"You do?" I ask, confused. If roles were reversed, I'd have a tough time being as understanding as she is at this moment.

"Yes." Her hand moves over my abs right before she pulls it away, but I can still feel the imprint of her dragging fingers. "I do. But, can I please ask you something?"

"Anything," I say, shifting.

"Can we still cuddle at night? I know I said that one time and, I understand things are strictly platonic between us, but it just felt nice to be held. That's one thing I'm missing through this pregnancy. Some human contact."

Jesus.

It will take the strength of a thousand men to get me through nights of holding her without actually touching her, but I also know what it means to desire human touch. Growing up in the attic of the barn, I'd wished for hugs goodnight and never got them, so I can understand her need.

"Of course, but—"

Before I can even get my sentence out, she's turning and backing up into me. The minute her ass hits my crotch, she makes a surprised sound.

"But give me a second," I say on a shallow breath.

"Oh my . . . *hello*, Eli."

Fuck, how embarrassing.

"Uh, sorry just . . . you know, calming down from the breast exam."

She chuckles, and instead of moving away, she just plants her ass against my lap and then pulls my arm over her stomach and lays my palm right over her belly.

And despite what's happening down south, there's a connection in the way I'm holding her, a feeling that beats through me that makes me feel possessive.

This woman, this baby, I'm not just living with them, going through the stages of the pregnancy. They feel like mine. Like they belong with me, in my life.

Whispering softly, I say, "You have the smallest of bumps."

Her hand falls on top of mine. "I know. I took a picture today. I could see a big difference. My window of being able to wear my regular clothes is closing, but oddly, I don't think I've ever felt sexier."

You look fucking sexy.

If I had it my way, we wouldn't be cuddling with clothes on. We'd be fucking with clothes off.

"If you weren't here, I'd probably be sleeping naked, feeling the silk of the sheets against my skin. Makes me want to take boudoir pictures or something."

Hell . . .

"Maybe I will, for me. I want to remember the way I feel now so when I'm thirty-nine weeks pregnant and uncomfortable, I can look back and say I am beautiful."

"You don't need pictures to prove that," I say, keeping my hand on her stomach. "You're always beautiful, Penny."

She halfway rolls to her back so she can look at me. She cups my face, and it feels like her lips are only a few inches away when she says, "Thank you, Eli." And then she presses the lightest of kisses to my cheek before turning around.

My pulse hammers in my throat as my stomach twists with desire. Those lips are going to be the death of me . . . if not her gorgeous tits. Or the way she makes me feel like a whole man, a man who isn't just desirable but also wanted. *Needed. Part of a family unit.* Hers.

━━━

"MMM, WHAT'S THAT SMELL?" Penny asks as she walks down the hallway in nothing but a goddamn robe that's barely secured at her waist. "Are you making French toast?"

This morning, I walked in on her in the bathroom, shaving her legs in the tub. Her robe was hanging loosely on her sexy frame as she had one leg up against the tub wall, shaving. I saw a great deal of skin, and it made me go fucking crazy with need . . . once again.

"I am," I say, keeping my eyes on the griddle in front of me. Eyes down, man. Eyes down.

She moves behind me in the kitchen, dragging her fingers over my bare back. "I hope you're making some for me."

"Of course," I say while she hops up on the counter and crosses one leg over the other, not bothering to fix her robe as it gapes open right at her hipbone. Everything important—is covered, but my mind is playing fucking tricks on me as it scans the immense amount of skin that's visible.

"Good, because I love French toast." She pulls on her shoulder and groans. "Ugh, I'm so sore. I think I slept on my neck wrong last night." She rolls her head side to side, causing the light wisps of her hair to dance along her collarbone. "It's going to be a long day."

I flip my last piece of French toast on a plate and turn off the griddle.

"Do you need me to help?" I ask, for some stupid, stupid . . . stupid reason.

"Really?" she asks. "You wouldn't mind?"

"Nah, I have some time before I have to be on the ice for my morning skate."

She hops off the counter and places her hand on my chest as her eyes beam up at me with appreciation. "I'd be forever grateful."

"Sure." I gulp as her hand fits into mine, and she guides me back to the bedroom. "Uh, where are we going?"

She chuckles, and the sound hits me right in the goddamn dick. "Don't worry, I just figured lying on the bed would be more comfortable. That way, you can straddle me and have better access."

Jesus.

Fucking.

Christ.

Remember when I said I was stupid? I meant it.

"You can use my lotion that's on the nightstand," she says.

Oh great, the lotion that makes me horny just from the smell of it. Awesome. Thumbs up.

"Probably best if I remove my robe."

Before I can protest, she whips it off, her back to me, and she wraps one arm across her breasts, covering them.

But that's the only thing she covers.

"Hope you don't mind that I'm wearing a thong. Not like you haven't seen my ass before." She laughs as she lies down on the bed on her stomach.

Yup, I've seen it before, but I haven't had sex in a few months. MONTHS. This feels like a modern-day torture device, just staring back at me, begging for my hands. *Fuck, I want her.* And her thong, if that's what you want to call the three thin straps of red clinging to her soft skin.

Fucking red.

There's something about that color, pressed so tightly to her skin that ignites an ember inside me. That and the blatant display of her ass.

I want to spank it.

I want to sink my teeth into it.

I want to see if she'd take my fingers . . . my cock.

I want to spread her legs wide and glide my hand along her seam to see if she's wet, if she's as needy as I am.

"Is something wrong?" she asks, lifting up and turning just enough that I can see the slightest curve of her side boob.

"No." I let out a low cough. "Nothing's wrong." Reaching over to the nightstand, I grab the stupid, sweet-smelling lotion and squirt a solid amount on my hands. I'm going to be smelling this all goddamn day, even when I'm getting dressed for the game. I can feel it already.

Then I climb on the bed and straddle her body. "Am I pressing down on you too hard? I don't want to hurt the baby."

"No, you feel good, Eli."

My nostrils flare, and I take a deep breath. Just rub her shoulder. That's all you have to do, rub her freaking shoulder.

I reach down and move my hand along her tight muscles.

"Oh, yes, right there," she moans as her hands curl into the blanket beneath her. "That feels so good, Eli."

Holy mother of God.

When I agreed to do this, I didn't think she'd sound like she was mid-orgasm. If I'd predicted that, there's no way I'd have offered to massage her.

But too late now.

"Is the, uh . . . pressure okay?"

"So good," she says on a heavy breath. "Oh Eli, your hands, they feel amazing."

I squeeze my eyes shut as I try to keep a handle on things. Think of gross things, things that won't make your dick hard like . . .

Posey eating a bologna sandwich.

And . . . Taters showing me that hairball from the locker room showers the other day.

And . . . the gash in Pacey's knee that one time we played hockey on his hometown lake.

Blood. There was so much blood.

Lots and lots of blood.

"Yes," she whispers. "Right there. Ohhh, Eli. I owe you so much after this."

BLOOD!

He needed six stitches.

They did it without Novocain.

"You're giving me chills." Her butt lifts up against my cock.

TOENAILS.

He didn't cut his toenails. I remember telling him he should have cut them in case of something like going to the hospital for stitches ever happened.

Because blood . . . all of the blood.

"Eli?"

"Yes?" I croak.

"I . . . I'm a little embarrassed, but . . ." She turns and covers her breasts as she makes it all the way to her back, and I'm straddling her, staring down at her gorgeous, blushed face. "I'm incredibly turned on right now. This is crazy, but hey, my doctor told me to give in to the urge, so, could you hand me my vibrator that's in the nightstand and give me a little privacy?"

My mouth goes absolutely dry.

My ears sound off a ringing tone that I'm not sure where it's coming from.

And my arousal spikes to an all-new level.

"I know, awkward, but if I don't take care of this before work, I'm going to have a really rough day. I'll be quick, and then we can enjoy some French toast."

"S-sure," I say, stumbling over my words as I reach into her nightstand and find a pink vibrator. I stare at it for a few seconds, completely and utterly jealous, and hand it to her.

"Thank you," she says as she switches it on.

The buzzing sound drowns out every other sound in the apartment, and I watch, fixated, as she brings it close to the small triangle of her thong.

She chuckles. "Uh, are you going to stick around for a show?"

"What? Oh, shit . . . sorry, no. I think I'll go wash the lotion off my hands." I quickly disappear into the bathroom and shut the door as the buzzing sound echoes through the apartment. The only thing separating us is this door as I hear her masturbate.

She's pleasuring herself, and I have nothing to do with it.

"Ohhh, yes," I hear her say.

My dick pulses against my briefs, and before I can even think twice about it, I press one hand against the door and release my cock with the other.

It aches against my palm, so sick of my hand, wanting me desperately to plow through this door and bury itself so deep inside Penny that we might not ever return.

"Mmm, God," she moans, and the bed slightly creaks beneath her.

Is she moving her pelvis? Are her nipples hard?

Is her chest arching off the mattress?

If only I could see, if only I could be the one making her wet . . . making her come.

But I can't, and that's so fucking infuriating.

I smooth my already lotioned hand along the tip of my cock where precum has settled, and I rub it along my painful length that has grown with the mental images of Penny naked flashing through my mind.

"Oh, I'm going to come," she says. It isn't loud, almost a whisper, but just loud enough for me to hear, for me to indulge.

I pump my hand faster, tugging, pulling, jacking so hard and so fast that I don't have a moment to breathe as I feel my orgasm bloom at the base of my spine.

Jesus, it's right there.

My balls tighten, my stomach bottoms out, and my dick grows even harder as I frantically pump.

"Oh my God," she cries out, and I know, I know she's fucking coming all over that vibrator. But I envision it differently.

It takes me back to my bedroom, where my dick is so deep inside her sweet pussy that I can barely think straight. She's pulsing around me, milking my cock until there's nothing left inside me.

Her smell.

Her taste on my lips.

Her intoxicating moans.

The grip her pussy has on my cock.

Fuck . . .

My hand stills, and my cock swells right before I come, my orgasm tearing through me with such force that I have to drop my head to the door for support.

"Fuck," I whisper, catching my breath. I slowly pump a few more times and then drop my hand from my cock and place my forearm on the door in front of me.

That did nothing for me.

Sure, it was a release, but it didn't help this burning desire racing up and down my spine.

It doesn't relieve the need I have for *her*.

It only took a tiny edge off.

Not sure it will be enough.

Hell, I know it's not enough.

Because if it were my choice, I'd burst through this door and make her sit on my goddamn face until I made her come three fucking times with my tongue.

That would be how I'd spend my morning. Instead, I'm cleaning up the bathroom and washing my hands, then knocking on the door, asking her if I can come out.

When she says yes, I open the door to her putting her robe back on and tying it loosely at the side. When her eyes meet mine, I notice her flushed cheeks and pleased smile. Walking up to me, she once again places her hand on my chest and sighs happily. "Thank you so much, Eli. I know this is weird for us, but I'm so glad I can be comfortable enough to do that in the other room. I feel better. It might be like this for a while, given the sexual drive I have recently. So I appreciate you being cool about it."

It might be like this for a while?

How long is a while?

Because I'm not sure I can take another day like this.

She's walking around this apartment like a goddamn goddess, her sexual magnetism a ten out of ten, and tempting me with every smile, every time our eyes meet, and every sashay of her hips.

If this is going to last longer than today, then I'm royally fucked.

Chapter Twenty-Four

PENNY

"He's not breaking," I say as I take a seat at the bistro table Blakely and Winnie are sitting at.

"Who's not breaking? What are we talking about?" Winnie asks, looking between us.

Blakely and I exchange glances, and I give her a curt nod.

"Winnie," Blakely says. "We love you, and we want you to be in this circle of trust, but there's a slight conflict of interest. You're dating Penny's brother, and what we're about to discuss can't get back to Pacey. So, we know this is asking a lot from you. Do you think you can keep this information in this circle, right here?" Blakely motions between all of us.

"Are you asking . . ." She pauses and glances over her shoulder and then whispers, "To form an alliance?"

I slowly nod my head. "A bosom buddy alliance." I point at our chests. "We all have boobs. This is information only for those who have boobs."

Winnie rubs her hands together. "I've always wanted to form

an alliance. This feels right. Should we touch nipples to seal the deal?"

"Or we can shake on it," Blakely says.

"I mean sure, not as fun, but sure." Chuckling, we all shake on it, and then Winnie says, "So, what are we talking about?"

Chiming in like the best friend that she is, Blakely says, "Our dear pregnant friend over here is attempting to break Hornsby's will."

"Oh, that sounds like fun. In what way?"

"I want to have sex with him," I say. "Badly."

Winnie chuckles. "If I were in your position, I'd want to as well. Oh, wait . . . is this why you texted me the other night? Is Hornsby not having sex with you because of Pacey?"

I nod. "Your boyfriend is being a wet blanket on my sexual appetite."

"And I'm assuming by this killer dress that does wonders for your cleavage, you're trying to break Hornsby with your feminine prowess."

"Exactly," I say, "but it's not working."

"Not that you want to hear this, but all I had to do was kiss Pacey, and that was the end of that. Have you tried kissing Hornsby?"

"Been there, done that," I say, waving my hand in dismissal. "He kissed me back for a second, and then it was as if my brother was sitting on his shoulder, reminding him of what he shouldn't be doing. He pulled away. It was absolutely humiliating."

Winnie's brow knits. "That's awful. I'm so sorry. And because of Pacey?"

I nod. "Yes, because of him. But I've taken that humiliation and let it light a fire under my titillated ass, and now I'm determined to break him, but he's not cracking."

"What have you done?" Blakely asks while Winnie still has an irritated look on her face. "Maybe we can help you come up with new ideas."

"What have I not done?" I ask, exhausted, just as a server

brings us salads. Blakely ordered ahead so we wouldn't have to wait long for our food. She's thoughtful like that. "Let's see, I've worn see-through tank tops. I've asked him to hold me at night again. I've worn a robe, loosely tied around my body and then asked him to massage me. I made all these moaning noises—"

"Classic, well done," Blakely says.

"Yeah, but all it did was turn me on, so then I was like, fine, I'm turned on, I'll take care of it. I asked him to hand me my vibrator from the nightstand, and that's exactly what I did."

"In front of him?" Winnie asks in dismay. "And he still didn't do anything?"

"He was in the bathroom. I'm pretty sure he jacked off while in there, but still, he didn't do anything to me. Oh, and I had him feel my boobs to see if they were bigger. He concurred they were, and that was it."

"Wow," Blakely says, sitting back in her chair. "I feel like the boob thing would have easily cracked him."

"Nope." I stuff some lettuce in my mouth. "And I've never felt sexier than right now. I always read that the second trimester is magical, but I didn't think it would feel this great."

"You look amazing," Winnie says. "Seriously, I'd do you."

"Thank you." I toss my hand up in the air. "This dress alone should make him want to take me against a wall."

"Has he seen you in the dress yet?"

"No, not yet. He bolted out this morning before I got dressed. And I'll say this, I think he's at his limit. I think he's right there, and if I just push him a little more, he will fall over the edge. But I'm just not sure how to do it without grabbing his penis and sticking it in my mouth."

"I mean, that is an option," Blakely says.

"And what do I say? Oh, sorry, I thought it was a lollipop? My bad."

"Pregnancy brain is a funny thing," Blakely says. "My sister once served me a glass of milk when she was pregnant, but it wasn't milk. It was her car keys. She legit had no idea. So slinking down and putting his dick in your mouth could possibly work."

Deadpanned, I say, "I'm not doing that. He'd stop me before I even started."

Winnie taps her chin. "Hmm, what if we get you some new sexy nighttime wear? Something that when you wake up, your boob is not even covered because the fabric is so loose?"

"That's a good idea," Blakely says. "Isn't there a lingerie shop around the corner? We can see if they have anything."

"I bet there's a short nightgown that would work."

"I feel like I tried that," I say.

"But you said he's on the edge, which means, if you keep pushing a little harder, he'll crack."

"Oh, and have you flirted with other guys in front of him?"

"No." I push my salad around with my fork. "We haven't been around a lot of people."

"Well, don't you need to do some material before the game tonight? In that dress, you could easily make him jealous."

"I could do that."

"And hey, isn't your birthday in a few days?"

I nod. "It is."

"Well, if we don't crack him by then, this very well might work. He'll want to celebrate your birthday, but   ." As if a stroke of genius hits her, Blakely grips my arm. "You don't tell him it's your birthday."

"Ohhhhh." Winnie claps. "Yes, that's the way to go because then halfway through the day, we can plant the seed somehow that it is your birthday, and he'll feel awful and want to make it up to you."

"Exactly." Blakely slaps the table. "Oh, this is good. That will make him crack, especially if you say something like you're going out with the girls."

"And then we do go out," Winnie adds. "And we dance, and he sees you dancing, and he won't want anyone else dancing with you, so he'll swoop in. And that's when you rub your ass all over his crotch. He'll take you to the bathroom, and that's where you stick your hand in his pants and feel how hard he is. He says something like 'you've been a naughty girl', and you say 'well, spank me then', and you bend over, and he whacks you on the ass, once . . . twice. Three times! You moan, and then he moves you against the stall of the bathroom and lifts your skirt—"

"Umm, Winnie?" I say.

She blinks a few times and looks up at our staring faces. "Did I go too far?"

"Just a bit," I say.

She fans her face. "Sorry about that. Been reading some spicy books with Pacey lately, and my mind seems to be working in a different way at the moment. But, uh, yes, birthday. I think that's the winner."

"I think that's a last resort," I say.

"And I think it might be better if I tell him I have nothing planned. You and I, Winnie, will have to have separate emergencies that take us away from Penny because there is no way I'd leave her alone on her birthday," Blakely says to Winnie. She turns to me. "So, maybe we cancel our plans with you last minute."

"Gah, yes, and then he'll make sure he does something for you."

"Well, that's if they aren't in Washington. My birthday is supposed to be on game five of the series."

"If he is in Washington, it will only make it better for when he comes back home," Blakely says. "The guilt will eat him alive."

"True," Winnie adds. "Wow, this bosom buddy alliance really works fast. We have flirting in front of him, new nighttime wear, and then of course, a last-resort, birthday mishap. I must say, ladies, we might be able to run the country with the kind of work we do."

Blakely holds up her water. "Agreed. We know how to get work done. I'm proud of us. Now, we just need our friend Penny to execute agreed plans."

They both eye me, and I set my shoulders back, puffing my chest. "I shall do my best in getting this man to stick his penis inside me."

"That's all we can ask for." Blakely smiles. "And then you have to tell us about it."

———

NEW NIGHTTIME WEAR?

Check.

Cleavage on full display?

Check.

Hair fluffed and looking devastatingly silky?

Check.

Lipstick applied?

Check.

Confidence to flirt?

Surprisingly, check.

This new sense of confidence has really rocked me, and I'm riding it.

I need to gather some pre-game coverage of the boys for TikTok to get the fans pumped for the rest of the series. They're all aware I need to bother them and have scheduled a few minutes in the media room for me, which is where I'm headed right now.

Just as I round the corner to the hallway that leads to the media room, I run right into the man in question, Eli Hornsby.

"Wow, sorry about—" His words fall short when he sees that it's me. His eyes land on my cleavage and then quickly meet mine again. "Uh, wow, Penny. I didn't know that was you."

"Hey, Eli." I smile up at him, acting as casual as possible, even though his eyes are burning me up with their perusal. "Are you ready for the game?"

He pulls on the back of his neck. "Yeah." His eyes flit down to my cleavage again and then back up. "Little tight in the hamstrings, but stretching."

I playfully tap his chest and smirk. "If I knew your hamstrings were tight, I'd have rolled them out for you last night." My hand slides down his chest, and then I move past him, heading toward the media room.

He jogs up next to me. "So, uh, what do you need from me for TikTok?"

"Just going to ask you a few questions. Have you do some things to help get the fans pumped. Nothing too strenuous. Don't worry, I won't work you too hard." I wink at him, and I watch him gulp. "That is . . ."—I lean into him, my breasts pressing against his arm—"unless you want me to work you hard."

He swallows and then starts coughing just as Posey joins us. He pats Eli on the back and says, "You okay there, bro?" He spots me, and his eyes widen. "Penny, wow, didn't see you there over this brute."

Okay, time to do your thing, Penny. Make Eli jealous.

Very, very, jealous.

"That's okay, I'd like to say the same, but it's hard not to notice when you're in the room."

"That's what I keep telling the guys," Posey says as Eli turns toward me with a quizzical lift to his brow.

"Clearly the most good-looking of the bunch, they have to bring you down a notch somehow."

"Very true." He nods in agreement just as we make it to the media room. "I feel like you see me, Penny."

I drag my hand down his arm—God, I'm nervous—and say, "I always see you, Levi." And then, I walk over to the media table where mic packs are set up.

My hands are shaking as a tall figure stands next to me.

I don't have to look up to know who it is.

"What was that?" he whispers.

"What was what?" I ask, keeping my eyes turned down.

"That . . . situation with Posey?"

Turning toward him now, I act completely confused. "What are you talking about?"

"You called him Levi."

I slowly nod. "Yes, that is his name, isn't it?"

"And you touched him."

I chuckle. "I didn't know he was untouchable." I hold my hand up. "Is there a disease on my fingers now? Should I go wash my hand?"

"I'm being serious, Penny."

"About what?" I ask.

"About . . . all of that."

"I'm sorry, I don't understand," I say, batting my eyelashes.

"You . . . you . . . acted like, you know . . ."

"I really don't. Now, if you'll excuse me, I have a job to get done." I move past him, making sure to brush my shoulder along his, a smile passing over my lips.

When the other guys walk into the media room, I give them all hugs and joke and tease with them. The entire time, Eli stands off to the side, arms crossed, watching my every move. And I can't help but revel in his stare because, if I didn't know any better, I'd say he's . . . jealous.

Just what I was looking for.

—————

"ARE you going to wait for Hornsby?" Blakely asks as we move through the hallways of the arena.

"Yeah, but not really wait for him, if you know what I mean."

"Make him think you're doing something else, and he just runs into you."

"Exactly." I pull on the ties of the shirt I'm wearing. "How do I look?"

"Honestly . . . really hot."

"Yeah?" I give a turn and say, "Does my stomach show too much?"

Blakely shakes her head. "Not too much. You're good. This was a great idea. A change of outfit. And that push-up bra we got today? Seriously, I need to get one for myself."

"I feel like my boobs are tickling my chin."

She laughs. "They're not, but getting close, and Hornsby

might die when he sees you wearing his name on the back of your shirt."

"That's the plan."

Before the game started, I changed out of my dress and into a pair of black maternity leggings, black booties, and a purple Agitators shirt that dips quite low in the front. And of course, it has Hornsby's name on the back. I considered wearing a different name, maybe Posey, just to grate on his nerves, but I thought having his name on my back would make him think of claiming me, so . . . here's hoping.

"Oh, look, they're starting to come out of the locker room." Blakely nods toward their locker room door.

I turn toward her. "Everything in place?"

She gives me a quick once-over and then nods. "Yes. And you smell amazing."

"Perfect." I give her a wink and then head over to the wall that's across the locker room and lean against it, one foot propped against the brick.

Eli's usually one of the first guys to walk out, so I hope I don't have to wait here much longer.

The boys won tonight, thank goodness. We needed the win badly, which means they will be in Washington on my birthday. I'm a little sad about it, but I'm also hoping Eli being away works to my advantage.

The door to the locker room opens, and just as I look up, I'm greeted by the smooth swagger of Eli Hornsby. Decked out in a deep purple three-piece suit and black button-up, forgoing the tie to pop the top few buttons of his shirt, showing off his beautifully muscular chest.

He's the only man I know who can literally steal the breath from my lungs.

He's adjusting a cuff under the sleeve of his jacket when he glances up and makes eye contact with me. He pauses mid-stride, and like he did earlier, his eyes scan me up and down before he says, "Hey."

I push off the wall. "Just the man I was looking for. Was

hoping for a quote I could use for a post about the win. Think you can help a girl out?"

"Yeah, sure."

"Thank you," I say. "Can you just text me one on your way out to your car? I have some things to finish up quickly, and then the girls and I are headed out."

He frowns, his brows pulling together. "Headed out where?"

I smile. "To celebrate, of course. Agitators are coming back." And then, I turn away from him and start walking away. If only I had a camera on him to see his reaction to my shirt. I give it a few seconds, and then I glance over my shoulder to see a stunned Eli, his hand dragging over his mouth. "See you at home," I say.

Smiling to myself, I take off, quickly walking toward my office where I'll hang out and watch *Bridgerton* until I've wasted enough time making him even more jealous.

Part of me deeply hopes that he won't resist me for much longer. Not just because I'm incredibly horny and want Eli something terrible. But because of what I didn't show Blakely and Winnie. If he does reject me again, if this isn't just about what Pacey says, I don't know what I'll do with that. I'm fairly sure it will rip a tiny piece of my heart out, though

———

ELI: *Hey, just checking on you, making sure you're good and don't need anything.*

Eli: *Not trying to be a nuisance or anything, but it's getting pretty late. You good?*

Eli: *Penny, just let me know you're alive.*

Penny: *Alive, coming home soon. <3*

———

BAGS OF LINGERIE in hand and feeling like I'm totally owning this situation, I walk through the door of my apartment and kick my shoes off.

Eli whips around from where he's sitting on the couch in only a pair of athletic shorts. His hair is messy, as if his fingers have been pulling on it all night, and his eyes are searching me. For what, I can't be sure, but they're looking me over frantically.

"Hey, I didn't think you'd still be up."

"Of course I'm up," he says. "I was worried about you."

"Worried about me?" I ask with humor. "Why? You realize before you came along, I was more than able to take care of myself and make it through a night without any worries."

"But you're pregnant now."

"Yes, I am, and that doesn't mean I'm incompetent or have to be a hermit, Eli."

"I'm not saying you're incompetent or have to be a hermit, I'm just saying . . ." He trails off. I don't think he knows what he's trying to say.

"Okay." I work my way into the bedroom and set my bags down in the closet. I reach in and pull out the cream-colored silk nightgown the girls liked the most, and I quickly change out of my clothes and into the nightgown. I bought four others just like it, and honestly, they're really comfortable. They have a very thin strap, and the neckline dips down to skim just above my areolas, leaving nothing to the imagination. And the hem hits me mid-thigh, offering enough coverage so if I so choose, I don't have to wear underwear. Which is exactly what I'm doing tonight.

I free my hair from my ponytail and let it fall over my shoulders before ruffling my hand through it to break up the waves a bit.

And of course, because I thought ahead, I spritz a little perfume on my wrists and rub my wrists down my neck and over my cleavage.

Pleased, I step out of the closet, half expecting to see Eli, but when I see he's not in the bedroom, I walk out into the living area, where he's sitting on the armrest of the couch. The TV is shut off, and he's massaging his forehead. When he looks up, his hand falls to his side as his eyes narrow in on me.

"Just grabbing some water, and then I'm going to head to bed. You must be tired. Get all of your adrenaline out?"

"No," he says through a clenched jaw.

"Oh, okay, well, feel free to stay up as long as you want." I move past him and his blazing eyes, fill up a glass with water, and walk back to the bedroom, where I grab my phone and text the bosom buddy alliance while I brush my teeth.

Penny: *I think we might be at a breaking point. There's some serious anger brewing in that man.*

Blakely: *Really? Wasn't happy about you "going out"?*

Penny: *Didn't seem like it. He texted me several times, and now, he looks absolutely distraught. I kind of feel bad.*

Winnie: *Don't! He's being ridiculous. He's trying to uphold some stupid promise to Pacey, which Pacey has no right making in the first place. Break him, Penny. BREAK HIM!*

Blakely: *Agreed. He clearly likes you. You're just pushing him into the light.*

Penny: *Okay. P.S. this nightgown is fire, ladies. Oh my God, I've never felt sexier. I'm not wearing underwear.*

Blakely: **WHIPS BRA OVER HEAD* Yeahhhhhh, girl, get some!*

The door to the bedroom opens, and I spit out my toothpaste, rinse my mouth, and turn off the light.

"Oh, I thought you were going to stay up longer," I say when I spot him.

His gaze falls to me as he pulls on the back of his neck, his veins tense, straining.

"No. I'm just going to try to get some sleep."

"Great. Well, the bathroom is all yours."

"Already brushed my teeth."

In a cheery tone that is probably driving him nuts, I say, "Oh nice." I move to the bed and flip down the sheets and comforter. "You really did play such a great game tonight. It was fun seeing you out there on the ice."

"You watched the whole game?"

"Most of it. There were some things I had to take care of, but yeah, I watched most of it." I slip under the covers, and I can feel the fabric of my nightgown play dangerously close to exposing my breasts, but I honestly don't care at all.

It's so crazy to think about how shy I was the night of Eli's birthday. How I could barely look at him because he's so handsome, and now I'm at a point in my life where I couldn't care less if I flash him my boob. I actually welcome it. I welcome all of him.

"Cool," he says before pushing his shorts down, revealing his black boxer briefs, and then climbing into bed. I switch off the light on the nightstand, and instead of turning toward him like I normally do, I keep my back to him, and I scoot closer.

"Mmm, I can feel your warmth already," I say as I snuggle my back into his chest.

He makes an incoherent sound before I take his arm and wrap it around me.

"I look forward to this at night," I say, bordering friendship and what I want. "Some human touch. You know? The days are long and just knowing I have this comfort for when I get home, it's nice."

I move in closer and press his hand to my stomach.

Once again, he's stiff at first, but after a few seconds and some deep breaths, he's melting right into our hold.

"Is, uh, is this nightgown new?" he asks, his fingers slowly dragging over the fabric. The movement—which is so small—makes me fully aware of how much I need a man right now. Not just any man, but this man.

"It is. I told you I had to get some new bras. Well, the girls and I went to the lingerie store, and I found these. They looked so comfortable, and they are. Do you like it?"

"Uh, yeah, I mean . . . it's nice on you, and it feels good."

"So good, and they're just long enough that I don't have to wear underwear."

"You're"—his voice cracks—"not wearing underwear?"

"No. It's gotten so uncomfortable recently. I think I'll be forgoing it altogether. But the new bras I got feel like butter wrapped around me. I wore one with my shirt today. Did you notice?"

"Hard not to notice, Penny."

I turn just enough so I'm on my back, looking up at him. "You say that as if it's a bad thing?"

"It's not." His hand doesn't lift from my stomach. If anything, his grip on me grows wider, stronger. "You just . . . well, you looked really freaking good today."

"Aw, thank you, Eli. I've been feeling so good lately. So you liked the dress? Not sure how much longer I'll be able to wear it."

He shakes his head as his eyes grow heavy. "No, the shirt. I really liked the shirt."

I knew he would. Eli is a type A alpha. It's written all over his personality. He's sweet, kind, and an extrovert, but he also has this alluring, domineering side. I knew if I wore his name on my back, he'd not only find it sexy. Hopefully, he'd find peace that I'm communicating, in some ways, that I belong to him too.

"Oh yes. I liked it too. Wearing your name . . . it felt special." His breathing picks up as he swallows hard. I have him right where I want him. "Anyway." I lift and kiss the side of his cheek. "Good night, Eli."

And then I lower back down to rest my head on my pillow.

I try not to hold my breath as I listen for any indication that he might crack. Break. Maybe even bend. I'll take a bend at this point.

I know I've played with his head enough tonight. I'm just waiting to see the effects of it.

But when he doesn't say anything, when he doesn't even make the slightest move, disappointment rips through me.

What is it going to take for this man to do something? To break that promise with Pacey? To give in to his obvious desires?

There's got to be something—

He shifts behind me, and his hand slides up my stomach so his thumb rests right below my breast. My breath seizes in my lungs.

Oh God, is he bending?

Out of pure fear that I'll scare him away, I hold my breath, waiting . . . hoping . . . begging.

He's so close.

I barely hold in a moan.

His fingers dance so dangerously near me that I can feel the heat coming from them.

And I want it.

I want him.

I want him to touch me.

One more shift. One more inch.

One more breath.

Anything.

Please, just anything.

And then his thumb moves, the tip rubbing gently across the underside of my breast.

Yessss.

My eyes squeeze shut as a wave of arousal pools between my legs instantaneously.

Just like that. I'm ready for him.

I just pray it wasn't an accident . . .

Chapter Twenty-Five

ELI

Don't fucking do it, man.

Don't.

But . . . hell. I can't fucking take it anymore. My mind is full of images of her, recent images that I'm surprised I was able to clear out for the game because they've been running on repeat.

Her asking me to feel her breasts. Her perfectly heavy, magnificent breasts. Her in the damn robe. The dress . . . my shirt. Massaging her. Her moans. Her orgasm. The little touches. The teasing. The fucking flirting.

And now, this nightgown, the one she's wearing with no underwear. I don't think I can hold out. Especially when she smells this good. I move my head closer to hers, and before I can stop myself, I say, "Are you doing this on purpose?"

"Hmm?" she asks as her ass rubs against my crotch.

"Are you fucking with me on purpose?" I repeat, my thumb once again caressing the underside of her breast because I can't seem to control myself.

The question makes her turn, causing my thumb to drag completely over her breast. "How am I fucking with you, Eli?" she asks, her voice full of curiosity.

"I don't know," I say, my mind so fucking confused, I don't even know where to begin. "But . . . you're making me want things I shouldn't want."

Now she turns completely, and her hand falls to my chest. "And what exactly do you want?"

My tongue wets my lips as I grow hard just from her touch, from her proximity, from the way I can see her nightgown barely cover her breasts.

Don't do it.

Don't fucking touch her.

You made a promise to your friend.

Her hand falls over my pec, her thumb rubbing across my nipple, and I nearly scream out in frustration.

Fuck!

I'm hard.

I'm desperate.

And I'm so head-over-heels infatuated with this damn girl that I don't think I can keep acting like she doesn't affect me.

My hand falls down her side to her hip, where I grip the fabric of her nightgown.

Her fingers dance across my chest again. "What do you want, Eli?"

I'm going to lose it. I can feel it.

I want her lips. I want her moans. I want her delicious pussy. I want everything this woman has to offer.

But I can't . . .

"Your silence makes me believe you're not ready for what you want." Her hand slides up to my cheek. "That's okay. Sometimes it takes a bit to figure out what we want." And then she slips away from me and out of bed.

"Where are you going?" I ask, watching her petite frame walk away.

"Checking to make sure I locked up." She disappears down the hallway, and I inwardly groan while pulling on my hair.

Fuck.

This is maddening.

I flip the covers off and go to the kitchen for some water. As I walk down the hallway, she walks toward me, but her head is down, so she doesn't notice me until we're a few feet away.

"Oh." She presses her hand to her chest. "You scared me."

I stare down at her, my fucking need skyrocketing so fast that I can physically feel my will slipping.

She drags her finger down my abs as she asks, "Everything okay?"

And I stop her hand, grip it tightly as I quietly say, "You are toying with me."

"What do you mean?" she asks.

"That kiss, you wanted more, and now you're trying to get it."

"Wh-what are you talking about?" she asks, stumbling now.

"The way you've been dressing. The touching. The flirting with other guys. That's all to get my attention."

"Oh my God, Eli, I have better things to do "

I press her against the wall, pinning her hand over her head. With my other hand, I set her hips against the wall as well. Her gasp is followed by a series of quick intakes of breath.

"Don't fucking lie to me. You want my attention. Don't you?" When she doesn't answer, I move my hand to the hem of her nightgown and slip my fingers under the silky fabric. "Now that I call you out on it, you're going to go shy on me?"

"I don't want your attention."

"Bullshit," I seethe, my irritation and pent-up frustration creating my mood. I move my hand farther up her body, dragging the fabric with me until I reach her hipbone. "You're doing everything you can to drive me crazy. Do you realize how infuriating that is?"

"If you think I'm putting on some show for you, you're wrong."

I lower my forehead to hers. "I don't fucking believe you." My voice is so strained that I barely recognize it. "You know exactly what you're doing by walking around in a nightgown like this, by wearing my name on your back." I let out a heavy breath, my hand moving toward her belly button. "Do you know how hard it made me, seeing you wearing my name?"

She shakes her head just as I glide my hand another inch.

"Feel me," I say. I take her pinned hand and bring it right in front of my hard-on. "Fucking see how you make me feel."

She wets her lips and then cups my cock. I squeeze my eyes shut and push her harder against the wall. Her fingers run along my length, a feather-like caress, and then pull away before I can sink into her touch.

"Do you see?" I ask.

"Seems like something you need to deal with," she says before patting me on the chest and moving away from me. She slides by me and heads back into the bedroom.

Is she fucking kidding me?

Is she really going to deny what she's been doing?

I tear away from the wall and go back into the bedroom, where she's slipping under the covers.

I should rip those covers off, push that godforsaken nightgown up, spread her legs, and show her just how much she's charged me up.

But with what little control I have left, I watch her settle, her petite body nuzzling into position. I half expect with how she's lying through her teeth about toying with me that she'd sleep on her side, attempt to ignore me. But no, she nestles in the middle, where I'd normally hold her.

It's the only reason I proceed with proving her wrong. I'm going to get it out of her. Even if it means taking her naked body into my goddamn hands, I'll make her confess.

Set in my intentions, I slip under the covers as well and pull her into my chest. To my chagrin, her ass nestles right against my cock. Shit, that feels so goddamn good. Just enough friction to drive me wild, to make me prove her wrong even more. Slowly, I slip my hand under her nightgown, my fingers curling over her hip.

With my lips right next to her ear, I say, "What turns you on, Penny?"

She doesn't answer right away. She steadies her breathing before she says, "Do you think that's an appropriate question?"

She's so fucking infuriating. She's trying to act all innocent now when she knows damn well what she's been doing to me.

My fingers move forward, coming close to her pubic bone, and she doesn't even flinch. "If you were wearing a turtleneck, no. But when you're wearing this . . . yes."

"It's comfortable for me."

"It's fucking sexy, tempting, and driving me nuts. But that was your intention, wasn't it?"

"Never." I move my hand right over her pubic bone now, and her leg bends, creating more room for me.

"You're such a liar," I whisper into her ear. "If I were to touch your pussy, how wet would you be?"

She doesn't answer. She doesn't move. I'm not even sure if she's taken a breath. So I slip my finger just a little bit closer . . .

"How wet, Penny?"

She lightly groans before arching her back into me. "So fucking wet, Eli."

Christ. I inch my finger forward to the top of her slit, where I toy with her, barely dipping my finger.

"Yes, Eli," she says, wiggling.

"Tell me the truth. Tell me you've been taunting me, and I'll make sure you find the release you so desperately want."

"I don't . . . I don't know what you're talking about," she says again, causing a roar of frustration to ripple through me, and before I know what I'm doing, I'm rotating her to her back and pinning her, so I'm hovering above her, my body now between her legs.

Tell me, tell me you've been taunting me.

I take both of her hands and plant them on either side of her head as I drop my pelvis against hers. From my hasty fumbling to get her in position, one of her breasts slipped past the fabric of her nightgown.

Nipple hard, her tit just begging for my mouth, I lower my head down and suck the little nub past my lips. Her back arches, thrusting her breast deeper into my mouth. I suck her in, all of her, taking every ounce she's willing to offer me.

I suck.

I lick.

I bite . . .

"Yes," she cries out.

I pull away an inch and say, "Tell me, tell me you've been taunting me."

She shakes her head. "You said you didn't want me."

I pin her with my stare. "I never fucking said that. I'd never lie about wanting you. Because I want you, Penny. I wanted you the day I first met you, and I wanted you the night of my birthday. I've craved you ever since. Don't put those words in my mouth."

"Then prove it," she says with such sass, such power, that I feel that last wave of restraint slip away. And then I thrust my hips over her spread legs.

My covered cock to her wet, dripping pussy. The connection is so palpable I can feel all the way down to my toes.

"Fuck, you're so wet. I feel it through my briefs."

Testing me, she asks, "Don't you want to stop this, Eli?"

"Why the fuck would I want to stop this?" I ask, now rubbing my dick along her exposed pussy, soaking up every ounce of pleasure.

"You stopped our kiss. Told me you can't." She spreads her legs even wider. "Why not stop now?"

I pause despite my thrumming body. "Do you want me to stop?"

"I'm clearly aroused and needing release. Do you really think I want you to stop?"

"I need a clear answer."

"You need a clear answer, but don't you think I deserve one?"

Even though I know I shouldn't keep going, I can't stop myself. I thrust harder, faster, the friction between us building.

"You're driving me crazy, Penny." I lower my forehead to hers as I thrust. Our linked hands grow tighter, her fingers pressing into the back of my hand. "I know, in the back of my mind, I shouldn't be doing this, I shouldn't be touching you, let alone rubbing my cock along your pussy, but fuck, I can't take it. I can't handle you walking around here, in practically nothing, flaunting the body I've been craving for months."

"Yes," she whispers as she hooks one leg around mine, bringing her closer to the friction between us. "More, Eli."

My name, rolling off her tongue like that, unleashes something in me.

I'm now thrusting frantically, and nothing could stop me at this point.

Not one damn thing.

Her breathing increases.

My groans become more intense.

And as I keep pace, I hold my breath, afraid I'm going to miss one moment of this if I search for air. Because this feels like a dream, like this can't possibly be real. I've thought about this, over and over, having her in my arms, feeling her, searching out a release with her.

I'm afraid if I blink, it will all disappear.

But when I hear her feral cry fall past her beautiful lips followed by her legs clamping tightly around me, I know this is real.

Every last second of it.

And I soak it all up.

How she clings to me.

The sounds of her moans.

The way she wets my boxer briefs . . .

It's all I need to bring me to the precipice.

I move my covered cock over her, faster and faster until my

balls tighten and I climax. All of my pent-up frustration is released as I groan in her ear, riding out my orgasm until my body is completely sated.

And that's when I realize what I've done.

"Fuck," I mutter as I slowly lift to look her in the eyes. "Fuck, Penny. This was not supposed to happen."

"Why?" She challenges me with a chin tilt even though her eyes are still heady with pleasure.

"Because we're only supposed to be friends."

At that, she scrunches her eyes shut, pulls at her hair, and growls. *Yep. Growls.*

Oh, fuck. She's not only hurt but angry now too.

"Don't. Give. Me. That. Crap. There is something else, and you're not telling me. What is it?" When I don't answer, she says, "Is it Pacey?"

I glance away, not confirming, but that's all the answer she needs.

"I knew it." She releases my hands and slips out from under me. "You know what, Eli, just forget this happened."

"If only it were that easy," I mutter.

"What?" she asks when she whips around.

"It's not that easy, Penny. I can't just forget this happened because I know I'll relive this moment for months."

She holds her hand up. "Cut it with that shit. I don't need you telling me all these dreamy romantic things when I know they mean nothing."

"They mean something."

"If they meant something, then nothing would block you from taking what you want."

"You're not the one losing out if I act on what I'm feeling," I say, growing angry. "If I actually take what I want, if I claim you as mine and only mine, I lose a friend. A close friend, practically family. You're never going to lose your brother."

She takes a step forward and motions between us. "Pacey does not control this. What happens between us is just that, between us." And then she walks over to the closet, where I hear her rummaging around. After a few seconds, I hear the sound of a zipper, and everything in me freezes. Is she leaving?

I hop out of bed, change out of my briefs, and slip into my shorts. When I head to the closet, she pops out, wearing sweats and a T-shirt and rolling a bag behind her.

"Where are you going?"

"That's none of your concern."

"The fuck it's not." I stand in front of her, blocking her from going anywhere. "You can't just leave."

"Actually, Eli, I'm a grown woman, and that means I can do whatever the hell I want. I have a mind of my own, unlike you."

Walked right into that one.

I push my hand through my hair. "It's not that easy, Penny."

"Why not?" she yells at me. "Why is this so hard on you?"

"Because . . ."

"Because why?"

"Because I don't want to be fucking alone," I shout. "Because Pacey will always be your family, no matter what, but I don't have a goddamn family. My friends, they're all I have, and I'm not about to fuck that up." I pause, attempting to swallow down my painful truth. "I almost lost him once. I can't go through that again."

She rears back, and I can see the minute she understands what I said. The anger in her shoulders dissipates, and her expression immediately turns soft. I bring her into my arms, as there's nowhere else I want her to be right now. *Ever.*

"I'm sorry, Eli. So very sorry."

I rub her back as I press my chin to her cheek. "Don't apologize. It's fine."

She steps away, far too early for my liking, and takes my hand in hers, giving it a good squeeze. "I'm really sorry. Things are just crazy for me right now, and my hormonal libido is insane. I let that take over my brain." Her cheeks stain pink as she says, "I was trying to get your attention, drive you nuts, and I shouldn't have done that. I should have honored your promise to Pacey. I really am sorry."

"You were driving me crazy before this, just so you know." I place my palm on her cheek. If I wasn't the fuckup, the man not good enough for this woman, the man her own brother didn't want near her, I'd grab her and never let go. She's . . . perfect. And I'm . . . *not*. "If things were different, I wouldn't have held back for so long. I would have taken what I wanted the first night I was here. But things are different, and I want to respect that."

"I get it," she says sadly. "I truly do." She looks away, but not before I see tears in her eyes. *Fuck. I've gone and hurt her again.*

"Penn—"

"Well, I'm going to clean up and then get to bed." She sniffs back her tears, and I feel like I just shattered her in some way. *She deserves so much more than I could ever give her,* but I hate this. Before I can add anything, she asks, "Do you want to use the bathroom first?"

"No, go ahead."

She gives my hand one more squeeze and then slips into the bathroom while I take a seat on the edge of the bed and filter my hands through my hair, pulling on the strands out of pure frustration.

I don't think I've ever wanted a person as much as I want Penny. And it's not just the attraction I feel toward her. It's so much more. She's warm, funny, generous . . . unfailingly kind. Somehow, she crept into my life and captivated me. *She's all I think about.* She fills in the broken and cracked parts of my soul . . .

If things were different, she'd be mine.

But they're not, and I have no right in saying that either because even if she was mine, I'm pretty sure I'd fuck that up somehow.

It takes us a few minutes, but once we're both cleaned up and ready for bed again—her wearing a pair of shorts and the same T-shirt now—we climb under the covers. I move to the middle, but she keeps to her side. *Not happening.* Will she allow me to hold her, though? Because I'm not sure I can sleep without her touch now. Did I fuck that up too?

"Hey," I say, tugging on her hip. "What are you doing?"

"Eli, I'm not going to make you hold me, not after everything that happened." I hate that the sass has gone from her voice, that she sounds so subdued. *Teary*.

"First of all, you didn't make me do anything. Secondly, I like holding you at night. I like the human touch. So please, come over here."

She doesn't even pause as she slides back into me. I wrap my arm around her stomach and hold her tightly against me.

"Thank you," I whisper.

She doesn't say anything, but her hand falls to mine, and then we both drift off to sleep.

Chapter Twenty-Six

PENNY

"The plan is off," I say as I sit down in Blakely's office.

She removes her blue light blocking glasses and folds her arms on the table.

"What plan?"

"The bosom buddy alliance plan, the one to get Eli to break."

Her brow crinkles. "Why? It was such a good plan."

"It was until I pushed Eli to dry-hump me last night."

Blakely breaks out into a grin. "Oh, an old-fashioned dry-hump. God, what I wouldn't do for one of those right now. They're so raw, so dirty, yet so innocent. I believe I shall convince Perry to dry-hump me later, or maybe I'll just do it myself. How did it happen? Give me some pointers."

"Are you even listening to me?"

"Uh, yeah, you said you dry-humped, and forgive me for wanting more details. How did it happen?"

"I don't even know at this point. There was a lot of touching, a lot of frustration from the touching and showing skin, and then before I knew it, he was pinning me against the bed and rubbing his penis over my"—I motion to my southern region—"area."

"And how did it feel?"

I sigh heavily and melt into the chair just thinking about him on top of me. "Freaking amazing. I was done in seconds. But during and after, we were pushing each other, trying to get the truth from one another, him wanting me to admit that I've been taunting him, and me wanting him to admit why he's put up a roadblock between us."

"Was it because of Pacey?"

"Yes, but not for the reason we thought." I sit up again and lean forward. "It's because he has no family. He lost his mom when he was twelve, and his dad was never in the picture. Grew up in the attic of a barn practically by himself, and now he treats his teammates as his family, so he doesn't want to mess that up."

Blakely grows serious. "Oh hell, I never would have thought about it that way. I thought he was just accommodating Pacey's sensitive man feelings."

"Me too," I say. "But now . . . well, as I said, the plan is off."

"Ugh, that's devastating for your vagina."

"Tell me about it. She's still weeping."

"At least he was honest with you."

"Yeah, I'm glad he was because I was really starting to get annoyed. But now that I know that, we can just focus on what's important, the baby."

"And what about the mom? You have needs."

"Which will be met by my trusty friend, the vibrator. And hey, I ordered that other device—"

"The clit stimulator?"

"Yeah. That should give me everything I need." I stand from my chair and straighten out my high-waisted black pants.

Blakely chuckles.

"What?" I ask her.

"It's just a vast difference from what you wore yesterday.

Pants and a turtleneck. You went from sex kitten to HR's best friend in seconds."

"I'm showing arms. It's a tank turtleneck."

"I love you, Penny, but I'm going to tell you right now, no one wants to see your arms when you have a rack like that." She points at my chest with her pen, causing me to laugh. I shouldn't feel I can't flaunt the girls just because of Eli. I can wear things that make me feel sexy simply because I want to feel good about myself. But if what Eli said is true, it's more difficult for him when I show extra skin. And honestly, he's a good man, even better than I first thought, so I don't want to do anything that makes him struggle against his attraction to me. Hence the turtleneck.

"Well, these boobs are currently off the market. That means keeping them hidden from the world."

"Such a shame. I liked staring at your cleavage."

"There's something seriously wrong with you," I say before taking off and heading back to my office.

━━━

ELI: *Was going to make tortellini for dinner. Are you going to be home for dinner?*

Penny: *Yes, but you don't have to worry about me.*

Eli: *If I'm already making dinner, you can have some.*

Penny: *Okay, sure. Thanks.*

Eli: *Are things weird between us again?*

Penny: *I want to say no, but I think they are.*

Eli: *How can we make it better?*

Penny: *Uh . . . I ate an apple?*

Eli: *LOL, that's a start.*

Penny: *Unfortunately, I just think this is how it's going to be, Eli. And we have to accept that.*

Eli: *We can be friends.*

Penny: *I don't think we can be the kind of friends you're hoping for. And that's okay. As long as we're friendly, that's all that matters. And you* *need to stop focusing on me and concentrate on your game for tomorrow. You guys have to win.*

Eli: *But things don't feel right between us.*

Penny: *Not sure they ever will.*

⬛▭

"CAN I ASK YOU SOMETHING?" Eli says as we're lying in bed, his arm protectively around me of course.

"Sure," I say as I clutch his pillow.

Dinner was a disaster, we didn't know what to say to each other, so instead of talking, we just sat there and ate. I tried to do the dishes after but he wouldn't let me. So then I ended up just scrolling through TikTok and replying to comments from trolling fans with just enough sass not to get me fired but to make everyone laugh.

"Have you ever thought about being a parent? Before all of this? Were children in your future?"

Oh . . . I wasn't expecting him to ask that. Something so deep.

"Um, I assumed that I'd probably have kids one day once I was married and settled. I never expected to have a kid like this. But yeah, I'd say at some point, I'd probably have kids."

He's silent for a second before he says, "I always swore I wouldn't. It's why I lived the type of lifestyle that I lived, never really attaching to anything. It was easier that way."

Quietly, I say, "Can't lose something you don't have."

"Exactly." He squeezes me a little tighter. "But things have changed. I don't have a choice other than to accept this new person into my world, and that freaks me the fuck out. I don't want to do this alone. And it's fucking with my head that things are weird between us again. I just . . . I need you to promise me that no matter what happens between us, we'll always be there for each other. You can count on me, and I can count on you."

"Why are you bringing this up now?"

"Because I can feel us drifting apart after last night, and that fucking scares me. All of this scares me, but knowing I had you at my side made it easier. If that's taken away from me, I don't think I can be the man I need to be."

Needing to look him in the eyes, I turn toward him and press my hand to his cheek. "Eli, you don't need me in order to be the good man you already are."

Vulnerability flashes through his eyes. "This is overwhelming for me, Penny. You have your parents to help navigate you through all of this. I don't have that. I don't have someone to guide me. And I'm so fucking scared that I'll fuck this up. That I won't be a father this baby deserves. I need someone to lean on, someone to guide me when I'm being an idiot."

"Eli, you're not going to do this alone. I promise. Whatever happens, we will make it work."

"Promise me," he says, his voice so heavy with concern that it nearly splits me in two. I now understand this man very well. He's terrified of being alone again. Even though he lived a fun and seemingly carefree life, I've caused a disruption that terrifies him. I'll do anything I can to ensure he has his family intact.

"I promise, Eli."

"Thank you." He leans in and presses a soft kiss to my forehead before pulling away.

From the outside, Eli looks like a well put together man. He appears strong and confident like nothing fazes him as he struts through life in his three-piece suit. He's easygoing with a solid head on his shoulders, the first guy to welcome you. In getting to know him, I see that yes, he's all of those things, but he's also incredibly vulnerable, a young boy looking for someone to love him, someone to take his hand and walk him through this life, so he's not alone. And that right there . . . that breaks me. Because I am fairly certain I wish I could be the woman to do that for him. To love *him*.

Chapter Twenty-Seven

ELI

"Dude, what the fuck is going on?" Posey whispers as we sit on the bench, watching another loss unfold in front of us. "Your head isn't in the game."

It's not.

I've tried so fucking hard to prepare for tonight, to mentally get to where I need to, but I can't seem to push past my worries where Penny and the baby are concerned. My conversation with Penny last night hit me hard, leaving me feeling raw and exposed. I voiced my concerns, and now that they're out there in the world, I'm scared.

This morning, Penny and I ate breakfast sandwiches together that I picked up from the coffee shop around the corner. She asked me questions about the game, everything felt normal from the outside looking in, but it's not normal. Nothing is fucking normal.

Because what I realized very quickly is that I like this girl. I really fucking like her, and I don't think I can do anything about it. I'm not relationship material, I wouldn't even know how to be in one if I was, but being this close to Penny, clinging to her every night, leaning on her for help? It's making me think. It's making me want . . . more.

I want to be a better man.

I want to be an amazing father.

I want to be an equal partner in this parenting adventure.

And fuck me . . . I want Penny.

And that's the problem. I can't have all those things, especially Penny. I would be too damn scared to lose her. Too damn nervous to see her slip through my fingers.

That's what's been playing in my head all day.

That's why I can't get it together on the ice to save my life, and that's exactly why we're down by two goals, with a minute left in the game.

Coach pulled my line, and I don't fucking blame him. We've been playing like shit. He's been pacing the back of the bench, a rolled-up piece of paper in his hand, ready to strike any second. I can feel his anger beating down on me.

Why are you fucking up, Hornsby?

Because I can't get my head on straight.

I press my hand to my forehead. "I'm all kinds of fucked up," I say to Posey.

"Dude, we need to talk after this if we have any chance of staying in this series."

"Yeah, I know."

The countdown begins, we all know we lost, and when the final buzzer sounds, the disappointed fans hang their heads low as they trudge up the stairs and out to their cars while we, the team, collectively gather our shit and head into the locker room.

We're flying to Washington tonight. Coach wanted to get us there as soon as possible to get adjusted, and I'm sure it will be a silent-as-shit flight.

There isn't much talking in the locker room. We all know where we went wrong. We all know where we need to improve. The only thing that is said is from Coach when he pokes his head into the locker room and tells us we have "forty-five fucking minutes to get our asses on the team bus" that will take us to the airport. Would we have preferred to drive ourselves? Take our time? Of course, but we aren't afforded that luxury when we lose like we did.

We all put it into high gear and strip down, take showers, and pack up. Our gear will be rank when we open it up tomorrow because it didn't have time to dry. Lucky equipment managers. Since I don't have to do much after the game, I spend a little more time under the pounding water of the shower and then fit myself into my suit, which is the last fucking thing I want to put on right now.

I don't mind the tradition of wearing a suit before and after the game. Still, after a brutal loss and everything hanging so heavily over my head, I just want to slip into a pair of sweatpants and then cuddle into Penny under her silky sheets.

"Meet me on the bus," Posey says. "We have some talking to do."

Great.

Just what I want to do.

Talk more.

I pack up, place my bag over my shoulder, and head out of the locker room behind a couple of guys only to hear my name called. Normally, I wouldn't look up, but I know that voice.

Penny.

I pause and turn around to find her standing against the wall wearing that shirt again, the one with my name on the back. An instant flood of relief and comfort pulses through me as I walk over to her.

"Sorry about the loss," she says when I move in only a foot away.

"I played like absolute shit," I reply.

"We all have our bad days."

"I've been having quite a few."

"It's been done before, Eli, a win when you're down like this. There's still hope."

"I know." I blow out a heavy breath and reach out to take her hand in mine. She lets me, thankfully. "Are you good? Everything okay?"

"Yeah. I know you guys are leaving, so I wanted to catch you before you left. I have something for you."

"You do?" I ask.

She nods and then opens her purse and pulls out a bag of gummy bears. "Just in case you don't have any for the away trip."

I take the bag from her and stare down at the ridiculous candy that has been a huge part of my game since my mom gave me my first bag. I then wrap my arm around her shoulder and pull her into a hug. "Thank you, Penny. This means a lot to me."

She hugs me back, the warmth of her body something I desperately wish I could bottle and use whenever I'm feeling lonely or afraid. "Of course." She pulls away and pats me on the chest. "Now, stop losing and go give us a win."

I chuckle. "If only it were that easy." I let out a heavy sigh.

"Is everything okay with you, Eli? I'm sure it's the last thing you want to hear, but you really didn't seem like yourself out there."

"I know. Just lost in my head right now. Posey wants to talk about it on the bus, so . . . mentally preparing for that conversation."

"Well, if there's anything you need from me, just let me know."

"Thank you," I say. God, I wish I could kiss her. I wish I could curl her into me, lift her chin, and taste her lips one more time. I wish I could show her the affection that pulses through me whenever I see her, rather than holding back and opting only for a hug. I wish I could walk out to the bus, holding her hand, and give her a kiss goodbye like I see the other wives and girl-friends do. But I don't have that privilege. I'll never have that privilege, and one day I'll see Penny in another man's arms as a result. *Fuck.* "I'll text you."

"Sounds good." She takes a step back. "Safe flight, Eli."

Because I can't seem to get this girl out of my head, I close the space between us one more time, and I hug her, pressing a kiss to the top of her head.

"See ya, Penny."

I release her, and when I turn around, my stomach nearly drops to the floor as I spot Pacey, standing outside the locker room, staring back at us.

Fuck.

⬜

"IT'S NOT WHAT YOU THINK," I say when I get on the bus and take a seat next to Pacey in the very back. "Nothing is going on between us. I swear, dude."

He keeps his gaze straight ahead, staring at the seat in front of him. "You care for her."

It's not a question. It's more of a statement. And from the stillness of his body and the direct way he's making sure not to make eye contact with me, I honestly can't tell if he's angry or not.

So I tread carefully.

"I do. I care about her a lot. She's the mother of my child, Pacey. I don't take that lightly."

There's no response. Just staring.

Sweat forms on the back of my neck, and I attempt to figure out how to navigate this.

"Pacey, she was just giving me—"

He turns toward me. "Do you like her?"

Yes.

A lot.

I like her more than I should.

"It's, uh . . . it's complicated," I answer.

"How is that complicated? It's either a yes or a no."

"It's complicated because you're her brother and my best friend, that's why."

"If I were out of the picture, what would your answer be?"

"But you're not. You're right here, completely in the picture."

His nostrils flare. "Stop avoiding the fucking question and answer it."

I turn away, watching the other guys climb onto the bus, clearly avoiding the back of the bus where tensions are high.

I bite down on my lip and then say, "If you weren't in the picture, yeah, I'd allow myself to like her, but I told myself I wouldn't go there. I don't want to lose our friendship."

"Does she like you?"

I grip the gummy bear package that's in my hands as I think about the other night, hell, the last week. The way she'd touch me, smile . . . cuddle in close. How she'd tease me with her outfits, flirt with me in her texts, and smile at me when we watched *Ozark* together. Our late-night conversations, our confessions . . . how close we've become. She's the first person I think about texting when I have news, and she's the only person I want to hear right before I go to bed.

"I think she does," I say quietly.

From the corner of my eye, I can see him slowly nodding.

"But I'm not doing anything about it." Besides dry-humping her one night, but we don't have to get into that. "I know she's off limits, man."

He reaches into his backpack and pulls out his headphones. Before he puts them over his head, he says, "Don't let me get in the way of anything." He then looks at me. "But if you fucking hurt her, you're dead to me, got it?"

And then he silences me by putting his headphones on and starts typing on his phone.

Uh, what just happened?

Did he just give me permission to explore things with Penny? That can't possibly be right . . . can it?

I want to tap him on the shoulder and ask him what he means by that, but he's shut down, and I know if I push him, it might not be good for me in the long run. So I lift from the seat and move to where Posey is sitting and sit next to him.

"Do I want to even ask what you two were talking about?"

I shake my head and whisper, "I think he just gave me permission to be with Penny."

"That doesn't seem like him." Posey looks over his shoulder to the back of the bus. "Is he running a fever?"

"I don't know. He caught me in the hallway with Penny." Posey gives me a look. "We weren't doing anything but talking. And sure, I hugged her, but that was it." It wasn't it. Not really. I *needed* her hug like I needed my next breath. Just like it always is for me. "He asked if I liked her."

"Do you?"

I nod slowly. "Yeah, and I think that's what's fucking with my head. I've never really felt like this before, man, toward anyone, and I don't know how to process that."

"That's what's been going on? You have feelings for a girl, and you don't know what to do?"

"Yeah. We both agreed we don't want to be in a relationship, but I swear to God, Posey, every day I spend with her, I feel like I *could* try a relationship with her." Are we not almost in one anyway? Living together, sharing meals together, talking about and doing life together. Isn't that what a relationship is?

Posey slowly nods. "That's the problem, though, man. She's not the kind of girl you *try* something out on. Either you're all the way in, or you're out. There's no in-between."

Unfortunately, I know he's right. Penny isn't a guinea pig for my lack of dating. She isn't someone I should test the waters with. She's the long-term girl you commit to, and I just don't know if I'm the man who can commit.

"You're right," I say before letting out a heavy breath.

Fuck.

PENNY: *How are you feeling about tomorrow? You guys can do this. So what, you have to win three straight games in a row. That's doable.*

I stare at the text. It's the third one she's sent me today that I've left unanswered. I know she'll start to worry, but I don't know how to react to her. My head is telling me not to fuck this up. Keep things platonic. But my fucking soul is asking for a chance with her.

And I've been sitting in my hotel room since we left the arena for practice, doing nothing but festering in my own thoughts. I'm longing for interaction . . .

But I don't want to lead her on. I don't want to say something stupid.

Then again, if I don't say anything, she'll think something's wrong.

Something is wrong, though.

All of this is wrong.

I wasn't supposed to develop feelings for this girl. I wasn't supposed to enjoy seeing her after a game, waiting for me. I wasn't supposed to crave her warm body at night instead of this cold hotel bed. And I wasn't supposed to prefer watching a show after a game with her, rather than going out to a bar.

But fuck, everything has changed.

I set my phone down and stand from my bed. I slip on a pair of sandals and a hoodie, flip the hood over my head, and grab my wallet. There's a convenience store just outside of the hotel. Maybe if I grab myself a snack and a drink, that will clear my mind.

With a key card in hand, I head out of my hotel room and walk toward the elevator just as Posey rounds the corner. His hair is disheveled, and his shoulders are completely slumped.

"Hey," I say, causing him to look up.

Surprised to see me, he pauses and then asks, "Where are you going?" He glances around. "Dude, please don't tell me you're headed down to the bar."

The bar is where all the single guys on the team go given all the ladies know what hotel we're staying at and where to find us if we're looking for some fun.

"Do you really think I'd do that?"

"I don't know. You're in a weird headspace."

"I could say the same about you."

I'm not the only one on the team acting weird. I know the weight of our losses doesn't rest solely on my shoulders because I'm not the only one struggling. And it's showing right now, with the etch in Posey's brow and the droop in his normally uplifting demeanor.

He moves his hand through his hair. "I'll be fine."

"You made me talk about my shit," I say. "Maybe we should talk about yours."

He shakes his head. "No, I can't."

"Were you downstairs at the bar?"

"No. I went for a walk." His eyes meet mine. "Catching feelings is bullshit." He moves past me, but I press my hand to his chest, halting him.

Catching feelings? Where the fuck is this coming from?

"Dude, who do you have feelings for?" I wrack my brain for a clue, anyone he might have run into, fucking anything, but I'm coming up short, and I can't be sure if it's because he hasn't said much to me or because I've been so caught up in my life, that I haven't been paying attention.

Maybe a bit of both.

"Nothing we need to worry about. It's probably just a stupid crush that I'll get over. Just drop it."

"Posey—"

"Seriously, Eli, drop it." And there it is, my first name. Whenever we pull that out, we know it's serious.

"Okay, but if you need me, you can talk to me. I know I'm going through my own shit, but I'm here for you."

"I know," he says. "I appreciate that. And you swear, you're not about to do something stupid?"

"I was going to grab a drink and a snack, but now I'm thinking maybe not. Is it crawling with people in the lobby?"

"There's no way you'll be able to walk a few steps without being bombarded. Try the vending machine."

"Yeah, I think I'll do that." I pat him on the shoulder. "Thanks. I'll see you in the morning."

I start walking toward the vending machines when he calls out to me, "Hey, Hornsby?"

"Yeah?" I look over my shoulder.

"I have a bad feeling about tomorrow."

"Yeah . . . I think everyone does."

He slowly nods and walks away.

I take the next five minutes to wrestle over what I want from the vending machine, and I settle on a water—boring—and a bag of Dot's Pretzels. When I reach my room again, I kick off my sandals, lie down on my bed, and pick up my phone to see another text from Penny.

I swipe my phone open and read it.

Penny: *I'm sorry to keep bothering you, but I just want to make sure we're okay.*

Just what I thought, she's worried.

But I don't know how to respond to her. I don't know how to act other than fucking pine over the damn girl. I can't leave her hanging, though. So, I send her a quick text back.

Eli: *Sorry, busy prepping for tomorrow. Trying to focus.*

I feel bad. Every other away game, I've always talked to her, but I'm the jackass who can't seem to make sense of things, despite trying to work through them with my therapist. *He* agrees with me: trying something new with someone important isn't the best idea.

My phone beeps.

Penny: *Oh, sure. Sorry. I'll leave you alone. Good luck with the end of the series.*

Groaning, I toss my phone to the side and push my hands through my hair in pure irritation.

Why is this so damn difficult?

Probably because you have abandonment issues and refuse to let anyone else in your life that you could lose.

Yup, that seems accurate.

Chapter Twenty-Eight

ELI

Blakely: *You're an asshole.*

I stare at my phone, wholeheartedly agreeing with her text.

I am an asshole.

I ended the conversation with Penny last night rather abruptly and haven't texted her since, and the text from Blakely tells me Penny was affected.

I text her back.

Eli: *I know.*

I scoop a pile of eggs into my mouth while I watch the three dots on the screen, taunting me, preparing me for a response.

Blakely: *Going dark on her, especially now. You're all kinds of messed up, Hornsby. Don't worry, I'm picking up the pieces you keep breaking off her.*

I pinch the bridge of my nose and let out a heavy breath.

Fuck.

Eli: *It's not what you think.*

Blakely: *You don't WANT to know what I think, especially about* *you. I should never have left her alone with you on your birthday. I'll forever regret that.*

Eli: *Probably the right verdict.*

Blakely: *Seriously, what's wrong with you?*

Eli: *Still trying to figure that out.*

Blakely: *Do me a favor, at least call her today. Out of all days, call her today.*

Call her.

Hear her voice?

Dip into the one thing that I crave . . . no. I can't.

I set my phone down and finish eating my eggs. Focus on the game. We have to win tonight.

We can't lose. If we do, we're out. That's the end of the season, and if the season ends, then I have to face the one thing I don't want to right now: my feelings for Penny.

THE LOCKER ROOM is eerily quiet as we prepare for our game. We're an hour away from the puck drop and are now finishing treatments, warming up, and attempting to get our heads in the right mindset.

I haven't spoken to Penny since her last text last night, and I haven't been able to stop thinking about it. Should I have spoken more to her? Did I do the right thing?

Should I have called her like Blakely suggested?

Pacey walks into the locker room after getting his hamstrings stretched. He's been sore lately so he's been spending extra time in the training room.

Instead of walking over to his assigned locker, he walks toward me and takes a seat. Stretching his legs out in front of him, he says, "So what did you do for her today?"

Huh?

"Do for her today?" I ask. "What do you mean?"

Pacey slowly turns toward me. "For Penny."

I wrack my brain for what the hell he might be talking about.

Blakely's comment about calling Penny comes to mind. What the hell is today? Did she have a doctor's appointment and not tell me?

"I'm assuming you sent her something," Pacey adds.

Sent her something?

Dread creeps up the back of my neck as my mouth goes dry.

"Dude . . . I . . . I don't know what you're talking about."

Pacey's brows narrow. "It's her goddamn birthday, and you didn't send her anything? You said you care about her."

"It's Penny's birthday?" I ask. All the color in my face completely drains. "She didn't say anything to me. I had no fucking clue."

Then again, you shut her off before she could even say one word to you. She tried striking up several conversations with you yesterday, you fucking moron, and you didn't engage.

"Holy fuck." I scramble in my locker to find my phone, and when I have it in my hand, I move past a fuming Pacey and straight to the phone room designated for the guys to talk to their families without the raucous of the locker room in the background.

Half-dressed for the game, I shut the door behind me and quickly dial her phone number. I listen as it rings.

And rings.

And rings.

"Hey, it's Penny. Sorry I couldn't get to the phone right now, but leave a message, and I'll get back to you as soon as I can. Thanks."

Beep.

I hang up, not bothering with a message.

Pacing the room now, I dial up Blakely and listen to it ring and ring until voicemail picks up.

Fuck.

I try to call Penny again when my phone buzzes with a text message.

Blakely: *I'm at the movies with Penny. What the hell do you want?*

My fingers fly over the keyboard as I text back.

Eli: *It's her goddamn birthday? I didn't fucking know. Can you ask her to call me?*

Blakely: *Uh . . . no. She'll call you if she wants to call you. And yes, it's her birthday. Way to make her cry on it, you piece of human garbage.*

Eli: *Blakely, I swear, I didn't know. Fuck, I need to talk to her.*

Blakely: *Honestly, just leave her alone. We finally got her to have some fun. You texting her will only ruin it. Just focus on your game, like you told her you were doing last night.*

Eli: *I was doing that.*

Blakely: *Bullshit. And I'll say this right now, if you're out there living your single life, I'll actually murder you.*

Eli: *I'm NOT! Jesus, I care about Penny. I'd never do that to her.*

Blakely: *But you will ghost her on her birthday. Even better. I hope you break a rib tonight. Peace.*

"Fuck," I yell just as the door opens and Pacey peeks his head through. "Man, listen—"

He walks into the room and shuts the door, only to lean against it. He folds his arms over his chest and says, "No, you listen. We have a game in less than an hour. We need you to be present. You can worry about Penny later."

Feeling like I was just hit by a goddamn truck, I say, "Dude, I really fucked up."

"Good, you recognize that. You're just going to have to beg for forgiveness later."

"You're not mad at me?"

"As Winnie pointed out to me, I can't insert myself in the relationship you have with Penny. You two have to figure that shit out. And like I said, hurt her, and you're dead to me. I know hurting her today wasn't intentional. After we're done with all of this, I expect you to make it right."

"I will." I swallow hard. "I fucking will."

"Good. Now, a fuck-ton of people are relying on us to play our best hockey. Get your fucking head on straight so we can go win this, Hornsby."

"Got it." I have a job to do, so I'll get my shit together.

And then, hopefully, I can fix things with Penny.

Chapter Twenty-Nine

PENNY

The door opens, and I hear it quietly click shut.

I glance at the clock and read that it's just past one in the morning.

The boys lost tonight, eliminating them from the playoffs. I didn't watch the game. I couldn't even stomach it. I know they lost because I receive alerts on my phone about the Agitators, and I saw the headline. I sent a quick text to Pacey, letting him know how sorry I was that they lost, and he apologized for losing on my birthday and that he plans on celebrating me when he gets back.

Winnie and Blakely came over to spend the day with me. I moped around for the first half, crying a few times because I honestly didn't know what I did wrong. Did he get weird because I gave him gummy bears? I was just trying to be nice. All morning, I tried to think of the moment I messed up, when I should have done something different, and all I came up with was the gummy bears.

I want to say that not hearing from Eli didn't really affect me at all, but it did. I've come to the realization that no matter how hard I try, I like the man. And those feelings probably won't ever go away, which is sad—because I picked the wrong person to fall for.

He's so easily detachable from my life, despite me wanting to cling to him. And the worst part of it is that he doesn't even realize how much it pains me to see him walk away, to watch him distance himself.

I can hear him move around the living room, and for a second, I wonder if he's going to sleep on the couch. I almost wish he went straight back to his place, where I don't have to have this twisting ball of anxiety pulsing through me, wondering what he's going to do.

And then . . . he starts toward the bedroom.

Oh, God.

Panic ricochets through me. Should I act like I'm asleep? Keep my eyes open? Confront him? Ask him to leave?

I don't have enough time to decide before he opens the bedroom door. From the light of the moon, I see he's removed his suit jacket, and the buttons of his shirt have been undone, offering a view of his devastating, well-defined chest and abs.

Just like that, tears form in the backs of my eyes, and I curse myself for being so emotional over this man. For letting him hold rent all day—*every* day—in my head, twisting and turning my emotions until I can barely breathe.

I watch as he moves toward me carefully, and when his eyes meet mine, he pauses. Quietly, he says, "Are you awake?"

Holding back tears, I say, "Yes."

"Penny . . ." He closes the distance between us. "Why didn't you tell me?"

"I don't want to talk about this," I say, my voice wobbly. "Maybe you should just go to your place."

He reaches the bed and stands over me. "I'm not going anywhere."

Of course he's not. Because he doesn't want to be told what to do . . . because he does *everything* on his time.

Pushing the blankets off me, I sit up on my knees so I can look at him better. His eyes quickly fall to my nightgown, the one that he loves so much, and then back to my eyes.

"I am barely holding it together, Eli," I say. "Please, just leave."

But he doesn't move.

Nor does he reply. Slowly, his eyes flit over me, taking in every last inch. They fall to my chest, my collarbone, my neck . . . my lips. His breathing grows heavier as the air in the room seems to still, and silence captures both of us.

What is he doing?

Why isn't he saying anything?

Why does he keep staring at my lips?

Before I can ask, he takes a step forward, and I gasp just before his hand slides behind my head, and his lips capture mine in one unexpected yet powerful kiss.

A kiss that lasts only a few seconds before I'm pushing him away.

"What are you doing?" I ask.

He glides his tongue over his lips as if he's granting himself another taste of me. "Giving in."

"Giving in to what?"

He turns away, and I don't miss the uncertainty in his tense shoulders and the way he pulls ferociously on his hair before turning back around.

When his desperate eyes meet mine, he says, "No matter how hard I try, Penny, I can't separate my feelings from being the co-parent you need. I like you, want you . . . need you, and I'm a fucking moron for not saying it earlier, for trying to push you away instead."

My heart stills and I feel my lungs beg, plead for a breath.

"Wh-what are you saying?" I ask.

He cups my cheek as he says, "I can't stay away anymore. I

want your lips, I want your body, I want . . . you." His other hand grips my hip and then rises to my rib cage, where he holds me tightly, in place, not letting me stray any farther away from him. "I'm sorry for everything. For pushing you away, for fucking up your birthday, and for making you cry when you deserve nothing but happiness." His nose passes over mine. "Please, Penny, please tell me I have a chance."

His lips are a whisper over mine, never taking, just taunting.

I want to hurt him. Tell him to leave, to take his hands off me, but even though there might be some satisfaction in seeing him sulk away, I don't think it outweighs the satisfaction of giving in to his touch.

"You hurt me," I say quietly.

"And I'll spend however long it takes to make it up to you." His lips nip at mine, his hand traveling farther up my ribs until his thumb is stroking the bottom of my breast.

"I have feelings for you, Eli. I don't want to get hurt even more if I give in."

"I don't want to fucking hurt you, ever, Penny." His nose drags over my cheek and then to my ear. His thumb passes over my nipple, and I arch into his grasp. "I'm so goddamn sorry for everything. Let me show you the kind of man I can be for you," he whispers.

My hands fall to his chest, then rise to his shoulders. I slip them under the fabric of his dress shirt and slowly move the fabric over his shoulders and down his arms. He assists me in taking it off, only for his hands to return, one just beneath my breast, the other now at the arch of my back.

"Are you going to push me away again?" He shakes his head as his lips glide over my jaw, and his hand moves up over my breast and pulls down the fabric of my nightgown, exposing me.

"No, I can't. I tried that, and it just made me both miserable and need you even more."

I slip my hands down his back and under the waistband of his pants. "I'm scared."

His mouth moves over mine, never kissing, just teasing. "Me too, Penny."

"I like you, Eli, a lot."

He pauses and then connects our foreheads as he pushes the nightgown straps over my shoulders and down my arms. "I like you so goddamn much," he says.

"Don't hurt me." *Please, please don't hurt me. I won't survive it.*

"I won't," he says. He then slides the rest of my nightgown down my body until it pools at my knees, leaving me completely naked.

Eyes trained on each other, I move my hands to the front of his pants, and I undo them, fumbling with the zipper as it rides against his thick erection. When they're finally undone, I inch my hand down the front and grip him tightly, causing him to hiss with satisfaction.

"Fuck, Penny." His nose rubs against mine again, his lips testing mine with the smallest of kisses. When I kiss him back, he loses all self-control and pushes me back on the bed, removing the rest of my nightgown. "Please tell me you want this, you want me," he says as his hand slowly moves up my stomach, his lips passing over mine.

I pull his cock out past the waistband of the boxers, the tip pressing against his stomach. "I want this, Eli. I wish I didn't, it would be so much easier, but I want you."

He peppers kisses down my jaw and over my neck as he says, "This is new to me, Penny. These feelings, they're so strong, I can't fucking let you go. But please, help me navigate them."

He teases my hardened nipple with his fingers.

"I will." I arch into his hand.

He kisses along my collarbone and then down my chest until he pulls my nipple into his mouth.

"Yes," I call out, sifting my hands through his hair. "God, Eli, I've wanted you for so long. Wanted this."

He sucks and pulls . . . and nibbles, and when he lifts up, he says, "I've dreamed of having my mouth on your body again. Yearned for it. *Craved* you."

He moves to my other breast. His hand slides down to the swell of my stomach, where he pauses for a second and then continues down, then pushes my legs open. I let them fall as wide as I can, giving him all the access he wants.

His mouth still on my breast, he glides his fingers down my center.

"Fuck, Penny, you're so wet."

"And sensitive," I say as I feel my orgasm already start to form. "I come fast, Eli."

"Perfect." He brings his mouth back up to mine and presses his thumb to my clit. His lips cover mine, swallowing my gasp as his tongue dives into my mouth and tangles with mine.

My hips have a mind of their own as they rotate against his thumb. A pressure immediately builds in my core, causing my limbs to feel weightless. It's as if they don't even exist, and the only thing that matters is the way his tongue dances against mine and his thumb massages my clit.

Up and down.

Sliding.

Gliding.

Building the pressure so deep inside me that I'm panting against his mouth.

"Eli, I'm . . . oh God." I can't get the words out before I'm coming on his fingers. I moan loudly, gripping his hair until I can't take the pressure anymore, and move his hand away so I can catch my breath. "Oh my God," I say as my body melts into the mattress.

He kisses me tenderly on my lips, then my cheeks, my chin, my eyes . . .

And he pulls away. I glance up at him to see his erection looking painfully hard. He pushes his pants and briefs down just enough to release his cock from its confines and begins to stroke himself while staring down at me. It's the most erotic and fascinating thing I've ever seen.

He doesn't just stroke. He rotates and pulls, passing his hand over the head of his cock every so often and then bringing his hand to his balls where he gives them a gentle squeeze before repeating the process.

"Aren't you tired of your hand?" I ask him.

He smirks down at me. The devil himself could be tainted by that look. God, I have missed that grin. "Yes, this cock wants your pussy more than you can imagine, but I know my limits, what I've earned, and it's not that just yet."

"Says who?" I sit in front of him and drop his pants and briefs all the way down his legs. He keeps a hold on his cock as he steps out of them.

"I say."

I move my finger over the contours of his abs. "And who made you the decision maker?"

"No one, you literally control me, Penny. You have to know that."

"If that's the case." I bring my finger down to the tip, where I catch his precum, continuing slowly down the side of his cock. I reach forward, my mouth a few inches in front of him, and run my tongue over the tip. He hisses in reply. "I want your cock in my mouth."

"Penny . . . no—"

But I have my mouth over the head before he can even protest. My hands fall to his hips, and I hold him steady as I bob my head over his cock, licking and sucking just enough to drive him crazy.

"Jesus," he groans as his hand sifts through my hair. "Fuck, Penny, I don't deserve this. I don't deserve you."

"You don't," I say as I pull my mouth from his cock, "but that doesn't mean I don't want you."

I move up his body, dragging my hands with me until I reach his face. I grip his cheeks, and I bring his mouth to mine. He pulls me against his erection and returns the kiss. And we stand there, holding each other, our mouths doing all the work. I can't remember the last time I just made out with someone, enjoyed the feel of their warm body against mine, or the welcoming hold of a man.

But it's addicting, and it's turning me on all over again.

"I want you in me," I say against his mouth.

He grips my hips and turns me around, a one-eighty against his body so my back is to his stomach and his head is draping over my shoulder. With two fingers, he snags my chin, pulling me to the left until I find his lips again while his other hand plays with my breasts.

Our tongues clash.

Our breaths sync.

And his cock presses against the seam of my ass. The sensation of his girth sliding over my skin causes sweat to break out across my neck. There's a yearning so deep within me to pulse with such overwhelming need that my kisses grow faster as I move my hips against him.

"Shit," he mutters as his hand glides gently over the column of my neck. "Penny . . ."

"Hmm?" I ask when he pinches my nipple.

He moves his mouth to my ear and slowly and deliberately says, "I want to fuck you . . . bare."

"Do it," I say as I rest my head against his strong shoulder, his hand playing carefully with my neck. "Fuck me, Eli. I want to feel all of you."

His fingers pass over my trachea before moving to the back of my neck. With his hand at my waist, he bends me forward by holding my hips back and pushing me down so my hands land on the mattress in front of me.

That's when he steps away and smooths his hand over my backside.

"I want you to be mine, Penny. If I fuck you, right now, that means you're mine."

My head drops as I spread my legs a little wider for him. "I've been yours since the night of your birthday. That has never changed."

"Good answer." His hands run up my back and then down again, where he lifts it, only to return a light smack to my right ass cheek.

"Oh God," I yelp in surprise right before a wave of lust rocks through me. "Eli . . . I—"

Smack.

"Oh fuck," I moan, my back arching, my pussy so wet now that I fear what will happen next.

I await his next smack, but instead of it coming, I hear him behind me, sifting through my nightstand. I glance over my shoulder and see that he has my clit stimulator in hand.

"I won't need that," I say. "I'm already on edge."

"I didn't ask if you needed it. I know you'll come with only my cock. But I want you to have it," he replies before landing another spank on my ass.

"Oh God." I nearly cry as my clit pulses between my legs. "Eli, I'm right there, ready to come. Please, just fuck me."

"You want my cock?"

"Yes."

"Good," he says as I feel his tip at my entrance. I angle my ass up, giving him better access, and he slips an inch in.

"More. All of you."

His hand smooths over my ass where he's smacked it. "Patience, Penny."

"You don't understand. I need to come, my clit . . . it feels so heavy, I need the release."

"Then maybe I should just fuck you with my tongue."

"No," I cry out. "Give me your cock."

"Fucking Christ," he mutters. "That's the sexiest thing I've ever heard." And then he plunges his cock inside me in one giant thrust.

"Yessss," I cry out just before my clit stimulator is turned on and placed exactly in the right spot. It sucks my clit, and my legs quiver from the pressure of my orgasm building. "Eli, I'm going to come, please, fuck me."

"Goddammit, you're pulsing around me."

"Fuck me," I say, trying to hold back, trying to wait.

Please, just fuck me.

He grips my hip with his free hand, and in seconds, he's pounding into me. The sensation of his bare girth sliding against my walls and the feel of the stimulator sucking on my clit over and over again. It's too much, and I'm coming in seconds, calling out his name as I grip the sheets on the bed.

The stimulator falls to the ground, rattling against the floor as he grips both of my hips and thrusts into them over and over, prolonging my orgasm until he stills and groans over me.

"Motherfucker," he says as his cock swells. I can feel him release, grinding against me until he's completely done. After a few moments, he leans forward and presses a kiss between my shoulder blades before releasing himself from me.

I'm about to stand when he bends down and lifts me into his arms. Out of instinct, I put my arms around his neck and look into his eyes.

"What are you doing?" I ask.

"Taking care of you," he answers as he walks us to the bathroom. He sets me down on the counter and then steps between my legs. His hands smooth over my hair, and he leans forward, connecting our heads. "Penny?"

"Yes?" I ask, my hands now on his chest.

"I'm so sorry I fucked things up."

"I know," I say as I detect the vulnerability in his voice. "But we're moving on."

His eyes meet mine. "And you're moving on with me?"

"Yes," I answer, bringing his lips to mine. "I'm moving on with you, Eli."

We make out for a few more minutes, just like that, me on the bathroom counter, him holding me tightly, exploring my mouth, never letting go.

"Missed you, Penny. So fucking much."

"Missed you too, Eli."

We spend the next few minutes cleaning up and getting ready for bed. I reach for my nightgown, but he pulls it away and kisses my shoulder, asking me to sleep naked with him.

I couldn't think of anything better than to be skin on skin with this man.

We both get under the covers, and when he pulls me into him tonight, instead of my back to his stomach, I rest my head on his chest and curl my arm around him.

"Do you have any plans tomorrow?" he asks as he softly strokes my skin.

"Well, I was supposed to work, but the team I work for was eliminated from the playoffs tonight."

"They didn't deserve to be in it. Most of them didn't have their heads in the game."

"You being one of them," I say as I drag my finger over his abs.

"Yeah, my heart and head weren't in it. I'd never say this to the guys, but I'm glad we're done."

"Uh . . . yeah, don't ever say that to the guys." He chuckles, but I ask, "Why are you glad?"

"It was too much to figure out, everything between you and me, the unknown, and walking on eggshells around Pacey. I just needed a second, you know? But you can't have a second during the season. It's a constant grind."

"I get it. So, then why are you asking about tomorrow?"

"I want to take you out for your birthday. I royally fucked up and want to make it up to you."

"That's not necessary, Eli."

"It is for me." He tilts my chin up so I have to look him in the eyes. "Please, let me do this for you."

I sigh heavily and curl into him again. "I mean if you must."

He chuckles. "I must." And then he kisses the top of my head. "Penny?"

"Yeah?" I ask as my hand wanders farther down his abs. "I hope you realize, I'm going to fuck you again . . . and again . . . and again. I hope you aren't planning on sleeping."

"Wouldn't even dream of it."

"GOOD MORNING," I say as Eli hovers over me, a smile on his face.

"Happy Birthday."

"It was yesterday," I groan as I attempt to close my eyes again, but he's not going to have anything to do with that as he pulls the covers off my body.

"Eli, this is not how you wake someone. I'm naked and cold."

His hand slides up my back. "Quite aware you're naked. That's why I'm going to need you to sit on my face."

"Huh?" I ask, opening my eyes just as he lies back on the mattress.

"I said, sit on my face." In one fell swoop, he maneuvers me out of my comfortable curled-up spot, and he positions me on his stomach.

"Eli, what on earth?"

"Babe." He gives me a look as the nickname makes my stomach feel all warm and fuzzy. "I want that pussy. Now sit on my goddamn face."

He grabs my hips and moves me closer until I'm right up against the headboard, my pussy right at his mouth.

"Perfect." He parts me with his fingers and then presses his tongue to my clit.

"Oh Jesus," I say, knowing once again, it's going to be quick for me. This pregnancy has made me hypersensitive.

"Fuck, I can feel you getting wet on my tongue." He laps at my clit with long, languid strokes. It feels so good that I start to move my hips, searching out more. He does the same as he presses two fingers inside me.

"Oh, Eli," I moan, my hands fully on the headboard now, gripping hard, while I'm riding his tongue. "God, this is . . . I've never done this before."

And then something occurs in my mind. If I'm this turned on, how turned on is he?

From over my shoulder, I check on his cock and see that it's hard as stone and stretching up his stomach. The veins desperately search for any kind of relief from the blood pooling inside them.

I lift off him, and just as he protests, I rotate and stick my pussy back near his face as I lift his cock and suck him hard into my mouth.

"Fucking Christ," he moans as his thick quads flex beneath me. "Ahh, baby, you're so good at that. So fucking good."

I swirl my tongue over the head of his cock three times before flicking my tongue on the underside. While squeezing the base, I repeat the motion over and over again.

His tongue has slowed down on my clit, now just tenderly flicking it, driving me nuts as he pushes his hips at me.

"Shit, I'm sorry. You're just . . . fuck, you're making me forget."

He spreads me again, and this time, he sucks my clit into his mouth, and I nearly fly right off his cock. A feral cry falls past my lips. He does the same from the squeeze I have on him, and then together, we try to make each other come faster.

Him sucking on my clit.

Me sucking on his cock.

We moan together.

We rock together.

When we can't take anymore, pleasure rips through us, and we both come in each other's mouths, riding out the last of our orgasms until nothing is left.

Breathing heavily, I roll off him and lie flat on the bed, my back on the mattress. I stare at the ceiling and press my hand to my heart.

He crawls over me and presses a soft kiss to my lips. "You taste so fucking good, Penny." Then he moves down my body and kisses my stomach. "You have a little bump."

"Yeah, it's really popped out in the last couple of days. I need to get some more maternity clothes because things aren't really fitting that much anymore."

"Then I know exactly what we're doing today," he says,

pressing another kiss to my stomach. "Shopping spree." He wiggles his eyebrows, and I laugh out loud.

"Why do you seem more excited about the prospect of shopping for clothes than I do?"

"You're not?"

"No, I am," I say. I stand from the bed, he holds out his button-up shirt to me, and I slip into it as he puts on a pair of shorts. I only bother with a few buttons because what's the point, really? I just sat on the man's face. "But you seem *really* excited."

He lifts my hand to his lips, where he presses a light kiss. "I'm just excited about spending some time with you."

"You know, some hockey players would be mourning the season."

"Sometimes, there are more important things than hockey, and I'm staring right at one."

"The charming side of you is dangerous, and if I can remember, that's how I got pregnant in the first place."

He laughs and pushes me down the hallway to the kitchen, where he gently lifts me up and places me on the counter. I yelp from how cold it is at first but then quickly get used to the chilly stone on the backs of my legs. It's relatively easy to ignore because the man in front of me is the Eli I recall from months ago. He's stupidly sexy and joyfully confident again.

"What do you want for breakfast?" He opens the fridge to absolutely nothing. With a brow raised, he looks over his shoulder. "Uh, there is no food in here."

"Been kind of busy freaking out over the boy who wouldn't talk to me on my birthday."

He winces and straightens. "Can we never talk about that again? It legit gives me a stomachache."

"Too soon to joke about?"

"Too soon."

I bring him in close and wrap my legs around his waist. "Sorry, but it is the truth."

"I know." His hands smooth up my thighs. That's all I need. That little touch and I'm lit up again.

I wrap my hand around his head, and I bring him close so I can open-mouth kiss him. He, of course, matches my kisses, my tongue strokes, and when I peel out of his shirt, he moves his mouth down my chest to one of my breasts.

"Seriously, babe?" he asks when his fingers find just how wet I am.

I lean back on the counter and spread my legs as he undoes the last button of the shirt and flips it open.

"I need your cock," I say.

"Christ," he mutters as he brings his cock out of his pants and gives it a few strokes. I watch as it grows in his hand, thicker and thicker. My mouth waters from the prospect of having him inside me. Stretching me. Pounding into me until I'm coming all over again.

"Eli, fuck me."

He growls something deep in his throat and then lines his cock up to my entrance only to pull my hips down and insert me on him.

"Yes," I cry out as he pulls me off the counter and flips us around so we're pressed up against the wall.

"Is this okay?" he asks.

"God, yes. Please just make me come."

He doesn't say anything else as he grips my thighs and moves me up and down against the wall.

Pushing.

Pulsing.

Grunting.

Our sweat mixes, our groans compete with each other, and when my orgasm builds, I kiss him until I'm moaning so loud I can hear my voice vibrate off the walls as I come all over his cock.

It takes him a few more strokes, but he's right there with me, falling over the edge.

After a few deep breaths, he asks, "Are you okay?"

I sigh into his hold. "More than okay." I bring my hands to the back of his head and play with the short strands. "Really freaking okay."

He smirks, and I'm a messy puddle of goo. I'm not sure how I got to be in this position. In Eli's arms, it feels like a blur, but now that he's here, I don't want to let him go.

Chapter Thirty

ELI

Taters: *Drove up to the cabin this morning. Come when you want.*

We spent the latter half of the day shopping, once I was able to get Penny off my dick. No joke, I can't tell you the number of times we've had sex since early this morning. We got her quite a few new outfits, things she'd be comfortable in, and then I took her out to a late lunch followed by some ice cream. We ran into a few fans, but nothing too overwhelming. I was worried about lashing out, but everyone was pretty cool, giving us space, and I appreciated that.

But it was nice, holding her hand as we walked down the street, going from shop to shop. I wasn't worried about being caught, about touching her wrong, or even saying something that wasn't appropriate. I was able to breathe . . . be happy.

And fuck, it felt good.

Since Penny is in the bathroom, I quickly text him back.

Eli: *I don't want to leave Penny. Can I bring her?*

Taters: *Might as well. If Pacey can get Winnie to talk to him, pretty sure she's coming too.*

My brow pinches together.

Eli: *What do you mean she's not talking with him?*

Taters: *Did you think our star goalie was just sucking because he was getting older? No, Winnie put a break on their relationship after you fucked his sister.*

Eli: *What? It seemed like they were fine.*

Taters: *Just this last week or so. He put on a happy face, and so did she, but they weren't sharing the same bed. He told me everything on the flight home.*

Eli: *Holy shit. I wonder if that's why he told me he didn't care If I pursued Penny.*

Taters: *Yup. Winnie thought it was ridiculous that he was inserting himself into your personal life. So, basically, the women in our lives ruined this playoff season for us.*

Eli: *Did they? Or did we ruin it by not doing the right thing with them?*

Taters: *In my case, the women ruined it.*

Eli: *I'm assuming you're talking about Sarah.*

The toilet flushes, and Penny comes out of the bathroom wearing one of my shirts, looking fine as hell as she walks toward me without an ounce of makeup on her face and freshly fucked hair.

Taters: *Yeah, let's just say I came up here to make a change. To stop making the same damn mistake over and over again.*

Eli: *Good. Let me ask Penny, and I'll get back to you.*

Penny takes a seat directly on my lap and moves her hands over my bare chest. One of my favorite things about her is she has no problem showing affection. The way she touches me, kisses me, even hugs me. She just takes what she wants at that moment, and I fucking love it. I haven't had affection in my life for such a long goddamn time that to have someone who actually shows it moves me in a way I can't even describe.

"Everything okay?" she asks.

"Did you know Pacey and Winnie were on a break?"

Her hands pause from smoothing over my shoulders. "What?"

"Yeah, Taters just told me. Winnie hasn't said anything to you?"

"Not a thing." She goes to move off my lap, but I hold her in place.

"Don't bother them. Taters made it seem like they were working things out. Let them."

"But why were they—" She pauses and then says, "Oh, because of us, huh?"

"Seems like Winnie wasn't happy about Pacey meddling."

"She never said anything to me."

"Probably because she didn't want to stress you out any more than you were. But that would explain his sudden change of heart."

"Change of heart?" she asks. "What are you talking about?"

"You know, it's not something we need to worry about. Let's talk about the appointment tomorrow."

"Wait, no, don't pass this off. What kind of change of heart did Pacey have?"

Christ, me and my big fucking mouth.

"Penny, I don't want to talk about it, we're in a good place, and I don't want you to get angry."

"Is it something that will make me angry?"

"Honestly, I have no idea."

She folds her arms over her chest while straddling my lap and says, "Well, tell me, and we'll see."

I drag my hand over my face and let out a heavy breath before saying, "The night you gave me gummy bears, Pacey saw us, and I was afraid he thought something was going on between us, so when I got on the bus, I told him that nothing was happening. I was holding up my promise to him. But then he asked if I liked you and if you liked me, and . . . well, I told him the truth. I do like you, Penny. I always have. That's when he said that I shouldn't let him get in the middle of it."

"So he gave you permission."

"Yeah, I guess."

"And then, instead of calling me up, you went silent on me."

See, this is exactly why I didn't want to say anything. It looks really bad on my end. Well, that's because it is bad.

"Penny." I rub her thighs slowly. "I, uh . . . I've just been trying to handle all this shit in my head, and sure, I didn't handle it well, I see that, but the only reason I pushed you away was because I wasn't sure how to handle the feelings I had for you. It's stupid, but it's the truth."

When my eyes meet hers, understanding flashes through them. "Is this the first time you've had feelings for a girl?" she asks.

"Yes," I answer. "Sure, when I was growing up, I had some crushes, but that's all they were, they were nothing like what I feel for you, and it's frankly been terrifying."

"Why?"

"Because," I answer, "I've lost pretty much every important person growing up, and I don't want to lose anyone else."

"You have your boys."

"That's out of necessity, but even at that, I still panic from time to time when they get hurt."

She smiles at me and curls into me, resting her head on my shoulder. "Well, sorry, but you have me now and this baby, and we're always going to be a part of your life, so you better get used to it."

"I'm starting to find great comfort in the idea," I say while I drag my hand over her back. "And about tomorrow, are we going to find out the sex of the baby?"

"What do you think? Do you want to know?"

"I do, but if you don't, I can wait. Practicing patience has been my MO lately."

She chuckles. "I want to find out. I'd rather mentally prepare myself for what's to come."

"Me too. And then we can bicker over names."

Her hand caresses my chest. "Do you really think we'll bicker over names?"

"Well, let's see. If the baby is a girl, what is your first name choice?"

She's silent for a second and then says, "I really like Betty. Classic and sweet."

"Uh-huh, and here I'm thinking Crystal would be a good name."

"Crystal?" She pushes back to look me in the eyes. "No offense to all nice Crystals out there, but that's a bonafide stripper name."

"No, it's not."

"Uh . . . google it. Type in top stripper names and see what comes up."

I grab my phone and type in top stripper names. And sure enough, the first thing that shows up is Crystal, followed by Tiffany and Amber, both names that I think are nice.

"See." Penny points. "Stripper name."

"What is the validity of this website anyway? Just because it's the top link on Google. That means nothing."

"It means everything. Face it, we're going to fight over names."

"Why are we even having this conversation? I thought we figured this out. Peggy Leggy and Johnny Jim."

She laughs and curls back against my chest. "If you think we're actually going to name our kid that, you need to seriously rethink every decision in your life."

"Are you going to hate me if I say they're starting to grow on me?"

"Yes. Oh my God, Eli, we're not naming our kid Johnny Jim or Peggy Leggy."

"You say that now, but when it's zero hour, and they need a name for the birth certificate, you might be singing a different tune."

"Keep telling yourself that."

—

"SO YOU, uh, you just show off your belly like that?" I ask, staring down at her exposed stomach.

She chuckles. "Yes."

"And then Dr. Big Pecs is going to walk in and put his hand all over your stomach?"

"Well, he'll use a wand thing, but yes, and guess what?" She leans in and whispers, "He's seen my vagina as well."

"Why did you have to say that? Now all I'm going to think is that he's been digging around in there."

"Well, first of all, there's been no digging, and second of all, that's his job."

"You know what I mean."

There's a knock on the door just as Penny whispers, "Be cool."

The door opens, and lo and behold, Dr. Big Pecs comes strutting in, computer in hand, hair slicked back, wearing one of the tightest shirts I've ever seen. Well, of course, his pecs will look big when he wears a shirt three sizes too small for him. Can he even breathe in that thing?

"Penny, how are you—" He looks up and makes eye contact with me. "Oh, we haven't met. I'm Dr. Bigpeckus. You must be the absent father."

Uh, excuse me? Absent?

That's a bold fucking statement.

But not wanting to start anything, for Penny's sake, I brush off the comment and take the man's hand in mine. "Eli, nice to meet you."

He studies me for a second and then asks with a tilt of his head, "Eli Hornsby?"

"Yes, sir," I say out of pure habit.

"Well, no wonder you haven't been to any of the appointments. You've been busy playing hockey."

What's this man's problem? Does he have something against hockey players? I want to ask Penny, but she places her hand on her stomach and says, "I'm glad he's here for this appointment, the most important."

"All of them are important, Penny, especially in this new journey you're going through."

"I would have been here if I could," I say, feeling the need to put that out there. "Our schedules never matched up, unfortunately."

"And now that you were kicked out of the playoffs, you have all the time in the world to dedicate to your baby." He smiles, but it's a pompous smile. The type of smile that would get your jersey pulled over your head by the opposing team if you were on the ice. "And of course, Penny, you look amazing." He places his hand on her stomach, and I know that's his job, but that doesn't mean I need to like it.

We know she looks amazing. *We don't need you moving your hands all over her.*

"Thank you so much. I feel pretty great. I know all the books say the second trimester is the best, and I really feel like that's the case with me."

Hand still on her stomach, he asks, "Are you experiencing a heightened libido?"

How is that an appropriate question?

"Do we need to talk about that?" I ask. "Maybe we can just, you know, get on with the baby X-ray thing."

Big Pecs looks at me and says, "I know this is your first appointment, but it is common and necessary to talk about everything significant that pertains to her pregnancy, including heightened libido, breast growth, and anything else that might make *you* uncomfortable. And it's not a baby X-ray. It's a sonogram."

Uh-huh . . . I don't like this guy.

Penny takes my hand, probably sensing my agitation, and gives it a squeeze before saying, "I have had an increase in libido. Lately, it seems like I can't get enough. I'm very aroused most of the time."

So we're, uh . . . we're talking about it.

"Has Eli been able to keep up?"

"Yes," I nearly shout and then realize the volume of my voice. "I mean, yes. Of course I've been able to keep up."

Big Pecs eyes me very seriously before turning back to Penny. "Well, if he can't, there are ways to get your needs met."

"I can keep up," I say with an edge, leaning in closer to Penny now. "Very much capable of taking care of her . . . uh . . . arousal." I cringe saying the word out loud in such a sterile environment.

"Please, I'd like to hear from Penny." His goddamn hand is STILL on her stomach. "Is he able to make you orgasm?"

"What kind of question is that?" I interrupt once again. "Of course I can make her orgasm."

Big Pecs holds his hand up. "First of all, it's a very important question. It would do her no service if she isn't able to orgasm. And secondly, I'd like to hear from Penny because even though you might think she has an orgasm, she could be faking it."

She's not fucking faking.

I can feel her pussy convulsing around my cock.

Her pussy is always dripping wet.

She nearly kicked me in the face the other night when I was going down on her because her orgasm was so strong.

She's fucking satisfied, you slicked-back, shirt-too-small prick.

"I'm not faking anything," Penny says, holding my hand even tighter. "Honestly, I've had the best sex of my life with Eli. I'm completely and utterly satisfied. Nothing to worry about on that front."

"Good," Big Pecs says while giving me some serious side-eye.

Hear that, motherfucker . . . my girl is satisfied, so go take your goddamn side-eye somewhere else.

Honestly, what is this guy's problem? Because I couldn't come to some appointments, he's going to be a dick? How unprofessional.

Someone is going to get a riveting Google AND Yelp review after this.

Big Pecs is incredibly intrusive, obsessed with holding pregnant bellies, and has a poppyseed tooth. Bedside manner is lacking, shirts far too small for his monster truck chest, and shows blatant hate toward hockey, which is a sin in Vancouver. One out of ten: would not recommend him.

We spend the next few minutes talking about other pregnancy things while I watch his hand move over her belly, smoothing, gliding . . . stroking. The back of my teeth grinds down out of pure, jealous rage. Call me crazy, but I think Big Pecs has it out for me.

Maybe he thinks I'm some deadbeat baby daddy. That could not be further from the truth. I want to meet our baby. And I've formed a bond with Penny that I never expected, never believed was possible. *Especially for me.*

"Okay, so you two want to find out the sex of the baby?" Big Pecs asks.

"We do," Penny answers, looking me in the eyes. "Right?"

"Right," I answer.

"Well, I don't believe you should find out, so I'm going to hold on to that information." He sets down the sonogram thing in his hand and stands. "You both have a good day."

Uh . . . what? Penny looks at me with panic and confusion as a wave of fury beats through me in seconds.

First, he's going to be a dick to me.

Then he's going to have his hands all over her stomach.

And question my ability to make my girl come . . .

And now this?

Oh no, he fucking doesn't.

Not on my goddamn watch.

My hockey aggression rises to the surface as I stand from my chair and say, "We didn't ask what you wanted. We're telling you what we want to happen, and as people who are paying your goddamn bills, you will provide us with a service. Now tell us the sex of the baby, you big pec-ed motherfucker."

The words flow right out of me, unfiltered, straight from the inner beast inside me as my fists clench at my sides.

This guy wants to try to tell us what to do. Well, he's going to have to go through me first.

"Eli." Penny tugs on me.

"No," I say to her. "I'm not going to let this guy dick us around." I pick up the sonogram wand, shove it at him, and say, "You fucking tell us if this baby has a vagina or a penis right fucking now, or I'm going to show you what it's like to be defended by me on the ice."

"Eli, please."

Big Pecs holds his hands up and says, "Slow down there, big guy." Throwing down the big guy, yeah, I'll show him just who the big guy is. "It's a joke I play on my patients. It's just a joke. Of course I'm going to tell you the sex of your baby."

You would think that would defuse me, but it doesn't.

"It's not a fucking funny joke. Usually, people laugh at jokes. Do you see anyone laughing? Not to mention, it's incredibly unprofessional. You've been a total nightmare this entire visit, and it's taking everything in me not to slam you against the wall for the way you've spoken to me, the way you've degraded me in front of Penny, and this—"

Penny tugs on my arm. "Eli. It's okay."

"It's not okay, Penny. He's been dicking us around."

"Eli." Her eyes meet mine. "He's been joking this whole time."

Wait . . . what?

Big Pecs holds his hands up still, looking more startled than anything. "Penny asked me to give you a hard time, said you were feeling inferior about your chest compared to mine. I thought it was funny, so I went along with it."

She . . . uh . . . she what?

I glance down at her, and she winces. "Sorry." She attempts to smile. "Got . . . you."

I sit in my seat, nostrils flared, and turn toward her. "I hate you."

She chuckles. "No, you don't."

"Right now. I do."

She wraps her hand behind my neck and brings me to her, where she presses a gentle kiss to my lips. "You don't hate me," she whispers.

I groan and kiss her one more time before saying, "No . . . I don't."

When we part, Big Pecs holds his hand out to me, and reluctantly, I give it a shake. "Sorry, but it was all her idea. For the record, huge fan, man. Sorry about the loss. I was really hoping you guys could bring The Cup home this year."

Still salty toward the man, I say, "Yeah, well, next year maybe."

He nods and then clasps his hands together. "And I guess congratulations are in order. You're having a boy." He turns on the monitor and circles a portion of the baby. "Right here, clear as day, he's spread-eagled showing off his manhood."

And just like that, the anger and irritation drain away. An odd sense of pride surges through me as I look closely while Penny says, "Just like his father."

I chuckle as she loops her arm around mine.

Big Pecs prints out a few pictures and then lets us clean Penny up in private. She reaches for the wet towel, but I stop her and take the cloth in hand. "You, ma'am, are in so much fucking trouble."

She lets out a long thread of chuckles. "I'm sorry, but things have been so weird and up and down. I haven't pranked you in a bit. I really wanted to lighten things up between us."

"Lighten things up? Penny, I almost checked your doctor into the wall."

She covers her mouth and chuckles some more. "I think I saw steam come out of your ears, but I'll say this, it was really hot seeing you stand up for me like that." Her hand falls to my cheek, only for her thumb to pass over my bottom lip. "Really freaking sexy, Eli."

I wiggle my eyebrows at her. "Turned on, are ya?"

She nods her head. "Very."

"Good, I'll be sure to take the long way home so you don't have any relief anytime soon. Serves you right for putting me through that shit."

"Where's your sense of humor?"

"Something you should know. Don't fuck with the things I care about, and I care about you, Penny."

Her eyes soften, and she wets her lips before saying, "And you care about our son."

My heart warms immediately, and all the irritation falls to the wayside as the word "son" starts to sink in.

"Holy shit," I say, gripping her hand. "We're having a boy, Penny."

"I know." She smiles, and it's the most beautiful, genuine smile I've ever seen. "We're having a little boy, Eli."

I bring my forehead to hers, where I rest it and press a gentle kiss to her lips. "The little guy is going to be like me, I know it. He's going to be such a troublemaker."

"No." She gently shakes her head. "He's going to be kind-hearted, funny, and handsome . . . just like his father."

I'm not one to cry, really ever, but as I stare into Penny's eyes, relief and appreciation pulse through me. I am *so* fortunate that *she's* the one I'm going through this journey with. She makes me feel wanted, like I'm not a damaged soul trying to navigate his way through life, but rather someone who can contribute to this world and not just through his hockey talent.

"Fuck, Penny." Tears well up. "You mean so much to me, do you know that?"

She smiles. "No, but it's really good to hear."

Chapter Thirty-One

PENNY

"So this is the infamous cabin?" I ask as Eli pulls his Tesla into one of the six garage bays. "Not very cabin-like if you ask me. More like a mansion in the mountains."

"Yeah, but Taters, for some reason, thinks it's a cabin."

"He's wrong."

Eli chuckles as he puts the car into park.

After our doctor's appointment, Eli "punished" me for my behavior, but I didn't think it was much punishment at all, well, besides not letting me come for what felt like ten minutes. I was so turned on that when I did come, it dragged on forever. Probably one of the best orgasms I've ever had. So really, I think I won twice.

He then asked me if I wanted to come up to the cabin with him for a few weeks. It took me two weeks to wrap some things up at the office, but lucky for us, the Agitators always give staff time off once the season is over since we put in so many hours during the season. My mini vacation starts now.

The drive up was supposed to be eleven hours, doable in a day, but because I like to pee a lot, we split the trip up into two days, and we stayed at a hotel in Kamloops where we shared a giant cookie in bed while watching the final season of *Ozark*.

It was simple and nice.

And of course this morning, I knelt in front of Eli and gave him a blow job that brought him down to the ground, only for him to return the favor after he caught his breath.

Before getting out of the car, Eli turns toward me. "I haven't said anything to Pacey about us being here . . . together. I haven't really talked to him much at all, so I'm not sure if he's coming up or not."

"Do you not want to tell him?"

"I wanted to feel you out and see what you wanted to do. I'll back whatever your decision is."

"Well, I want to be with you. I don't want to have to sneak around, hold your hand when no one is looking, or pretend we're not together for the sake of someone else's feelings." I take his hand in mine. "I just want to be normal."

He smiles softly and brings our connected hands to his lips, where he presses a soft kiss. "I want the same thing."

"Good. So if Pacey does come up with Winnie, we can pull him to the side and tell him."

"Or, I can text him."

I pause for a second, thinking about it. "I mean, I'm not opposed to it. Better than having a long, drawn-out conversation."

Eli picks up his phone, and he opens up a text message with Pacey. "Let's craft a text right now."

"Perfect."

He pauses. "And you're sure you're okay with this?"

"Listen, I think I've been making sure everyone else is okay during this pregnancy. I think it's time we worry about ourselves for once."

"Good answer," he says and then starts typing while reading out loud. "Dear Pacey—"

"Oh my God, do not start it like that."

"Why not?" he asks.

"Because that's not how you speak to him. You want to be as casual as possible."

"Right." He starts typing again. "Hey, dickwad—"

"Starting things off with an insult isn't great either. Maybe something like . . . hey man."

He smirks. "Ah, you're a clever one, Penny Lawes." He types again. "Hey man, Hornsby here."

"Oh my God." I rip the phone from his grasp and do the dirty work myself. "'Hey man, wasn't sure if you're coming up to the cabin or not, but if you are, heads-up, Penny and I are a thing now.' Annnd send," I say while pressing the blue arrow. "There, done. Now we can go make out in the kitchen."

"Yeah, we won't be doing that. I don't need Taters staring us down, which . . . babe"—he pins me with a glare—"if we're going to have sex in this house, which I'm assuming we will, given the way you nearly gobbled my dick this morning—"

"Hey, I did not gobble it." I push at his shoulder, causing him to laugh.

"But given your voracious appetite for sex, you need to be fucking quiet, which I know will be hard for you, but you can't be screaming like you normally do. Taters will bring it up since our rooms are near each other."

"Not scream? So I don't have to fake it anymore?"

"Shut the fuck up with that shit. You're not faking."

"How do you know?" I lift a questioning brow.

"Because"—he leans in close to me—"when you come, I can feel your pussy clenching around me, and it's one of the sexiest feelings I've ever felt."

My cheeks heat while my body follows closely behind. "The sexiest?"

"Yes," he says, his voice lowering.

I lean in even closer and bring my hand to the back of his head just as his phone beeps with a text message.

"That's Pacey," he says, pulling away. He lifts his phone and reads the text out loud. "'Not sure I'm going to make it up there. Winnie's not talking to me still, and she's staying at her friend's house. Just don't hurt Penny, like I said.'"

"Winnie isn't even staying with him? What the hell happened that it could be that bad?" I ask. "And why hasn't she told me it was this serious?"

"I don't know. Should I ask?"

I nod. "Yes. Ask him. Also . . ." I poke his chest. "Listen to my brother, and don't hurt me."

He presses a soft, lingering kiss to my lips. "Never." And then he types back. "Dude, what happened? Also, I promise I won't hurt her."

His response is immediate, and we read it together.

Pacey: *My shit to worry about. Have fun in Banff.*

"I don't like that answer," I say. "I'll text Winnie in a bit to see if there's anything we can do."

"Hey," a voice shouts from inside the garage. We both turn to see Taters standing in the doorway with only a pair of shorts on, holding his arms out. "What the hell are you doing? I've been waiting here to greet you for fucking ever."

Eli opens his car door and says, "Sorry, just texting Pacey."

Taters nods in understanding. "Spoke to him this morning. Things aren't great with Winnie. Not sure they're going to make it up here."

"What the hell happened?"

Taters moves to the back of the car and opens the trunk. He peeks past the seats and says, "Hey, Penny."

"Hey, Silas," I answer as I get out of the car.

"They got in a huge fight. It started with Pacey's neediness to control the situation between you two." Taters motions between us. "But then turned into so much more. Pacey has been withdrawn, apparently because he's been trying to plan his proposal. He hasn't wanted to give anything away. Winnie took it the wrong way, and now everything's gone to shit." Taters pulls our suitcases out of the back. "He actually made me bring the ring here because he didn't want Winnie to see it."

"He was going to propose?" I ask. "Why didn't he say anything to me?"

"Probably because we had enough going on," Eli says. "Fuck, that's brutal. What's he doing to get her back?"

"Working with her best friends right now and telling them what happened, asking them not to spill the beans. It will be a miracle if they come up here from the sounds of it."

I glance over at Eli. "I feel awful."

"Don't," Taters says, closing the hatch. "Trust me when I say, he brought this upon himself, and he'd be the first to admit it as well. This is no one's fault but his." He pops up the handles of our suitcases. "But I'm glad you're here. Holmes drove up with me, and all he's done is read his goddamn books since we arrived. I need some company."

"Is Stephan here?" Eli asks.

"Who's Stephan?" I ask.

"Our chef," Taters answers. "He comes up on Friday. He was here when we first arrived, but had to fly out and help his mom into her assisted living. Until then, I do have food this year, and to my demise, I have bologna as well."

"Where's Posey?"

"Driving up on his own. He'll be here later today." Taters looks between us. "Am I guessing you're going to need some privacy?"

My face blushes as Eli steps in and says, "Can we take the loft?"

"That was my plan. I don't need to be hearing you two." And then he pushes our luggage toward the house. Eli takes my hand in his, and together, we walk in as a couple for the first time in front of his friends.

—

"WOW, I can't believe Taters owns this place. How did he even find it?"

"Not sure," Eli answers as he stretches across the bed, hands behind his head, looking so delicious that I'm having a hard time keeping my eyes off him. "But we all signed a contract that states if he ever sells it, we're the first in line to purchase. We don't want it ever leaving our circle."

"I can see why." I stare at the beautiful vaulted ceiling with wood beams and an understated black-framed candle chandelier. "This place is stunning."

"Yeah, I can think of something more stunning." I look over at him. His eyes are trained on me.

"Are you flirting with me, Eli Hornsby?"

"I'm appreciating you." He sits up on his elbows. "I know you can have your pick of any goddamn guy in this world, and for some reason, you're choosing me, a choice I'm not sure I'll ever understand."

I move toward the bed and climb up on it so I'm straddling his lap. "You should talk. I'm sure there were girls lined up at your hotel room, waiting to get their chance when you were away."

"There weren't," he says. "They all hang out at the bar, and I was nowhere near that."

"I wasn't implying—"

"I know," he says. "Just want to clarify any chance I get."

I move my hands under his shirt. "You have been more than vocal about that." My hands glide over his abs and then up to his pecs. He doesn't move, doesn't even blink as he lets me feel his impeccable body. "But thank you for appreciating me. Do you think you can appreciate me in the bathtub?"

"You want to take a bath?" he asks.

I nod. "My back is sore from the drive, and there's a huge tub in the bathroom calling my name. I also saw some lavender salts." I smooth my fingers over his nipples. "I'd love for you to join me."

His brow creases. "Are you allowed to take a bath?"

"What do you mean?" I ask.

"Well, doesn't it, you know, boil things if you sit in hot water?"

"Oh my God, Eli, I don't have an actual egg inside me."

"I know that," he groans. "I just thought, you know, it could hurt the baby."

"No, baths are completely normal."

"Are you sure? Maybe we should ask Big Pecs."

"Do you really want to call him?"

Eli winces. "No."

"That's what I thought. Seriously, it's okay, and I could really, really use one right now. Please."

"Babe, you naked and wet is not something you need to beg for. Just fucking show me the way."

Chuckling, I lean down and press a kiss to his lips before getting off his lap and heading to the bathroom, him trailing behind me.

I start the tub, toss some salts inside, and then turn toward him and lift my arms up in the air. "Help me?"

"You realize you're going to make me hard, right?"

"Nothing wrong with that." I smirk at him.

Deliberately, he moves my shirt up and over my body and drops it on the floor. He squats down in front of me, presses both hands to my growing stomach, and kisses it gently before helping me out of my pants and underwear. His fingers drag up my inner thigh, and as he stands, he carefully turns me around so my back is to his chest. His hands glide up my sides, then down to the clasp of my bra, where he undoes it, then removes the thin straps from my body. The bra is tossed with the rest of my clothes right before his hand reaches around and grasps my breasts.

I arch into him and sigh. "They're so sensitive."

"I've noticed," he says. "It's really fucking hot, Penny. Everything. Especially your newfound confidence. You were so shy on my birthday, but I could see what you wanted that night. Now I don't have to dig for it. You just tell me." He's not wrong. I'm still amazed Eli chose me, I'm not going to lie, but he's given me so much . . . sexual confidence. Like I told him all those months ago, I hadn't believed I was "good" at sex. But Eli has proven me wrong. It's all about the chemistry between the couple that determines how good sex is. *And we are explosive.*

His fingers play with my nipples, pleasure tearing through me with each pass. "You're not as intimidating to me anymore. I feel comfortable with you." I turn and loop my arms around his neck. He slides his hands down my back to my ass, which he holds tightly. "I feel like I can talk to you about anything now. We've built that trust."

With a look of utter contentment, he places a kiss on my forehead. "You're the first person I've trusted outside of hockey. I don't ever trust anyone, but you've been able to slowly change that perspective."

"That means a lot to me," I say as I stand on my toes and kiss him on the lips. Still holding me close to him, he returns the kiss, deepening it by opening his mouth and swiping his tongue over mine.

I groan into him and slip my hand down between us to his pants, where I feel his hardness through the fabric.

"I really want to take a bath," I say as I move my hand past the waistband of his jeans.

"Then let's take a bath," he says right before pulling his shirt over his head. God, he's so freaking ripped. I don't think I've ever seen a more perfect body. He's sculpted and chiseled in all the right spots. His arms are strong and thick, while his waist is narrow and defined. He has the pinnacle V that I'm sure isn't easy to accomplish.

He strips out of his pants and briefs, and I watch as his cock strains forward, searching out a release.

I reach for it, but he steps away. "You need the relaxation, and we're going to do that in the tub first."

"But you're hard."

"I'll survive."

He turns off the water. He then steps in and leans against the back of the large soaking tub. When he's settled, he holds his hand out to me and helps me climb in. The water is warm, the perfect temperature for relaxation, and as I sink down between his legs, I can feel my body start to melt into him.

"Are you comfortable?" I ask him, his hard-on pressing against my back.

"Very," he answers as he gently rests my head on his chest. "Are you?"

"Mmm, yes, I could fall asleep like this."

"Then do it. I'll take care of you." He wraps his arms around me and kisses my neck.

It's been a journey to get here, where Eli is openly affectionate, not holding back or chastising himself for having feelings, where we can simply enjoy each other with nothing hanging over our heads. I know this pivotal moment is a big step for us.

This is intimacy.

This isn't just us tearing each other's clothes off. This is more than that. This is us becoming one, and as he slowly laps water against me, I know this is a moment I'll remember.

"Are you awake?"

"Yes," I say as I place my hands on his.

"Your stomach is really starting to grow. I hope this doesn't sound weird, but it's exciting."

"That's not weird at all."

"Have you felt the baby kick?"

"I have," I answer. "It feels like a flutter, but I've felt him in there. And like Dr. Big Pecs said, he's measuring quite big already, bigger than the average baby, so I think he's going to have your height. Which, of course, makes me think about my apartment situation. I really need to find a bigger place, especially since Blakely and Winnie are already talking about having a baby shower for us. I won't have any space for everything."

His fingers trace up and down my arm as he quietly says, "I have space."

"Which is so great, you won't have to worry about having any issues with fitting things in your place. My landlord got back to me, and there are no current two-bedrooms up for rent. There's a three-bedroom, but that's way out of my price range. So I'll have to find a new building, which is sad."

"Penny, I have room," he says again.

I give his hand a squeeze. "Yes, you said that."

"You don't understand what I'm saying." He draws my chin so I'm forced to look at him. "I have room, for the baby . . . and you."

Wait . . .

"And me . . . as in . . ." I swallow. "Like I move in?"

"Yeah," he says, his eyes completely sincere.

"But . . . you don't want that, me barging in on your personal space."

"What have I done for the past few months?" he asks. "Barged in on yours."

"It's different."

"How?" he asks.

"Because you're, you know . . . this professional hockey player who I'm sure has better things to do with his life than move his baby mama into his apartment."

"What are you saying?" he asks, confusion knitting his brow.

"I'm not trying to say anything, I'm just, I don't know . . . I didn't bring it up to pressure you or anything."

"You didn't ask me. I brought it up. It was my idea."

"Still." I shake my head. "I don't want to do that to you."

I turn back around, but he's no longer holding me tightly. Instead, he's stiff and unmoving and not in a good way. "What exactly do you think you're doing to me?" he asks. "Because from where I see it, I'm trying to figure out what happens when the baby comes, and I just figured you could move in with me. But it seems as though you don't want that."

"It's not that I don't want that, it's just . . . I don't know, Eli. What if you get sick of us? I don't want to move out and deal with all of that. I'd rather just have my own place."

He nods slowly and leans back against the tub, tilting his head back, looking up at the ceiling. "Do you think that's going to happen? That I'm going to get sick of you?"

"I honestly don't know. And I don't want to hold this against you because that's not what I'm trying to do at all, but you said it yourself. This is the first time you've actually let someone into your life. This is all new to you. I don't want to overwhelm you by moving in, taking over your private space, and then bringing a baby into that. It's not fair to you."

"Do you know what's not fair?" he asks. "You making that decision for me."

Sensing his frustration building, I turn in the tub and straddle his lap as best as I can. His eyes avoid mine until I force him to look at me. "I'm trying to help you understand where I'm coming from."

"You just said you trust me," he says, hurt lacing his words. "Now, it seems like you don't trust me at all."

"No, that's not the case." I backtrack, trying to figure out a way for this to make sense. "I trust you, Eli. I just want to make sure you're ready."

"Me telling you I think you should move in is me being ready."

"Yes, but how long have you been thinking about this? We can't do a spur-of-the-moment—"

"For a month."

"A month?" I sit back on his quads. "But we haven't, you know . . . been intimate for that long."

He reaches out and grips my chin, holding me steady. "Just because we haven't been intimate for that long doesn't mean I haven't been thinking about you. Thinking about ways to keep you. This might seem all new to you, but it's been on my mind for a while. I want to be there for you, Penny. I want you close to me, as much as I can get you. I want you to move in."

I pause as my breath hitches in my chest, his words sinking in. "Wait, you're serious."

He drags his hand over his face. "Jesus Christ, Penny. Yes, I'm serious."

"For like . . . for how long?"

"As long as you want."

"Would we . . . share a bed?"

"Uh, do you really think you'd move into my place and not share a bed with me?" His hands fall to my side, his thumbs rub against my stomach. "I want the same setup we have now, just at my place instead. We can set up the baby's room and ensure we have everything we need. I have plenty of storage and two parking spots so you don't have to worry about that." What I can't get over is that he's been thinking about this for a month. He has shown me time and time again how much he wants *us*. But it's still hard to fathom.

"So the same thing we have now." Perhaps a stupid question, but I have to know the parameters. To see what he believes we've had at my place and what it means to him.

"Yes." His hands inch north until his thumbs press against my breasts. "Just more space, more closet space, more kitchen space. A tub just like this."

"Ooo, I like that," I say as I shift against his lap, feeling him stir alive. "Have you used it?"

"Only for sore muscles, never like this." His thumbs now pass over my nipples. "Never with someone else."

I rub my clit against his length. "Never had sex in it?"

His eyes darken. "Never."

Reaching between us, I take his cock in my hand and gently stroke it up and down before sitting up and placing him at my entrance. "Are you opposed to it?"

"No," he says, his voice desperate as I slowly lower on top of him. "Fuck," he whispers once he's all the way inside me. "Penny, nothing has ever felt this good. Fucking nothing."

"Same," I say when I rest my hands on his shoulders, angling myself better so his cock hits me in just the right spot. "No one has ever made me come the way you do." *Nor made me feel so sexy* and *treasured*.

He growls right before latching on to my neck with his lips. "Tell me you want to move in, Penny." He kisses up my neck to my ear. "Tell me when we get back, we can pack you up. Tell me you want me just as much as I want you."

"I want you," I say breathlessly. "So much, Eli."

"Then say it." He moves me up and down on his lap now, my stomach rubbing against his. "Say you'll stay with me."

My hand falls to the back of his neck, keeping him close as I thrust up and down on his cock. "I want to move in," I say, the answer to his question feeling right.

"Promise me," he says, our pace picking up as water sloshes around us.

"I promise, Eli."

He pulls away from my neck and moves his lips to my breast. "You're mine," he says right before wrapping his lips around my nipple and sucking the nub.

As I move over him, slowly, his sentiment rings through my head.

You're mine.

You're mine.

I feel that truth, now more than ever, as he holds me close. Never letting up on his grip, he kisses me and loves on me more than he ever has. His lips explore my body from my breasts to my collarbone to my mouth, where his tongue laps at mine, only for him to return to my jaw, back down my neck, and to my breasts again.

The sensation of him not being able to get enough and needing more blazes through me, lighting me up.

"I need more," I say to him, my fingers sifting through his short strands.

"Different position?" he asks me.

I nod. "Yes. From behind."

My favorite position.

He lifts me off him and then helps me out of the tub. He emerges from the water, droplets dripping from his gorgeous skin and his rock-hard cock. I roll my teeth over my lip just as he steps up behind me, and bends me over so I'm holding the edge of the tub.

His hand smooths over my backside while he lines his cock up with my entrance. Angling me up, he enters me in one smooth stroke. I call out his name from the thrust and then drop my head as he continues to work in and out of me. Aware of what I like, he reaches forward and pinches my nipple between his fingers. The harsh but satisfying sensation sends a flood of pleasure through me, causing me to moan louder than I should. He told me to be quiet, but everything feels so heightened, and it's hard not to express how he's making me feel.

"God, Eli, you're so good."

"That's right, baby. Tell me how you feel."

He thrusts, and I groan some more. "Your cock is so big. It makes me feel so full."

Another thrust as his hand falls to my pussy, where he presses his thumb to my clit, and I scream out his name, forgetting all about common decency. "Eli . . . oh God, I'm going to come."

"Me . . . too," he says just as his pace picks up, and together we push and pull, taking what we need, our climax building and building and building until our orgasms crash together, our names falling off our tongues.

His hips still, I feel him deep inside me, while my pussy contracts around his length. We stay like that for a few more seconds before he slowly lowers his lips to my back and presses a kiss. When he stands and removes himself, he turns me around and pulls me into a hug, one hand around my back, the other cradling my head.

"Babe."

"Hmm?" I ask, seeking out his warmth.

"You were way too loud."

I chuckle. "I know. I'm sorry."

"Just be glad your brother wasn't here, but also"—he tips my chin up to look me in the eyes—"you're going to move in with me."

"I am."

"Are you worried?"

I shake my head. "Not even in the slightest."

"Good. I promise, Penny, I'll do everything in my power to make you happy and comfortable."

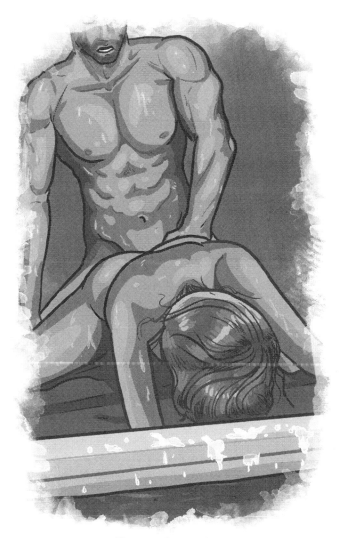

Your cock is so big.

"I believe you, Eli. I really do."

Chapter Thirty-Two

ELI

"So . . . you and Penny are really going at it, huh?" Taters says as the orange of the bonfire in front of us lights up his face.

Taters, Posey, Holmes, and I are all circled around the fire pit, staring into the flames, beers in our hands. Pacey and Winnie haven't made the trip yet, despite Pacey's valiant attempts to make things better. Stephan has been a wizard in the kitchen, especially catering to Penny's cravings. Having her here has made this one of the best trips to the cabin ever.

Not just because of the sex. I mean, don't get me wrong, that's been life-altering, especially the morning sex. Fuck, when she's all warm . . .

But having her here to take walks with, to cuddle into next to the pool, and even to have someone to talk to at night, it's just made this visit special, and I'm so fucking glad she came with me.

She's been exhausted lately, though, so she went to bed early, leaving me with some guy time for the first time since we got here over two weeks ago.

"Do you really think I'm going to talk about that?" I ask Taters.

"No, but just pointing out, we can all hear you."

"I'm starting to wake up hornier now than ever," Posey says while rubbing his hand over his leg. "Dude, this is not healthy for me."

"I told her to try to be quiet." I shrug. "That's all I can do."

"Or you can give the girl a break," Posey says.

"Dude, it's not me. She's the one who initiates."

"Really?" Taters asks while scratching his chin. "Sarah was never like that."

"Sarah was made from ice," Holmes chimes in.

"Penny is also in her second trimester, which increases, uh . . . how she feels," I say, to put it nicely. I'm not about to give the boys specifics. That's between Penny and me. But I'll say this, she loves sucking my cock, and she easily, hands down, gives the best blow job I've ever had.

Nothing comes close.

She can make me come in fucking seconds. It's embarrassing.

"Well, can you let us sleep in tomorrow morning?" Taters says, disgruntled. "You two are waking the whole house up, and it's getting on my goddamn nerves."

"Is that what's bothering you, or is it the shop girl you can't stop thinking about?" Posey asks.

"Shop girl?" I bring my beer bottle to my lips. "What's this about?"

"Nothing," Taters dismisses. "So what's going on with you and Penny? You guys a full-on couple now?"

"We're seeing how things go," I say, unsure honestly of where we stand with labels. "I, uh, asked her to move in with me when we get back."

"Aren't you already living together?" Holmes asks.

"We are, but we need a bigger place for the baby, and my place is plenty big, so I asked her to move in."

Taters straightens up in his chair. "Dude, are you ready for that?"

"What's the difference? I've been living with her for a few months anyway."

"Yeah, but this is in your space."

"So?" I shrug. "I don't see a problem with that."

"So wait." Posey leans in. "Does this mean you're going to marry her?"

"Marry her?" I ask incredulously. "Posey, we're still getting to know each other. Having her move in is just a small step, more transitional than anything since we already live together. It will give us more room and the ability for me to continue to be there for her."

"And still have tons of sex," Taters adds.

"There's more to us than sex," I say, growing angry. "Stop disparaging her like that."

"Sorry," Taters says while letting out a loud sigh. "Christ, I think I'm fucked in the head."

"You're just realizing that?" Holmes asks.

"Bro, we've known for a while," Posey adds. "We've just been waiting for you to realize it. And you did for a second before you got back with Sarah this season, which we all agreed was a huge mistake on your part."

"I thought you guys liked her," he says.

"Not after the way she manipulated you," Holmes says. "I think it's good you're trying to clear your head up here. It will be healthy to finally break away from her."

"Facts," Posey says while pulling a sandwich from a bag next to him. He holds it out to us. "Bologna, anyone?"

"Christ, how can you eat that?" I ask.

"Easy." He takes a bite and smiles at us while chewing.

"You're sick," Taters says and then turns back to me. "So . . . it's safe to say that things are getting serious with Penny. You like her."

"A lot," I answer. "And I'm going to see where that feeling for her takes me."

"Have you found out what you're having?" Posey asks.

"Yup." I smile.

"Wait, you have?" Holmes asks, looking more lively than ever.

"And you haven't told us?" Posey bellows. "Dude, that's some messed-up shit."

"Why haven't you said anything?" Taters asks.

"Because we're just keeping it to ourselves right now."

"That's some bullshit," Posey says, mouth full of bologna. "How do I know what kind of presents I should get you?"

"You're going to get me presents?" I ask with a raise of my brow.

"We're not assholes," Taters says. "Of course we're going to get you stuff. Blakely invited us to the baby shower, so we're not going to show up empty-handed. And it would be helpful if we had some direction."

I chuckle. "I can't imagine you three walking around a baby store, picking stuff out."

"Why the hell not?" Posey asks, offended. "We know things about babies."

"Oh yeah? What do you know?"

"Uh . . . that they shit," Taters says.

"They take naps," Holmes offers.

"They suck on boobs," Posey adds. "Basically, they're mini versions of us."

"Well put." Taters gives him a nod.

"That's awkwardly accurate," Holmes says.

"Oh, yeah?" I say. "When was the last time you've sucked on a boob?"

Holmes shifts in his seat. "Doesn't matter."

Posey thumbs toward Holmes. "Talk about blue balls. I walked in on this guy taking a shower during the season, and his balls were like two mini Violet Beauregardes hanging from his junk. The hue of his balls was frightening."

"Shut the fuck up," Holmes says, kicking at Posey, who's laughing now. "Just haven't been into that shit recently."

"You haven't been into fucking anyone? Wow, interesting." Taters shakes his head.

"I've been dealing with things, don't have time for that."

Whispering, Posey says, "Yeah, dealing with things, aka, crushing on someone who has a boyfriend."

"Dude, shut the actual fuck up," Holmes seethes.

Taters and I both whip our heads to look at Holmes, who, even in the light of the fire, is blushing.

"Holmes, you crushing on someone?" I ask.

He's practically trying to murder Posey with his eyes, and it's not affecting him at all as Posey gleefully eats his bologna sandwich.

"Who is it?" Taters asks.

"No one's goddamn business." Holmes leans toward Posey and says, "I swear to God, if you tell anyone, I'll murder you."

Posey pretends to zip his lips and toss away the key.

"Well, we have one clue," Taters says. "She's attached. Who do we know that has a boyfriend?"

"It has to be in our circle," I say. "Because Holmes never goes out."

"Could be someone in his building, though, like a neighbor."

"True." I nod. "Has he worked with anyone recently that could have caused him to form a crush?"

"Can we stop talking about this?" Holmes asks.

"Uh, not that I recall," Taters says, ignoring Holmes completely. "He's only been working with Penny . . ." He trails off, and Holmes quickly holds up his hands.

"It's not Penny, I swear. Posey, back me up."

"I thought you were going to murder me?"

"Tell them it's not Penny."

Posey deeply sighs. "It's not Penny . . ."

"Why did he trail off like that?" Taters asks, pointing at Posey.

"There was a trail," I add. "He's alluding to something. But what?" I wrack my brain as Holmes shifts uncomfortably in his seat.

"Uh, how about Pacey and Winnie? Has anyone heard anything from them?" Holmes asks, trying to change the subject.

We both ignore him. "If it's not Penny, maybe someone close to Penny," Taters offers.

And just like that . . . I snap my fingers and say, "You fucking like Blakely, don't you?"

Holmes groans and slowly sinks into his chair, covering his eyes with his hand. "Fucking hell."

We glance at Posey, who taps his nose, indicating that my guess is correct.

"Holy shit, you like Blakely," I repeat and then say, "Dude, she has a boyfriend."

"I know. We established that. And it's nothing. I just mentioned that she was pretty, that's all. Can we drop it?"

"He said more than she was pretty," Posey mumbles.

"Drop. It," Holmes says in a stern tone and then looks at me. "You can't fucking tell Penny. I don't want Blakely finding out. It's nothing, okay?"

"Don't worry, I'll keep that one close to me. But seriously, you like her?"

He lifts from the chair. "This is exactly why I stick to my books."

"Sit down," Taters groans. "Stop being a diva and just talk to us about it."

"I'm good." He stuffs his hands in his pockets and maneuvers around the bonfire. "See you in the morning."

Once he's out of earshot, Taters leans forward. "Now that was some interesting shit. Halsey Holmes has a crush on an already-taken girl. I might just stay tuned in to see that unfold."

I don't think he's the only one.

———

"YOU SMELL LIKE CAMPFIRE," Penny mumbles as she curls into me the moment I slip into bed.

I spent the past five minutes tiptoeing around the bathroom, getting ready for bed, not wanting to wake Penny, but it seems like I woke her anyway.

"Want me to take a shower?"

She shakes her head against my bare chest. "No, I like it." Her hand falls to my stomach as she presses a kiss to my pec. "Have fun with the guys?"

"Just talked." I swallow down the knowledge about Blakely, even though it's slowly eating away at me. Halsey likes Blakely. I couldn't be more shocked. Not just because the guy hasn't expressed interest in anything but hockey and books, but because Blakely would be the LAST girl I'd consider for him. She's loud and opinionated and very outgoing where he is very quiet, doesn't like to talk much, and would prefer to be a hermit for the rest of his life.

"What did you talk about?"

"Just stupid shit," I answer. "Well, and you, of course."

"I figured as much. You tell them we're moving in together?"

"Yes, but they were confused and pointed out that we already lived together."

"It's different," she mumbles.

I stroke her hair, letting the silky strands fall through my fingers. "That's what I told them, but they were still confused. They were pissed I didn't tell them about the sex of the baby."

"I don't want to say anything until Winnie and Pacey are okay."

"I know, babe." I kiss the top of her head. "Did you talk with Winnie tonight?"

"Yes." She sits up on her elbow so she can look me in the eyes. And under the light of the moon, in this dark room, I can't help being in awe at how goddamn beautiful she is. Not an ounce of makeup on her face because she doesn't need it, and her hair falls over her cheek, like a picture frame, molding her into a work of art. "Why are you looking at me like that?"

"Like what?" I ask.

"All dreamy-like."

I smile. "Because you're beautiful, and I was just thinking about how beautiful you are. And that's not a line. It's the truth."

"You can't say things like that," she says, her hand sliding down my stomach.

"Why not?"

"Because it makes me want to do things to you, and I'm trying to tell you about Pacey and Winnie."

Her hand reaches the waistband of my briefs, and instead of stopping her, I place my hands behind my head and say, "I won't take it back because it's real. True. The image of you, fresh from bed, looking gorgeous as hell, it's ingrained, and I'm one fucking lucky guy to be privileged to sleep in the same bed as you."

"Ugh, Eli," she groans as she straddles my lap now. "You're turning me on."

"I'm not trying to, babe. I'm just telling you the truth."

"I know." Her hands lay flat on my stomach as she moves over my hardening erection. The only thing between us is my boxer briefs. I know this because she never wears underwear to bed anymore. She thinks it gets in the way. Which . . . is true. "God, Eli, I don't think I'll ever get enough of you."

She leans back and slips me out of my briefs before positioning me at her entrance and sitting down on my length.

I'll never get enough either. Until my dying day, I don't think it will ever be enough to satisfy this craving I have for her.

"I love your cock."

I bite down on my lip as she rocks over me, her nipples pressing against the fabric of her nightgown, her hair falling over her shoulders in waves.

"Babe, slow down."

She shakes her head. "Can't. Already . . . there."

Her hips roll faster, and I'm trying to think of a scenario where I can prolong this, where she doesn't come as fast because fuck, I want to live out this feeling. So I lift and halt her hips from moving.

Her eyes round with surprise as I move her off me and to her side.

"What are you doing?" she asks, disappointed.

"Slowing you down." I gently put her on her side and then lift one of her legs so the bottom of her foot is pressing against the mattress, spreading her just the way I want. I wiggle in behind her after completely removing my briefs, and then place my cock right where it needs to be. Her head falls back against my shoulder as she moans.

"This will not slow me down."

"It will if I don't enter you."

"Eli, don't."

I gently drag my fingers up and down her stomach, then whisper, "I know how wet you are, but are you throbbing yet?"

She shakes her head.

"Then we have some work to do."

"Eli, please, just let me fuck you."

"No, baby," I say while I press a kiss to her shoulder. "I just don't want to be fucked anymore. I want to feel you. Every part of you. I don't want quick, I want to drag out the best feeling I've ever had in my life, and that's being inside you."

I drag my fingers over her breasts, circling her nipples, then moving down her cleavage to her stomach again and repeat the route. My cock plays with her entrance but is never fully inserted, despite the urge I have to thrust deep within her.

"You're . . . you're making me breathless, Eli."

"Good," I answer while leaning forward and pressing a kiss to her shoulder. "Keep talking to me."

She reaches back and loops her hand behind my neck, keeping her close. "I feel so safe with you, Eli. When you're around, I know nothing will happen to me."

My fingers pause at her breasts and then gently cup them.

"I look forward to the moments when I get to hold your hand."

I press her nipples between my fingers.

She groans. "God, I love it when I wake up to you wrapped around me."

With just enough pressure, I roll her nipples between my fingers, causing her to arch against my back.

"You make me feel seen for more than Pacey's sister."

I pause and then whisper into her ear, "Because you are, baby, you are so much more than that title."

Her breathing really picks up, and her grip on the nape of my neck grows tighter. "I'm throbbing, Eli. I'm so wet. Please . . . please give me what I need."

"And what is that?" I ask.

"You," she answers just as I slip inside her. "Yes," she moans loudly. "Oh God, Eli, this, you . . . it's amazing. It's all I want."

I thrust into her tight center, feeling the beginning of her pussy contracting around me, throbbing against me.

"Fuck, baby, you feel so good."

"Tell me you want me," she says, panting now.

"I want you, Penny. No one else, only you."

"You make me happy, Eli," she says while bringing my hand back to her breast and forcing me to squeeze hard. "Oh . . . oh . . ." She clenches around me.

My cock surges and swells as her orgasm starts to peak.

"More, I want more, all of you," she cries out as I thrust faster and faster until she's crying out in ecstasy.

Her pussy clenches, my balls contract, and then I'm coming inside this woman I can't get enough of.

White-hot pleasure rips through me, creating the most blissful feeling of my life, wrapped up in this woman who cares so deeply about me.

After a few seconds, we both slow our movements and catch our breath.

"God, Eli," she mumbles, her voice sounding dreamy now. "I love you so much."

And that's when I still, freeze, make no movement whatsoever because she just . . . she . . .

Fuck.

Those three words. I can't remember the last time I heard

them. The last time they were said to me from a person I trusted, a person I knew wouldn't hurt me.

There they are.

Hanging in the air.

Reverberating in my head, beating me down until I can't feel a thing.

My legs.

My arms.

My heart . . .

I can't feel any of them.

I'm like stone, unable to move one inch.

What do I say? What the hell do I do?

Penny moves off me and then slowly sits up and turns toward me. Hand on my chest, she leans forward and presses a kiss to my mouth, before getting up and walking toward the bathroom.

Fucking hell.

I madly push my hands through my hair, wondering where that came from and . . . did she truly mean it?

Of course she did. Penny doesn't say things just to say them.

So that means . . . she loves me. And I have no idea how to react to that other than to hope this doesn't end us.

Chapter Thirty-Three

PENNY

"Why are you whispering?" Blakely asks.

"Because I can't have him hear me."

"Who? Eli? Why not?"

I rock back and forth, holding my knees in close to my body —as close as I can get them with my belly.

"I accidentally told Eli last night that I love him."

"What?" she shouts. "Holy shit, Penny. Did you mean it?"

I roll my lips together as my eyes squeeze shut, tears forming in the corners. "I did. I've felt that way for a while now, but I swore I'd never say it, not to him, not when I know his past still haunts him. But we were having this intimate moment, and it just slipped out."

"What kind of intimate moment?"

"Sex, Blakely. What do you think?"

"Well, I don't know what you're doing up there. You could have been enjoying a peaceful sunset, and you said it. But saying it during sex? Oof, that's rough."

"I know," I whisper-shout.

"What did he do?"

"Went completely rigid. Pretty sure I short-circuited him. I pretended as though it didn't happen, cleaned up, and then acted like I fell asleep quickly, which, in reality, I did not. I was up almost all night replaying the moment in my head over and over again. It's been absolute torture."

"Where are you now?"

"In the closet in our bedroom, wishing I could be washed away with the laundry." My emotions start to bubble up on me, and my throat grows tight. "What am I supposed to do, Blakely?"

"Well, not hang out in the closet all day, that's for sure. How were things this morning?"

"Fine, maybe slightly tense, but I don't know if that's just me or the both of us. We had breakfast together, and then he went to work out, and I'm in the closet. I don't think I can stay here. What I've done is so detrimental, I'm not sure I can recover."

"Are you just embarrassed?" she asks.

"Well, yes, because who shouts that out while having sex? Especially with someone who has never been in a relationship before. I mean . . . he doesn't even call me his girlfriend, and here I am, mentioning love. God, that was so stupid. All of this was stupid. I blame this godforsaken baby. I would never have said something like that before, but here I am, his fingers pinching my nipples, and I'm calling out to the heavens above that I love the man."

"You do, though."

"I know that, but he doesn't need to know that." I press my fingers to my forehead. "Please, Blakely, please help me fix this. I can't be here."

"What are you going to do? Run away?"

My head perks up. Run away. That's . . . that's a great idea. "Blakely, you're brilliant."

"Penny, I was kidding."

"No, that's exactly what I need to do. I need to run away. Go back to Vancouver."

"And what happens when Eli calls you to see why you left? Because you know he will."

"You don't know that. He might be freaked out just enough not to want to be near me at the moment."

"That won't be the case. He'll chase after you."

"Then . . . I'll give him a reason. Some sort of . . . oh, I know. I'll visit my parents, oh, and make Winnie meet me there. Tell him I'm doing some sort of recon mission to get her and Pacey back together. Think she'd go for that?"

"You know, it's a good shot. She's been staying with her friend Katherine, the safety police, and I think she's about done with her. Why don't you call her up? But I'll say this, I think it might be better to talk to Eli."

"No, no, it won't. But thanks for the idea. I'll keep you abreast."

"Please don't say abreast."

"Talk to you later, bye!"

I hang up and quickly dial Winnie. The phone rings twice before she answers. "Hello?"

"Hey, Winnie. I know things are weird right now with you and Pacey, so I thought, why not come on a little girl trip with me to my parents' house where we can sleep in my bunk beds and stare at the pictures of Jess from the *Gilmore Girls* hanging on my wall and toss peanut butter pretzel balls in our mouths and drink lemonade while wearing slippers and pajamas and not worry about boys at all? We can relax and do each other's nails and sing karaoke on the karaoke machine I got when I was twelve and then do some latch hook because a girl hang is nothing unless you do a mindless craft together."

"Uh . . . wow. Okay, first of all, hi. And secondly, Penny, is everything okay?"

"Nope. Please meet me at my parents'. Please, I'll explain later. And I know you probably need the break from Katherine."

"Yeah, that is very much true. Okay, but aren't you in Banff right now?"

"Don't worry about me. Just get a flight out today. I'll meet you at the airport."

"Okay . . . are you sure you don't want to talk about what's going on?"

"Let's save the raunchy details for later when we see each other. Text me your flight details. Bye."

I hang up and set my phone down, feeling momentarily relieved but now, I have to pack and leave without Eli trying to stop me.

———

ELI: *PENNY, ANSWER YOUR GODDAMN PHONE!*

It's the tenth text I've received in half an hour, not to mention he's called me several times.

I'm only ten minutes away from the airport. I can hold out. Lucky for me, Eli was still working out, running actually, when I packed up and then convinced Stephan, the chef, to drive me into Calgary because Eli—*conveniently*—wasn't going to be home in time. He went right with it and said he needed to pick some things up anyway, so it worked out for him. I loaded up in his truck, and then on the way down the mountain, I booked a flight after I gained service again. I just needed out of the house as soon as possible. Eli must have been on a really long run because it took him a very long time to text me.

My phone buzzes again.

Eli: *Penny, this isn't fucking fair to me, to disappear like this with no explanation. You know I have abandonment issues. You can't just fucking leave like that.*

Oh God, I didn't think about it like that.

Guilt immediately swarms me, and I find myself texting him back right away.

Penny: *Just got service. I'm sorry, Eli. Headed to my parents' place with Winnie, as she needed some time away. I'll call you later.*

There, short and to the point, and there are no I love you's anywhere to be found. Hopefully, that will help me gather myself before talking to him on the phone.

"Are you sure you're okay?" Stephan asks. "You've been incredibly quiet."

"Just thinking. I'm fine. Thank you."

My phone buzzes, and I glance down at the text message.

Eli: *STEPHAN TOOK YOU? What the actual fuck? He's not going to have a goddamn job when he gets back here. The boys are furious.*

Oh, shit. Stephan is an innocent bystander in this mess. I don't want him getting in trouble because of me.

Penny: *You all were working out, and Holmes was reading. Stephan had to go to Calgary, so I just hopped a ride with him. Don't be mad at him.*

Eli: *You couldn't have waited for me? What the hell is even happening? Why did you leave so abruptly?*

I look up at the road and see the airport come into view, thank God. I hold off on answering Eli as we pull up to arrivals.

"Here we are. Let me grab your bag for you."

"Thank you," I say as I exit the truck. I move around to the back and give Stephan an awkward hug. "Thanks for all the great food. Your waffles are another world."

He smirks. "You're more than welcome. Hopefully, we see each other again."

"Hopefully," I say before waving and moving my suitcase inside the airport. I have three hours until my flight, so plenty of time before I need to seriously consider getting to my gate. I move my suitcase to a quiet corner, and I stare down at my phone just as it starts ringing again.

Eli.

Might as well get this over with.

"Hello?" I answer.

"Jesus Christ," he says, his voice irritated and relieved. "Penny, what the hell are you doing?"

"Headed to my parents', I told you that. Going to meet Winnie there. She needed some alone time. I tried to tell you how Winnie was doing last night, but we kind of got distracted."

But yeah, she called this morning, and I said I'd meet up with her. You were out running, so I thought a note would suffice."

"You thought a note would be fine? Just a note? How the fuck did you think that would suffice?"

"Can you please calm down?"

"Calm down? Penny, I went for a goddamn run and came back to an empty room, your things gone, and a note. Excuse me if I'm freaked out right now."

"It's not a big deal," I tell him, trying to pass it all off as nothing, even though I can hear the panic in his voice, the same frenzied panic pumping through me at the moment. The panic from knowing that I told this man I loved him and he not only didn't say anything back, but he didn't say anything at all and went catatonic on me.

"It's a big deal to me, Penny. I thought . . . hell, I thought we were spending time together."

Another wave of guilt hits me hard. But how am I supposed to know how he feels after what happened last night, or the way he acted this morning? A little cold . . . distant. This is the first time he's gone on a long run since we got here. How could it not correspond to what I said to him?

"I don't know, Eli, I just figured after last night that . . . it would be okay. That maybe you just needed some space."

There, I put it out there. The elephant in the room.

And of course, he's silent, just like he was last night.

This just confirms my thoughts. I freaked him out, and despite him not liking the way I took off, he's not in the same commitment headspace as I am.

Sure, he says he wants me, but wanting someone and loving someone is completely different.

Wanting someone is founded by lust.

Loving someone sits on top of a foundation of trust, desire, attachments, and intimacy.

Just from his cold, distant mood this morning, I can tell, he doesn't love me. He just *lusts* me.

I'd like to say I'm okay with that, but I'm not. I'm . . . hell,

I'm embarrassed. Again. Even though he's the one who insisted I move in with him, I often feel as though we're a step out of sync with each other. I tried to kiss him, he pushed me away. He didn't want to risk his relationship with Pacey, and then the next minute, he gave in. He's . . . impulsive yet uncertain. I think I want him to catch up. He thinks I'm running. We're not in sync, but I sincerely hope we might get there one day.

Unable to take the silence or the wondering, I say, "I don't want to miss my flight, so I should get going. I'll text you when I land."

"Penny, hold on," he says just as I hang up the phone.

To my horror, tears fall, and I quickly wipe at them and take a deep breath. It's fine.

You're fine.

Everything is fine.

This is a minor bump in the road, nothing you can't get through with some help from your parents.

⊏⊐

"MOM, WHERE ARE YOU?" I say into the phone as Winnie and I stand outside, freezing our buns off.

"What? Honey, it's windy. I can barely hear you."

"Where are you? I'm outside the door."

"What door?"

"Your door," I shout into the phone.

"You're in Scottsdale?"

"What? No . . . wait, are you in Scottsdale?"

"Yes. Where are you?"

Groaning, I say, "At your house."

"Why on earth are you there? We're in Scottsdale."

"I gathered that." I shake my head at Winnie. "When are you returning?"

"Not for a week. We just got here. Honey, you should really tell people when you're stopping by."

"Starting to understand that. Okay, well . . . I guess we'll figure something out."

"Talk to Marybeth at the corner store. She'll be able to house you."

"I'm not going to talk to Marybeth, but thanks."

"She'll probably give you homemade cookies."

"Thanks, Mom, love you." I hang up and lean against the house. "They're in freaking Scottsdale. God, Winnie, I'm so sorry."

"That's okay." She looks off to the side. "You know, we can find a hotel for tonight and then fly back together tomorrow. At least we'll have one night together."

"That works. God, I'm so embarrassed."

"Don't be. It was fun flying on a whim and getting out of the house as far away from Katherine as I could get. And we can order in tonight, chow down, talk. Might be good for both of us."

"Yeah," I say sadly as I move my way down the stairs with my luggage. "I'm craving some tacos. What about—" My bag wheel gets stuck on my way down, and I trip over it and careen down to the ground. Thankfully, I'm able to roll to my side, so when I land, it isn't directly on my belly.

"Oh, my God," Winnie shrieks as she comes to my side and places her hand on my shoulder. "Penny, are you okay?"

"I . . . I think so," I say, groaning as I place my hand on my pretty prominent stomach. I take a few deep breaths. "Just . . . wow, I feel dizzy all of a sudden."

"Don't move, okay?" Winnie says, pulling her phone out.

"What are you doing?"

"Calling 911. What does it look like?"

"Winnie, I don't need an ambulance. Just give me a second."

"No way, I'm not chancing anything. You just fell down the stairs. As a pregnant woman, we're calling an ambulance."

"It was two stairs."

"Which is more than enough." As she speaks to an operator, I feel myself succumb to the dizziness. I'm not sure if it's the sun beating down on me or the cool sidewalk, or the fall . . . but before I know it, my eyes are closed, and I'm drifting off to sleep.

———

"IS SHE IN HERE?" I hear a deep male voice ask.

"Sir, she's sleeping right now. Can I ask who you are?"

"Eli," he says. "Can you tell me anything that happened?"

"Are you her husband, boyfriend?"

"Uh . . . what? No . . . I mean, I'm the baby's dad."

"Ah, okay. Well, unfortunately, I can't tell you anything, but you're welcome to sit next to her until she wakes up."

"Thank you."

There's a soft click of a door, and then I feel a warm presence come closer, only to sit on the edge of the bed. My hand is covered in his.

My eyes slowly flutter open, and Eli's handsome face comes into view. "Jesus," he says right before pressing his forehead against mine. "Penny, are you okay?"

It takes me a second to figure out what's going on. I'm in a hospital bed. Eli is sitting next to me, and beeping machines fill the silence. I look down at my stomach, and that's when I catch Winnie sitting in the corner, legs drawn into her chest, looking scared.

"Winnie," I say, holding my hand out.

She's quick to her feet and takes my hand. "I'm so glad you're okay."

"What's going on?" I ask her, ignoring Eli for the moment.

"You fell down the stairs at your parents' house, remember? You passed out, and I called an ambulance. I told Eli because I felt like he needed to know. From what I've heard, the baby is fine." She points at the monitor. "That's the heartbeat."

More tears fill my eyes as I stare at the monitor and see the line bounce up and down. My hand caresses my stomach as I glance down at it. "I'm so sorry," I say to our baby boy. "I'm so sorry I was careless."

"It was an accident," Winnie says. "And you actually twisted so you didn't land on your stomach. You did good, Mama."

I let the tears slide down my cheeks. Glancing at Eli, I say, "How did you get here?"

"Private jet," he answers and brings my hand to his lips. "Penny, are you okay?"

"I think so," I answer just as a doctor walks into the room.

"Oh, you're awake. That's wonderful. How are you feeling?"

"Okay," I answer. "Just a little confused."

"That's to be expected. You took a bit of a tumble, and given that you're seven months pregnant, that makes things slightly more risky. Thankfully, your friend did the smart thing and called for help." She glances at Eli. "Am I free to speak right now?"

I nod. "Yes."

"Okay, well, we checked on the baby, and he seems to be doing just fine. Tough guy in there. You did have some spotting, which is why we want to keep you overnight, just for observation, but other than that, you look pretty good."

"Spotting, is that going to be an issue?"

"It doesn't seem like it will be, but as I said, we just want to keep you overnight to observe, just in case."

"And the baby, he's okay?"

"Yes, he's quite fine. Nothing to worry about, Mom. Next time though, let someone else handle the luggage." She smiles at me and then takes off out the door just as I hear her say, "Oh, almost ran into you there."

"Sorry." I hear Pacey's voice say just as he walks into the room as well. He first glances at Winnie, and then he comes to my side. "Penny, are you okay? Is the baby okay?"

"Yes," I answer. "Everyone is okay. The doctor said he's a tough guy."

"Guy?" Pacey asks, his eyes welling up. "You're having a boy?"

I smile and nod. "We are."

Carefully, Pacey leans down and gives me a hug. "That's so

fucking great, Pen." He lifts up just enough to look me in the eyes. "Jesus, don't scare me like that again."

"I'll try not to," I say as he pulls away and lets out a deep breath.

He places both hands on his head and says, "Fuck, I need some ice cream." He looks over at Winnie and holds out his hand. "Will you join me?"

I half expect her to say no, but I feel satisfied when she nods and takes his hand. I wouldn't ever want to fall again while pregnant, but I'm sort of glad that it looks like the scare might have brought them back together.

When they're out of the room, Eli leans in closer and presses a soft kiss to my lips. "Penny, I was so fucking scared." He cups my cheek. "I can't tell you how relieved I am that you're okay, and that the baby is okay."

I wet my lips as I stare into his beautiful eyes, but all I can think about as he stares back at me is what he said to the nurse.

That he's not my boyfriend.

Just the baby's father.

If that doesn't speak volumes, I don't know what does.

"Will you talk to me?" he says. "Please, Penny?"

Not wanting to start a scene here, I say, "Sorry, still a little stunned."

He continues to cup my cheek. "Don't apologize." He scoots a little closer. "Is everything okay between us? I feel like the past twenty-four hours have been a whirlwind of insanity that I just don't quite understand."

I swallow deeply and nod, willing back the perpetual tears. "Yes, Eli. Everything is fine."

"Okay, because . . . you just left, and I don't know. I thought that we were having a good time, you know? Enjoying each other."

A good time.

That's what this is to him.

A freaking good time.

I should have seen that coming, especially after his reaction from the night before.

"We were. I just wanted to help Winnie out, you know?" I nod toward the door. "But seems like I helped out in a different way."

"He was a disaster to deal with when he found out you and Winnie came out here."

"You know, we're grown women, and we can do what we want," I say.

"I know, but I think he was worried about losing Winnie, and hell . . . I was worried about losing you too."

I don't understand it. When he says things like that, it feels like he feels the same love that I have for him. He makes me believe there could be so much more, but when prompted, I don't get the same response.

His thumb drags over my cheek. "When we're allowed to take you out of here, where do you want to go? Back to Banff, or do you want to go home?"

"Home," I say, not wanting to return to Banff, to the room where I confessed my love for this man. I don't want to be reminded of that moment, a moment I'm trying desperately to forget even happened.

"Okay." He leans in and presses a kiss to my forehead. "Then we'll go home."

Chapter Thirty-Four

PENNY

"What do you think?" Eli says, holding his arms out as he shows off his apartment.

While we were in Banff, he had movers pack up my place and move me into his apartment.

Normally, such a grand gesture of not having to move would be applauded, but as I stare at his apartment, where my décor and personal items have been expertly placed and used as decorations to make his apartment mine as well, all I feel is irritation.

Intense irritation.

An irritation so consuming that I can actually taste it on my tongue.

Why would he do this?

I'm not his girlfriend.

I thought that we were having a good time, you know? Enjoying each other.

He doesn't love me.

He's the baby's dad.

"It's . . . uh . . . it's done," I say as I walk around the apartment. I run my fingers over the back of his long gray couch draped with one of my throw blankets. Behind the couch is the console table from my apartment, decorated with some of my favorite books and picture frames. It seamlessly goes together, which irritates me even more. The curtains in his apartment have been switched out to ones that are similar to mine, and the art above the mantelpiece is colorful, pulling the many hues from my apartment together.

"It's done?" He chuckles, not sensing my mood. "Babe, it's more than done. It's us."

Us.

Well, that doesn't seem like an appropriate word since I'm not even considered his girlfriend in his mind. But we're an us. Isn't that swell?

"And look, the kitchen is a perfect combination of your things and my things, and of course, I had them use your dining room table because frankly, I liked it better."

Yup. It is better. And the wood grain softens the room surprisingly, making it feel less modern and more homey.

The bowl of lemons on the table, and the rug under it that's mine, pulls it all together.

Who has a bowl of lemons anyway? Are those fake?

They can't be real.

What a waste.

When I pick one up, it's light and plastic-like in my hand. Huh, fake. He must have a good designer to find such a lifelike fruit.

"And come with me," he says, taking my hand and walking me toward the hallway. My eyes land on the fireplace, the space in front of it where this started. The French silk pie, the flirting, the way he looked in his suit, the need to be with this man.

If only I knew it would end up like this, me walking around with this belly full of baby, attempting to enjoy a surprise that my non-boyfriend created for me. And uncomfortably at that.

In what felt like seconds, I went from feeling sexy and

425

amazing to uncomfortable in my own skin, where everything seems to irritate me.

Everything.

He walks me past a few doors and into his bedroom—well, I guess our bedroom. A bedroom for two people not in love but living together and sharing a baby together, a bedroom where there will be sex because, even though just looking at him makes me want to roundhouse kick his crotch off, I still want my mouth on his cock.

The hospital actually kept me for a total of three days. Eli stayed by my side the whole time, and every kind gesture, every kiss, every hold of my hand, made me so angry.

Very angry.

Irrationally angry.

Because it's confusing. I feel like he's playing with my heart, and I don't know how to handle it. And the more upset I get, the more I want to cry. The more I want to cry, the more he wants to hold me and be affectionate. It's a vicious circle, and for the life of me, even though I know he doesn't love me, I keep holding his hand, I keep snuggling into him. Because, despite him not loving me, I still very much love him and I can't stop my heart from seeking him out.

That's why I'm here, in his apartment, not running away.

He opens the door and smiles as he walks me in. The center of the room is his enormous bed, but with matching bedding as I had in my apartment. The nightstands have been switched out to reflect mine, and the rug on the carpet is new, but again, it ties everything together. The art on the wall above the bed is from my bedroom, and on the nightstands—each of them—is a sonogram picture framed. It's a sweet gesture that once again irritates me.

What if I wanted a different picture there?

What if I don't want our baby staring at us when he's plowing into me from behind?

What if I didn't want that freaking swirly art above the bed, but rather a mirror, so I could see myself while I deal with the irritating fact that I still want this man inside me, all the time? *Even though* . . .

He comes up behind me and wraps his arms around my stomach as he places a kiss on my neck. "What do you think, babe?"

I think it was a huge invasion of my privacy to have some stranger move all of my things, but I can't look like an ungrateful wench because frankly, I've inserted myself into this situation, so I say, "It's nice."

It's all I can muster.

It's all my heart can take.

"Nice?" He laughs. "Just nice? Man, I thought there'd be a bigger reaction than that. Do I need to show you the closet space you have to warrant a 'really nice'?"

"Just soaking it all in," I say.

"Well, I have one more thing to show you." He takes my hand and brings me to the door on the left just outside our bedroom. He opens it up, and lo and behold, it's a white room with beautiful hardwood flooring, the same as the entire apartment, with large windows and a single white crib constructed in the very middle. "It's for our little guy."

Okay . . . listen up, ladies. This right here, this gesture is cracking my shell of indifference. The irritation is melting into a puddle at my feet, and in its place, an emotion so intense, so palpable starts to take over.

Happiness?

Joy?

Anticipation?

He didn't decorate this room. He's done absolutely nothing but leave it as a blank canvas, something for both of us to do together. That was sweet. That was thoughtful.

That right there is why I can't seem to take a step back from him.

It's why I'm so confused.

Why my heart is breaking with every breath that I take. With every warring ounce of love I feel. Worry laces his eyes as I walk toward him. I gently place my hand on his face, stand on my tiptoes, and place a very soft kiss on his lips. His hand presses into my lower back, keeping me in place as he reciprocates the kiss, reminding me just how much I'm addicted to him.

To his taste.

To the way his body molds against mine.

And to how he makes me feel protected . . . loved, despite how he truly feels.

My mouth parts, and I slip my tongue against his lips. He parts his mouth as well, and our tongues collide, but not in a frenzy. We're calm, exploratory, appreciative. His hands slide up the back of my shirt as our kiss deepens even further, pulling the hem up until I lift my arms above me and allow him to take it all the way off, leaving me in my bra and shorts.

He then runs his hands over the clasp of my bra, and in one swift motion, he undoes it and the fabric falls off my body.

"Do you love it?" he asks as he takes me closer, pressing my sensitive nipples against his shirt.

"I do," I say and then pause to look him in the eyes. "Thank you, Eli."

His smile stretches across his face right before he bends down and lifts me into his arms. Our lips lock, and he takes me into the master bedroom, where he gently lays me across the bed and pulls my shorts and underwear off, leaving me bare.

From behind his head, he pulls his shirt off and then undoes his jeans and drags them down his thick thighs along with his briefs. His cock juts forward, and he grips the base. "What do you want me to do to you?"

Love me.

Make love to me.

Tell me that I'm the only woman you ever want in your life.

Truly make me yours, brand me, mark me, make sure it's obvious I belong to no one else but you.

Eliminate this tormenting feeling that's pulsing through me every time I look into your eyes.

Don't leave me alone in this world of love, wondering, hoping, begging that you'll open your eyes and see how much I can offer you.

I swallow and say, "Fuck me."

"That I can do." With a smirk, he bends between my legs and brings his mouth to my pussy. My head falls back against the mattress, and I let myself forget my tumultuous emotions, focusing on his mouth and how he's making me feel at this moment . . . taken care of.

———

PENNY: *I want to punch him.*

Blakely: *Punch who? Eli? Why?*

Penny: *He's sooooo irritating.*

Blakely: *What's he doing?*

Penny: *Do you want the list?*

Blakely: *I kind of do.*

Penny: *Well, for one, it's called a shirt, man. Wear it. No one needs to see your perfectly defined abs all the time or round, disc-like nipples. Also, can he stop making me all of this food? Like, breakfast. He makes these eggs that are so delicious. Just stop it. No one wants your eggs. Oh, and get this . . . he's always leaving the toilet seat down. What kind of crap is that? And then he's like oh, can I massage your feet for you? Can I get you anything from the store? Hungry at 2 a.m.? No problem, baby, what do you need? And what's with the baby shit? I'd rather him call me Mistress of the Dark or Dragon Breath, but baby? It's honestly puke-worthy. Ugh, and he brought home all of these paint samples for the baby's bedroom, thoughtful paint samples that I talked about. Like . . . he actually listened. And to top it all off, he's still making me come so hard that I honestly feel my eyes rolling to the back of my head. I don't want to come that hard. No one, and I mean no one, should have the right on this planet to have that many orgasms in a week. And he's always giving me oral, like every time. He's trying to show off. That's what he's doing. He's showing off how good he can fuck me with his tongue, and frankly, it's getting on my nerves. Congratulations, buddy, you can make me squeal with delight by only using your tongue. Slow clap for you.*

429

Blakely: Ummm, don't hate me "Dragon Breath," but it seems as though he's actually doing all of the right things.

Penny: EXACTLY. He is.

Blakely: Okay, so, once again, "Mistress of the Dark," don't slaughter me, but I fail to realize how there is a problem.

Penny: Uh, isn't it obvious?

Blakely: No. No, it's not.

Penny: He's being too perfect!

Blakely: Ah yes, what an absolute fucker. How could he *possibly* be so awful to you? Damn him all to hell.

Penny: Are you patronizing me?

Blakely: Can I ask you a question?

Penny: Might as well.

Blakely: You're seven months pregnant, right?

Penny: If you say this has to do with my pregnancy, I'm going to slice you with a rusty knife.

Blakely: You're seven months pregnant, which means you're entering the third trimester, and your patience is going to continue to shrink until nothing is left.

Penny: My patience level is fine. I'm just asking him to stop being so goddamn nice. He doesn't even like me, Blakely. I said that in a hissing tone. If he loved me, then sure, dote on me all you want, but he's making me believe he's this nice guy, and then what happens when I have the baby? Huh?

Blakely: He's a nice guy. We established that. And I do think he likes you. He just doesn't know how to say it, so he's showing you instead.

Penny: You realize how completely useless you are at the moment?

Blakely: Wow . . . welcome to the third trimester. I hope Eli is mentally prepared.

Penny: Ugh . . . I'm sorry, okay. I just . . . I can't stop thinking about how he's doing all of these nice things, but why? Why bother?

Blakely: Because, sweetie, like I said, he likes you, but he doesn't know how to say it, just show it.

Penny: It's slowly eating away at me. I can feel it. The angst of it all. I don't want him to do nice things for me. I want him to love me.

Blakely: It takes some people longer.

Penny: Or maybe, Blakely, he just doesn't like me like that, and all of *this has just been a way to stay closer to the baby. And get laid very, very often.*

Blakely: *Do you really think he'd do that?*

Penny: *I honestly don't know. What I do know is that with every day that goes by, I'm growing more and more irritated, more angry . . . and more sad.*

Blakely: *Penny, please don't be sad. Give him time.*

Penny: *Hard not to be sad when all I feel like is an incubator. Someone he can have sex with. And of course, the means to an end.*

Blakely: *Do you need to meet up? Should we go somewhere to talk? You don't sound great.*

Penny: *I'm fine. I'm going to take a bath. I'll talk to you later.*

Blakely: *Penny, don't shut down. Please just talk to me . . .*

"YOU LOOK HOT," Eli says as he comes up to me in the kitchen and places a kiss on my shoulder.

"I'm wearing a five-year-old sports bra and underwear. Explain to me how this is hot?"

He pauses mid-kiss to my neck and pulls away. "Is everything okay?"

"Fine," I snap at him as I shove a brownie in my mouth and walk to the living room.

"I'm smart enough to know when a woman says fine, she doesn't mean it." He joins me in the living room and sits across from me on the coffee table.

Mouth full of brownie, I grip my large stomach and say, "This looks hot to you?"

"Babe, you're easily the most attractive woman I've ever laid eyes on."

"Oh, yeah, sure . . . okay." I roll my eyes and reach for the remote, but he stops me.

"There seems to be a problem, and I'm not positive what it is. Mind if you help me?"

"Help you what? Understand a woman? Why do I need to be your educator? Read a book."

Now he rears back slightly, blinking. "Hey, Penny, what the hell is going on? Did I do something wrong?"

"Oh, you finally realize you did something wrong? Wow, Eli, it only took you seven freaking months."

"Wait . . . what are you talking about?"

Chalk it up to the hormones, possibly my defense mechanism to how destroyed I feel inside, but I can't seem to control my emotions.

I love him.

But I hate him.

I hate him so much for putting me through this. For being so caring, attentive, and appreciative, but that's it. There's nothing else, and that is what's making me sad.

That is what's making me cry whenever he leaves.

That is what's fueling the fire to the raging flames burning through me.

"If you don't know what I'm talking about, then I can't help you."

He pauses, blinking a few times, and it's almost comical, watching him try to process all of this. Isn't it clear as day why I'm irritated? How come no one can understand besides me?

"I'm sorry, Penny, but I really don't understand."

"Typical," I say while I tug on my bra that, despite being five years old, still has the elasticity of a brand new one, causing my boobs to feel so confined that I can't even take it, so I tear it off over my head and drop it to the side. Leaving me in nothing but a pair of underwear.

I watch as Eli's eyes drift to my chest and then quickly back up.

"Was it the bra? Do I need to get you a shirt or something?"

"Uh, are you saying I need to cover up?"

"No," he says, his tone deepening. "I'm just trying to make you comfortable."

"Well, me comfortable, is sitting here in nothing but my underwear. What do you think about that?"

He smooths his hand over his jaw. "Honestly, I think it's hot. Your tits are fucking sexy."

There he goes again.

"Ugh." I toss my hands up. "What am I? A piece of meat now?"

"Jesus Christ, did I say that?" The timid voice he was using has now turned to irritated.

Join the club.

"Might as well have. Am I just a vessel for your sexual needs, Eli?"

"Yeah, Penny," he says sarcastically. "You're just a hole to stick my dick in."

I point my finger at him. "I knew it."

"Jesus . . . fuck, you're losing it."

"Excuse me?"

"Yeah, you heard me. You're fucking losing it. And I'd say I've been pretty fucking good the past two weeks since you moved in. I've been at your beck and call, given you everything you want, even fucking you whenever you hopped on my lap—"

"Oh, I'm sorry for all of the sex. You poor, handsome millionaire, having to have sex with a horny woman. You are so put out."

"You know I didn't mean it like that. Stop putting words in my mouth."

"How could I put words in your mouth when apparently the only thing I put in there is my pussy." I stand from the couch, and he grabs my hand before I walk away.

He stands as well, his chest inches from mine. "What the fuck is going on with you, Penny?"

"As I said, if you don't know, I can't help you." I snap my wrist away from him and head toward the bedroom. "I'm going to put a shirt on now so you don't have to be subject to my feminine wiles."

"YES, ELI. HARDER. HARDER."

"Fuck," he says as he pulses, pulling on my hips as he thrusts into me. "Babe, I'm going to come."

"Eli!" I yell as my orgasm rips through me, splitting me in half and causing me to lose all sense of what is right. He stills behind me and groans as he comes, and I slowly lower my forehead onto the counter to catch my breath.

"Holy shit," he mumbles as he leans forward and kisses my cheek. "Are you okay?"

"Yes," I answer.

Like we're two robots, he removes himself from me, and I straighten up, fixing my new maternity nightgown over my stomach and ass. I had to get some that would fit over my belly, and they have left nothing to the imagination. Cut low so my cleavage is on full display, I walked out of the bedroom after changing, only to see Eli's eyes turn dark . . . hungry.

I was torn in half as my heart wanted him, but my mind tried to ignore him. It was seconds before my heart—and my libido—won out. I walked up to him, stuck my hand down his shorts, and pulled him out before bending down and placing him into my mouth. He let me suck him for a few seconds before he carefully bent me over the counter.

This, of course, was after we were fighting about who got to do the dishes. I stormed off, irritated that he wouldn't budge from the sink, and put on my nightgown.

"Do you want me to grab you a washcloth?" he asks.

"I'm more than capable of cleaning myself up," I say.

"Didn't say you weren't."

"You implied it," I counter.

"Actually, it's called being a nice fucking guy."

"You know, you've been playing that card a lot lately. The nice guy. How do I know it's nice, and you're not just stacking up evidence?"

"What kind of evidence?" he asks, looking confused. God, he's a good actor.

"The evidence you'd use against me?"

"For what?" he nearly shouts.

"Uh, to prove something."

"To prove what?"

"Oh . . . you know." I cross my arms over my chest and nod.

"Holy fucking shit. I really don't."

I don't stay to listen, though. I go to the bathroom and clean up before brushing my teeth. I consider going to bed, but I'm really not tired. I go back out and find Eli finishing the dishes.

Hand on the wall, I ask, "Are you satisfied?"

He glances up, and his hair falls over his forehead, making him look that much sexier. "Satisfied? In what way?"

"Well, let's see, satisfied sexually and satisfied that you got to do the dishes."

He turns the water off and dries his hands before resting them on the counter in front of him. His triceps fire off under the recessed lighting. "Am I satisfied sexually? Yes, I can barely keep up with you. Do you make me come harder than anyone ever before? One thousand percent. Hands down, no questions asked, my dick is a slave to your pussy, and it will do anything you ask." Good answer. "Am I satisfied with doing the dishes? It doesn't matter to me. I just want you to take it easy."

"Why? Are you saying if I don't take it easy, I breathe too hard?"

"What?" he asks, wincing and blinking at the same time. "How the fuck did you get that from what I said?"

"It is what you said."

He shakes his head and tosses the dish towel on the counter. "I don't know what to fucking do with you, Penny."

"What do you mean?"

"Nothing." He turns off the kitchen light and walks toward me. When he reaches me, he pauses, presses a kiss on my forehead, and then keeps moving toward the bedroom.

"Where are you going?"

"To bed," he answers and then is out of sight as he slips into the bedroom.

To bed? Why doesn't he want to hang out with me? We usually watch a show at night together.

I lean against the hallway wall and tilt my head slightly back.

God, I hate myself. This is just not me. Yes, I'm an emotional person—passionate, one might have said. But this . . . erratic behavior is not who I am at my core. And I hate that this is what I've become. *I used to love who I was.* I hate that I keep picking fights with him to push him away, even though my heart wants to drag him closer. In my mind, if I keep him at arm's length, I can convince myself that I don't need him, that I can exist without his love.

Maybe you're acting like a monster because you have no idea how to control the burning pain that is so deep in your bones. Especially because I can't leave.

I've never had to wish someone would love me before. My parents, my brother, Blakely, their love has always just been there. Unconditional. And I don't think that makes me spoiled, but rather unused to this one-sided love that promotes sadness and disappointment.

But standing here, knowing he's upset, it breaks me.

I don't want to be broken.

I don't want to feel like this.

This . . . out of control.

I move toward the bedroom, where I find him in the master bath, leaning against the counter, brushing his teeth. When he spits out his toothpaste, he asks, "Do you need something?"

I nod. I can feel my tears start to surface, but I hold back, not wanting him to fret over me all over again.

He rinses his mouth. "What?"

"Are you really not going to watch a show with me?"

"Do you want me to watch a show with you?"

I nod. "I do."

"Okay."

He finishes up and then leads me back to the living room,

hand in hand, where he reaches for the remote. "Do you want to pick?"

I shake my head. "I just want to sit on your lap."

"Okay." He takes a seat on the couch. I sit on top of him, and he lays a blanket over the both of us. I rest my head on his shoulder, and he curls his arm around me. Not turning the TV on, he quietly says, "What am I going to do with you, Penny?"

"Get rid of me," I answer sadly.

"Never," he says, kissing the top of my head. "I wish I could understand what's going on in your brain, though. You've been a little up and down lately."

I wish I could understand what's going on in your brain, Eli.

"It's the hormones." I lift my head and kiss his jaw. "I can't control them."

"I can understand that, but I want you to know, I'm not here to pick battles with you, I'm here to support you, and no matter how much you try to push me away and fight about meaningless things, I'm not going anywhere. I'm here, babe."

"Are you sure you want to be?"

"Of course," he answers. "I'm all yours."

I sigh into him, and I can feel my ugly emotion start to trigger again. "I wish that really were the case," I say, causing him to force me to look at him by lifting my chin.

"Why do you say that?"

"Because it's the truth."

"No, the truth is, I'm yours. No one else's, and I'm not going anywhere. Even when this baby is born, I'm still yours."

If he's mine . . . then why doesn't he feel like it?

Because he doesn't understand the definition of love, Penny. His actions show love, but maybe he simply doesn't know that.

And there's absolutely nothing I can do to help him understand.

———

ELI IS A VERY NEAT PERSON.

What am I going to do with you, Penny?

I realized that from living with him in his apartment. He likes to fold his shirts a certain way, his jeans are always hung, and his shoes must be lined up properly. Suits are all stored in protective bags, and socks are folded together, not inside each other, and then lined up specifically in his top drawer.

I've never seen anything like it.

Drawer open, I drag my finger over the fabric of his socks, wondering what would possess a human to spend so much time perfecting the appearance of a sock drawer. This seems like such a waste of time. And would he even notice if something was out of order? What if I put one of his ankle socks with a dress sock— why does he even have dress socks? I never see him wear them. Nonsense.

Never hurts to conduct a few experiments.

I pick up a few of his running socks and replace them with some dress socks. I then open his underwear drawer and gag at the organization. He folds his underwear into little squares. What an annoying habit. It's underwear. Toss it all in a drawer and be done. Why, as a civilization, have we found it necessary to fold underwear?

Irritated with the mere sight of it, I stick my hand in the drawer and make an utter mess of it all. Smiling, I shut both drawers. That's better.

Needing something else to do, I wander over to the baby's room, where I lean against the entrance and stare at the perfectly neat sample squares of paint Eli painted on the walls the other day. Variations of gray on one wall, blue on another, and green on another. They're so precise.

And he's starred the ones he likes.

Presumptuous if you ask me.

Inside the bedroom, I spy one of the paint cans with a paint-brush on top.

Don't mind if I do.

I pick up the paintbrush, pry the can open with a paint can opener, and see it's the dark gray that Eli didn't really like. It's so dark, it's almost black.

Well, at the moment, I think it's quite nice. And babies really only see black and white at first, so why not give him a color that he can appreciate?

I dip the paintbrush inside and then lift it to the wall where the blues are painted. I slap the gray onto the wall and start writing with it. I don't bother taking my time. Instead, I let the paint drip down the wall in gobs as I scroll across all three walls. It's cathartic.

It's been a month and a half since the day I told him I loved him, since I confessed my most confident of secrets. And a month and a half since he visibly froze with fear. Has he changed his mind since? Not that I can tell. Does he blow steam up my ass every day?

Yes.

Should I be happy? Probably.

But I'm sad.

I feel . . . depressed.

Used.

Nowhere close to the woman I once was.

Blakely thinks I'm insane.

Winnie believes I should give him more time.

My mom even chimed in and told me that it might be harder for him to express his feelings.

But at this point, I'm not even sure I love him anymore.

God, could you hear how bad that lie was? Because it was a very bad lie. I try to convince myself that I don't love him. I try to tell myself all of the annoying things that he does, but they don't seem to have an impact, and with every day that goes by that he doesn't say it to me, I feel like I'm nothing more than a sexy buddy who's carrying his baby, I get angrier. More frustrated. More irritated.

More depressed.

More needy for something more. Anything that will make me feel whole again.

Hence, the sock drawer, the underwear, what I'm currently doing, and the smoothie I made him this morning before he went to work out that I "accidentally" put salt in and then happily watched him make a queasy face as he swallowed. I don't think I've ever been more satisfied than watching him try to figure out how I ruined his drink. Pure gold.

And I can't seem to stop myself. Call it the hormones, the embarrassment, the loneliness, the rejection, or the inability to be loved by someone else, but it's all getting to me.

I set the paintbrush down and step away to marvel at my work. I smile to myself as I read, "This room belongs to Johnny Jim."

Now that is what I call decorating.

Satisfied with the change, I walk into the living room and survey the space. A few pictures of him shaking hands with some famous hockey players hang on the walls. Frankly, a little pretentious if you ask me.

So I decide to change them since I'm on a roll.

I take a seat at the desk in the corner of the living room, and pull out a Sharpie and some paper. Getting comfortable in my seat, I uncap the Sharpie and then tap my chin, thinking what to draw.

Anything could be better than a stodgy picture of two men shaking hands.

Smirking, I press my pen to the paper and start my first commissioned art piece. Commissioned by me, of course, and as I continue to draw, ensuring there's specific detail, I know my customer will be very satisfied.

I repeat the same drawing but make some adjustments here and there.

And then one more.

When I'm done, I cap the Sharpie and stare at my drawings, chuckling.

One picture is of a penis, flaccid, looking very sad and almost weeping because it's so sad.

The next one is a picture of just a pregnant belly and boobs, coming from the side of the paper. The penis is now happy.

The third picture is the backside of the pregnant woman,

walking off the paper, hair floating in the wind, the penis is sad again. Talk about portraying a story through art. Doesn't get better than this.

It takes me a moment and some finagling—the frames were held down with what felt like glue—but I add my new art to the walls and step back.

"Wow," I say to myself. "Those look amazing." I snap a picture with my phone and send it to Blakely.

Almost instantaneously, my phone beeps back with a message.

But it's not from Blakely, but rather a friend I haven't talked to in a while.

I swipe open the message and read it.

Remi: *Hey, gorgeous. I'm in town. Are you free for dinner this week?*

I read the message a few times and feel a sense of . . . nostalgia pass through me. Maybe it's because I'm in such a dark place right now, but before I can stop myself, I text him back.

Penny: *Hey you, I'd love to see you. Just let me know when and where.*

Remi: *Perfect. Tomorrow night, I'll come pick you up. Send me your address.*

Absentmindedly, I text him back, and then on a deep, satisfied breath, I set my phone down. It will be good to see an old friend, maybe get me out of this rut that I'm in. *At least it will get me out of this perfectly decorated apartment.*

Drumming my fingers again, I turn toward the kitchen. "What next?"

I spend the next half hour taking all the throw pillows apart so they're just the filler pillow rather than the pretty sham. I move his phone charger into the fridge because it felt right, and I take one of his shoes and repot a succulent in it and set it at the window. I take another picture and send it to Blakely, telling her I might be onto something with the succulent shoe. Eli walks through the door just as I'm about to rearrange the coat closet by turning it into a mini rave space, disco ball included.

"Hey, babe," he says when he spots me halfway in the closet, halfway out. He places his hand on my back and kisses my cheek. "What are you doing?"

"Nothing." I slam the closet door and fold my arms together. "Why do you ask?"

He eyes the closet and then me. "Just wondering. Why, are you trying to hide something?"

"What would I hide?"

"I don't know. You just slammed that door pretty quickly, as if you're hiding something."

"I'm not hiding anything, Eli."

"Then why did you slam the door?"

I laugh maniacally as if I can't even believe what he's saying. "Me? Slam the door? Maybe you walked into this apartment so fast your breeze from opening the door actually slammed the door. Ever think about that?"

"What are you hiding in there?" he asks, growing more irritated.

"Nothing."

He tries to open the door, but I swat at his hand. "Don't you dare go in there."

"Penny, I'm not fucking around anymore. What's in there . . . or who's in there?"

"Who?" I shout, my eyes widening. "Are you really asking if there's a who in there?"

"You're acting like a who is in there." He gestures to the door.

"You're making me act like there's a who in there."

He grips his hair, tugging on the strands. "Who the fuck is in there?"

"No one!" I shout.

"Then open the goddamn door and show me."

"Or what?"

"Or I'm going to do it myself."

I step away from the door and gesture toward it. "Have at it."

Eyes on me, he swings the door open and then looks into the

closet to find all the coats on the ground, but not a body in sight. Confused, he meets my eyes again. "What the hell?"

"Did you really think I'd hide someone in there? Or even want anyone but you?" I push lightly at his shoulder.

"You were acting weird. What am I supposed to believe?"

"Uh, how about the fact that I freaking told you I loved you in Banff? Wouldn't that be evidence enough that no one would be in the freaking coat closet?" The minute the words slip past my lips, I regret them. Just like before, he freezes, his eyes widen, and it's like the word love makes him turn catatonic.

This right here . . . this is why I'm losing it.

This is why I feel like crying every time I look him in the eyes.

Because it's as if he's completely and utterly horrified I even muttered the words.

"God, I can't stand you." I move past him to put on my shoes, then I grab my wallet and head to the door.

"Where are you going?" he finally asks.

"Somewhere not near you." I walk out the front door and slam it as, once again, embarrassment consumes me.

Flipping through my phone, I pull up Blakely's phone number and press send.

It rings three times and then, "What have you done now? Change out his shampoo for mayo?"

"Blakely, I need you."

Her voice grows serious. "What's wrong?"

"Meet me at Mabel's Ice Cream . . . please?"

"Give me ten minutes."

"Thank you."

WAFFLE CONE in hand with a giant serving of peanut butter cookie dough ice cream, I say, "You have to admit, the shoe succulent was a good one."

She bites into her homemade ice cream sandwich—two double chocolate cookies with strawberry ice cream in the middle

—and then says, "I did kind of like it. Didn't mean it was right, though."

"What do you mean?"

"Do you really think messing with his stuff is going to fix things?"

"I'm not messing with his things. I'm nesting. Ever heard of it?"

"I have, but you're not nesting. You're being vengeful."

"How so?"

She pins me with a look. "Don't do that runaround bullshit with me, Penny. I'm your best friend. I've known you long enough to understand when you're hurting and deflecting, and that's exactly what you're doing."

"I'm not hurting," I say, biting into my ice cream. She asked me if everything was okay when we arrived, and I lied. Told her I just needed to share ice cream with her. We then went into the fun things I've been doing around the house, avoiding the one main issue, how I truly feel.

"So you're telling me you're not hurt at all from him not telling you he loves you or claiming you as his girlfriend?"

"No. I'm fine." I look away, unable to answer truthfully.

Because I'm hurt.

I'm hurting so bad.

"You're such a liar. Why don't you talk to him about it?"

"Oh yeah, that seems like a stellar conversation." In a whiny voice, I say, "Eli, why won't you love me?" I shake my head. "No freaking way. Not to mention, I let it slip earlier, the elephant in the room. I brought up the *I love you*, and you should have seen him, Blakely. It was like the first time all over again. The guy absolutely freezes. Let's face it, commitment is not his thing."

"So what, you're just going to stay there, fuck up his things, and then hope that maybe someday he'll find his way to an I love you?"

I shrug. "Maybe. I don't know." I pause. "Remi texted me."

"Remi? As in Remi Gasper? The man who Eli apparently absolutely hates?"

"Yes."

"What the hell did he want?"

"He's in town, asked if I wanted to go to dinner."

She pins me with a glare. "What did you say?"

I shrug. "That I was free. It's just a dinner between friends."

"Is that *all* it is?" she asks.

"Yes, Blakely."

"Penny, I don't think that's a great idea. It will only make Eli mad."

"Heaven forbid we make Eli mad," I say, growing irritated.

"Think about what you're doing, Penny. Remi isn't just some friend from the past. There's a history between them. You're going to end up hurting Eli."

"He's hurting me," I shoot back at her, pointing at my chest. "He's hurting me every goddamn day, Blakely. How come no one sees that? Why is no one on my side here? Why am I the only one who sees how painful it is to live with a man, day in and day out, and not be loved by him? I'm in this purgatory because of the baby, but I wouldn't have stuck around if there was no baby. Who would, Blakely? Who *would* stay with someone who doesn't love them? Would anyone offer their heart every single fucking day and have it stomped on? Because that's what it's like. For me. Every. Fucking. Day."

"Penny, I didn't mean—"

Tears well in my eyes. "I just want this nightmare to be over with. I want this feeling to be washed away. I want to be out of this monotony where I wake up to his warm arms every morning, to his soft kisses, knowing damn well they mean absolutely nothing. It's unrequited love, Blakely, something you haven't—thank God—experienced. And it's breaking me. I don't want to go to dinner with Remi to be vindictive or mean to Eli. That's not what I want to do at all. But if having dinner with an old friend breaks Eli and me, breaks the vicious cycle I've been living in, then it might be exactly what's needed."

I don't want to be an obligation anymore. Someone Eli stays with simply to *look after* and *be there for the baby*. I'm not ungrateful.

I know I'm so lucky compared to others who are left pregnant and alone. I'm simply hurting.

It's like living with a daily wound so deep that a Band-Aid can never heal it, yet a Band-Aid is all I'm given.

And I don't think I can live with this sorrow.

I swipe at my cheeks as my tears run down them.

"Okay . . . okay," Blakely says, reaching out and taking my hand. "I'm sorry. I wasn't aware that it's been that bad for you."

"It has been," I say between sobs. I suck in a deep breath and try to steady my voice. "I'm not in a good headspace, and I just need something, anything to help me through this."

"Why don't you talk to Eli? Tell him how you really feel."

"I did," I say and shake my head. "He just goes still, quiet. Because I know he doesn't feel that way about me. And for the sake of the baby, he's probably just sticking it out."

Blakely doesn't say anything right away but instead grips my hand tightly.

She doesn't have to say anything, because I think we both know the answer to all of this . . . there's nothing I can do.

Finally, she lifts her head up and says, "What was it that he said to you about living in the barn for all those years? Wasn't it that he felt so lonely, but rather than dwelling on that, he convinced himself that he didn't need anybody to survive? That he didn't seek their love once he realized they wouldn't give it to him?"

I take a deep breath and think about that conversation we had. It feels so long ago now. He accepted his living situation as a foster-like situation. Even though they were blood family. It brings more tears to my eyes, just as it did then. He was only a little boy when he lost his mom, when he was cast aside and treated like a stray. *Not loved like a son or nephew.*

"Yes, he believed it was weak to want a hug. To ask for anything more than the scraps of *home* life he was given."

"Well, maybe he just needs love, Penny. He needs to be reminded every day that he's loved, that it's not some fluke, and that it's real. Maybe he needs to see your actions match your words."

"And then what? Every day I say I love him, but I remain broken, battered, and even more heartbroken?"

"Maybe . . . but also, maybe he finally sees that he's not the abandoned, cast-aside child he once was, but instead, a man who is wanted. A man worth spending time with. A man worth loving."

Chapter Thirty-Five

ELI

You're such a fucking moron.

Of course she's not hiding anyone in the goddamn closet. She has proven more than once that she cares about you and only you. That she wants you. She seeks you out more than any woman ever has, and at night, when her mind settles down, she curls into you, soaking in your warmth.

Why would I even suggest that she was hiding someone?

Probably because with each passing day that goes by, I feel more possessive over her. I feel the need to show her how much I care about her. How much I want her in my life.

Yet every time she brings up the word love, I fucking freeze.

I become so self-aware of my inadequacies that I don't know what to do other than to not say a goddamn word.

Because how could she love me? She's so much more than I'll ever be. She's so smart, so loving, so open to giving her heart. And every day, when I wake up with her in my arms, I wonder how I get so goddamn lucky to be able to spend my days with her, even when she's acting out or fighting with me.

I'm the one who's fucked up.

I'm the one who could easily mess this up.

I'm the one who needs to figure out how the hell to be in a relationship.

Hating myself for being so goddamn stupid, I kick my shoes off and place them in the closet before hanging all the coats back up. When I turn toward the living room, I spot one of my dress shoes on the windowsill.

What the hell is it doing there . . . and what is that in it?

She's . . . planted something in it.

What the fuck?

I pick up the shoe and examine the expensive leather that is now full of soil and . . . yup, she watered it.

I put the shoe back down because I'm not sure there's much I can do about that at the moment. Instead, I pull my phone from my pocket and dial Posey.

"I just left you. You miss me that much?" he answers.

"Dude, I keep fucking up."

"What did you do this time?"

I pace the living room while pulling on my hair continuously. "Accused her of hiding a man in the closet."

"What?" He chuckles. "What I wouldn't give to be a fly on the wall in your apartment. Between the insane fights you get in, and the weird things she does around the place like hide the remote control from you—"

"Found it in the freezer, by the way."

"I just think it's a goddamn fun house over there. So what made you think she was hiding a man in the closet?"

"She was acting suspiciously when I got home and slammed the door to the closet and then acted like I shouldn't go in there. When I confronted her about it, she finally said I could go in. I had my hand cocked at my side, ready to plow my fist through whoever was in there, but when I opened it, all I saw were all the jackets on the ground."

"Weird. What was she doing?"

"No goddamn clue, but I did just find one of my shoes on the windowsill with a plant in it."

"Ha, really?"

I grow serious. "Dude, she brought up the I love you." I heave out a sigh as I sit on the couch and prop my feet up on the coffee table.

"Oh hell, really? I'm assuming since you called me, you didn't say it back."

"I didn't. I fucking just stood there, staring at her. She, of course, vanished after that, so I'm really doing a good job at life right now."

"What the hell is your problem? Don't you love her?"

"I mean . . . I don't know, Posey. I can't fucking even remember what love is at this point. How can I say it to her if I don't even know what it is? What I do know is that I'm obsessed with her, even when she's planting something in my shoes." I drag my hand over my face. "I'm so fucked in the head over this. And it's only getting worse. I feel like every day that goes by, she's becoming more and more agitated with me. And also . . . she seems sad."

"Could it just be the pregnancy?"

"Possibly, but I don't think I'm helping the situation. The only thing that's keeping me calm, that's reminding me that I won't lose her, is when we go to sleep at night. She sleeps on my chest, using my body to help keep her comfortable. It keeps me feeling connected, recharged, ready for—" I pause as my eyes focus on the pictures on the right-hand side of the fireplace. "What the fuck?"

"What? Is there another shoe with a plant in it?"

"No," I answer as I head to the pictures. "She . . . she covered my pictures with Lewis, Farwell, and Kavinsky, with what I'm assuming are her own drawings of a penis being aroused by a pregnant woman, only to be passed up and sad again."

Posey laughs out loud, the boisterous sound filling the phone.

"Oh shit, I'm going to need a picture of those."

"Why would she do that?"

"Why would she plant something in a shoe? Oh hey . . . maybe she's nesting."

"I don't think that's what nesting is. That's when she puts together the baby's room, right?"

"I think it's everything around the house. Oh shit, go check the baby's room, see if anything changed in there. I'm kind of hoping she made bedding out of your suits."

"Why would you hope that?"

"Because it's fun for me."

I head toward the baby's room, just as my eyes focus on the throw pillows. "Wait, all the throw pillows are missing their covers."

"Ooo, that seems almost psychotic."

"Maybe she spilled something on them."

"That's logical, but it's Penny we're talking about here. I think logic is out the window."

I hate to admit it, but I think he's right.

Ignoring the pillows, I go to the baby's room and stop dead in my tracks when I see words splattered across the walls in gray paint—shocked that it's not red with the way it's scrolled out.

I swallow hard and then say into the phone, "Posey, man, I think I'm in way over my head."

"What did she do?"

"You don't want to fucking know."

———

THE FRONT DOOR OPENS, and Penny steps inside, holding a bag in one hand and her phone in the other. She takes her shoes off and sets them in the closet, and then moves toward the master bedroom without saying a word.

I'm standing in the kitchen, holding my phone charger and trying to figure out why she put it in the fridge, when I set it down and follow her.

She drops the bag on the floor and then slips under the covers of our bed and rests her head on the pillow before letting out a deep sigh. Her eyes close, and I contemplate what to do.

Should I let her be?

Should I cuddle up behind her?

Should I talk to her?

When I see how peaceful she is, I know exactly what my next move will be. I pull my shirt off, and fold it, setting it on the dresser before getting in the bed behind her. She makes more room for me, and I situate the blanket over both of us before slipping my arm around her stomach. She scoots into my front and then rests her hand on mine.

"I'm sorry," I whisper into her ear.

Quietly, sadly, she says, "I know, Eli."

"It was stupid, and I should never, ever question how you feel about me. That's not fair to you."

She sighs but doesn't say anything, so I take that as she just wants to sleep. Not wanting to let go of her, I stay with her tucked into my chest, and as I rest here with her, I realize that nothing is better than this.

Not a night out with the guys.

Not a last-second score to win the game.

Not even a fucking championship.

Nothing beats being with Penny. Absolutely nothing.

And then . . . I hear her sniff.

I still.

When I hear it again, I gently squeeze her and ask, "Babe, is everything okay?"

She shakes her head. "No."

"Hey," I say softly. I try to tug her to face me, but she doesn't move. She stays put. "Penny, what's going on?"

When she answers, all I can detect is the pain in her voice, and it nearly destroys me. "I just want to be your girlfriend, Eli. I just want to be loved."

Oh . . .

Her wants seem so simple.

Yet to me, they feel monumental. *Impossible.*

Commitment has never been easy because that means I'm allowing myself to own something . . . someone in my life. Someone I could lose.

Mentally, I don't believe I'm stable enough for that. To allow Penny that close because if I lose her, it will destroy me.

But haven't you already let her in?

"And I know you don't want that," she adds, her voice so full of sorrow that it physically pains me. "But I don't know how to change how I feel. So . . . there you go. I love you, Eli, and I'll probably love you forever."

She sighs heavily and then cuddles in closer, not saying another word. She drifts off into a deep slumber, one she doesn't wake up from until the next morning. Not me, though. I lie awake the entire night, playing her words over and over in my head, trying to muster up the confidence, the ability to feel the same way.

⸺

"HEY," Penny says quietly as I walk through the door and set my gym bag down on the entryway floor.

She's sitting on the couch, wearing a pair of leggings, heels, and a maternity blouse that looks really fucking good on her. She curled her hair, leaving it in long waves, tumbling down her shoulders, and she's wearing makeup. It's very natural, nothing too bold, just accentuating her beautiful features.

Smiling, I say, "Baby, you look gorgeous."

"Thank you," she says softly as she drums her fingers on her phone.

"Not trying to say that you need to go anywhere to look like that, but . . . do you have plans or something?"

She nods. "Going out to dinner."

"Yeah?" I walk up to her. "Need me to go get dressed quick?"

Looking away, she shakes her head. "No, I'm, uh, I'm going with someone else."

I'm about to take a seat next to her when I pause mid-stride toward the couch. "With someone else? What do you mean by that?"

"Just a friend," she says, clarifying.

"Oh . . . okay."

But she continues to avoid eye contact, which unnerves me. After her confession last night, things have felt tense. She's been very quiet and not her normal, bubbly self. We haven't fought, and she didn't even attempt to have sex with me this morning like she always does. Sure, it put me on alert because that didn't seem normal, but before I left for the gym, she walked up to me, completely naked, and dropped to the floor, pulling my shorts down with her. She held me against the wall and sucked me off, not letting me pull away but instead making me come in her mouth. Afterward, I lay her across the couch, spread her legs, and propped them up, only to dive my head between them. I played with her nipples and watched her come all over my tongue until she was completely satisfied. I reveled in having the taste of her on my tongue all goddamn day.

But after, her texts were short.

Her communication was vague.

And now, well . . . now, it seems like she's avoiding me.

There's a knock on the door, and before she can get up, I say, "I'll get it."

"Eli, it's fine, I can," she answers as she struggles slightly to get up.

But it's too late. I'm at the door before her. I open it, and the minute I see the bouquet held by the man I absolutely despise, my vision turns completely red.

"What the fuck are you doing here?" I ask.

Remi smirks at me. "Hornsby, I should be asking you the same thing. Isn't this where Penny Lawes lives?"

"It's where we both fucking live," I seethe.

Penny's hand touches my back as she moves to the side of me. Remi's eyes go to her stomach, widen, and then he looks back up at us. "Well, looks like we have some catching up to do."

He chuckles and hands her the flowers. Before she can take them, I swipe them out of his hand and toss them on the floor behind me.

"Eli," Penny scolds, but I don't care.

I turn toward her and say, "You're not going out with this motherfucker."

Her eyes narrow on me. "Eli, that is not your decision to make."

"The fuck it's not. You live with me, Penny. We're having a baby together. That is very much my decision to make."

"I live with you because we're having a baby together, and we're having a baby together because of one drunken night. You have made that quite clear that that's all we are."

I can feel Remi's eyes on me as he listens. "We're more than that."

"Are we?"

"Yes," I say, pulling on my hair. "And to hell if you're going out with him."

"I'm not going out with him. We're catching up because we're friends and he's in town. It's that simple." She steps forward, and I grab her hand.

When her eyes meet mine, I quietly say, "Don't do this, Penny. Don't do this to me."

Her eyes search mine, and for a second, I think she's going to stay with me. Then she says, "I'm not doing anything *to* you, Eli. You need to own your own reaction, here, that's all." And then she snaps her hand from mine and walks out of the apartment with Remi at her side.

ELI: *She hasn't come back yet. It's been two fucking hours, and she's not home.*

   Posey: *I don't know what you want me to say.*

   Eli: *Tell me what the fuck she's doing.*

   Posey: *Surprisingly, I don't have a homing device hooked up to her leg.*

Eli: *Don't be a fucking dick.*

Posey: *Well, what the hell am I supposed to say? Am I supposed to feel bad for you? Because I don't. She told you several times how she felt, and you did nothing. This is on you.*

Eli: *I know . . . I know it is. But I don't know how to fix it.*

Posey: *Seems pretty easy to me. She told you she wants to be your girlfriend. She wants to be loved. The writing is on the wall.*

Eli: *It's . . . it's too much.*

Posey: *Then I hope seeing her going out with other men is something you get used to because that shit will not stop. You're attracted to her because she's fucking gorgeous. And other men will see the same thing. She might be living in your house, but she's still single, man.*

———

THE FRONT DOOR OPENS, and I spring up from the sofa where I've been pulling on my hair for the last half hour, rocking back and forth, begging and pleading for her to come home.

She shuts the door behind her and locks up. When she turns around, she comes to an abrupt stop when she spots me standing in the living room, with nothing but the light of a side table lamp illuminating the space.

"Eli, you startled me." She takes her heels off and then sets her purse down on the console table.

I'm a goddamn wreck.

My heart is in my throat.

My limbs feel numb.

And when I go to speak, my throat is so tight from holding back on my emotions.

"Did you . . ." I clear my throat as I'm hit square in the chest with the thought that passes through my mind. "Did you kiss him?"

She turns away. "I don't see how that's any of your business."

"Penny," I say desperately, tugging on my hair. "Please, please just fucking tell me."

Instead of answering, she heads to our bedroom, where I hear her getting ready for bed.

"Fuck," I say out loud before picking up a pillow from the couch and throwing it across the room. I plop back down on the couch and dive my hands into my hair.

Nausea roils in my stomach from the thought of her lips on someone else's. Of another man holding her hand. Hugging her. Thinking they have even a shot at being hers, let alone Remi fucking Gasper.

What did they do? Did they talk about me? About my fucked-up head?

Did they hold hands during dinner? Stare into each other's eyes? Make fucking plans for future dates?

Agony rips through me just as I feel her step in front of me. She bends at the knees and lifts my chin to look at her.

No longer in her date night outfit, she's changed into her nightgown. Her face is clear, and her hair is tied up into a messy bun.

"Just . . . just tell me," I say, my voice choked.

Her expression turns soft as she closes the space between us and presses her lips to mine. My hand slips to the nape of her neck, and I hold her in place, opening my mouth, my tongue swiping against hers.

With her hand on my chest, she pushes me back on the couch and then climbs on top of my lap. Her belly makes it a little harder for us to connect, but I still keep her in place, making sure she knows this mouth of hers is all I ever fucking want, nothing more.

When she pulls away, her finger drags across my cheek as she softly says, "I didn't kiss him, Eli. I didn't even give him a hug goodbye."

Relief washes through me as I slowly lower my head to her chest, where she hugs me tightly.

"Fuck . . ." I quietly say as I hold her.

I'm not sure how long I hold her for, but I do. I hold on tight.

I allow myself to soak her in, to remind myself that she doesn't belong to anyone else, that she's here, with me, on my lap, in my arms.

She's mine.

When I finally lift my head, she presses her hand to my cheek and leans in for another kiss. This one is more demanding, more needy, and I feel the same way. My hands fall to the hem of her nightgown, and I lift it over her head. I waste no time and quickly take one of her breasts into my mouth.

My lips travel over her skin, kissing, licking . . . sucking.

I nibble up her chest, I bite tenderly on her nipples, and when I reach her neck, I spend a moment marking her, letting every goddamn person in this world know that she belongs to me.

And she lets me.

She tilts her head to the side, offering me her delicate skin, letting me take charge.

And when I feel satisfied, when I know she's been branded by my possessive self, I stand her up, bend her over so her hands are gripping the armrest of the couch, and I release my cock from my shorts

In one smooth thrust, I enter her, bottoming out immediately.

Her back arches, and she lets out a long moan right before I pulse inside her.

Hard.

Thrusting.

Taking.

Claiming.

I fuck her, over and over again until she's yelling out my name, her perfect, little pussy gripping me.

It's at that moment that I know . . . she's mine. She will always be mine.

I just need to figure out how to keep her.

"CAN I ASK YOU A QUESTION?" Penny says.

Naked and in bed, I'm spooning her from behind, drifting off to sleep.

"Anything, baby," I say, kissing her shoulder.

"Remi . . . why do you hate him so much?"

Hell, I knew she was going to ask this question. It was only a matter of time. A part of me thinks that I should just tell her the semi-truth, how he's a horrible player, harp on that again because that's what I've told her before. But I know, deep in my bones, that if I'm going to work on keeping Penny in my life, I need to start owning up to the truth.

My thumb moves over her stomach as I say, "You know Holmes had a twin brother, right?"

"Holden?" she asks.

"Yes. We were all pretty close actually. Not sure if you knew that. This was obviously before you worked for the Agitators. But it was during All-Star weekend. Holden came to visit. We were going to watch Halsey in the game together. Anyway, we were out the night before, and we were drinking. I wasn't aware that Holden had a drinking problem. Halsey never spoke about it, so I never thought much of it. I just thought he liked to toss back quite a few on a night off. That night, Remi came into the bar. We already hated each other because of how he acted on the ice, so when I saw him, in my drunk state, I grew angry."

I pause because fuck, it's painful.

Penny, though, she squeezes my hand and gently says, "It's okay. Take your time."

After a few more moments, I say, "Remi and I got into it, so bad that we started fighting, and we were kicked out of the bar. I can't fucking remember much of what happened after that because we were torn off each other, there was some media shit I had to deal with, and before I knew it, Holden left. We were supposed to leave together. It wasn't until the next morning that I found out he was in a car accident and died."

"Oh, Eli," Penny says as she turns in my arms and faces me.

"I . . . fuck . . . I couldn't even look at Halsey for a goddamn month because I knew it was my fault. I knew if I hadn't let Remi get to me, that Holden would have never driven drunk."

"No." Penny shakes her head. "His death is not your fault. You can't hold on to that, Eli. Holden had a problem, and if it wasn't that night, it would have been another night. You can't blame yourself for that."

"I do, though. And I blame Remi. Fuck, I blame Halsey and Holden too. They should have told me. I never would have taken him to the bar, and I never would have left him." I choke up as I say, "He . . . he was like a brother to me, and once again, I lost another person in my life. But this . . . this was my *adult* life, and fuck, it felt even more painful than before because I knew I could have prevented it. If I'd made smart choices, I could have prevented it."

"Eli." She forces me to look her in the eyes. "I love you, you know this, I love you so, so much, but you can't control other people. You can't control the choices they make, and yes, you made a choice to fight with Remi, but Holden made the ultimate choice that night, and he chose to drive when he shouldn't have. There is nothing you could have done about that."

Tears well up in my eyes, and before I can stop them, they fall down my cheeks, but Penny is there . . . she's right there, to kiss them away.

And that's exactly what she does. Every time a tear falls, she presses her lips to my cheeks. When she's not doing that, she's holding me . . . loving on me as the sorrow that's been building in my body since the morning of Holden's death finally starts to release.

Because of this woman.

Because of the unconditional love she gives me.

Because, even though I can't seem to vocalize how I feel . . . she vocalizes it for the both of us.

And for that, I know I'll never ever let her go.

"EVERYTHING LOOKS GREAT," Big Pecs says before turning toward Penny and me. "But I'm sensing some tension between the two of you. Am I right?"

"Everything is fine," I say just as Penny sits up on her elbows.

"He's lying to you. Everything is not fine."

After one of the worst nights of my life, which turned quickly into one of the best, things have been better between Penny and me. It's almost as if she's starting to understand me, and even though I might not say what she wants, she still tells me every chance she gets how much she loves me.

And every time she says it, I think it's sinking in more and more.

Big Pecs crosses one leg over the other and says, "Care to talk about it?"

I hold my hand up. "Seriously, everything is fine."

"Say fine one more time," Penny seethes at me, nostrils flared, looking like she's ready to eat me alive.

Oh, did I mention that she's gained that crazy back again? Yeah, in full force. The sadness seems to be slowly fading away, and in its place, she's starting to show her—to put it nicely—third-trimester self.

Big Pecs sets his hand on her arm and says, "Why don't you tell me what's bothering you?"

"Fine . . . he won't use an anal plug on me."

"Jesus . . . Christ," I mutter as I drag my hand over my face.

"Oh, I see. And is there a reason?"

Penny rolls her eyes. "Says he doesn't want to hurt me, that he doesn't have enough experience. I told him to read a fucking book and just shove it up there. Still won't do it. And I'm telling you, Doc, I've never wanted something more in my entire life."

He nods, understanding written all over his face. "I can understand the craving for something different in your sex life. Maybe find something you're both comfortable doing."

"I told him I'm sure I could find someone on Craigslist who could help."

"And I told you that's not a goddamn option," I hiss at her.

462

Gesturing to me, she says, "See what I'm dealing with?"

"Penny, I think you're starting to enter the anxious phase of pregnancy, and instead of dealing with those feelings, you're trying to fill them with other things, like sex. Let me ask you, how many times are you two sharing sexual intercourse?"

"Not nearly enough." She folds her arms with defiance.

"Three to five times a day," I answer.

"Wait . . . a day?" Big Pecs asks.

"Yes," I say, exasperated.

"Told you not nearly enough," Penny says.

Big Pecs clears his throat and shifts on his chair. "Penny, three to five times a day is more than enough. The most I've actually heard."

"See." I poke her. "Told you."

"What does he know?" Penny motions to Big Pecs, who is literally two feet away from her.

"Uh, he's a doctor."

"Just a title."

Fuck, she's in a mood today. Although, I'd take this Penny over sad Penny any day.

Big Pecs and I exchange a look, and then he stands from his chair. "Well, I don't know what to say to you other than good luck. If you do decide to use an anal plug—"

"We won't," I say.

"Oh, we will," Penny adds.

"Then please just be careful. Other than that, the baby is measuring great. Call me if there are any problems."

"Thank you," I say while Penny stays silent.

When the door clicks shut, she turns to me. "Let's do it here."

"Let's do what here?" I ask.

"The sex."

"What? No, Penny."

"Oh, it will be really quick. You shoot off early sometimes."

"That was one fucking time, and it was because you put a vibrator against my balls. I wasn't prepared for that sensation."

"Well, guess what I have in my purse?"

"Jesus," I groan. "No, Penny. We're not having sex in the doctor's office when anyone could walk in."

"Isn't that the thrill of it?"

"No." I shake my head. "Not even a little. I have a reputation to maintain, and I can't be found with my pants down at my ankles, fucking my girlfriend in the doctor's office."

"Wait . . ." She slowly sits up, and I offer her some help as she maneuvers with her belly. "Did you just . . . did you just call me your girlfriend?"

I think back to what I said, and hell . . . I did. It just slipped out.

"Uh, yeah. I did. Is that okay?"

Tears well up in her eyes. "Eli, you called me your girlfriend." She takes my hand and pulls me between her legs. "Your actual girlfriend." The smile that stretches across her face is so beautiful that I have a really hard time looking away.

I press a kiss on her forehead. "You're mine, right?"

"I hope so."

"Then yeah, you're my girlfriend."

Her teeth roll over her bottom lip. "And you're not just saying that?"

"Do you think I'm the type of guy who would just say something for the hell of it? There is meaning behind my words, Penny. You should know that by now."

"I do." She cups my cheeks and brings my mouth to hers. "So does this mean we're in a real relationship?"

"You live with me, babe, doesn't get more real than that . . . oh wait, it does. We're having a baby together."

"Little Johnny Jim."

I chuckle. "Yeah. Little JJ." I kiss her lightly and pull away before things can get too deep. "Let's get you dressed, and then I can take you out to lunch. How does that sound?"

"Perfect."

"BABY, please, I don't want to come in your mouth."

She smiles up at me and then releases my cock from her lips. She climbs up my body and straddles my lap to position my length at her entrance.

"Fuck, Penny, you're so goddamn beautiful."

She slides down on top of me and lets out a long, beautiful moan as her head falls back, her hair floating over her shoulders. It's one of the most erotic things I've ever seen. This beautiful, confident woman, carrying a child, seeking out her own pleasure. I've never seen anything like it, and I'm addicted.

I'm addicted to her.

To the sounds she makes when I'm deep inside her.

To her sweet scent that consumes me when I'm buried between her legs.

And to the way her touch feels like a warm hug all over my skin.

I can't imagine a day without her.

And when I called her my girlfriend today, I meant it. I don't know why I didn't say it before. I don't know why I was holding back because it felt so right the moment I said it. It felt like everything was in place.

Her hands land on my thighs behind her as she arches her back, seeking out more pleasure. This has become her favorite position in the last week. All she wants is to sit on top of me. And I fucking love it too, because I get to stare at her and watch her beautiful tits bounce with her movements. I get to experience her face turn into shock every time her orgasm rocks her. And I get to feel her love pulsing through me with every thrust, every moan.

"Eli, it feels so good. Too good."

"No, baby, it's never too good," I answer as I help her rock her hips. She's been more tired lately but never tired enough to not connect with me on this level.

"Oh . . . oh, Eli. I . . ." Her pussy clenches around my cock, and my orgasm hits me square in the chest, unexpectedly.

"Fuck," I yell as I squeeze my eyes shut and pump into her, my body filled with pleasure.

And together, we slowly float down until she's lying on her side, curled into me, kissing my chest.

"I love this, us," she says. "So much, and I'm so worried that when the baby comes, it will be gone."

"What?" I say, lifting up to look her in the eyes. "Penny, why would you think that?"

"Insecurities," she answers. "Don't you have them?"

"I do," I say, "but babe, you have to know I'm not going anywhere. I'm not sure how many times I have to say that."

"Maybe every day," she answers.

"Then I'll say it every day." I kiss her nose and then lie back down to pull her into my chest.

"What are your insecurities?" she asks, her fingers dancing along my chest, playing with the very short strands of my chest hair. It's been a while since I've had a waxing appointment, but she's told me she likes my chest hair, so I've kept it.

"Honestly?"

"Yes." She nuzzles into my neck. My hand finds the back of her head where I play with her hair.

"Not being good enough for you."

"Come on, Eli," she says in such a tone that makes me think she doesn't believe me.

"I'm fucking serious," I reply. "I've thought that from day fucking one. The first time I met you, Penny, I knew you were way out of my league. Not just because you were Pacey's sister but also because you were this intelligent, funny, beautiful woman who I wanted more than a few minutes with. When I saw you at the bar on my birthday, I fucking knew that was my moment to talk to you. And I did. I was not going to go through the night without spending time with you."

"Eli, I was such a mess that night."

"You were so goddamn perfect, Penny. You have no idea the kind of energy you brought that night. It was authentic, and I fucking loved every moment of it. After that night, I felt . . . fuck,

I felt empty, like I was missing something. And I slowly realized it was you. You were what I craved, what I needed in my life. And when I saw you walking around the arena, talking to the guys, barely even looking in my direction, I knew . . . I wasn't fucking good enough."

"I wasn't avoiding you because I didn't like you, Eli. It was because of what we did."

"I still felt insecure around you. Not because of anything you did, but measuring up to you and the love and empathy you pour out of you. Fuck, I felt lucky to even catch a glimpse of your beautiful eyes. And even now, holding you in my arms, I know I'm lucky, I know I don't deserve you, I know that I fucking hit the jackpot even when you're insane and painting weird things on the baby's wall, planting God knows what in my loafer, and desecrating significant pictures." *I am not going to mention her crazy mood swings.*

She chuckles. "Don't call a pregnant lady insane."

I sigh and squeeze her.

There have been times when I've wanted to call her more than insane. But then I consider the many nights she's gotten home before me and cooked dinner, despite being tired from a busy day. The times she's checked in to see how I am after my morning skate when she knew my knee had been in pain the night before. The moments we've had on the couch—before we were fucking all over said couch—simply watching a damn TV show to make sure I was relaxed before I tried to sleep after a game. Those things are just as sacrificial as what I've done for her, but she could have made little effort to get to know me over the past few months. She could have kicked me out of her apartment—or at least tried—but she didn't.

Yet I can't find the words to express what she means to me. "I wish I could be better for you."

"You are, Eli." I shake my head.

And then I sit up on my elbow, so I'm looking down at her. "I know that you're waiting for me to say those three little words, what you've said to me."

"That I love you?" she asks, her tone easy, unfazed.

Me, on the other hand.

I swallow and nod. "Yeah, those three little words. I just . . . hell, Penny, I can't remember the last time I said it. I can't recall ever feeling that way. It's been so long. I've been so lost. I'm afraid to let myself explore those feelings out of fear of losing you. Because I know I can, easily. You could have your choice of any man, and you choose me. That doesn't go unnoticed. And even when I struggle to find my feelings and tap into a side of me that I'm certain I shut down when I was twelve, you still choose to be with me. You choose to be with me when you're frustrated, when you want nothing more than to plant multiple succulents in my shoes, or mess up my freaking underwear drawer every day. You keep choosing me."

"Because you keep choosing me, Eli. Don't you see that? This isn't all one-sided. I love you because of the man you are, because of the way you make me feel, because of the way I feel at peace in your arms. I know"—she tears up and pats my chest —"when I'm here, right here, right next to you, that nothing will ever harm me. And . . . that I'm home."

A tear streaks down her cheek, and I pass over it with my thumb, rubbing the wetness into her skin. "Is that what love is, Penny? Feeling safe, protected?"

"Part of it," she says. "Love is a multitude of things."

"Can you . . . can you help explain it to me?" I ask, my insecurities once again rising to the surface as I realize what a stupid question it is. "Never mind—"

She gently rubs her thumb over my heart. "Love is intimacy, Eli. Love is feeling protected, trusted, secure with yourself. Love is feeling like you're home. Like there is nowhere else you want to be than in your person's arms. Love is feeling this unbridled connection with another human, a connection so strong that when they're not around, you feel . . . empty, incomplete. And love grows with intensity as your relationship grows. It starts small, like this tiny kernel needling at your back, bringing awareness to your brain that something is taking over and that an emotion is growing inside you. And as time passes, that kernel blooms into something bigger, something that eclipses your heart and takes up room in your chest, so when you see your person, all you can do is let out a deep breath of relief because they're there. With you. For you. And if that person is the right person, if they're truly the match to your soul, then they will make sure that nothing bad ever happens to you. That no matter what life throws at you—death, joy, heartache—they will be there, by your side, holding your hand, and reminding you that despite what you might be going through, there is always a home in their arms." She brings my hand to her lips and kisses my palm. "Love is what I feel for you. It's what I felt for a while, and I know it's what I'll feel forever."

I don't realize I'm crying until Penny lifts up and smooths her thumbs over my cheeks. My mind twists with her words, the dots connecting, the clouds parting, and light shining down on that exact feeling she's talking about.

The breathlessness when she's not around.

The feeling of peace when she's near me.

The need I have to hold her hand, to walk through this life with no one else but her.

The knowledge that no matter what happens in my day, I can count on her beautiful face, her charming wit, her empathetic heart to carry me through all life's challenges.

The kernel needled me from the first day I met her.

And if I'm honest, it's grown over time.

On my birthday, I was struck so goddamn hard by that kernel blossoming into so much more.

And now, all I can think about is her. All I want is her. And I can't even fathom a day moving forward when she isn't mine. When I can't call her, kiss her . . . love on her.

Holy . . . shit.

"Penny?" I ask, my voice choked up.

"Yes, Eli?"

"I think . . ." I swallow hard, pushing down the lump forming in my throat. "You mean everything to me. Your smile." I kiss her lips. "Your heart." I kiss her chest. "Your mind." I kiss her forehead. "I couldn't go a day without knowing that they belong to me. I'm so sorry it took me so long to figure it out." Her eyes well, and I quickly kiss them and push her gently on her back. "Baby, I love you . . . Jesus Christ, I can't believe it took me so long to say it, to acknowledge it. But fuck, Penny, I love you."

"Don't apologize," she says. "I just hope that I didn't push you."

I shake my head. "You didn't, Penny. You opened my eyes, you let me figure it out, and you never fucking left me. You never gave up. Even when I could see the pain in your eyes, you never gave up on me."

"I couldn't," she says. "Because I love you and that strong bond that I have for you in my heart, it's unbreakable, Eli."

Smiling, I let a tear fall down my cheek right before I press my lips to hers. "You make me so goddamn happy. I didn't know what I was missing in my life until you, Penny. You've parted the clouds that were hanging over me, and you let the sunshine in." I kiss her again. "Thank you."

"No need to thank me, Eli. Just loving me is enough."

With that, I smooth my hand over her stomach and between her legs. She spreads for me as she sinks into the mattress. My mouth finds hers as I press my thumb along her slit.

"I love you," I say again, the words falling off my tongue with ease now. "Just you and me, Penny. Just you and me."

She reaches for my hardening cock and starts stroking me. "You and me."

I move over the top of her and spread her legs, trying not to put any pressure on her growing stomach, but the position doesn't quite work, so I slide us both down to the edge of the bed where I stand in front of her. Getting the perfect angle without pressing on her stomach, I bring my cock to her entrance, and I tease her with my head, running it along her clit for a few strokes.

"Make love to me, Eli. Please . . . make love to me."

"That was the plan, baby."

And then I enter her, and I can feel my world changing around me with each deep stroke.

With each connection of our eyes.

With every beautiful sound that falls past her lips.

She's mine.

Forever.

Epilogue

ELI

I shift in bed and reach for Penny, but when my arms come up short, on the cold side of a bed, I quickly sit up and look around the dark room.

She's not in bed, nor is there a light on in the apartment anywhere.

Worry immediately strikes me as I stand from the bed and go straight to the bathroom, where I flip the light on. She's not here.

I slip on a pair of shorts and then quickly stick my head into the baby's room. She's not there, either.

Next is the living room, dining room, kitchen area. I turn on the light, but she's not here, either.

What the hell?

Are her keys here? I check the console table near the entryway and see that her keys and wallet are missing. She left?

I jog back to our bedroom and pick up my phone to dial her number. When her phone on the nightstand rings, I curse loudly.

Checking the time, I see that it's three in the morning. Where could she be at three in the morning?

Would she go to the hospital without waking me up? That doesn't seem right.

I walk back into the living room, keeping my phone close, and I attempt to figure out where she'd go just as the front door opens. She pauses when she sees that the lights are on.

"You're awake?" she asks.

"Jesus, yes, I reached for you, and you weren't in bed, so I looked for you. Where the hell were you?"

She steps all the way into the apartment with a brown bag. "I went to find a donut," she answers casually. "I wanted a chocolate one. You'd be surprised how hard that was to find. I went to four different stores." She holds up the bag. "Don't worry though, I got a dozen."

"You . . . you went to get a donut at three in the morning?"

"Technically, when I left, it was two, but the answer is yes. I didn't think I could sleep without one." She takes a bite of one. "You look sweaty. Are you okay?"

"Penny, you didn't take your phone with you, so I didn't know where you were. Please don't fucking do that to me again."

"I didn't do it on purpose," she says, taking another bite. "I just really needed a donut, Eli. You can understand that."

"Babe, ask me to do it next time."

"Uh, no. I'm not going to do that. You don't need to be parading around Vancouver looking for donuts. Trust me, I had it handled."

I step up to her and take the bag. Gripping her chin, I say, "Next time, wake me up, or there are going to be some serious problems."

"Are you . . . threatening me, Eli Hornsby?"

"Yes."

"Ooo." She smiles. "And what exactly is the punishment? A solid spanking?"

"No . . . your punishment would be no more sex."

Her face falls. "You can't do that to a horny pregnant woman who needs the help of your penis at least three times a day."

"And you can't scare a frightened boyfriend who loves you deeply and wants to protect you."

She taps her chin. "I can possibly see your point."

Chuckling, I wrap my arm around her. "God, Penny, you're going to drive me so fucking nuts."

"Good thing you love me, right?"

I kiss the tip of her nose. "Good thing."

"DO we really have to paint? I kind of like the motif we got in here."

"Penny," I deadpan, looking around the room. "It looks like a freaking crime scene in here."

"Crime scene would need red. I used gray. I think it's quite fetching, announcing him in here. Don't you think it has this avant-garde look? Very original."

"It has a *psychopath was here* look that I'll not allow my son to live in. We are painting."

She groans and then takes a seat on the floor. "Well, at least take your shirt off and make this interesting for me."

"No," I say as I pour the dark gray paint she loves into the paint pan. "Every time I've attempted to paint this room, you've asked me to take my shirt off. I've obliged, and then you've somehow managed to get your hand down my pants, we have sex, and then the painting is forgotten. Not happening this time."

"Wow, so you're just going to deny me of the finer things in life now?"

"Flattery is not going to work in your favor as well."

"Well, what if I get undressed, just lie here naked, maybe grab that clit stimulator you love using on me so much when your tongue is tired?" She waggles her eyebrows at me.

"Do what you want. If I have to paint this room with a goddamn erection, then I will. We have one month, babe. We have all this stuff from the baby shower. We have to start nesting."

"Aw, look at you using the terms."

"I'm serious." I dip the roller in the paint and soak up the gray. The room has already been edged and taped off. I just have to get the main space of the walls done. It shouldn't take me that long, at least that's what I'm hoping. You can never tell with the woman sitting in front of me . . . now circling her nipples.

"Oh my, look at this, my nipples are getting hard."

I pause and turn toward her. "Penny?"

"Hmm?" she asks while waving her legs open and shut.

"Why don't you want me to paint this room?"

"I told you," she says, exasperated. "The room is unique."

"That is not the reason, and you know it."

"Well, that's the reason I'm giving you."

"Penny . . ."

"Eli . . ."

"Fine." I turn away from her and start painting the wall in one big stroke of gray. "Don't tell me. That's fine. Don't tell me anything. We'll just remain two people in love who don't tell each other everything. That is just fine."

"Wow, Eli, trying to throw down the guilt trip?"

"Nope, just letting you know how it is."

I continue to paint while I feel her watch me, watch my every stroke, my every move until she says, "If this room is painted, then it's all real."

I pause the roller and turn toward her. "What do you mean, it's real?"

"I mean . . . this is the last thing we need to do, and I don't know if I'm ready, Eli. I don't know if I can handle this. Giving birth . . . being a mom. It's all too scary."

"Baby." I set down the roller and squat in front of her. I grip her shoulders and say, "You're the strongest woman I know, and there is no doubt in my mind that you're not only ready for this but you're also going to be the best mom out there. You have so much love to give, so much heart, so much patience. You're more prepared than you know, and I can't wait to see you hold our little guy, to watch the bond you have with him grow every day. This is real, it's so fucking real, and you're going to excel."

"You really believe that?"

"I know it, babe. I fucking know it."

She smiles shyly. "Would it be appropriate to lay you down and make love to you because of your sweet comments?"

I chuckle. "After I'm done painting, my body is yours, but I'm getting this done first."

<hr />

I STEP off the elevator and make my way toward the apartment after a very difficult practice. The new season's started. Coach is punishing us, warning us that we better not have the fallout we had last season. We won't. We're looking strong.

After Penny's fall down the stairs, Pacey basically told Winnie that he was a wreck without her and begged her to come back. She did. That same week, they went up to Banff, to the cabin, and Pacey proposed with some help from the boys.

Taters, well, he met someone. Someone way different than Sarah. She's reserved, so goddamn smart, and a breath of fresh air.

Posey, God, he's in a world of mental anguish, but lucky for us, he's learned how to deal with that torment while playing at the same time. All I have to say is . . . don't fall in love with a legend's daughter. It's high expectations to live up to.

And Holmes, last I heard, nothing has changed with Blakely. She's still dating that Perry dude, and Holmes is still crushing.

A few steps away from the apartment door, I notice a very potent smell of pumpkin. Is that . . . is that coming from our apartment?

Can't be, right?

Penny is currently on maternity leave and has been an absolute mess. Every day I come home, it's something new. There was the day she was sobbing on the couch while watching reruns of

Family Feud. She said someone guessed cucumber as the most popular vegetable, and she couldn't fathom how an eggplant might feel from being left out. I sat there and consoled her the best I could.

Then there was the time she was in our bedroom, folding every article of clothing in the apartment. EVERY article. Including underwear, which she normally thinks is such a waste of time. And when I asked her what she was doing, she said she was on her fourth round of folding it all. Fourth fucking round. She said they weren't folding right, and she wasn't going to be done until it was all folded correctly.

And then there was the time I found her on the bathroom floor, holding her naked breasts and asking God why they were leaking.

She also made some more art for me. She sat in paint and then sat on a canvas and gave it to me. It was just a blob of paint. She cried for an hour about it. Found out, she'd been on the phone with her mom, which made her sad because she missed her mom. And because her mom likes painting, she decided she'd paint for me. Needless to say, I rang Tina and asked her to console her daughter and promise an urgent visit.

So as I approach the apartment door and the smell of pumpkin grows, I worry about what I'll find on the other side. I've been gone for a few hours, so I can only imagine what she's managed in that time.

I unlock the door and slowly open it. "Babe?" I call out just as I step into the apartment.

"Over here," she calls from the kitchen.

I glance over there but don't see her. The smell of pumpkin is so strong, I worry she's purchased a few and torn them open in a frenzy to find the perfect seed—wouldn't put it past her.

I round the counter and find her sitting on the floor with a dozen muffin tins resting around her, all filled with baked—what I'm going to assume are—pumpkin cupcakes.

"What, uh, what are you doing?" I ask her, terrified of the answer.

"I wanted to make you cupcakes, but they weren't coming out right."

"What do you mean? They smell amazing, and they look great."

"I made five batches, and I can't remember if I put sugar in any of them."

"Okay, well, I can try one if you want."

She nods her head. "Please, and tell me the truth." I won't tell her the truth if my life depends on it. No way in fuck am I about to make her feel bad about forgetting the sugar. Even if they are the worst thing I've ever tasted, I'll be eating every single one. *For months.*

I sit down next to her and reach for a cupcake. When I pick it up and start peeling the wrapper off, I casually ask, "Why are you on the floor with the cupcakes?"

"I was sniffing them."

"On the floor?"

She nods. "It was easier than standing once my water broke."

"Your what?" I shoot to my feet. "Your water broke? Penny?"

She nods as she pushes her hair out of her face. That's when I notice she's still wearing oven mitts.

"Jesus Christ, Penny, we need to get you to the hospital."

"Do we, though?"

"Yes," I answer in hysteria. "Penny, if your water broke, you're in labor, and we have to get you to the hospital. When did it break?"

She shrugs as she leans back on her elbow and grips her stomach with a wince. "Like half an hour ago? Can't be sure."

"Holy fucking shit, Penny, why didn't you call me?"

"You were at hockey."

I'm going to freak out.

But instead, I lean down, take her oven mitt-covered hands in mine, and lift her to her feet. "Are you having contractions?"

"Totally. They don't feel good."

Keep it together. Don't freak out on her.

I need to get her to the hospital as quickly as I can. I can have Winnie or Blakely come grab the things we need.

I scoop her up into my arms, and she protests. "What on earth . . . ooo, God, this one really hurts."

Panic pierces through me as I forget about her shoes, forget about jackets, forget about everything. My phone is in my pocket as well as my wallet, and I rush her out of the apartment, not even bothering to lock up. I rush her down to my car, buckle her up, and head to the hospital in minutes. On the way, I hold her hand while driving and call Blakely.

"Hello?" she says over the car speaker.

"Blakely, Penny's in labor. I'm taking her to the hospital." She squeezes my hand and groans as she holds her stomach. Jesus Christ. "I didn't lock up, there are cupcakes all over the place, and we don't have our bag."

"Don't worry, I'm on it."

"Thank you so much," I say before hanging up. "Ten minutes, babe, are you going to be okay?"

She shakes her head. "I'm not ready, Eli. I can't do this."

"Yes, you can, Penny. Remember, you're so strong. You're prepared. You're going to be the best—"

"Don't bullshit me, Eli," she says in a strange, demonic-like voice. "It's going to hurt. It already does. You're not going to want me after this. I'll be an ugly, flappy-vagina woman after this record-size watermelon comes out of me."

"Baby, listen to me," I say, keeping my eyes on the road. "It will hurt. I'm not going to lie about that. But I can guarantee you, no matter what happens, I'll always love you, I'll always want you, and even if you are a flappy-vagina woman, whatever the hell that means, you will be my flappy-vagina woman."

She groans again, this time buckling over. "Oh God, you're so good at saying all the right bullshit things. I love you."

If I weren't so scared, I'd laugh. "I love you too, Penny."

479

PENNY WASN'T wrong about the record-sized watermelon that came out of her. Our boy was so big that there was no way she could deliver him naturally, so she had to have an emergency C-section. Prepping for that was scary because I knew there was some risk involved. But I kept it together, and as I stared into her eyes, holding her hand, I kept telling her how much I loved her, how strong she was, and how I'd still have sex with her after—her demands, not mine.

And then . . . the cry of a boy pierced through the room, and tears immediately hit us. They held him above the barrier, and we both held on to each other while looking at our son for the first time.

After he was cleaned and wrapped up, they brought him over to us while Penny was being stitched up.

I'll always remember Penny's speech about love, how it grows and intensifies, starting as a kernel and turning into something so much bigger than you can imagine. With our son, it was different. It was like a tsunami of love just tackled my heart in a matter of seconds. One look at his tiny face, and I was done.

Love at first sight . . . just like his mom. But this time, I actually knew what that feeling was.

Now that we're in our room, Mama is doing great, baby is latched on, and I'm cradled in next to my family . . .

Fuck, my family.

It's been so long since I could claim such a notion. But here I am, sitting next to my girl—my soon-to-be wife hopefully, if I have any say in it—and my son, and I couldn't feel more whole.

Fulfilled.

Life is funny. You never really know what you're missing until you get a taste of something good. I got a taste of what it felt like to be wanted, to be a part of something bigger than myself, and there was no turning back for me. Once a player, now a father, a man so far in fucking love with his girl that I can't dream up a situation where I'm not one of the luckiest guys on this planet.

"He looks like you," Penny says softly as she raises her hand to the back of my neck. "He looks just like you, Eli."

My family . . .

"He does," I say, getting choked up. "I can only hope he has your heart."

"Funny, I hope he has yours." She leans back and presses a soft, gentle kiss to my lips. "I love you," she whispers.

"I love you, too." There's a knock on the door, and Pacey and Winnie quietly walk in with balloons and flowers. Right behind them are Posey, Taters, Blakely . . . then Holmes.

And there they are, my support system. The people who first taught me about loyalty and dependability. The guys who have been there for me through thick and thin, my second family. This is what it's all about. This right here, the love in this room, is overwhelming, and it only took a moment for me to recognize it.

"Hey," I say quietly. "Do you guys want to meet our son?"

They all nod.

I kiss Penny's forehead and move aside, giving them a view of my sweet baby son with his beautiful mama. *God, I love her. And him.* "Meet Holden Hornsby," I say, my eyes falling on Holmes, whose eyes are lit up with tears. "We thought the name should live on."

And it does.

The name lives on to be one of the greatest there is.

Our son will be great because he'll know unconditional love from his first breath to his last. He'll be given hugs and never believe they make him weak. He will never be discarded, but affirmed and believed in.

And he will know those things because of the incredible woman beside me. The woman who persisted and didn't give up on me until I fully understood what love meant. A woman who is quirky, cute, and sexy. A woman who never stopped believing that one day I'd be able to say those three little words that are true game changers. Words I now live by. *Forever.*

Made in the USA
Columbia, SC
17 May 2024

9d7561d3-cb5c-4140-98d7-3e05c295d77dR01